FLYING TO VALHALLA

Other Books by
Charles Pellegrino

HER NAME, TITANIC

FLYING TO VALHALLA

CHARLES PELLEGRINO

An AvoNova Book

William Morrow and Company, Inc.
New York

To Jim Powell. This book is all your fault, and I dedicate it to you with hopes and prayers that as we throw open the doors to a new wilderness, the keys you and I have begun to forge do not also open the gates of Hell.

AVON BOOKS
A division of
The Hearst Corporation
1350 Avenue of the Americas
New York, New York 10019

Copyright © 1993 by Charles Pellegrino
Published by arrangement with the author
Library of Congress Catalog Card Number: 92-45642
ISBN: 0-688-12506-9

Library of Congress Cataloging-in-Publication Data:
Pellegrino, Charles R.
  Flying to Valhalla / Charles Pellegrino.
     p.   cm.
I. Title
PS3566.E418F57   1993   92-45642
813'.54—dc20   CIP

First Morrow/AvoNova Printing: June 1993

AVONOVA TRADEMARK REG. U.S. PAT. OFF. AND IN OTHER COUNTRIES, MARCA REGISTRADA, HECHO EN U.S.A.

Printed in the U.S.A.

ARC   10   9   8   7   6   5   4   3   2   1

Contents

————\\\\\\————

I. Breaking Glass

1. Valkyrie Dawn   3
2. The Alphan   13
3. The Pod   19
4. Who Speaks for Earth?   24
5. Welcome to Tunaland   47
6. In the Darkness of the Forest   54
7. The Architects of Eden   60
8. Death at Tranquillity   68

II. Time and Time Again

9. Teacher's Pet   83
10. The Keynamers   92
11. On the Origin of the Fittest   97
12. Warning Signs   102
13. Who Speaks for A-4?   114
14. Her Name, *Enterprise*   125
15. The Chemist   137

16. The Astronomer   143
17. Her Name, *Titanic*   147
18. Trinary   161
19. The New Alphans   173
20. Random Poisoning   177

III. Monsters From Earth

21. Softly Come the Dragons   193
22. Strawberry Plague   197
23. A History Lesson   218
24. The Other People   230
25. Ice   232
26. Sorry to Interrupt the Festivities,
        But Someone Is Trying to
        Tell Us Something   238
27. Sun Diver   243
28. Chandelier   246
29. Valkyrie's Web   252
30. Secret Wars   257
31. 2057: The Crash of Three Worlds   262
32. The Fallen Sky   272
33. Like Dreamers Do   275
34. Trinity   284
35. The Fear of God   289
36. Your Words as Slow as Light   292
37. 2061: Split Ends   295
Afterword   299
Acknowledgments and Notes   329

Chronology

SPRING, 33,552,442 B.C.	FIRST CONTACT.
AUTUMN, 33,552,365 B.C.	First coherent light from Alphan probe reaches A-4.
AUTUMN, 33,551,882 B.C.	Effective end of Earth; formation of Caribbean tectite fields.
WINTER, 15,007,283 B.C.	Formation of Ries Basin.
WINTER, 700,652 B.C.	Formation of Ghana Crater, Austral-Asian tectite fields; beginning of *Homo erectus* diversification.
WINTER, 522,295 B.C.	Construction of reed-and-wood structures in Spain; mammoth hunters learn the many uses of fire; beginning of elephant extinctions.
WINTER, 14,391 B.C.	Nomadic herdsmen inhabit the Nile Valley; invention of pottery, lamps, ropes; cave paintings become widespread.

SPRING, 6299 B.C.	First Cities.
SPRING, A.D. 1912	*Olympic* and *Titanic* become world's first ocean-crossing cities; Harriet Quimby flies solo across the English Channel.
SUMMER, A.D. 1945	Physicists learn the many uses of nuclear fire; end of Second World War; effective beginning of U.S.-Soviet Mutually Assured Destruction pact.
SPRING, A.D. 1953	"Galileo" and Richard Tuna are born.
SUMMER, A.D. 1969	Spaceship *Eagle* lands on Earth's moon.
SPRING, A.D. 1984	Richard Tuna and James Powell reveal plans for Valkyrie antimatter rocket.
WINTER, A.D. 1990	First antimatter engine concept tests at Brookhaven National Laboratory; first medical applications of genetic manipulation of human cells (to treat immune dysfunctions) signal that human beings are on the verge of being able to dictate their own evolutionary destiny.
SPRING, A.D. 2008	First successful antimatter engine tested in lunar orbit; science of immunogenetics flourishes.

SUMMER, A.D. 2009	Construction of first international lunar base; perfection of Asimov Array robots begins.
SUMMER, A.D. 2011	Christopher Wayville is born; U.S.-Israeli war begins.
SUMMER, A.D. 2019	First antimatter-driven interstellar probe launched from lunar orbit.
WINTER, A.D. 2048	First crewed antimatter rockets set forth to explore Alpha Centauri system.
AUTUMN, A.D. 2054	Starship *Beagle* lands on fourth world of Alpha Centauri A; SECOND CONTACT.
SUMMER, A.D. 2076	Exodus Fleet; effective end of Earth.

If you live in human society and you twitch or stand out from the crowd, or show signs of intelligence—watch out. They're going to get you. And if we cannot treat our own species with decency, why should we expect any better treatment from total strangers, up there? You young astronomer types who are so hopeful about discovering new civilizations—you dream a dangerous farce.

—THE CHRISTCHURCH WIZARD

Pellegrino, Powell and Asimov's Three Laws of Alien Behavior:

Law No. 1

Their survival will be more important than our survival.
If an alien species has to choose between them and us,
they won't choose us. It is difficult to imagine a contrary
case; species don't survive by being self-sacrificing.

Law No. 2

Wimps don't become top dogs.
No species makes it to the top by being passive. The
species in charge of any given planet will be highly intelligent, alert, aggressive, and ruthless when necessary.

Law No. 3

They will assume that the first two laws apply to us.

I

Breaking Glass

1

Valkyrie Dawn

———\\\\———

Autumn, A.D. *2054*

At FIRST GLANCE, THE THING THEY CALLED VALKYRIE looked nothing at all like a rocket. Its designers must have been crazy. Manufactured in and launched from space, it resembled two, half-kilometer-diameter spiders' webs anchored at opposite ends of a ten-kilometer-long string. Its engine was not at the rear, where any self-respecting rocket motor ought to be. It *pulled* the crew compartment and all of its supporting equipment along on a tether, like a motorboat towing a water skier, as if its creators had been intent on turning the field of rocketry literally inside out. Valkyrie was a giant kite whose sail was a magnetic field. It flew on a muon wind of its own creation.

Frail, and impossible, the "star wisp," as her detractors called her, had been decelerating at twenty meters per second for close on six months—skidding through space with her brakes on *full stop*. Cradled near the forward web, the lander *Beagle* carried in her belly only two passengers: Clarice Wayville and her husband,

3

Christopher, who carried in his own gut an odd, vague sense of superstitious dread.

And thus did the Wayvilles come screeching down through the light-years, finally detaching their engine of coils and tethers near the ice world, Powell, then moving on in their little winged crew compartment, *Beagle*, toward one of the galaxy's rarest, most beautiful jewels. Like Earth, Alpha Centauri A-4 was an accumulation of lucky accidents: she orbited just the right distance from just the right kind of star, and though there were two suns in her sky, the farther, dimmer one never approached close enough to exert any real influence over the world's climate. A-4 possessed just enough mass to maintain a grip on her hydrogen, so that even when bathed in the yellow glare of A's habitable zone, she could maintain just the right kind of atmosphere. Water had been upon her surface for billions of years.

Oh, God, Chris told himself. *Don't let me screw this up.*

The continent he'd named Bardo was down there, but the ocean beyond was hard to see. Westward, an unbroken expanse of white clouds caught the last rays of the setting suns and threw them back into space. Directly below, only three hundred kilometers away, a river larger and wider than the Amazon snaked through a thick carpet of evergreens.

Chris shook his head. Part of his mind cried out for Clarice to stop, so strongly that he almost cried out himself. To that part of his mind, it would be so easy to turn the ship around and leave A-4 the way they had found it; but even if he could convince himself totally that they should not land, after traveling more than four light-years, they'd come much too far to retreat. Once before, when that part of his mind cried out even louder, he'd pressed for turning back, and Clarice had responded by drugging him to sleep—repeatedly. Now that they were in orbit around the jewel, fascination had taken command of both their imaginations, and Chris guessed that if he raised the subject again, he'd find himself on the receiving end of history's first extrasolar divorce, if not more drugging.

Yet for a moment it did seem possible, even sensible, to stop; to let whatever lived in the forests below go its own way before something sorrowful and irrevocable, and perhaps even a little terrifying, happened. For that moment Chris understood how easy it would be to destroy it—to destroy all of it—with just the slightest mistake, without ever knowing what they had done wrong. *Leave it alone*, that part of his mind begged. He tried to shake free of his disquiet, but it settled deeper just the same: *Hurry! Tell her! There is almost no time left!*

And he sensed that it already was too late.

ALPHA CENTAURI A-4 HAD NO SATELLITES—THAT IS, NO NATUral ones. There were two advance probes from Earth, weighing less than thirty kilograms each and orbiting the world since 2042. There was the *Beagle*. And then there were the Alphan pods—three of them in all.

On the planet below, someone had built what appeared to be a dam made of giant logs. Breached, it had lain unrepaired for centuries, certainly unused for as long. In one small corner of a continent, trees had been cleared and single-story reed-and-wood structures had gone up. No one in that village appeared to be broadcasting on laser or radio wavelengths. Night revealed no electric lights anywhere upon A-4. Nor did *Beagle*'s spectrographs reveal any atmospheric or oceanic chemicals suggestive of past or present industrial development, nor did her imaging radar show abandoned highways overgrown and hidden beneath the forests. And yet as recently as 2049, a new pod had climbed out of the atmosphere and joined the rest of A-4's unnatural satellites.

Chris first spotted one of the pods on his wallscreen at a distance of 160 kilometers. By then Clarice had got a clear fix on it and was calling out orders to the ship's computer. The gap closed to eighty kilometers, and at normal magnification, with unaided eyes, Chris could see the thing glittering out there in the sunlight. They passed through Alphan sunset into darkness and did not see the pod again until they were fifty-five kilometers closer. *Beagle*'s searchlamps cast a focused beam, which was reflected back as a single light flashing on and off, on and off, in the night. Some irregularity in the pod's surface was producing a rapid, cyclic fluctuation in brightness: the object was rotating. As the distance shrank to ten meters, with the relative speed between the two objects falling to zero, Chris saw that the pod was bullet-shaped, about a meter in diameter, and twice that in length. It was turning end over end, and this movement within the beam had produced what at first glance resembled the flash of a navigation beacon. Clarice positioned *Beagle* for docking, took aim, and fired her thrusters forward. Two spiderlike robots extended three hastily constructed poles, capturing the thing in a web of black tethers that looked for all the world like a cat's cradle.

Clarice burst out laughing. Her excitement spilled over to Chris, and for a moment he almost joined her in laughter. The pod's skin was a dull, drab brown, and covered with a transparent resin. As Chris turned the *Beagle*'s cameras, he saw that the pointed end terminated in a conical nozzle, and three long ropes snaked out from the edges of the rounded end. He searched, but there was nothing else on the whole surface—no insignia, no projecting antennae, no windows, no visible hints of a hatch. Nothing.

Chris was not normally the superstitious sort, but this close to the realization of all his dreams (and at least one persistent nightmare), he could not help but feel that it might all be taken away from him, that it might all go so terribly wrong. Even Clarice, a devout statistical theologian and onetime managing editor of the *Skeptical Inquirer,* was showing signs of occasional uneasiness, not all of them owing to the sheer rigors of a six-year drive—two years, as experienced by the crew—from Earth to Centaurus. Of all the planetary surfaces revealed by all the robot probes which had gone out ahead of her, A-4 was uniquely alive. And with that realization, long before her ship nudged itself out of lunar orbit, she knew enormous responsibilities lay ahead, even if the A-4 forests bore nothing more intelligent or more threatening than termites.

Clarice also knew that Chris did not seem to be bearing up very well under the responsibilities. Already mistakes had been made, and a great price paid. *Beagle's* sister ship had exploded into a relativistic hellscape two light-years out, and Chris had never fully recovered, saddling Clarice with yet another responsibility. From time to time her husband had become more hindrance than fellow explorer. His overworked imagination seemed to be nagging ruthlessly, building mountains out of what barely qualified as anthills, sometimes reverting her to the role of baby-sitter as he invented one reason after another for not going down to A-4, for not touching or changing anything. Although his panic had abated during the long months of deceleration, leading Clarice to suspect a temporary and hitherto unanticipated "relativistic psychosis" that increased proportionally with Chris's closeness to the speed of light, he still seemed to be preoccupied with tracking down the source of some interior and probably wholly imaginary alarm bell.

"Is everything going to be all right?" Clarice asked as she scrawled orders on a liquid crystal pad and the pod was drawn down to *Beagle's* roof.

"I hope so, love," said Chris. I hope so, he thought, but I really don't think so.

THE FOREST WAS PECULIARLY STILL THIS EVENING, THE AIR sticky and close, with not the whisper of a breeze coming off the ocean. The astronomer had made his way up a hill just outside a cluster of reed-and-wood structures. For several nights now, a newer, brighter point of light had been racing overhead. The others did not often look at the stars, as they were too preoccupied with the trees. The astronomer was sure that this new, wandering star was important, that it heralded a great change, but no one would believe him.

Judging from his careful charting of its motion, and from its increasing brightness, he understood that the object was getting closer every night. Whatever it was, it was coming down; but this latest fact he did not even attempt to explain to the villagers. He was, to their minds, A-4's afflicted. He thought in strange ways, and spoke of strange things, and they had long ago given up trying to bang it out of him. To his own mind, though he'd lived in close quarters with hundreds of his brethren, he trusted and was trusted by only one, known to the others as the chemist. But even she had declined to join him this night.

Resting on his haunches, he felt for the disks and rods in his carry-bag, drew them out, and assembled them with blindingly quick precision. He looked at his invention for a very long time, considering the new star, much as the Earthly king Montezuma had stood in another forest on another autumn evening, considering the approach of the first Spanish ship. As the king watched a floating mountain coming over the horizon, had he truly realized that the Aztec Empire was about to fall?

The astronomer mounted his machine on a tripod, and pointed it into the flight path he'd calculated for the new star; like Montezuma, he was becoming just another page in history. All he knew was that truly there was no knowing what changes the star might work. All he could do was turn the page. So he did, putting his face to the polished quartz lens and following the newcomer as it flashed in his sky magnifier.

Somewhere far below *Beagle*, in the darkness of the Takahashi Forest, a glittering yellow eye, catlike and aware, suddenly opened wide and turned toward space, searching.

NOW, ANCHORED BY A MECHANICAL SPIDER TO *BEAGLE'S* hull, an array of cameras closed in on the pod.

Clarice tapped Chris on the elbow and pointed. "What's that?"

He looked at the cardboard-thin liquid crystal screen lying on her lap. The spider was shining a light onto a swath of parallel grooves that showed through a glaze of resin.

"That's impossible," Chris said. But as the magnification steadily grew, he could not deny that he was seeing grain, the kind of grain found in—

"Wood!" Chris said quickly. "Impossible! They built a spaceship out of wood?"

Unconsciously, Clarice put a hand to the side of her head and began to rub. "This is nuts. Just what in God's name are they doing down there?"

Suddenly even the wildest of Chris's forebodings paled to foolishness. Nowhere in his untamed imagination had there existed anything so wild as the Alphan pod.

"Still wish we'd stayed at home?" said Clarice.

"Not on your life."

She handed him the flat. "Okay, love. It's your move."

"FU," he called into the screen, getting the computer's attention. "Commence with sonoscan." That fast, he was an explorer again. What other choice was there?

he thought. What do you really want to do, Chris? Toss
the pod away and go home?

—a spider attached scans to the pod's hull—

Without seeing what's inside?

Something shadowy and strange took shape on the
screen. Clarice let out another burst of laughter, and
this time Chris did join her. Another sonoscan attached
to the pod's hull. Then another. And another. And though
little rags of disquiet still clung to Chris, he was able to
ignore them and plunge on.

THE ASTRONOMER'S FULL NAME WOULD HAVE BEEN IMPOS-
sible for any human to recall without the aid of a liquid
crystal flat. It was strung together from the keynames
of more than a hundred ancestors, and would require
several minutes to recite aloud, or to write in letters
of the English alphabet. Japanese script would have
been easier. The Alphans spelled with pictographs, and
transmitted them by touch.

Now, the astronomer's season had come to A-4—star
season—the time of year when both suns set together,
when the world saw true night, and when each person or object cast only a single daytime shadow. The
astronomer loved his stars. He had catalogued in his
brain the position and brightness of every one of them.
His favorites were the ones that changed. The brightest
of these was known on Earth as Proxima Centauri. It was
the slowest-moving of "the wanderers," which traveled
from "week" to "week," from constellation to constellation, sometimes doing slow loop-the-loops in the sky.
Though he could trace their movements thousands of
years into the past and the future, the astronomer had
only the vaguest idea what they were, and no idea where
they came from or how they worked. And now there was
this new wanderer, a strange, fast one that appeared only
during the "hours" immediately after sunset and before
sunrise. It had moved the astronomer to work feverishly

toward perfection of his little assembly of mirrors and magnifying lenses.

Tonight he'd climbed the tallest hill in the Valley of Wells, bringing with him the sky magnifier. As he shifted the device's aim so that it would interrupt the next anticipated flyby of the new wanderer, something rustled in the dense brush behind him. It was his friend, the chemist. So she'd decided to join him after all.

Without a word he put forth his arms, inviting her into the clearing; then he rubbed a hand over the chemist's arm, sketching the stars with his fingers, plotting the wanderer's course against them, and marking off at even intervals how many pulsebeats of travel time would be required for it to scratch a path from horizon to horizon.

It's going to be here and gone fast, she sketched back.

Yes, but you look this time. You look first.

He put an arm over her back and motioned her toward the magnifier. She submitted.

As he'd predicted, it came racing out of the west precisely on time, shining against the heavens. It flashed for an instant in the mirror's field of vision, and when the chemist drew back from it, her eyes were wet and bright. She didn't know what to make of what she'd seen. She had devoted her life to becoming the world's leading authority on the environment inside a melting snowball—and the astronomer had told her that all wanderers were round, like snowballs. *But this,* she explained, *it looked like a triangle.*

Excitedly, the astronomer told her of his new wanderer's other strange qualities. The triangle, which he sometimes called the Fourth Fast Wanderer, was now following the same path as the First Fast Wanderer.

The keyname for the First Fast Wanderer was "Dim."

The Fourth Fast Wanderer had appeared ten nights ago, following its own, separate course until tonight, when the astronomer watched it chase down Dim. He was certain that the Fourth Fast Wanderer had devoured Dim. He now added the names Triangle and Dim to the Fourth Fast Wanderer, and gave it the keyname "Devourer."

The keyname Devourer was pronounced "Chris."

2

The Alphan

THE POD WAS AS SILENT AS A COFFIN—AND ACCORDING TO the spider's ultrasonic images, that's exactly what it had become. Something floated inside, rigid, clutching a pillowlike object. There was no pulsebeat, no respiration, no hum of air circulators, no electrical currents. In fact, there seemed to be no hint of life-support equipment, or electronic devices of any kind.

"Immortality," Clarice suggested. "The Pharaohs tried it with pyramids. King Hussein arranged to have his body launched into space."

"Good thought," Chris said. "Maybe we've found a royal burial, or a sacrifice." He studied the latest sonoscan on his flat. The creature blurred almost into nonexistence as it drifted away from the pod wall. Dead, he told himself. All the air had leaked out into space.

"Well, Chris, are we going to open it?"

"Nobody on Earth can tell us not to. Might as well give *Spider* the go-ahead."

"It's agreed, then?" FUQ2, the ship's computer, queried one last time.

"Yes," Chris said.

13

"Yes," Clarice said.

Slowly, cautiously, the spider started to cut a rectangular door into the curving hull of the pod. Three orbits later, the door was opened, and a swarm of brilliant white particles emerged into vacuum and sunlight and floodlamps. They tumbled end over end, fanning out in every direction. Many looked like strands of hair. Others, Chris realized, were globes of desiccated vomit. Clumps of it stained the fur around the Alphan's mouth, indicating that the creature had still been alive when its tomb was rammed into orbit.

Once we bring that thing inside, Chris thought, we're totally committed. He was thinking about extraterrestrial diseases. Great care had been taken to guarantee that no Earthly plagues would be introduced to the Alpha Centauri system. The *Beagle* had been sterilized like nothing that flew before her. Not a single virus particle or bacterium had survived. Even Chris and Clarice were free of all cells not manufactured by their own DNA or descended from well-ordered, healthy tissues. They possessed the most watchful immune systems ever devised. Their bodies sought out and devoured the viruses of herpes, arthritis, warts, and the common cold.

And cancer cells.

And plague.

And *E. coli* bacteria.

Not all of the effects were beneficial, however. The useful bacteria of the intestines were destroyed with the same haste as *Streptococcus*, so that Folsome drugs had to be manufactured to avoid massive attacks of diarrhea—which in a zero gravity environment was almost as unthinkable as nuclear war.

Theoretically, the same immunogens that prevented Chris and Clarice from introducing chicken pox to the Alphans would also protect humans from the Alphan equivalent of measles or typhus. That was all well and fine in theory. But in practice? Who knew? It had never been practiced before.

Chris grimaced, recalling one doctor's hair-raising prediction about what would happen if their immune systems could not recognize and destroy Alphan microbes. If that (*unlikely*—oh, please, impossible) speculation turned out to be true, within a few hours of their bringing the alien aboard, A-4's normal bacteria of decay would eat their lungs, while their skin, bloated and purple and hot, would exude the stench of rotting meat even as they still lived.

But sooner or later they would have to expose themselves to Alphan germs (if such existed). They'd *have* to. Now that they had flown more than four light-years, with the loss of one starship and its crew into the bargain, and come upon a people who were building spaceships—wooden but functional spaceships nonetheless—exposing the rest of A-4's secrets was a mission worth even the price of suicide. No bridge had ever been built that had not cost lives. If that was the price of bridging the stars, the Wayvilles and their ship were expendable.

THE CREATURE WAS SMALL, 0.92 METERS FROM THE TOP OF its head to its feet, which were located at the ends of enormously powerful, kangaroolike legs. Its muscular tail measured 0.65 meters in length, and was curled up with the rest of the body in what appeared to be a fetal position. Uncurled, the Alphan no doubt stood upright, like a man, but it did not walk like a man. It hopped—prodigiously.

The creature wore no clothes. Its two hands ended in four delicate fingers, which were clasped together around a cushion that turned out to be a rolled-up parachute. Its body was covered with soft fur, except for the feet, which, like the feet of birds, possessed scales. If Chris were pressed to give a classification to

the animal, he would have guessed that it stood somewhere between reptiles and mammals, and probably
closer to mammals. But he knew that the guess was
ridiculous. This ill-fated cosmonaut had an ancestry one
hundred percent removed from Earthly evolution, and
could no more be related to an alligator or a kangaroo
than a kangaroo could be considered second cousin to
a petunia.

Still . . . the tendency to link Alpha Centauri with the
familiar was a temptation that refused to go away. Para-
sitic creatures had burrowed into the skin behind the
Alphan's ears. They looked like . . . like mites—like mites
from Earth. The Alphan's face was actually cute, like
something Clarice had seen in an old Steven Spielberg
movie. CAT scans showed the brain to have evolved
from a stem and limbic system, with the more recent
addition of an outer neocortex, just like the human brain.
There were subtle differences, such as the ominous ratio
of brain volume to body volume in the alien (twice that
of humans), but there were no wild differences—none, at
least, until the results of tissue samples came through.

Clarice was not sure she believed what she had found.
The sugars were a mirror image of Earthly sugars, as was
the DNA, which coded for proteins made of right-handed
amino acids.

All proteins on Earth, with the exception of the cell
walls of certain bacteria, were built entirely from *left-
handed* amino acids. Primordial biologists suspected
that this had not always been so, and perhaps the
Alphan was the proof they needed. They believed that
billions of years ago, when the Earth was in its infancy, the first self-replicating protocells were built from
both right-handed and left-handed amino acids, mirror
images of each other, much as human hands are mirror
images of each other. These, the biologists said, drifted
through newly formed seas in the same half-and-half
ratio one finds if they are created artificially, in a test

tube. As protocells fell under the dominion of cells, the assembly of useful proteins was made possible only by the uptake of one (and only one) of the two groups of building blocks. The geometry of long-chain carbon compounds did not permit random associations of both right-handed and left-handed components—not if you wanted to construct an insulin molecule that worked. On Earth, the left-handed variety won universal acceptance. Nobody knew how.

On Alpha Centauri A-4, life apparently took the other road.

The Wayvilles had no idea how.

What they did know was that Alphan biochemistry presented two strange, unanticipated consequences. The first was that if they landed on A-4 and died, and if their bodies were kept beyond the reach of scavenging creatures, they would never rot. The second consequence was that they could eat all the Alphan meats and vegetables they wanted to, and it would all pass out of their systems without being digested. They could bake sugar cakes and eat Alphan lobsters by the kilo and not worry about putting on a single gram. In fact, they could feast all day long for weeks on end and actually *lose* weight. The planet was a dieter's paradise; but it was also dangerous. For all the food that the Takahashi Forest was capable of providing, A-4 might just as well have been as lifeless as the Mariner Valley. Without *Beagle*'s Folsome tubes and hydroponics, the Wayvilles were doomed to starvation on a world whose every continent seemed to be carpeted with gardens.

"Well, how do you like him?" Chris said. "It is a he . . . isn't it?"

"Looks it. He sure seems to have all the right equipment, and I think it's a fair bet that they don't have more than two sexes. The big question is the brain—twice as big as ours. D'you think they could be smarter than us?"

Chris shrugged. "Nobody's quite figured out how brain size and intelligence measure up in humans—or even in computers, which keep getting smaller and smaller and smarter and smarter. I'll be damned if I know what it means in a group of aliens built from all the wrong amino acids. But there *is* this: if they are more intelligent than us, don't you think they'd be visiting the Earth, instead of the other way around?"

"I don't know about that. For all we do know, this could be their *1,000,000 B.C.*"

"Good point," FUQ2 said. "I've found something that might support that view." The computer flashed something onto Clarice's flat. "Here, look at this."

One set of graphs showed the Alphan's carbon-12 to carbon-14 ratios. Another showed its cosmic ray exposure age. He had been dead in space for more than fifty thousand years. He was out here, whirling around this world, long before Goddard, Columbus, and Alexander had lived on Earth, long before the Stone Age, and the Wood Age before it.

"Then there's this." FUQ2 plotted the orbit of the infrared flare observed by an advance probe, extrapolated it into the present, then flashed a telescopic picture of the object onto the flat. It was what the astronomer in the Valley of Wells knew as the Third Fast Wanderer. It looked identical to Dim, the dead Alphan's pod.

Clarice was now aware of two things:

The Alphans must have learned how to build and launch crewed spacecraft when her own ancestors were trying to figure out how to milk goats.

And they had made no technological progress since.

Bewildered, she cleared the flat and began her report to Earth.

3

The Pod

~~~~\\\\\~~~~

Excerpt From Log of Clarice Wayville, Starship Beagle
Broadcast 3 October 2054

CHRIS AGREES WITH ME THAT THE ALPHAN SPACECRAFT MUST
have been designed for a single suborbital flight, much
like Alan Shepard's first flight almost one hundred years
ago. On the whole, it appears to us that orbit was
achieved entirely by accident. There is no control panel
inside the pod, and no pitch and yaw thrusters that
need controlling. Nor is there any communications system, or life-support equipment, not even a space suit
or an oxygen tank. The Alphan cosmonaut apparently crawled naked into a crew compartment that was
empty, except for a parachute that could be used as a
pillow against the acceleration. His life-support system
consisted of whatever air was trapped inside the cabin
when they sealed him in. The Alphan died of suffoca-
tion and hypothermia, probably near the end of his
first orbit.

There is no telling how many Alphans have died
in a similar manner before their ships reentered the
atmosphere, or how many ships flew in other wrong

directions—horizontal—and crashed. No guidance systems . . . no frills, but the Alphan pods get you there—if you're willing to kill your crew about three out of four times.

If the Alphans are a typical example of extraterrestrial civilizations, we will have a very lonely time waiting for them to land on Earth.

Early notes and sketches by Clarice Wayville showing the Alphan pod and mission profile. Transmitted to Earth 3 October 2054.

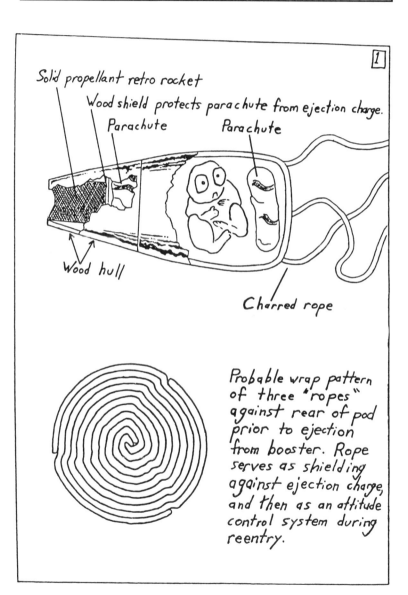

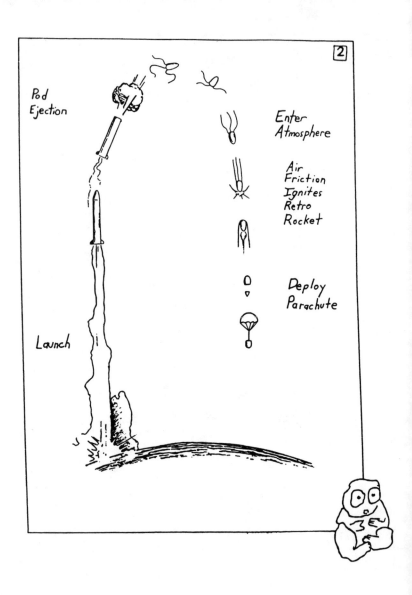

Pod
Ejection

Launch

Enter
Atmosphere

Air
Friction
Ignites
Retro
Rocket

Deploy
Parachute

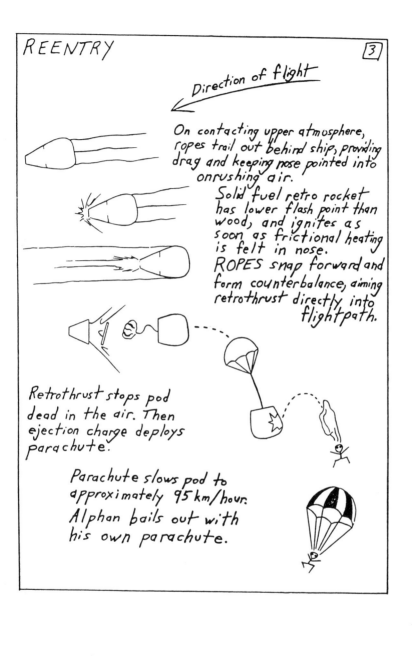

Direction of flight

On contacting upper atmosphere, ropes trail out behind ship, providing drag and keeping nose pointed into onrushing air.

Solid fuel retro rocket has lower flash point than wood, and ignites as soon as frictional heating is felt in nose.

ROPES snap forward and form counterbalance, aiming retrothrust directly into flightpath.

Retrothrust stops pod dead in the air. Then ejection charge deploys parachute.

Parachute slows pod to approximately 95 km/hour. Alphan bails out with his own parachute.

4

Who Speaks for Earth?

Spring, 33,552,442 B.C.

SOMEWHERE OVER SPAIN, THE POD LANCED INTO THE OUTER reaches of the atmosphere, booming and glowing, and shedding velocity as it went. Sixteen kilometers above Africa it stalled and bloomed like a yellow flower, roughly the size and shape of an orchid. Its petals rippled lightly as it parachuted into air of ever-increasing density and humidity. Its pistil recorded every detail of the landscape below, snatched up every odor from its surroundings, and broadcast its findings to the interstellar blackness whence it came.

Its four petals, which served presently as air foils and fine-tuned the robot's targeting abilities, would become extraordinarily efficient legs on the ground, permitting the probe to dart about on the forest floor, or even to clamber up the trunks of trees.

At the flower's axis, sixteen insectlike wings unfurled. Twenty stories above treetop level, the probe released four dragonfly-shaped robots, each barely longer than an inchworm. Three immediately gained altitude, speeding south and east toward new mountain ranges, and north

toward an unbroken ocean that was slowly narrow-
ing—at about the rate fingernails grew—to become the
Mediterranean Sea. The fourth machine winged west
and, after a kilometer or two, dropped swiftly and
deliberately into the forest, then came to an abrupt
stop in midair. On silent, shimmering wings it hovered,
rotating slowly in place, searching. It found other winged
shapes in the sky, some larger than itself, others much
smaller. All seemed to ignore the newcomer, on their
way to more important concerns.

A sudden commotion drew the probe to a pool of tree
sap. A butterfly had bogged down in the yellow resin
and a protomonkey—the newest and brightest thing
upon the planet's surface—was carefully removing the
insect. Hovering at barely an arm's length above the
monkey's brow, the probe watched as two hands made
certain not to tear the wings loose, and at the same time
not to smear any of the sap on the fingers. Grasping its
prize by the wings, the furry thing lifted the butterfly
to its nose, sniffed at it, bit it, then spat and threw the
insect away.

Just as quickly, it took notice of the probe and made
a swatting motion. The probe was quicker, and took
to the sky, uploading what it had seen to a distant
star, where minds that were beginning to regard all
life-bearing worlds with a sense of alarm would look
upon those manipulative limbs, and gaze into those
large brown eyes, and see immediately that here was a
world which bore further watching, for sooner or later
it was bound to spawn competitors.

The flier followed the Earth's magnetic field lines
west, leaving the forest behind and traveling over a
great sea, from which the land of Egypt would one
day rise.

A pulse in the air, not quite a radar beam, but something close to it, caused the probe to dive and twist
reflexively; but the pulse came on again, stronger and

quicker. Something had locked in, and a dark shape was twisting and turning in unison with the probe's movements. It was coming in fast. In those final seconds before contact, the probe diverted most of its energy to recording and uplinking high-resolution images of a creature that had not changed at all during the past thirty million years, and would not change at all during the next thirty-three million. It was warm-blooded, with dark, expressionless eyes and impossibly large ears. On hideous bat wings it zeroed in with a shriek that was more felt than heard. The probe attempted one final twist and dart, and almost saved itself.

Powerful jaws missed all the vital machinery, but clamped down on and shredded away the microthin wings on one side. The newcomer spiraled down, and down, and down.

NONE OF THE CONSTELLATIONS WERE EVEN REMOTELY FAMILIar in 33,552,442 B.C. Indeed, only a few of the stars were moving, relative to Earth, in their present directions at their present velocities. Brushing past each other's gravitational fields, whole solar systems were forever being whiplashed in random new directions, as if the galaxy's half trillion stars had been created simply to carry out a never-ending game of celestial billiards. The triple star system Centaurus, for example, was traveling away from the Sun and the Earth in the year an orchid-shaped probe from the fourth planet of Alpha Centauri A descended upon Africa. The system was then a dim point of light, seventy-seven light-years away in Earth's Northern Hemisphere sky.

During the next six million years, moving off at slightly more than sixteen kilometers per second, Alpha Centauri dimmed to extinction as it put another four hundred light-years between itself and the Earth. And then, beginning in 27,000,000 B.C., a complex series of close encounters with other stars nearly ripped the red dwarf star C from the Centaurus triad, and eventually flung the entire system back toward Sol.

By 1,000,000 B.C., when *Homo erectus* was fashioning stone hand axes near Thebes, A-4 passed once again within eighty light-years of Earth. About 2500 B.C., *Homo erectus's* descendants had begun building pyramids. Alpha Centauri was then a bright object in the Southern Hemisphere sky, only 4.6 light-years distant, and closing the gap at 23.3 kilometers per second. Forty-five hundred years later, A-4 would be three light-months closer to Earth, and if the Alphans of 33,552,442 B.C. could have waited until A.D. 56,600, they would hardly have needed interstellar probes, for a celestial trap shoot set in motion at the beginning of time had put their solar system and Earth's virtually on a collision course.

Autumn, 33,552,365 B.C.

A-4 orbited the larger, yellower of the two inner suns. Though the two suns revolved about a common center of gravity, the smaller sun, B, was to the larger sun, A, much as Jupiter was to Sol, except that B burned much brighter in the night sky, and never approached closer than a radius comparable to Saturn.

There were no Jupiter-like gas giants in the Centaurus A/B system, only stony, Earth-like, and Mercury-like worlds, and the Europa-like ice world, A-5.

On one of those worlds, life had surged out of the oceans hundreds of millions of years ago. Tens of thousands of years ago, creatures with scales and fur and unusually large eyes had begun erecting stone monuments in the Tiber Valley. Three thousand years ago they had spread over the face of the planet, and begun to broadcast to each other on radio wavelengths. Two millennia later, they sent the first artificial eyes and ears out amidst the stars, and were now drawing up plans to follow in crewed vessels.

Theirs was a world of two continents, covered from end to end with roadways, towers, and tier upon tier of farms and greenhouses. To any outsider, no matter how little learning he might have, it would be immediately apparent that this was a civilization pushed to the brink by its expanding numbers. Against the foundations of the highest towers, and within the apartments of the towers themselves, food was being grown. All the world's forests had been replaced by farms so many centuries ago that when naturalists attempted to plant trees on the slopes of the upper Tiber, they were vetoed by a public outcry, by the popular belief that trees would destroy the natural beauty of Tiber's grassy hills, upon which feathered, sheeplike creatures grazed. The public had forgotten that the hills they found so natural and so beautiful were in fact quite unnatural, for they had originally been covered with trees.

Celltrex was one of those who understood that very soon the two-kilometer-high city just wouldn't be high enough anymore. He lived in what he liked to call the Age of Irrationality.

It was a time in which an Alphan who had turned against and killed another who was in the process of beating and robbing him precipitated a continent-wide hunt by police, complete with composite photos on the evening news; but if that same unfortunate commuter had been killed, his assailant would merely have disappeared quietly into the night; and because the victim was an honest schoolteacher and in no one's debt, few would have troubled themselves over his loss.

It was a time in which the Alphans declared themselves a free people, yet still they condoned slavery.

It was a time in which the Alphans explored distant stars, and yet more than half of them clung to the ancient belief that the stars and planets were as gods and goddesses, and that their alignments at the instant of birth exerted a magical control over one's destiny.

Celltrex was beginning to wonder if the astrologers had been right about his own destiny, which was essentially none at all. On the very eve of his promotion to lecturer at Tiber National University, on the prestigious Mother Continent, he'd been fool enough to announce publicly that there were no immortal gods and goddesses, that nothing existed except atoms and empty space. Now his two laboratories lay in pieces, and secret reviews were being held against all of his published works in an effort to revoke his credentials. It did not matter that the ad hoc committee openly admitted to never having read the works—"for an actual reading of Celltrex's papers is not a prerequisite for reviewing them," they said. "We know they are rubbish."

And thus did Celltrex find himself a scholar without a school. He gathered whatever belongings he could carry in a bag and boarded a scramjet bound for the opposite continent, where a small group of scientists refused to recognize the revocations as legal, and managed to find for him some temporary consulting work on the data streaming down from a probe launched nearly two hundred years ago, toward a green world seventy-seven light-years away. It promised to be fascinating work; but as he pressed his nose against the passenger-seat window and saw the Tiber Valley and the towers of University Row shrinking with the distance—though he had every intention of eventually returning and clearing his name—a part of him knew that he would never see the place again.

He spent the forty-five minutes in orbit marveling over the latest printouts of the images coming down from the planet someone had, with a typically scientific lack of enterprise, named "Green." One of the little fliers had been attacked by a warm-blooded creature with huge ears and leathery wings. The robot lay now on the bottom of a sea, still sending back chemical analyses, reports of shifting water currents, and photographs of clam siphons protruding from a ghostly white ooze.

The orchid-shaped probe was still unharmed and completely mobile (or at least it had been seventy-seven years ago, according to the latest news), and from the treetops it had filmed a hauntingly beautiful sight, one that most assuredly was not duplicated anywhere else in all the galaxy. Green was a double planet, and the second, smaller world's apparent diameter matched almost exactly that of Green's sun. A billion other worlds there were, everywhere, but of such solar eclipses beyond Green there were none, forever. The three remaining fliers had calculated all future conjunctions, and would now spend the rest of their lives circling the world, chasing after Moon and Sun.

It occurred to Celltrex that if there had been sentient beings on Green, and if they had ever intercepted one of the probes and tried to infer from it what kind of civilization was capable of creating such things, they would not likely guess that somewhere out here someone like Celltrex was being punished for denying that the stars exercised some sort of conscious will over his destiny, or over anyone else's. Driven by microphotonics designed to last a million years, and able to recharge themselves from almost any energy source in their surroundings, Alphan space probes would have dared anyone looking at them to believe that, back home, A-4 was still a carbon-burning civilization. Industry was the global government, and the government knew what was best for the people, so two-kilometer-high city-towers were lighted by coal and oil. A-4's fabulous interstellar robots had been built too well, and might easily be taken by another culture as an anthology of Alphan civilization. They showed only the best half of an Alphan's face, and challenged the finder of a dragonfly or an orchid to guess from that what an Alphan looked like.

*   *   *

DOWN THERE, NEAR A-4, THE SHIP WAS A LITTLE WHITE triangle sinking toward a turquoise blotch, long known to the planet's inhabitants as the second continent. A mosaic of tiles—each so foamy and so light that, left alone in a field, it would have blown away on a gentle breeze—gave her skin a sinister, reptilian aspect. Burned indelibly into the scales, on both sides of her fuselage, the ship displayed her name in a bold red script—swept astern to give the illusion of speed. A hundred kilometers up, something shivered inside, and her wings flexed back, like the wings of a bird of prey descending on an unwary target.

As he had done a hundred times before, Celltrex opened the shade once the indicator light above his seat announced reentry. It was noon on the hemisphere below, and the daylight he let into the cabin disturbed fellow passengers trying to sleep beside him, and drew a look of annoyance from a steward. Celltrex ignored the look and the grunts, for not even a hundred reentries could make the view from high gate routine. Not even the data from Green could draw him away from it. He liked to imagine himself as an extraterrestrial visitor descending to A-4 for the very first time, wondering what impression the planet would make on such an observer. Each passing second the horizon climbed higher and higher into the sky, but even through the cherry-red glare of the wings, about fifteen meters behind him, the circles and rectangles of artificial islands offshore of the second continent were a sure sign of intelligent life. The largest of the floating cities was hundreds of kilometers across—a small continent in its own right, built as a series of concentric rings. It was the last Alphan-made structure visible to robot eyes heading out to the stars. If Alphan civilization survived, Celltrex guessed, they'd eventually rebuild the entire planet into geometric shapes. To him, this was not to be taken as a sign that civilization was advancing. He suspected that a truly advanced civilization would leave no mark at all upon the world.

Looking straight up from his window seat, he saw that the sky was brightening from black to violet, almost to a dark, dark blue. He'd once complained that space explorers lacked imagination, that the men and women who'd gone into the black, to the worlds of the B and C suns, rather than continue looking ahead into the deeps of unknown space, wasted too much time looking back at A-4.

After his very first scramjet flight to the edge of space, Celltrex realized that he had been wrong. He just couldn't help it. Always his gaze turned to the home planet. Presently, he was able to cover three ocean cities—fourteen million people—with a hand. On the continent ahead, two-kilometer-high city-towers rose out of the farmlands. A reddish-brown lens of filth hung over the pastures, almost as high as the towers. It grew thicker in the valleys. There was a particularly ugly deepening of color over the River Lethe, where uncountable oil-burning power plants were recharging the thing. It obscured the shoreline completely and streamed out one thousand kilometers over the ocean.

"Oh, nooo . . ." Celltrex whispered. "People are actually breathing that." And then a thought: in about three hours, after his plane had finished circling the cities, waiting for permission to land, he, too, would be breathing beneath the lens.

Spring, A.D. *1984*

Down there on Earth, during the first week of the third quarter of a much-prophesized but otherwise uneventful year, two protomonkey descendants brought the first detailed design showing what a relativistic rocket would look like to the Hilton meeting of the American

Association for the Advancement of Science. They were Brookhaven National Laboratory physicist Jim Powell and New Zealand astronomer Richard Tuna; and their rocket looked remarkably like the ones designed by Celltrex's people thirty-three million years earlier. This was not an act of coincidence. Just as all airplanes had wings, and all rockets designed to burrow up through the atmosphere would inevitably be missile-shaped, so, too, would all antimatter-driven rockets—at least in their earliest incarnations—look alike.

At first glance, the thing they called Valkyrie looked nothing at all like a rocket. Its designers must have been crazy. Manufactured in and launched from space, it resembled two, half-kilometer-diameter spiders' webs anchored at opposite ends of a ten-kilometer-long string. Its engine was not at the rear, where any self-respecting rocket motor ought to be. It *pulled* the crew compartment and all of its supporting equipment along on a tether, like a motorboat towing a water skier, as if its creators had been intent on turning the field of rocketry literally inside out. Valkyrie was a giant kite whose sail was a magnetic field. It flew on a muon wind of its own creation; and after six months of acceleration, Tuna and Powell explained, it would be sailing between the stars at ninety-two percent lightspeed.

Tuna had gained some small notoriety in New Zealand when evidence of a 15,000,000 B.C. asteroid impact, and an associated biological revolution, turned up in his fossil crab beds. Fifty million years deeper, the Nobel laureate Niles Filby found asteroid signatures linked with an earlier extinction and speciation event.

Filby returned to Berkeley, where strange ideas were easily welcomed, but for Tuna, the time and place could not have been worse. Creationism was a powerful force in New Zealand, and those university evolutionists in a position to oppose this force in Tuna's behalf had very jaundiced opinions about his speculations—which suggested that under the influence of asteroid impacts, nature sometimes made leaps; that evolution was not always a process of slow, stately change.

"You are challenging Darwin, Malthus, Glaessner, Mayr, and God knows who," wrote the very committee that was supposed to protect him. "You are too young to be pretending to be an authority."

"Even suggesting to a young scientist that it is somehow inappropriate to 'question Darwin,' " began a protest from Filby, "is the antithesis of what a young scientist is supposed to learn—to question virtually everything." Then, as Tuna found himself squeezed between creationists and neo-Darwinians, and as an ad hoc committee in New Zealand prepared to blacklist him, Niles Filby offered refuge at Berkeley . . . until Tuna began questioning Filby's ideas about periodic asteroid bombardments and mass extinctions. With practically his dying breath, as plans for the Hilton meeting were under way, Filby passed a memo to AAAS director Arthur Colby, expressing his opinion that rocket propulsion by antimatter-matter annihilation was "moonshine." Colby responded with a reminder of an old law: "When a distinguished but elderly scientist states that something is possible, he is almost certainly right. When he states that something is impossible, he is very probably wrong."

As Tuna and Powell entered the conference room, an undercurrent of laughter mingled with the word "antimatter" ran through the front rows, most of it directed at the younger Tuna. "Jedi Project," someone in front center called out, and then broke up into giggles. Colby was also in the front row. He stood and shook hands with the two "Jedi engineers," offering them seats beside him. Their detractors fell silent.

"All right, let's begin," the Cornell astronomer Frank Drake called out from the dais. "This is intended to be an informal brainstorming session and I would like to open with a reminder of Kerry Nock's suggestion from

JPL, that, crazy as some of the ideas presented here may seem, we must not discourage new ideas with our laughter, for one man's 'crazy' idea may spark a useful idea in someone else.

"Yesterday, Dr. Sagan brought up the question of interstellar migrations. Well, I've done some speculating on the subject"—he looked around the room—"and the truth of the matter is that, even at the very slow speeds of von Puttkamer's cosmic coral reefs, or arks, the picture begins to look like a wave of colonization that streams across the entire galaxy in a few tens of millions of years, which is nothing in terms of cosmic time. The implication of this, if even one of the many civilizations which have probably existed embarked on such an interstellar colonization venture, is that it would have taken over the galaxy, essentially instantly, but the fact is that such a colony has not come to Earth. Even if they came only as visitors, millions of years ago, where are their beer cans and soda bottles among our fossils? Or even so much as a lost key ring?"

A man in the third row stood up. Tuna recognized J. B. J. Bliss of the Creation Research Institute. "Do you know the story of Noah's Ark? I've heard of scientists who found pieces of it years ago, and it turned out to have rocket engines. They've been hiding it ever since. And what about that crashed saucer you've been keeping in an Air Force hangar since 1949?"

Drake tried to stifle a laugh, and was on the verge of braying, "Who let him in?" when Arthur Colby beat him to the punch.

"I can't let that go by without a comment," Colby said. "A friend of mine, who took charge of the CIA a few years ago, called its scientists together and said, 'Boys, I want the straight facts. What's the truth about UFOs?' And he told me two things. One: they all assumed there's a great deal of life out there. Two: there's not the *slightest* hard evidence that it's ever come here. And finally, if anyone thinks that a secret like that can be kept for one week, let alone several years, they don't know a damned thing about scientists."

"Which leaves us with the old question," Tuna said. "*Where is everybody?* Perhaps there is a galactic law that regards any life-bearing solar system and its nearer stars as the property of any intelligent life that may evolve there. You may observe and record, but don't you dare touch. And you have to admit that the most exciting thing you could hope to find is a civilization at the crossroads of interplanetary colonization and nuclear destruction. You'd want to watch very closely how other species came to terms with the possibilities."

Drake shook his head. He was a member of the SETI crowd, who envisioned extraterrestrial civilizations signaling to each other with radio waves and flashes of laser light, and he could not understand why anyone would waste the enormous energies required to actually cross interstellar space. Crossing his arms, he leaned forward and said, "In other words, Dr. Tuna, you think they have declared us a national park. They have not landed here because they find us so entertaining."

Unperturbed, Tuna answered, "It's sheer speculation, of course, but I can easily see *us* establishing similar laws if we were the first to move out into the galaxy. Humanity would not make a cancer of itself. As we mature, I think we will keep our numbers small, using only what we need, and turning our attention to preserving rather than subduing new frontiers." There was precedent for Tuna's belief. In his native New Zealand, one of the last pieces of land upon the planet to have been colonized, a shift in the people's way of thinking could already be detected. No matter how he felt about the way his countrymen conducted science and politics, he had to admit that they had left huge territories uncut even by roads. For the first time in history, a nation had said, "Gee, there's a whole new wilderness out there . . . Good. Let's keep it that way." They then declared most of the country a national park. Still farther south, when people began moving into Antarctica, they declared it an international continent, sovereign to no one; and there was talk of approaching the Moon and the planets the same way. Tuna anticipated that man's approach to the stars would not be much different.

"We will not go as conquering hordes," Tuna continued. "We will not grab everything in sight, and I think we can expect aliens arriving in our solar system to behave in a like manner . . . unless, of course, they perceive us as some sort of threat."

"In which case," Jim Powell added, "we would certainly have seen evidence of an alien visit by now, although I don't think we'd ever have known what hit us. In fact, I doubt any of us would have lived long enough to realize that we'd been hit by anything at all."

Colby whispered to Tuna, "What on Earth is your friend hinting at?"

"Relativistic bombs," Tuna whispered back.

"What?"

"Stay tuned."

"The explanation I prefer as to why the aliens have not left evidence of visits to our solar system," said Drake, "is simply that they are not here. And the reason they are not here is that it does not make economic sense to go to the stars."

Phil Morrowitz, another member of the SETI radio telescope crowd, broke in. "Right!" he said. "Travel to the stars is a hopeless proposal unless you're willing to expend about forty thousand years of the Earth's energy. That works out to about two hundred billion dollars' worth of electricity—at one cent per kilowatt-hour!" This drew a chorus of laughter from the gathering of three hundred. Some of them even clapped.

"All right." Morrowitz sighed. "I've heard rumors this morning that some people are willing to go the whole hog and consider using that kind of energy for a round trip to Alpha Centauri. I'm not. Listening for signals from space is more reasonable. If there are E. T.s out there, talking to them will cost us about thirty-four cents for the first three minutes. Exploration of other star systems is entirely another matter, for the fact remains that if a civilization is willing to consume all that energy, then it is *still* so much easier to communicate with radio waves—something like a few billion times more efficient. So if there are civilizations cruising around the galaxy in spaceships, there must be many more communicating."

"Getting the power may not cost us that much after all," said Tuna. "Not when you consider where computer science and robotics are headed during the next fifty to seventy years. A few days ago, at Brookhaven, we came to realize that it may cost us only the expense of developing about thirty small, self-replicating factories—which build factories, which build factories—which, when they reach a certain population density, switch over from building factories to building solar panels. We simply send them like a viral infection to the planet Mercury, and carpet one hemisphere with panels. You'd get more than fifty thousand times the U.S. energy budget there."

"Mercury rotates!" Colby called out.

"What?"

"Sorry, Richie," Colby said, "but you can't build your panels on one hemisphere only, because Mercury rotates. Where have you been? People have known that for ten years. I'm *sure* it rotates. Have I introduced you to the *natural resource*? Ask him."

"He's right," said Dr. Isaac Asimov. "Mercury rotates with a period of about three months, and the energy received per square foot, when Mercury is most distant from the Sun, is seven times what Earth receives. It goes up to ten times during closest approach. The interesting thing is that the one-eighty-degree and zero-degree longitudes do become gravitationally locked, alternately, during apihelion, and are exposed to the Sun almost three times longer than the longitudes ninety degrees away from them."

"Oh, no," Tuna groaned, flushing with embarrassment. "I don't believe it. We have to redesign the whole thing."

"Please," Asimov said, raising his hands above his head, as if to show that he bore no weapons. "Don't blame me. *I* didn't make Mercury rotate. Better to find out now than when you get there and look up in the sky and—'Hey! Why is the Sun moving?' "

Tuna groaned. "I don't believe I missed that. We *can* redesign it, though. We'll just have to cover a bit more surface area, and perhaps send three times as many machines to get the project started . . . make sure at least one cluster of them is in sunshine at any given moment . . ."

"And you'll certainly want to test and perfect the machines on the Moon first," added Asimov. "You know, it's just one more argument for building a permanent Moon base. By the time you perfect solar panel builders for Mercury, you'll already be beaming large quantities of clean energy down to Earth from the Moon . . ." He paused and smiled. "Incidentally, I wrote a science fiction story, way back in 1940, about an interrupted array of panels around the Moon's equator. So if you ever do build the thing, Richard, you can call it the Asimov Array."

"We can?"

"I insist on it."

"Well, I think it will be built—eventually. I also think I'm going to be writing on the blackboard when I go home tonight. *Mercury rotates. One hundred times.*"

"Slight miscalculation, eh?" said the man sitting next to Asimov. Tuna recognized him as Arthur C. Clarke.

"I know I've made some poor decisions lately," said Tuna. "But I'm feeling much better now."

Clarke let out a loud laugh. "Why don't you take a stress pill?"

Tuna detected an expression of mild annoyance on Drake's face, and rolled his eyes toward the ceiling, feigning innocence. "Fine," said Drake. "Let's say we get all the energy we want—from Mercury or somewhere— to build the ultimate propulsion system: a matter-antimatter rocket. There's still some small engineering problems. We take matter and antimatter, put them together—big puff of smoke. That propels the rocket. We have the passengers up front, in the rocket. Be sure to keep them far away from the engine so they don't get toasted by gamma rays. And let's say they're moving along at seven-tenths the speed of light. That's a nice speed because it means the passengers experience the same amount of time as it takes to travel at the speed of light to wherever they're going—one year to go one light-year. The problem is that, moving through space at seven-tenths the speed of light, you're looking into a particle accelerator, and dust grains begin to look like sticks of dynamite. *Can you believe this?* Not to mention that when one of these rockets lifts off from Cape Kennedy, it incinerates the whole state of Florida. And then—"

"I believe we've got most of those problems worked out," Tuna interjected. "First off, we don't lift off from Cape Kennedy. The rocket is built in lunar orbit. Second-ly, the crew is indeed far away from the engine, but not in front of it, as in a conventional rocket. Valkyrie is a space-ship on a string. The crew dangles ten kilometers behind the engine, with a shadow shield between the engine and the crew compartment. They receive no engine radiation at all. And any particles the ship accelerates into will first be ionized by a constant spray of coolant from the ship's engines. The ionized particles are shunted aside as they rain down with the reusable coolants upon the ship's magnetic field, which is what the ship is mostly made of: magnetic field lines. And, of course, we've worked out a similar solution for the deceleration phase of flight—"

"I hope you've worked them out better than the rotation of Mercury, kid!" called a voice from the floor. It was Bliss—again.

"I don't think the kinds of problems we're talking about have solutions," said Drake. "Relativistic rockets are preposterous. And it all tells us a rather sad thing: that Captain Kirk and Mister Spock have lied to us. You can't call up Scotty and order warp speed."

"I can foresee communication with extraterrestrial civilizations," added Morrowitz. "But as far as exploration of other solar systems goes, I'm afraid it's impossible."

Colby grinned knowingly, wanting to remind Morrowitz, as he had reminded Filby, of Clarke's first law, and especially of his second law: that the only way to discover the limits of the possible was to venture a little way past them into the impossible. But there was something more important afoot, something that had grabbed his curiosity and would not let go. "Excuse me, Chairman, but I'd like to ask Dr. Tuna what this relativistic bomb thing is I've heard about."

"It's rubbish," Drake said.

"Only assuming relativistic rockets can never be built," Tuna said. "But if they can, just think what will happen if you crash one of these things into a planet."

Colby's eyes widened. "God's teeth! And it's unstoppable."

"Exactly. And if we ever saw a relativistic gamma source approaching Earth, an expedition of exploration would be indistinguishable from an expedition of extermination, except in the minds of the visitors."

"Rubbish," said Drake. "Even if it were possible to build one of these things—and it's probably not—then I cannot agree that it's unstoppable. You simply throw a few nails in its path and blow it up."

"That's assuming you can predict its position and motion," said Jim Powell. "And you can't."

All heads turned toward him. Things were already interesting enough, but they were about to get even more interesting, and everyone knew it. "If I were to bring the equivalent of one space shuttle mass into the atmosphere above Manhattan Island at ninety-two percent the speed of light, all of North America and much of South America and Europe would become an instant microwave oven, and still the destructive potential of a relativistic bomb is but fractionally spent. Seconds later, the sheet of fire that cuts across the sky will probably destroy all life on Earth. But letting the entire bomb package come in one lump is not anywhere near as efficient as the shotgun approach." Powell looked around. The room was silent, and with good reason. What Powell described was strange, even downright creepy; but unlike Tuna, Powell had been around long enough to be proved right about a lot of other creepy things. This was the man who, while stalled in traffic on the Long Island Expressway, had shaken his head and said there just has to be a better way of getting around; and on the spot he had developed designs for a magnetically levitated train with a cruising speed of 575 kilometers per hour. Now, with his friend Tuna, he had graduated to tunnel versions of "Maglev" traveling so fast through vacuum that they'd have to run upside down between New York and Moscow, because they actually created a centrifugal force as they followed the curve of the Earth under the North Polar ice cap. And what was Valkyrie, ten kilometers long with its engines up front? It was just another train, of sorts; an interstellar train.

"If Richard and I really, really wanted to do an efficient job of Earth-wrecking," Powell continued, "then about fifteen light-days out, we'd separate the bomb package into two parts. One part, the part containing our last few kilograms of antihydrogen propellant, begins decelerating and will arrive about twelve hours after the leading bundle.

"At a distance of several light-minutes, an explosive charge (a minute quantity of antihydrogen) separates the leading bundle into ten thousand little relativistic bomblets that begin to spread across the 12,880-kilometer-wide disk of the Earth. If there are any doubts about the invulnerability of relativistic bombs, this scenario should remove them. Who is going to go after ten thousand invisible fragments spread out over twelve thousand kilometers?

"Each bomblet comes in at essentially the same time, producing the same effects as the large package, but distributing the capacity for death more evenly. Under ten thousand different epicenters, the surface of one hemisphere behaves like a very fast gas grill. New Zealand, Australia, and Japan enjoy twelve hours' respite in which to ponder why radio and television broadcasts from the Western Hemisphere have suddenly ceased, until the world slowly turns and exposes its eastern face to the second bundle of ten thousand crashing bomblets."

"Powell and Tuna must have fascinating nightmares," someone behind Colby said with annoyance. Colby was beginning to understand the undercurrent of animosity that seemed to be running against the two scientists. There were ugly truths that many people did not like thinking about, and Powell and Tuna were raking up examples more quickly than any audience could easily digest. The possibility that relativistic flight might become real had caused them to consider relativistic death, and the possibility of relativistic death had caused them to look upon this planet as if it were another, and then to contemplate the many ways of terminating human civilization. At Brookhaven National Laboratory, two men had sat over Coca-Cola and popcorn calmly and lucidly discussing magnitudes of annihilation far beyond the dreams of any nuclear weapons think tank. Scribbling mostly on napkins, in what must surely have rated as the most bizarre brainstorming sessions of any in human experience, they had drawn alien plans against all humanity. A scientific and supposedly rational, civilized part of humanity had ventured to think of humanity as if it were a noxious insect. Such thoughts were bound to make any listener livid because they were so belittling—and it should have occurred to all present that there was nothing new here except an alien perspective, that Pentagon and Kremlin wargamers had learned decades ago to look upon continental populations as if they were termite infestations. But the older perspective was a normal, everyday part of twentieth-century life, almost accepted, like background noise; few people even thought about it anymore. And if Powell and Tuna were right, Colby thought, then perhaps that was the very feature that should make aliens fearful of the human species ever becoming a relativistic one.

"If we were new explorers passing through a solar system," Powell said, "and if we found a planet like Earth at the stage of early electronic civilization, or in the Bronze Age, or even australopithecine man-apes, and we saw on Earth a potential future threat, and we were unsure just how dangerous the surrounding light-decades were, we could use the Earth to, as the saying goes, kill two birds with one stone. We'd simply use the world as bait. I think Tuna and I would set a small beacon adrift in the solar system, or several beacons, each sending out loud broadcasts on all wavelengths. Then we'd wait and see what happens. If, after a few years, forty pinpoint gamma ray sources are converging at relativistic speed from forty different directions, we will know that we wandered into the wrong neighborhood. At the same time we will have volunteered the services of unfriendly neighbors to take care of the *Homo sapiens* problem for us, and we've gotten a line on where the hostiles are . . ."

Colby thought of suggesting that the exploding galaxy SS433 was somebody else's SDI, but thought better of it when he looked up and saw that Chairman Drake was already seething.

" . . . now, some of you have been patiently listening for signals from other stars, and though the search is expanding every year, you've not received the whisper of a message. I can think of only two implications of continued silence. Either there is nobody out there, or there is somebody out there who for some reason is very reluctant to communicate. In the second case, if Tuna and I are wrong about relativistic flight being possible, and more advanced civilizations know this, then there should be no hesitancy about communicating and the sky should be alive with voices. Which of the two are you prepared to believe? Do you really think we're the only civilization in the whole galaxy?"

"Holy shit . . ." someone whispered. And aside from that, the room remained silent. It occurred to Colby that, under these ground rules, if a signal ever were received, it would have to come from a civilization that was dying, for one reason or another, and had decided to broadcast its music, its art, and perhaps even its accumulated wisdom to the stars. Only a people who had nothing to lose would be fearless of detection. The first sign of extraterrestrial life would thus be a death cry in the night. And if Powell and Tuna were correct, you wouldn't dare answer the signal. But . . . but . . .

"But—" Colby stood up and turned toward the others. "Our own radio signals have been leaking out for decades—all the way back to 1912. That first electronic shriek from the *Titanic*'s Marconi Shack was a sure sign of life on Earth. If we're so threatening to everybody, why are we still here?"

"I can think of four reasons for that," said Tuna.

"One: there is nobody else with relativistic capability within thirty or thirty-five light years of us.

"Two: they have not found us yet.

"Three: they have found us, but they do not consider us a threat.

"Or, four: we won't be here much longer."

5

Welcome to Tunaland

Autumn, A.D. 2054

Civilization was still here, but they were all gone now—*Powell, Tuna, Colby, Asimov, and Drake. Their names lived on in unexplored mountain ranges, continents, and oceans, to which the first Valkyrie starships had set sail. . . .*

Down there, near A-4, the ship was a little white triangle sinking toward a turquoise blotch, long known to the planet's inhabitants as the second continent. A mosaic of tiles—each so foamy and so light that, left alone in a field, it would have blown away on a gentle breeze—gave her skin a sinister, reptilian aspect. Burned indelibly into the scales, on both sides of her fuselage, the ship displayed her name in bold red script—swept astern to give the illusion of speed. A hundred kilometers up, something shivered inside, and her wings flexed back, like the wings of a bird of prey descending on an unwary target.

Inside the windowless vessel, wallscreens surrounding the Wayvilles' breakfast table (Clarice liked to call them her picture windows) showed a 360-degree view

47

of the ionosphere. A violet curtain was rising slowly around them. It outshone the stars. Far beyond the port bow, the northwest shore of the continent—they called it Tunaland—was rolling over the curve of the world and out of view. So were the mountains on the starboard, and the ocean aft. The horizon shrank with the diminishing distance, closed in from every direction. Strapped in their chairs, the Wayvilles listened to a mounting roar. Tunaland shimmered through a glare of rosy pink that suddenly flashed white. The flash was accompanied by a rapid-fire barrage of jolts. Is she supposed to do that? Chris asked himself. Such turbulence would not be normal for an Earth reentry, but this was not the Earth, and the *Beagle* was not a passenger ship. Chris hoped that FUQ2 knew what she was doing, and that the wings and heat shield, which had been assembled by spiders from cosmic ray tiles, would hold together.

"Dense pocket?" Chris asked.

"Yes," said FUQ2. "There is more activity in the upper atmosphere than you will find on Earth. The density differences are greater. There are strong, powerful, mighty big, and enormous convection currents, thirty-five-meter-per-second winds, sometimes blowing vertically, straight up and straight down—"

"I get the picture, FU," said Chris, with slight irritation. The computer had been trying its hand at creative writing lately, and was now discovering the synonym. He guessed it was only a matter of time before she stumbled upon that most irritating of all English devices, the exclamation point. It was going to be like watching the class clown standing on his desk and howling for attention from a substitute teacher.

"Look!" FUQ2 shouted. "The ionization! A growing force! Dazzling! Brilliant! Brighter than the suns! It is the fiery white heat of reentry! Hull pressure building against a hammerhead of air! It is like being in the middle of a tremendous neon light! It is like—"

"Shut up, FU!"

"Yes."

"Hull stress. Give me the short version."

"Fifty-eight percent of maximum specification . . . now sixty-two percent . . . fifty-seven . . . fifty-nine . . . fifty-seven . . . fifty-five . . . fifty-three . . ."

The turbulence slowly abated. Tunaland reappeared in the picture window, with a green X marking the Takahashi Peninsula. Then the whole continent tilted to one side as FUQ2 banked *Beagle* into its first S-turn. Clarice glimpsed a ripple formation of clouds. Glistening there, the intense white bands were marching on a chain of amber splotches—the Lagoons of Powell.

THE CHEMIST STOOD AT THE EDGE OF A NATURAL LIMESTONE pool, looking up at the place where the sky boomed. Something shot out ahead of the boom, something bright and triangular. It roared up there. She wondered at the intruder's queer growl, which did not come from the spot where the triangle appeared to be, but from a point that followed at a distance of several hands held out at arm's length.

She was even more confused by its shape. She remembered a hundred things that looked like it, including what the astronomer knew as the Fourth Fast Wanderer, Triangle, Devourer of Dim; but her mind could not make the connection, could not single Devourer out from any of the hundred other possibilities.

CLARICE TOOK OVER THE CONTROLS WHEN *BEAGLE* WAS TWO kilometers above A-4, with the Valley of Wells sweeping up ahead. Her takeover made for a good deal of extra work. Rather than sightsee, she now had to direct the final approach with her touchscreen pen and a series of verbal commands. Of course, FUQ2 was fully capable of finishing the landing without human assistance, and

Clarice knew it. Left on its own, the *Beagle* would touch down exactly in the middle of the selected clearing—not a meter to the right, not a meter to the left. "But dip me in shit," she told herself, "if I'm going to let the ship land itself. Four billion years of life on Earth have been leading up to this moment, up to the first landing on a world orbiting another star, and *no way* am I about to let an autopilot do it for me."

She rode down through clear air, pulled *Beagle*'s nose up at four hundred meters, and then kicked on the vertical thrusters. Streams of deuterium and tritium fired into blinding laser light. Green numbers flashed on the picture window, showing that more than ninety percent of the landing fuel remained. The ship was now hovering like an old Harrier Jump Jet, and it could do so for twenty minutes and still have landing fuel to spare.

It won't even be close, Chris thought. We'll be on the ground in one minute.

"Looking good," Clarice called up to Earth, but nobody on Earth was listening. It was 4 October 2054. Her words would not reach home until 6 February 2059. "Down a half . . . six forward . . . rad scans on . . . down two and a half—"

Chris called a down-facing view onto his flat. Grassy vegetation fluttered and shifted under gusts of deuterium fire. Something small and mouselike traced a hasty, zigzag retreat. The rad scans showed that it had received a lethal dose, and would probably be dead within a few days, assuming that A-4 life was anything like life on Earth.

"Altitude twenty meters, two and a half down . . . burning grass . . ."

The "mouse" would not live to die of radiation sickness—

"Three down . . . three down . . ."

—Chris watched it burst into flame.

"Wow! What a view!" said FUQ2.

"Altitude six meters," Clarice announced. "There's no stopping us now."

Chris ran two fingers over his left breast pocket, feeling a little square of gold foil inside, one of the very few souvenirs he had brought with him from Earth. He thought of the elderly woman who had given it to him, and the ship it belonged to, the ship her father had built: LM-5, the first one ever to land humans on a world that was not their own . . .

"We're down," Clarice said. "Engines stopped. Cooling system up full—"

LM-5 . . . Chris knew what words must be said. He spoke deliberately, interrupting Clarice, fully aware of the eerie familiarity that would be felt back home: "Port Chaffee. Takahashi Base here. The *Beagle* has landed."

THE ALPHANS CAME.

In the final seconds before touchdown a spider had gone topside. Through a haze of smoldering grass its cameras spotted two of them hopping near the edge of the clearing. Then there were more of them—more and more of them. The ship was immediately surrounded by aliens.

"This is amazing!" FUQ2 said. "Visitors to the A-4 forests will be struck with the prevailing blue-green hue of the evergreen vegetation and the apparent absence of flowers. Associated with this are rather active, almost mammalian creatures possessing a truly admirable intellect. The tiny, jointed beings move with swift precision under the incessant glimmer of an Alphan sky . . ."

The incessant glimmer of an Alphan sky? Chris winced. It was time to lobotomize the computer, starting with the Howard Cosell file. It would not be the first such assault in human history, or the last. Later, FU, later. There were the Alphans to deal with.

(Thumpa-thump!)

On the wing—two of them . . . five . . . eleven. Chris was puzzled by their lack of caution. They *did* look identical to the creature in the pod. They *had* to be intelligent. Of course they were, but why would intelligent beings come bounding headlong onto a starship without first taking pause to look it over, or at least to touch it and see if it was hot? It was as if the possibility of danger had never crossed their minds—and there *was* danger. There was residual radiation from the fusion jets. There was the seething hell that vented from the cooling ducts. Touch the ship there and you'd never use that hand again. To Chris's growing relief, an exobiologist on Earth had seen this possibility, and demanded that the ducts be put well out of (human) reach.

The Alphans were moving to and fro over the top of the ship, fiddling with the tiles, running their fingers over the seams, and sometimes trying to pry one loose.

"We'll have to watch out for that," Clarice said. "We won't need tiles for another reentry, but if they do start pulling them off, we're going to lose some of our cosmic ray protection for the trip home."

"We might have to let them pull until their little hearts are content," Chris said. Interstellar diplomacy had entered the mission profile, and if the Alphans chose to strip off the *Beagle*'s skin, there were only two choices: try to talk them into giving the tiles back, peacefully, or go find an island where there were no Alphans and try to build new tiles. You couldn't just lift off and dump the Alphans who were on top of the ship, fry the ones who were under it, and dose the ones who were around it; that would be a deadly insult to any intelligent species. If the price of avoiding hard feelings was to let the aliens wreck the *Beagle* from the outside in—again, the Wayvilles and their ship would be expendable.

And it looked to Chris as if it might come down to that. On the roof, six Alphans had surrounded the spider. The poor machine curled up into a ball at their feet. One of them snatched a camera from the robot's fingers and bounded off toward the stern.

The creature tried to remove the lens, and appeared to be having the greatest difficulty figuring out how to unscrew it. "How could a spacefaring culture be unfamiliar with the screw?" Chris asked. "It's one of the simplest machines . . . and yet we saw no screws on the Alphan pod."

Clarice shook her head. "I don't know, Chris. I don't know. I'd almost think these aren't the same creatures that built the pod, that we found an animal orbiting in space—their version of Laika the space dog."

The Alphan, the one known to his people as the astronomer, unscrewed the lens and moved it over his arm. His magnified fur seemed to arouse curiosity. He put his hand on the chemist's arm and signed excitedly. Considering Clarice's latest observation, the Alphans could have exploded an atomic bomb, and it would have been barely as jarring as the chemist's simple response to the astronomer's touch. Peering directly into the camera, she chirped one syllable, clear and bright and in the King's English.

"Chris," she chirped again. "Chris."

6

In the Darkness of the Forest

WATCHING THE ASTRONOMER MADE CLARICE DROWSY. Watching anything for fifteen hours, even an alien, would have made her drowsy, and this alien was proving to be a masterpiece of boredom. Clarice was bitterly disappointed. The creature sat alone with a female under a floodlamp on the stern. He did not speak. He had spent almost the entire night trying to take the camera apart, and appeared to be going about it in the most idiotic fashion. Each piece was pulled and twisted, first to the right, then to the left, and up and down until it came loose. The effort took forever. Lenses, levers, and photonic circuits lay all around him. From time to time, the female picked up one of the pieces and tasted it. Clarice's written commands to the ship's cameras had dropped off to nothing. Easing back into Chris's side of the bed, she let the video flat drop onto her belly. Within minutes it was rising and falling with the slow, steady rhythm of her breathing. Her sleep was deep and dreamless.

CHRIS DID NOT SLEEP, WOULD NOT SLEEP. HE FOUGHT VIOlently to remain awake. He had by now come to agree with Clarice that what appeared to be an alien creature calling him by name was merely a coincidental quirk of Alphan language. He convinced himself of this despite the inner disquiet that had preceded his arrival on A-4. Unlike science fiction and mystery novels, in which such things were strictly forbidden, real life was riddled with odd coincidence. The idea that an Alphan had anticipated his arrival was only an illusion, Chris decided. Coincidence. Nothing more. And now his disquiet was stowed and almost forgotten. Still, he had to stay awake. He had to see what the creature would do next. Had to.

He ran a hand over his left breast pocket for the second time that day. Next to the gold foil was a single laser-encoded coin—broken, with videos of himself, his son, Jonathan, and his first wife, Carrie.

The bond between him and Carrie had run deep enough that even a woman graced, as Clarice was, with the severest combination of intelligence and beauty would have been powerless to coax him away. But Clarice had been triply severe. She was guaranteed a position aboard one of the Valkyries, along with any partner she chose. She decided on first meeting that she wanted Chris, and she'd always had a way of having her way. She began as a ticket of transport to Alpha Centauri. And before he realized it, he was convincing himself that he loved her. Before he realized it, he did.

Now he had come where he wanted to be: to a planet orbiting another star. But the trip had cost him much.

Chris's little laser coin was badly damaged. Carrie had taken a hammer to it before he left, and Chris kept it hidden, not wanting to explain to Clarice how it got that way.

He inserted the family album into a flat. A New Year's Eve party flashed onto a corner of the wallscreen, full of data dropouts. There sat Uncle Dondi, and Carrie and

Jonathan. Chris ached. He had hurt them all. He tried to imagine what he and the family would be doing today if he'd stayed at home, and regretted that he would never know.

The cost of coming here, he told himself.

Wiping the corner of the screen clean and swinging one of the external scopes toward the sky, he focused on the Sun. The Earth was out there. It was too small and too dim to be seen at *Beagle*'s magnification. Even Jupiter was far too small. But somewhere up there his mother was buried, and he knew that his son probably cursed his name.

Under the circumstances, Chris had enough to think about that night without adding to it an alien whom no one had ever seen before calling him by his name.

(stow that thought)

But the thought refused to go away. What if—just what if Einsteinian time dilation turned out not to be very different from dying? he asked himself. Except, instead of lasting seconds, it dragged out through the whole relativistic phase of flight, pounding away at you for years. The newest hazard of near-light travel could thus be near-death hallucinations, and whatever impact they might have on the mind, and . . .

And what? Clarice never experienced an irrational disquiet, or bad dreams—

(time dilation and death)

—well, maybe it affects only some people, and not others. Or maybe, like most hot speculations, this one is all wrong.

(time and—)

—and that alien, up on the roof. Had she somehow shared my "relativistic psychosis"? Is that why the first and only words she—

She picked up the wrecked camera and reassembled it before Chris's eyes.

"What the—"

He cleared the flat and wrote, "FUQ2, check circuitry and operation of camera 2-D."

A second later, the computer flashed, "Normal."

"Any deviation from design plan?"

"None."

"It's identical?"

"Yes."

I couldn't do that, Chris thought. *No one* can put a camera back together that fast and make it work.

She handed the camera back to the astronomer, who immediately disassembled it and put it back together again.

NOON IN THE VALLEY OF WELLS.

The crowd about the clearing had diminished. In the shade of the *Beagle*, the astronomer and the chemist slept on a makeshift blanket, unaware that as they slept they inhaled a lingering residue of fusion products that would inevitably settle in their bones and glands. Above them, inside her ceramic shell, an alien named Clarice remotely examined and reexamined the camera, which the astronomer and his (friend? mate?) had taken apart and reassembled no less than a dozen times, with absolutely no variation from its original plan. She wondered how they could do that without a blueprint. They had put it back together entirely from memory, without error, but without invention either.

The astronomer was awakened by several sharp chirps that had risen from the general background murmur of boredom, and at the same moment he heard a peculiar humming overhead. The others drew nearer, and the astronomer and the chemist came bolting from underneath the ship. They stopped about ten meters away, and the astronomer looked back in puzzlement at the gaping, rectangular hole that had opened up in one side of the lander; and something moved restlessly within.

In there, hollow—a big hollow, the chemist signed. *In there, someone lives in the hollow.*

She was right, of course. It made sense, somehow; but he was mad at himself for not realizing earlier that *Devourer* must be hollow, and that someone, *Dim,* perhaps, could be in it.

The hole opened wider, and he pressed closer, as if the word "danger" had never existed, as if he expected to see one of his own townspeople emerging from the shadow—and he did expect to meet someone much like himself, perhaps someone from far away who signed in a different accent and whose hair might be a different color, but someone who was in all essentials just like him.

So he hopped right up to the cavity.

The two Things inside were—*ugly.* Their heads were small in proportion to their bodies, small and animallike. Four dark, brutish eyes were fixed on the astronomer's. One of the Things was grinning. The whole body, except for the head, seemed to be wrapped in a close-fitting blanket made from a fabric he had never seen. Their knees were on backward. They moved with surprising grace for creatures with such strange, deformed legs.

The astronomer was paralyzed by fascination mingled with a sudden chill of fear, fear such as he had not known since . . . since the fall that had left him half frozen on the Glacier Wear, dead, almost.

(dead? almost?)

Dead, the chemist had said—

(time and death?)

—dead. She brought you back from

(from that charred landscape?)

—back from Chris, back from the jaws of *Devourer.*

The chemist moved ahead of him and touched one of the creatures. It giggled, then touched back. Someone else came forward and touched. Then someone else.

Long seconds passed. The astronomer did not move, and one of the brutes had turned its face toward him.

"It's okay, I won't hurt you," the brute said—whatever that was supposed to mean. The astronomer's eyelids snapped shut as the creature made a move in his direction. He felt warm hands close softly around the sides of his face and work their way slowly to the back of his head. When he opened his eyes he was staring into that alien, hairless face.

And then the voice came to the astronomer from deep within. The words were incomprehensible, yet familiar. He had heard them before, on the ice, and now, again, the voice turned them outward and outward:

I am become Chris, the Devourer of worlds.

Outward and outward . . . suddenly, unexpectedly, Chris was sure that something in these peaceful-appearing creatures was about to die because of him, and he was similarly certain that he would die on A-4.

7

The Architects of Eden

Autumn, 33,552,365 B.C.

"WHAT DO YOU MEAN, CELLTREX, 'THEY'D ALREADY KNOW we are here'?"

"I mean, my friend, that three thousand years ago, before we began using cable networks and tight-beam laser relays, our planet was brighter than the suns at certain wavelengths. For hundreds of years our television programs and radar beacons were leaking out into space, spreading out in every direction at the speed of light."

"How far away do you think they can be detected?"

"That would depend on the quality of any extraterrestrial receivers. Green is seventy-seven light-years away. We could easily detect any primitive radio signals coming from there. I suppose a technology slightly more advanced than ours should be able to detect us at several thousand light-years."

"Nooo . . ."

"Yes," Celltrex said, pressing a fist against the side of his head in sympathetic consternation. "But that's a mixed curse. I think the Council Chiefs are making a big thing out of nothing. If there are extraterrestrial civilizations out there, then we've nothing to fear from them, because they've probably known about us for a very long time. If anyone out there wanted to harm us, we'd have heard from them by now. And Green? We've certainly nothing to fear from there. Yet what the Council considers doing to that perfectly harmless planet is the most extreme case of paranoia I have ever seen."

"Better not say that too loudly. You barely escaped hanging on the Mother Continent for being so outspoken. While we no longer have lynchings on this side of the world, we do have blacklisting and unemployment, which has the distinction of being slower and more torturous, and potentially just as deadly." Tyrell then pushed through a pair of priceless wooden doors, and led the way into one of A-4's most beautiful tea gardens. It was a geodesic half-dome, nearly three hundred meters across, and recessed into the side of a city-tower. Here, more than a kilometer above the farmlands, the air was dry and cool, and the dome's skin was silk netting that let the air blow through freely, yet kept the thousands of brightly colored flutter-fliers caged within. There were ramparts and bridges among the tallest trees, and a huge conference area nestled between two ponds. Three hundred Alphans—astronomers, geologists, geneticists, climatologists, zoologists, and botanists—were dining lavishly in front of a dais. Tree-ferns towered over them, and as Celltrex and Tyrell joined the gathering, something like an orchid broke free from one of the ferns, flapped its petals, and fluttered past a giant liquid crystal screen, scattering seeds as it went. At the dais, the President of the Commission was scrolling leisurely through pictures of eclipses and clam siphons on Green. She stopped purposefully at a close-up view of the protomonkey, froze the picture on the screen, and returned her attention to her meal.

An attendant brought warm tea to the two newcomers, took their orders, and returned with a lunch that went down very well.

It was the last thing that went down very well for Celltrex.

ON A CLEARING IN THE NORTH AFRICAN FOREST, THERE STOOD city-towers, dusty and red, and built by termites. Into this clearing came a troop of protomonkeys, and the largest of them pulled a weed out of the ground, stripped off the leaves with his teeth, and bounded deliberately toward a tower with the stem still in his mouth. The other creatures followed his example and, after wetting the stems with their spit, inserted them into holes in the towers and fished for termites. When the stems were withdrawn, dozens of writhing white shapes clung to them. These the protomonkeys licked off and swallowed; then they reinserted the stems and fished again.

The orchid-shaped robot did not stir as it watched from the clearing's edge. Following the command of its makers, it had sifted through teeming thousands of species, seeking out large-brained animals with manipulative limbs, and following after them. Its laser sent up a telescopic image of the toolmaking protomonkey—the only animal on all the worlds visited by all the Alphan probes able to create. Already in those dark brown eyes there was a dawning consciousness, a capacity for thought that was still latent on Green and could not possibly be fulfilled for ages; yet if the President of the Commission had her way, it might soon be extinguished forever.

PRESIDENT SUNRIGHT LEZ HAD LEFT THE TELESCOPIC VIEW of a protomonkey's face on the big screen throughout lunch, and even throughout her presentation, where it tacitly marshaled support for her view that Green was dangerous. The beast gazed out across the conference center like a giant subliminal message, and Celltrex felt that there should have been a law against it. But there were bigger issues to contend with, and to argue over the use of a still picture was to get tangled up in minor details—which, perhaps, was precisely the trap Sunright was attempting to bait the dissenters into.

Not that there was very much left for the dissenters to do. After decelerating from near-lightspeed and dropping off its orchid, the twenty-five-kilogram mother ship headed automatically to the Green-crossing asteroids. There it had constructed and planted charges, just in case they would ever be needed. Earlier scrutiny had revealed no signs of civilization within the system, and though the distances between stars required seventy-seven years for A-4 to receive the first pictures from Green, and another seventy-seven years for the mother ship to receive the appropriate response from A-4, no one on Green was anywhere near making even the crudest stone tools. Any danger the Commission could imagine was simply that: imagined. Yet the charges slept within the asteroids.

At last, President Sunright erased the protomonkey from the screen, and showed a close-up view of the first of several flying mountains that would be steered into the planet. In 512 years, the President announced, the asteroid was due to pass Green at a distance of 12.6 light-seconds. She explained that by applying a properly directed course change of twenty centimeters per second, added up over four successive explosions each time the asteroid crossed the orbit of the fifth and largest world, an actual collision, rather than a near miss of Green, could be arranged using only an equivalent two megatons of the mother ship's remaining fuel reserves. Sunright showed ever-closer views of the bowl-shaped crater into which the first antihydrogen charge had been placed, then began describing the crater in exhaustive detail, and all the smaller craters in the territory immediately surrounding it, reciting long names for each one.

"There you have it," Celltrex whispered to Tyrell. "There's your problem. The President is a keynamer."

Tyrell did not seem to welcome the interruption. He pressed a hand to his forehead and grunted disapproval.

"This is the safest course for us," Sunright continued. "Periodic asteroid bombardments should not entirely exterminate life on the planet, but they will make life extremely difficult for the toolmakers, and perhaps even drive them to extinction. Furthermore, should another civilization chance upon the Green system, they will look upon the impacts as a natural disaster. They will not suspect that we exist. It's final, nonrisky, and easy."

Celltrex rose up on his haunches. "Excuse me, President. But why?"

"Have we not sent a spaceship to Green at ninety-five percent lightspeed? You do understand the first implication of relativistic flight, do you not?"

Celltrex did understand the implication. Any spacecraft propelled to ninety-five percent the speed of light, or even thirty percent, even if its mass was no greater than an average-sized railroad car, became a planet cracker. If such a thing were to strike A-4 at that speed, even with its antimatter tanks empty, civilization, if not life itself, would be finished. Much of that railroad-car-sized mass, along with much of the matter it encountered as it dove through the planet's atmosphere, would be converted to raw energy. The numbers were staggering . . . a relativistic fireball radiating a trillion watts per square centimeter . . . a plasma boundary layer millions of degrees hotter than the suns . . . for hundreds of kilometers in every direction, the atmosphere is plowed away . . . walls of air pile up thousands of kilometers high, hovering at the edges of the strike, while all below is vacuum and backblast and ruin . . . a hemisphere of A-4 dances and sways, leaps and snaps and burns.

And there were worse things. A relativistic bomb was unstoppable. Truly unstoppable. You might hope to throw a few "smart rocks" in its path, but it was impossible to predict the exact motion or position of anything traveling at ninety-five percent the speed of light. If you could spot an engine burn two light-years away, the target would actually be only eight weeks away by the time you saw the burn. And by the time you saw it eight weeks away, it was actually four days away. And if it zigged and zagged ever so slightly, you would have no idea where it was coming from. A relativistic rocket launched offensively against a planet was certain to strike that planet. The attacked were always powerless to prevent it, given even ten million years of technological advancement beyond the Alphans.

"But the toolmakers of Green are far from becoming a relativistic species," said Celltrex. "They can pose no threat to us, and that will remain true for a very long time."

"But eventually, if they are left on their own . . ."

"Eventually what, President Sunright? What is the probability that we will ever see relativistic attack from Green?"

"Less than one chance in twenty-two thousand."

"Isn't that safe enough?"

"Considering the consequences, no risk is acceptable," said the President, and a murmur of agreement ran through the audience.

"Let's put it another way," Celltrex pressed. "You say one chance in twenty-two thousand. I take it that's the probability of the toolmakers ever evolving into a relativistic species like our own?"

"Yes, and every relativistic species will eventually come to fear the existence of any other relativistic species; and if possible, we must try to prevent the origin of others, who may become fearful of us and respond to their fear."

"How long, President, until the toolmakers evolve into a relativistic species?"

"At least twenty-three million years."

Celltrex was impressed with the President's ability to provide precise numbers, and to recite the names of hundreds, even thousands, of individual craters on an asteroid. It did appear to him to be a newly acquired ability, however; an ability that was spreading rapidly among his people—especially those in charge—and though he had little doubt that if he asked the President to estimate the number of sand grains that would be found on a given stretch of beach, she would instantly provide accurate upper and lower limits, her new powers seemed to be subtracting something from her thinking. They came at a price. Sunright had a clear focus on minute details, but she was missing the big picture, and Celltrex, heedless of whatever criticism he might draw from the only people in all the world who had given him refuge, was taking it upon himself to show her.

"At what speed," he asked, "are we moving away from the Green system?"

"40.887 light-minutes per year."

"So two things we know, President Sunright Lez. It will take at least twenty-three million years for a relativistic species to emerge on Green, and Green and A-4 are moving away from each other at some forty-one light-minutes per year—"

"No—40.887 light-minutes," someone interrupted from the floor.

"—which leads us to a third thing that you didn't know before. How many light-years away will Green be in twenty-three million years?"

"1,789.17," said President Sunright.

"Don't you see?" said Celltrex. "That's the point. By

the time they begin building even a Bronze Age civilization, we'll be nicely quarantined from the Greens. And if we're still around then, and if there's anything that worries us about these other people, we'll have nearly two thousand years to decide what to do about it. Let's not panic quite yet." He spoke these last words while pressing two fingers to his temple and smiling indulgently—a gesture of arrogance. If he had simply let the words stand on their own merit, logic might have prevailed, and Earth-crossing asteroids might have continued on their natural paths. But like most of history's great turning points, the outcome was not to be decided by logic. It was decided by a game of egos.

8

Death at Tranquillity

Winter, A.D. 2048

FOUR EPOCHS HAD PASSED, AND YET THE EARTH STILL remained green. Humankind now surveyed the universe from the same ledge upon which the Alphans had stood some thirty-three million years before. More than a dozen uncrewed probes had gone out ahead of the Valkyries. Two of them, each weighing less than thirty kilograms, had decelerated from ninety-two percent lightspeed and settled with unerring precision into orbit around the fourth world of Alpha Centauri A. From the nearest star shot two brilliant hairline spokes of microwave radiation. They spread six thousand kilometers wide through the intervening 4.2 light-years to Earth. Across the face of the planet, hundreds of little receiving stations caught the signals and translated them into pictures. To all outward appearances, A-4 was a pristine world never touched by industrial hands. There was no trace of the two-kilometer-high towers upon which Celltrex and Tyrell had once stood, contemplating the future. The artificial continents had long turned to mineral ores sandwiched between layers of sedimentary rock, and pieces of what had once been the Tiber Valley lay scattered in beds of siltstone on the tops of mountains. Forests grew everywhere. The space probes looked down upon a world of unusual beauty, sending back thermographs, analyses of oceanic currents and cloud patterns, and scans across the entire electromagnetic spectrum. But there was one thing no machine, outward-bound for the stars, could possibly convey to its creators, because there was no way of recording or interpreting the Lazarus Effect except through personal experience. It would soon shock the first interstellar travelers from Earth, as it had the Alphans, contributing much to the earlier civilization's historical misadventures.

As with most forms of seasickness and space sickness, some people were immune, most were not, and those who were not were affected to varying degrees. Prediction was difficult, and in the case of the Lazarus Effect, the only predictor was how one experienced the act of dying, for the experience of relativistic flight and time dilation, it turned out, was often a series of startlingly real "hallucinations" or "visions," not at all unlike some near-death visions, in which one's sense of time and reality could lose all meaning. If flight between the stars was a little bit like dying, the result was that you never wanted to send a susceptible explorer at relativistic speed and fully conscious to a place where he might encounter other civilized beings. The man who represented your civilization could very well be utterly disoriented by the time he got there. And from that perspective, he would be obliged to tell them about you.

If anyone on Earth had foreseen this effect, he need only have perfected the art of putting people into a deep, dreamless sleep and slowing their metabolisms, thereby keeping the Valkyrie crews unconscious as they sailed from star to star. But nobody knew these things in A.D. 2048. There was no way of anticipating, given only the experiences of interstellar robots, that relativistic flight could have psychological effects, or that one of the first interstellar travelers was also a man most likely to succumb to Lazarus sickness—which was ultimately unlucky for Earth.

FLOATING TEN THOUSAND KILOMETERS ABOVE THE MOON'S northern hemisphere, almost directly over the Crater Clarke, were history's first crew-rated interstellar rockets. One of them, the *Beagle*, cradled in full acceleration rigging, had just completed her twelfth uncrewed test flight out to a distance of fifteen light-minutes, just beyond the orbit of Mars. Her tanks, nearly empty now, were supercooled to within one-fifty thousandth of a degree of absolute zero, nearly three degrees below the faint echo of the universe's beginning, which still pervaded every cubic meter of space with a warm glow; hence some of the coldest places in the universe were of human origin.

Beagle's engines were little more than glorified electron microscopes—magnetic coils that guided and focused streams of particles, converting them into jets. The coils themselves were crawling with mechanical "mice" and "slugs."

Within the empty crew compartment, ten kilometers behind the engines, near the end of a tether, liquid crystal screens started to flash. Something big was moving out there in the night, coming in fast. *Beagle*'s scopes snapped with astonishing speed in the indicated direction. An instant later, the screens displayed an identification—

COMPOSITION: CARBONACEOUS CHONDRITE
    TYPE II
MASS: 2000 KG ± 400 KG
VELOCITY: 20 KM/SECOND
DIRECTION: LUNAR IMPACT, EARTH SIDE,

APPROXIMATELY EQUATORIAL 30° EAST LONGI-
TUDE

—and on the magnifier a dim yet steadily growing star burned in the shoulder of Polaris. The possibility of a collision with the ship should never have occurred to the computer. Even in the relatively cluttered plane of the solar system, space was so empty and vast that a dart tossed blindly into the Grand Canyon would have a greater chance of striking a specific grain of sand. Just the same, even as the *Beagle* realized that the meteor would miss her by more than a thousand kilometers, she sparked her main engine once, preparing for evasion. The resulting concussion of gamma rays and neutrinos became an expanding sphere that was, within one thousandth of a second, almost six hundred kilometers across. A fiftieth of a second later, a large, mantis-like machine conducting minerological surveys near the edge of the Moscow Sea detected a pinpoint gamma ray source high in the northern sky. As the sphere's expanding surface contacted the lunar far side, its gamma rays were intercepted by the first few centimeters of soil and bedrock, but the neutrinos did not behave like wavelengths of light. Born of reactions involving the so-called "weak force" that governs the decay of atomic nuclei, their interactions with all other matter in the universe were inconceivably weak. They traveled through the Moon like ghosts. At Tranquillity Base, trillions of them rose through the floor of the *Apollo 11* Monument. The three people gathered there felt nothing as the particles shot through their feet, penetrated their hearts and brains, and continued toward Earth. A second and a half later, they passed through the Earth.

THE MAN WHO WOULD SOON TRAVEL TO A DISTANT STAR AND bring his brethren to the brink of relativistic war—the man they called Christopher Wayville—was one of the three gathered at Tranquillity when *Beagle* prepared to make its dodge. The ship watched the object dwindle and vanish behind the rim of the Moon. No one else except *Beagle* seemed to be paying attention.

"Admiral Fitz Roy sends his compliments," a distant voice announced in Chris's suit radio. "You and Ms. Elmer Glue are to lunch at his office with Prime Minister Tam. Is thirteen hundred hours all right?"

"How long does that give us?"

"About two hours at Tranquillity, if you want it."

Chris turned to his companions. They nodded approval.

"Okay, Olsen. Thirteen hundred hours."

"Righto. Don't get your feet wet. Over and out."

The dusty moonscape lay all around them. About two centimeters of permaglass, and barely two millimeters more of empty space, separated Christopher Wayville's boots from Buzz Aldrin's bootprints. Not quite twenty meters away stood the abandoned shell that housed LM-5's empty fuel tanks, and the engine that had emptied them.

It seemed incredible to him that men could have accomplished so much with such primitive equipment . . . to come here in chemical rockets, not even knowing whether or not the surface would swallow them up. And what must the Apollo years have been like for her? The woman they called Elmer Glue stood beside him, scanning the horizon and trying to form for herself a clear image of the first rays of the lunar dawn on that last day of the old world, just before the ship had come out of the sky. She was currently the Moon's leading authority on Apollo, the only one old enough to have known the men who first came here. Her father was actually one of the builders of the ship in whose presence they now stood. His hands had touched it (through sterile gloves, if the history books were right), and he'd stood on Earth and watched it take to the sky, knowing that he would never go to the Moon himself, or even into space, but knowing also that something he had built was on its way. One of the astronauts, Fred Haise, who'd flown that hair-raising *Apollo 13* mission, had nicknamed her Elmer Glue; and for seventy-eight years the name had stuck.

Presently, she drew a silver pouch from her hip pocket. Bold red letters stamped into its surface proclaimed:

PROPERTY OF THE NATIONAL AIR AND SPACE
MUSEUM
SMITHSONIAN INSTITUTION

She unzipped the pouch, pulled out two shiny objects, and motioned the two cosmonauts to her side.

"These are for you," she said. "I've finally gotten permission, after, I might add, a good deal of effort, to give each of you a piece of the original *Eagle*, to take with you on your voyages."

Four centimeters square, and membrane-thin . . .

Anwar, who would next year be leading a party of four to Barnards Star aboard *Yamato* and *Calypso*, held his sliver up to the sun and turned it between thumb and forefinger. "Gold foil!" he shouted. "From *Eagle*? Really?"

"From *Eagle*," said Elmer Glue. "It's part of a larger piece they found about a kilometer from here, where the blast of the ascent engine had thrown it."

The whole bottom of the ship seemed to be draped in gold foil. It ran all the way down the legs and over the footpads. Anwar had heard that the Apollo people covered the surface this way to prevent heat from soaking up into the fuel tanks, or something like that. Something strange. But one question bothered him as he turned the little sliver over and over between his fingers: "Why gold? It's so expensive, and so heavy. Pushing all that extra mass around would have cost them a big penalty in fuel consumption. *Why gold?*"

"It's not gold, actually," said Elmer Glue. "They somehow plated aluminum onto mylar film. Nobody's sure exactly how they did it, either. It's sort of a lost art. The mylar had a yellow tint, and that's what made the aluminum look like gold. The mylar-aluminum combination was lightweight and cheap, and it provided good insulation, and reflected more sunlight than real gold. No fools, they."

She then removed a wallet-sized photograph of a fifteen-year-old girl from the pouch. It was she, as she had appeared almost eighty years ago, when her father, alone with *Eagle* only a few days before the launch, had slid the photo behind a sheet of gold foil and given to his child the gift of immortality. In the benign environment of the Sea of Tranquillity, in the absence of wind and rain and oxygen, she would probably have achieved a measure of endlessness beyond the dreams of any pharaoh. Long after the golden mask of Tutankhamen ceased to be even a memory, a little girl's smile would endure on the Moon.

But immortality was almost lost. At the beginning of the century, one of the first industrial expeditions to the Moon had returned the photograph to Earth, where it was displayed at Washington's Air and Space Museum. Some forty years of exposure to light, moisture, and oxygen had yellowed the film, and robbed some of the glitter from little Elmer Glue's eyes.

"This is what all those years of debate and court proceedings were all about," a voice beside the two cosmonauts radioed. "They said they were only making history more accessible to the public. Well, bullfeathers! They were only removing objects from their original historic context. They were *tampering* with history. You don't tamper with history, Chris, Anwar—no matter how good your intentions."

Now, very gently, she pulled several leaves of gold foil forward, and inserted her photograph exactly where the colonists had found it.

A Grumman "spider" nosed around the corner of *Eagle*, carrying under its belly a broad sheet of permaglass. It had a high, robust body about a half meter long, supported on six many-jointed legs that, to a newcomer from Earth, would have seemed impossibly thin. The machine took careful strides, avoiding Armstrong's and Aldrin's bootprints, while little whips near the tips of its legs erased its own prints. Other machines—spindly and barely larger than mice—scurried to and fro underfoot. They moved purposefully, erasing the bootprints of the first industrial expeditions, and leaving in their place the illusion of virgin Moon dust. Some of the colonists, behaving much like tourists on Hollywood Boulevard, had matched their boot sizes against those of the *Apollo 11* astronauts. If not for the NASA photo archives, no one would have been able to locate the position of Neil Armstrong's first step, and restore it. The American flag, too, would have to be replaced. Someone had stolen it. Christopher Wayville guessed that had Elmer Glue's photograph not ended up in the Smithsonian Institution, it would by now be as utterly lost as the flag.

The spider snapped the permaglass sheet into place, firmed it with manipulators, then headed around back for another sheet. In a few weeks, visitors would be able to retrace Armstrong's and Aldrin's footsteps without actually disturbing them. They could bring their fingers within touching distance of the ship's hull, but an almost invisible barrier of permaglass would prevent them from ever again touching it, pulling off pieces, and taking them away.

The contours of the permaglass matched the contours of the land so exactly that it was difficult to tell that the barrier existed at all. And all of this was Elmer Glue's doing. Now that the Club Med people had tested and discovered a lode of profits on the Moon, the Smithsonian had put her in charge of restoring the *Apollo 11* landing site. She chose not to disfigure the place with airtight domes and Maglev rails leading to Port Chaffee. Instead, people would arrive by truck, following a permanent road indistinguishable from the original lunar surface without infrared glasses. When they stepped out, they would step out in space suits, just like Armstrong and Aldrin.

"I always hoped to have my own museum one day," said Elmer Glue. "But I never imagined that by the time I got it, I'd be the oldest thing in it."

"It's beautiful out here," Chris said. "You've got it looking just like 1969 again."

"Very refreshing," said Anwar. "Especially after all those horror stories about how they were going to dome the whole thing over. What are you going to do for an encore?"

"Well, for a start, *Eagle*'s ascent stage is still up there in lunar orbit. But she's dropping altitude fast, and before she crashes I want to haul her down to Chaffee for display in the Samantha Smith Gallery. I was also planning to recover *Apollo 13*'s third-stage booster, but the Array robots got there before I could. It's all level plain and solar panels now. *Apollo 12* and *Surveyor* are gone, too."

"You're kidding," said Anwar.

"Afraid not. The very first landings, of course, had to be near the equator in order to guarantee enough fuel for a return to the Command Module, which was always in equatorial orbit. Unfortunately, the equator is also prime real estate for solar power production.

"And let me tell you something," she continued, turning toward Chris. "If a thousand Arc Angels came down and stood before me and told me that your friends at the Lunar Power Authority *accidentally* overlooked a few historical sites, I'd *still* call them liars. If I hadn't raised hell, all of this would now be under the Asimov Array. As it is, it practically covers this world. I remember when you could look up from Earth and see something romantic in the Moon. Now your eye goes right to that ugly streak across its middle."

Elmer Glue was a member of that so-called "new wave" of lunar colonists, and Chris had not yet decided whether they would become a blessing or a curse. For the most part, he wished the GreenPeace people would confine their activities to the one planet that was meant to be green and peaceful. One of the great advantages of places like the Moon and Mercury was their complete lack of rivers and forests and air—no environments to destroy. Now that solar farms were fueling starships from Mercury and beaming down clean electricity from the Moon, Asimov Array robots were said to be destroying the natural beauty of other worlds. Well, shit on them, Chris thought. There was plenty of natural, cratered wasteland to go around—at least in this solar system.

Chris lifted the sliver of gold foil to his faceplate and saw the Earth shining through it. "The metal is so thin," he was about to say, when the object *Beagle* had been watching impacted about twelve kilometers away. At more than twenty kilometers per second, it dove through more than a dozen meters of bedrock, excavated a thirty-meter-wide crater, and scattered pieces of itself and its surroundings for kilometers in every direction. Had it fallen upon Port Chaffee, it would easily have penetrated through to the subterranean chambers and hallways, causing grievous harm. But the nearest people were below the horizon, at Tranquillity Base, toward which an ejecta blanket of shards ranging from fist-sized down to sand grain-sized was arching. Without an atmosphere to slow them, the rocks continued flying at the same velocity with which the meteorite had originally catapulted them. Even the sand grains, which on Earth would have stalled in the air and collectively formed cauliflower billows of smoke, now carried with them stings like a volley of tiny razor blades shot from a cannon.

Without air to carry the sound of the explosion, and with the first splinters of rock arriving even before the thump of the impact could be transmitted through the basalt beneath his feet, Christopher Wayville neither saw nor felt, and barely had time to comprehend, what caused his death.

Hundreds of little white splash marks appeared in the permaglass, and simultaneously Chris became aware of a whistling sound in his suit. Air was escaping through a hole—it couldn't have been a very large one, otherwise he'd have been sucked right through it—but in space any hole at all was large enough. Almost immediately his ears began to pop, and he understood that breathing was going to become very difficult, very fast . . .

As his brain switches instinctively to maximum overdrive, snaps up and begins analyzing every new image, every new sound in search of a way out, each second stretches to the outermost limits, and Chris begins living in a netherworld of slowed time . . . One of those astonishingly long seconds he spends tending to an absurd detail: making sure the square of gold foil is zipped safely in his leg pocket as he begins his first forward leap in the direction of the truck . . . With his free hand he tries to find the hole and block the outflow of air . . . but the air continues to thin and a natural, deep-rooted reflex almost causes him to hold his breath . . . but no—a picture flashes up from his subconscious: Keir Dullea in that classic film, about to leap across airless space to lobotomize the computer HAL—but before the helmetless astronaut blows the explosive bolts, he hyperventilates and then holds his breath—NEVER, NEVER DO THIS! Chris warns himself—IN THE

VACUUM OF SPACE, AIR TRAPPED IN YOUR LUNGS WILL EXPAND INSTANTLY AND KILL YOU—it is against every natural instinct, but Chris exhales as he runs . . . and ahead of him he sees Anwar struggling with his helmet . . . a geyser of red mist is jetting through his fingers—GOD, NO! HAS HE HELD HIS BREATH? . . . A long second later, the question loses all meaning as Anwar's faceplate pops off and the outrush of air jets him backward onto the floor of the *Apollo 11* Monument . . . A head has grown out of the helmet, a head where it has no business being . . . In his world of increasingly slowed time, Chris does not even register a shudder as he dimly files away for future reference, somewhere in the back of his mind, that Anwar, though appearing to be merely asleep, must in fact be quite dead, for his neck has broken at a crazy forward angle . . . And then, as Chris exhales and inhales only vacuum, as he nears the truck and the rapid-fire evaporation of moisture from his skin makes his face intensely cold, he stumbles and falls and cannot get up . . . His eyes and ears are pounding, but he begins to lose interest in these new sensations . . . begins to lose interest in everything as an unlikely calm surges over him . . . and he's jerked up by the shoulders . . . it's Elmer Glue . . . she's pulling him toward the truck's air lock.

"You're going to be all right," she radios to him, but there is no trace of air to carry the sound in Chris's helmet.

Together with his suit, Chris weighs sixteen kilograms—"Thank God for lunar gravity," Elmer Glue radios again.

Still, she is ninety-five years old, and between the moment Chris stumbles and the moment he is surrounded again by sea-level air, a full minute passes.

II
Time and Time Again

9

Teacher's Pet

Autumn, A.D. 2054

THE WAYVILLES MOVED AWAY FROM THE SHIP. THE ALIENS followed, crowding around, hopping excitedly, impatiently, like little children expecting gifts from Grandpa. Behind them, very quietly, FUQ2 closed the doors, just in case the Alphans had any ideas about going inside.

Chris stopped in the clearing and pointed at himself. It was time for the language lessons. Pointing, he said, "Chris."

Chattering rose all around him. Some of the creatures scratched funny lines and squiggles on each other's arms. Simultaneously, a small alien hand brushed gently down the length of Chris's forearm, sketching lines with its fingers. Then they were all silent, and looked at him as if expecting an answer.

Chris didn't know how to answer. Nobody had ever contacted *aliens* before.

They're friendly, he told himself. They want to talk. But *how* do we talk? How do I tell them that when I point at something and say a word, it's a name?

Presently, one of them backed away. Chris recognized her (her?) as the one who had first touched him when he stepped out of the ship. She pointed (pointed? Th-that's *neat!*)—pointed behind him, at the *Beagle*, and uttered a string of words that included his name.

"No," he said, shaking his head. He turned and pointed where she was pointing: "*Beagle*," then, to himself: "Chris."

"No," she repeated, and then pointed at the ship: "*Beagle*." She pointed at him: "Chris."

"Yes. Yes!" he said, smiling. The Alphan seemed to smile back, pointing at herself and uttering a rapid-fire series of incomprehensible chirps. It lasted for about five seconds. Good God, Chris told himself. I hope that isn't her name. There's no way I can repeat it.

Clarice took the flat from under Chris's arm and said, "FU, did you get those last chirps?"

"Yes."

"Good. Can you identify the alien who sang them?"

"Yes."

"That's fine, FU. Now, when I point at her, I want you to play back the chirps."

Clarice pointed; the chirps played out. The alien immediately pointed to herself, hopped up once, and repeated the chirps. She cocked her head to one side and grinned.

Chris looked at Clarice and nodded approval. "Quick thinking," he whispered.

"Well, we've learned her name—I think. FU, I want you to begin a file on her, starting with her picture. Whenever I point at her, you repeat those chirps."

"Okay. Would you like me to file an Earth name with her?"

"Good idea. Good idea. That will make things much simpler. I think I'll call her Catherine—Catherine the Great."

"Chris. *Beagle*," said Catherine, pointing. Then she

leveled a finger at Clarice and went silent, seeming to invite an answer.

"Clarice," she replied.

"Clarice," Catherine repeated.

Then, pointing quickly, the other aliens recited, "*Beagle*, Clarice, Chris."

Taking the initiative now, Catherine the Great, Catherine the chemist, pointed to a tree and chirped. She pointed to another and whistled, then to another, and another, assigning to each a different pattern of noises.

Chris pointed to each of the trees Catherine had singled out, then added a few to the bargain and said, "Tree, tree, tree . . ."

Catherine made a surprisingly human gesture that reminded Chris of how an insensitive teacher might express impatience with a schoolboy who has failed to master a simple task. The Alphans had at least a dozen keynames for every tree in the forest. They transmitted the words, from time to time, through an abbreviated touchscript applied to the forearm, the same form of communication that Chris had just experienced and found so puzzling. Through keynames, each tree was known by its approximate age, its height, its location, its distinguishing characteristics, and even the keynames of its ancestors. The names of the trees alone were too complex for the human brain to hold. There were too many subtleties, too many things to be remembered. Only the ship's computer could hope to speak their language.

Even at this early stage, the Wayvilles understood that the quickest way to communicate with the Alphans would be to teach them English.

They'd better learn fast, Chris supposed. For already there were signs of trouble. One of the Alphans, the one who had acted so strangely when Chris touched him, had drawn away from the others and preferred to watch from the edge of the clearing.

Catherine pointed at the loner and seemed to invite him into the crowd.

The loner said, "No."

The little beasties picked that up fast enough, thought Chris.

7 OCTOBER, A.D. 2054.

Midmorning in the Valley of Wells.

A little white knot of Alphans was waiting when the Wayvilles stepped out of the ship, just as they had waited the morning before, and the morning before. Except for Catherine, the faces seemed to change each day, and the arrivals from the (village? encampment?) came with the ever-expanding collection of English words already in their heads.

They were good students. Point and say a word, and the Alphans would remember it. Then they'd go home and teach the other Alphans.

Catherine started the class by repeating one of Clarice's very first demonstrations. She held out a pebble and let it drop to the ground. "Fall," she said.

"Good," Clarice said.

"Clarice. Question: In *Beagle* today?"

Sure. Why not? Clarice thought. We've nothing to hide from them, and she understands English well enough that I can tell her not to touch something and she will obey.

CATHERINE, THE CHEMIST, WAS THE FIRST TO BE BROUGHT into the hollow of *Beagle*. She wondered at the room's queer furnishings. The things called "Bed" and "Table" were easy, but there was simply no telling what a "Chair" was used for until Clarice showed her. Creatures with backward knees and lacking tails could not sit on their haunches, *they had to sit on top of something*.

She was more puzzled by her hosts' unwillingness or inability to learn her language. They lived in a house that flew. They had to be intelligent. *Had to be.* Yet they were not smart enough, or attentive enough, to learn the trees, or even to learn her own keynames. Clarice, whom she now regarded with genuine affection, insisted on calling her by a name almost as dull as her own, or letting the "Flat" speak the keynames for her. The Wayvilles' memories seemed to be seriously impaired, like the minds of brain-damaged children.

Clarice led her to a "Wallscreen." It showed the outside, which was puzzling. From the outside, she could not remember seeing any large holes in Clarice's house, none except the "Door" through which they had entered. Yet here was a floor-to-ceiling window, clearer than ice, through which she could see all the way to the edge of the field, where the astronomer stood alone, still determined to keep his distance from the *Beagle*. She whistled across the field, then signed to him, but apparently he did not see her. How could a window see only one way? To own such a thing, they *had* to be intelligent, and they also had to come from far, far away, from a place farther than any rocket explorer had yet flown to and returned to describe. She liked to believe that they came from the very edge of the world; and if this was true (and, oh, what a big, beautiful IF), then there was no end to the fantastic things they would know and be able to teach.

Fantastic things lay all around. The chemist went directly to a rack of tubes, to which a crazy garden of alien plants clung. One of them gave off a most pleasant odor.

"Question," the chemist said, pointing at the plant.

"Strawberry," Clarice answered.

The chemist snatched a fruit from the vine—

"No!" Clarice said.

—and popped it into her mouth.

THE WAYVILLES MOVED A ONE-METER-SQUARE FOLD-OUT FLAT outside the *Beagle*. Chris explained to his "students"

how the flat must be protected from wind and rain,
and together they erected an enclosing lean-to some
forty meters from the ship. Forty meters was safely
beyond the "hot grass"—which Chris did not explain
to his students.

Now that they had picked up the words, it was time to
show them how sentences and paragraphs and conversations were made. The best way to do that would be to
show humans responding to situations, and to each other. FUQ2 printed off several stacks of children's coins,
to which Clarice added some of her favorite movies—
science fiction, all of them. The latest box-office smash,
the long-awaited sequel to *The Day the Earth Stood Still*,
was not among them. Michael Rennie had died almost
a century ago, yet he emerged from the memory of a
Hollywood computer as if alive yesterday. But at least
his comeback was dignified. Poor Norma Jean Baker
and John Fitzgerald Kennedy had been resurrected in
living color and three dimensions for a musical soft core
titled *Came-a-lot*.

With the fad for computer-resurrected actors, Clarice
thought that Hollywood had sunk to the lowest possible
depth, until the latest film broadcasts, fifty-two months
old now, started arriving from Earth. They'd brought
back Clark Gable and Judy Garland for the musical
version of *Moby Dick*.

Tacky, tacky, tacky, Clarice thought. What next?
Presidential candidates who don't exist, whose every
facial feature, mannerism, and habit of speech has
been meticulously crafted on a computer? Irresistible,
charismatic, and—no; she brushed the thought away.
For the present, there were the language lessons to
contend with.

Clarice guessed that she and Chris and the Alphans
would be having actual conversations in no time at
all. They'd absorbed the nouns and verbs immediately, without error and without effort. She'd never seen

anything like it. The Alphans learned everything.

"Flat," she explained, pointing to the screen. "You see movie. Say, 'FUQ2. Show me movie.' "

FUQ2 flashed a mountain scene onto the flat, drawing a flurry of chitters from the Alphans.

"Now watch," said Chris. "FUQ2, list movies."

One after the other, some twenty pictures flashed onto the screen. When Chris saw the one he was looking for, he called, "Stop," and then "Show."

It was one of Clarice's favorites, an old 2-D about a boy named Elliot and his friend from the stars.

7 OCTOBER.

Night in the Valley of Wells.

"FUQ2," the alien said. "Show me Clarice."

Inside *Beagle*'s tiled shell, Clarice took the towel from her wet hair and draped it over her shoulders. Mirroring the wallscreen, she sat at the breakfast table and began brushing out the knots. In the mirror, she saw Chris watching her from the shower doorway. Chris closed the door and moved up behind her.

"You're still worried about that strawberry, aren't you?" Chris said, then put his hands on the nape of her neck and began a light massage.

"Not a hell of a lot. I just wish we had more than FU's word on it that Earth food will not be bad for them. It's okay the other way around. All we do is stick a pin in any food they offer us and FU tells us in a flash if it's safe."

Chris raised a hand to Clarice's cheek. She leaned her head against it.

"Probably no harm done," said Chris softly. "She only ate one. And besides, everything in that strawberry is put together backward, from her body's point of view."

Clarice raised her own hand to the hand on her cheek and led it gently under the towel. Chris found his breath quickening as their fingers closed over an erect nipple.

"Anyway, it will probably pass through completely undigested," Chris continued.

"Right."

"Yeah, the whole biochemistry of this world is written in reverse. Did I tell you that FU found something close to chlorophyll in the grass?"

"Three times."

"It's backward."

Clarice made a soft sound as Chris's hand glided gently from one breast to the other.

"Even the sugars are backward."

"It's okay, then," Clarice said absently. "She'll be right, mate." She leaned back and nudged Chris's hands into a slow descent along her body.

"You know what I really want to learn from them?" One hand found her belly, the other found the soft curls of hair. He paused there, spreading his fingers, taking in the shudder beneath them. "One of the first things I want to ask them, when they can really speak English—"

"Is whether they believe in God," Clarice finished for him.

"Yes. You don't think that's silly, do you?"

"No."

"I'm glad. I think I'm really beginning to like this planet."

"Good. Then shut up and kiss me, fool!"

FUQ2 DISCOVERED THE UNAUTHORIZED STREAM OF DATA outflowing to the fold-out flat in the Alphan field. FU knew from her library that many humans were exhibitionists. She connected this fact with Clarice's request, back in 2048, that no ship interior scenes should be broadcast to Earth when she and Chris made love, and from this connection FU concluded that the present broadcast to the Alphans was a mistake. Yet even as she killed the broadcast, her passengers' moans were downlinked through the hull of the ship, and a tremendous cheer went up outside.

10

The Keynamers

Autumn, 33,552,365 B.C.

"**I** APPRECIATE YOUR OPINION," THE PRESIDENT SAID, AND then no one spoke to Celltrex or recognized his right to speak for the remainder of the conference.

He could not understand their way of thinking. When the Alphans first developed interstellar spacecraft, the best thing they had ever hoped to find was a spectacularly beautiful world just like Green. No one had planned to destroy such a world once it was found. But for three days the Commission had focused on the ludicrously small probability that a civilization capable of star flight might rapidly develop on Green. And once the danger was present, the argument went, there would be no stopping them. And it would also be only a matter of time before the other people became keynamers. They would begin to genetically redesign their own brains, artificially boost their intelligence very quickly beyond the capacity of anyone on A-4, and perhaps dream up devices even more frightening than relativistic bombs.

If Celltrex had been allowed to ask the President or her closest advisors about the probability of a starfaring civilization arising on Green in the space of a few hundred, or even a few thousand, years, they would have answered: one chance in several billion, or even a trillion. But probabilities did not enter into the argument. A kind of tunnel vision had settled in, and by alienating the President, Celltrex had reinforced it.

After the conference, Celltrex stayed behind in the garden, enjoying the feel of cool and relatively smog-free air ruffling his fur. It was night on A-4. A brilliant red star, almost a sun, cast a blood-red glow over the haze layer and the city-towers that protruded through it. Only Tyrell had stayed behind with him. For a long time the two Alphans said nothing. They just stood together, watching the dim, yellow-white star of the Green system setting behind a tower.

"The President is a keynamer," Celltrex said at last.

"And most of the Commission," Tyrell volunteered.

"And you?"

"I . . . I had no choice. They're walking encyclopedias. They remember everything. There was no other way to keep up with them."

Tyrell was right, of course. The new drug allowed one to store whole telephone directories in one's head, or to assign a different name to every crater on an asteroid, and to forever remember each name; but what good was knowing such facts, Celltrex wondered, if one did not also know how to connect them?

"You should take the I.Q. boost yourself," Tyrell urged. "There's no describing what it's like to feel your abilities enlarged every morning, to awake and see things you never saw before."

"But it's permanent," said Celltrex. "Your DNA is pumping out substances it never pumped out before— at least not in such large quantities. Your children are going to inherit those same qualities, and all the Council children, and in another generation, perhaps all the children of A-4. A mind-expanding drug that truly does expand the mind? Possibly, but at what cost?"

"Don't you see it, Celltrex? We have finally taken control of our genetic destiny. The age of random variation from generation to generation on this planet is over. We can begin to direct our own evolution. We can choose our future."

"I don't see it, old friend. And certainly I will not see it in my own family lineage—ever. If your abilities were really so enlarged, you would use your newfound eyes to view our planet as if it were another. A species attempting to program its own genetic destiny? What can be more dangerous? That's what will really wipe out a civilization. We needn't worry about relativistic bombs from Green."

Tyrell had used all of his influence to get Celltrex safely away from the Mother Continent, and to find him work. But his friend had responded, as he did almost everywhere these days, by pointing out the mistakes of even his own supporters. For an Alphan who at times tended to show glimmers of extraordinary insight, he had no knowledge at all about good politics, and within hours of stepping off a scramjet, had managed to create a generally shared mood of "let's get Celltrex." Even Tyrell was beginning to succumb to that feeling.

"The Commission members are agreeing with the Mother Continent," Tyrell said slowly. "You've cut your own guts out in a most public display. They're voting to revoke your credentials."

"And your vote?"

"I'm abstaining. But it won't make any difference. I'm afraid the vote will go overwhelmingly against you. In a day or two you'll have no degree."

"Do they think they can change my name so easily, as if I won't know who I am? Besides, most people's degrees are about as meaningful as the degrees on a thermometer." He grinned acidly. "And you know where you can stick a thermometer."

Tyrell, who possessed an advanced degree, bristled. But he was better at politics than Celltrex, and managed to contain himself. Besides, he felt sorry for his friend. Celltrex's career was finished, and there was nothing left for either of them to do.

"You know," Celltrex said, "if I really wanted to be censored out of existence, I could have kept my mouth shut and continued living in the Tiber Valley, where at least the scenery was a lot nicer."

A stiff wind came in off the ocean, lifting the smog layer over the summits of the towers. The trees rustled secretly. "You know, there is a way," Tyrell said. "If you take the drug—"

"Never!"

"Look, it's only your whole future we're talking about. If I can explain to the others that you are undergoing a transformation, they may at least *think* you're one of them. Perhaps they'll actually let you speak again; but more important, perhaps even you will see the world differently. Perhaps you really will be one of them."

"Not me. Or my children. Or my children's children's children. No matter what I do or say, there is no stopping the asteroids from crashing down upon Green; and if there is any genetic implant that can make me or mine agree with that outcome, then it's the geneticists and the rest of the world who have gone wrong, not me.

"It should be obvious to you, Tyrell. It should be obvious to everyone that by the time civilization does evolve on Green, our people won't be around to worry about it. I won't be surprised if by then the only trace of our existence is a few pieces of broken glass eroding out of some fossil-bearing stratum in the hills."

"How can you say that? We've built and launched starships. We've thrust giant towers into the sky, and covered the oceans with our cities. Look about you, and tell me that we cannot possibly last."

"Time will have its say," Celltrex said, pressing two furry fingers to his temple.

"Time will have its say," he repeated. "It always does."

11

On the Origin of the Fittest

No one ever listened to Celltrex again, and nearly five hundred years after he died of natural causes at an advanced old age, a fire lit in the sky over North America. The first asteroid fell into south central Florida, releasing about ten percent of its impact energy as air blast. It produced winds of five hundred kilometers per hour as far north as New York, where the wind blew for forty-five minutes. If this had been the twenty-first century A.D., the wind blowing across the East River could easily have toppled every building in Manhattan. Seen from the air, the only recognizable features would have been found near the air-scoured shambles of the World Trade Center Twin Towers: a shiny gridwork of smashed glass, two meters deep, marking places where streets once ran.

Across Nova Scotia and eastern Canada the winds were down to a hundred kilometers per hour, but they blew for sixteen hours. Billions of trees had fallen in rows from Florida to Massachusetts, but tall cedars still stood along the shores of Halifax, until the tsunami rolled over them.

The corresponding heating effects resulting simply from compression of the air were 70° C at eight hundred kilometers from ground zero, and 29° C at thirteen hundred kilometers. Large volumes of hot ash were also ejected and carried along with the blast, raising the temperature still higher. Direct thermal lethality extended across the Carolinas, Texas, and Mexico. Approximately 150 cubic kilometers of dust were injected into the stratosphere; it circled the globe. The sky's transparency changed. Sunlight striking the high-altitude particles began to radiate much of its energy far from the ground, triggering climatic effects that would span the centuries. In the wake of the North and Central American asteroid sauna, a false winter descended upon survivors in the Eastern Hemisphere. Meanwhile, atmospheric nitric oxide, a byproduct of rapidly heated air, began to erode the ozone layer so severely that when at last the sunlight did return in full strength, its ultraviolet rays penetrated through to the ground virtually unfiltered, killing much of the plant life and animal life left on the continents.

Thus did an event known to later generations as the terminal Eocene extinction begin. The North African forests teeter-tottered on the very edge of desertification, and most of the world's protomonkey tribes died off, along with many of the predator species that had long dominated them. Their numbers were winnowed down to the strongest and the wisest. Far from preventing the emergence of intelligence on Earth, the Alphans were unwittingly breeding monkeys to that very end.

By 15,000,000 B.C., the African plate was in collision with Europe and the Middle East. The continent's northward drift was pushing peninsulas and chains of islands into their first physical contacts with Iraq and Turkey. The animals living on either side of the junction were meeting for the first time. Antelope and horses, which had evolved in Asia, extended their range into Africa, passing elephants, monkeys, and apes coming from the opposite direction.

The planet gave the appearance of having fully recovered from the Alphan bombardment of 33,551,882 B.C. Across the forests and savannas of Europe, East Africa, and Asia had spread the cosmopolitan dryopithecine and ramapithecine apes. This was the zenith of apen radiation and diversification: a great branching of new lineages, most of which would be pruned out of existence in a very short time.

Dryopithecus africanus was a tree-climbing creature weighing about eleven kilograms. If nature had been allowed to follow its course, *Dryopithecus*'s environment might have remained forever dominated by the more brutish and relatively witless *Gigantopithecus*, which stood four meters high at the shoulders. But into their world came a great calamity.

Sandwiched between layers of Egyptian mud, a dragonfly-shaped robot sent beacons up into the sky, assisting five million tons of rock and rock-ice in its final course corrections. It came from the west, moving at thirty-two kilometers per second, and carrying with it all the explosive force of five hundred hydrogen bombs. Somewhere above France it slid into the atmosphere. A billion years of accumulated boulders and dust blew away from its surface like a spray of dazzling diamonds. It detonated on the forested hills near Stuttgart, in southern Germany, sending up a cloud of roiling black death. Thousands of kilometers away, the mere sound of the explosion left those few lucky dryopithecines that survived the collision with a permanent, maddening ringing in their ears.

And then, like clockwork, fifteen million years later, man's family tree was pruned still further when two more asteroids were guided in to carve out Africa's Ghana Crater and the Austral-Asian tectite fields. The lineage known as *Homo erectus* was around to witness these twin catastrophes. By this time, fifteen million years of earthquakes, wind, and vegetation had softened the features of southern Germany's Ries Basin, but still it was a recognizably saucer-shaped depression thirty kilometers across. At the center of the crater, natural moats and peaks made the land easily defensible by dryopithecine descendants. One of the world's most strikingly beautiful medieval villages would eventually rise there, changing little in appearance even into the twenty-first century A.D.

The Alphan dragonfly was still faithfully sending data up to its homeworld, every twelve thousand years or so, when Egyptian people carved huge blocks from the white-mud-turned-to-limestone, hauled the blocks away, and built from them the Pyramids. Cheops was cased in a glass-smooth shell of white marble. Its peak was solid gold plate, and silver inlaid hieroglyphs wider than a temple door descended each of its four sides.

By A.D. 1988, the gold and silver, and even the marble, were gone. Much of the limestone, too, had been removed—powdered and burned as lime and used to build habitations long turned to rubble. In that year, the Alphan robot lay barely a centimeter below the surface of Cheops' southeast cornerstone. Millennia of alternating heat, cold, burial under sand drifts, reexposure, and sandblasting had exposed a fossil clam lying immediately above it. The clam drew the attention of an American paleontologist who just happened to be passing through on his way to the buried city of Thera. As he began to pry the fossil loose, he came within five seconds of exposing an object that at first glance would have appeared to be a remarkably preserved insect, and at second glance an artifact from a civilization clearly more advanced than his own, and very, very old.

But the greatest discovery of his time slipped from his grasp as Britain's Prince Charles approached the site, led by an entourage of soldiers on camelback and men in black Mercedes limos. They were to pose for a thirty-second photo opportunity in front of Cheops, for which the army had cleared all the tourists out of the area. But no one had noticed the paleontologist among the limestone blocks, and he had failed to take notice of them, until it was almost too late. The soldiers nearly mistook him for an IRA assassin, and had they been men of lesser training, they would certainly have shot him on the spot. Instead, they let him raise his hands above his head and explain that he was harmless. Still, they held him under guard for two hours after the Prince had left, and he never did manage to return for the clam.

By A.D. 2048, the chance for discovery of the Alphan probe was lost. Egypt's Ministry of Tourism restored the Pyramids to their former glory, casing the limestone block at Cheops' southeast corner beneath two meters of polished white marble. The descendants of protomonkeys had, by this time, sent robot eyes of their own hurtling into the Alpha Centauri system, carrying with them *Voyager*-like greetings from Earth in the form of coin-sized laser discs engraved with Bach, Beethoven, and the Beatles singing "Here Comes the Sun," while huge infrared telescopes on the Moon scrutinized A-4, raising more questions than they answered. No one on Earth had guessed, or could easily have comprehended, that humankind owed its existence to periodic bombardments which had extinguished most large predators, along with many dominant primate lineages, and yet allowed man's apen forebears to tread upon the Earth and subdue it. If not for xenophobia, the twenty-first century might have seen a herd of giant deermice wandering through the forested wilderness of Manhattan Island, and there would never have been telescopes, music, or questions. But now the stars waited for the Children of Green.

They had been waiting for a very long time.

12

Warning Signs

———————

Autumn, A.D. 2011

CHRIS COULDN'T SEE ANYTHING THROUGH THE BLUR OF WHITE light into which he awoke. His eyes simply refused to focus. There was music playing somewhere nearby: "Rock-a-Bye, Baby," in a little windup music box.

He remembered freezing and suffocating. He remembered thrashing in vain on the surface of the Moon, and Elmer Glue hoisting him up by his shoulders. He must be at Port Chaffee, he guessed, in a hospital bed, fully repressurized and revived. Fixing these most probable bearings in his mind, he groped for a blanket or an IV needle, anything that might confirm his location, and quickly became thoroughly disoriented. His arms would not move in any rational direction. His legs, either. And when he tried to call for a nurse, he discovered to his horror that he had absolutely no control of his facial muscles. All he could do was shriek.

It was neither a nurse, nor his wife, nor Elmer Glue who came for him. It was a woman he'd buried close on twenty years ago, a woman whose warm, gentle hands were slowly turning to dust.

"Mom . . ." Chris tried to say, but the word came out

only as a gurgle. He wanted to tell her that her difficult child would one day make her proud, if only she would live long enough. All those early troubles with his teachers would be forgotten by the time *Beagle* came along.

The initial confusion Chris felt upon waking had given way to fear that the Tranquillity accident had left him paralyzed, and fear in its turn was giving way to bewilderment mingled with grief.

(Mom . . .)

For days and days, between long intervals of overmastering sleep, he tried to come up with an explanation for the strange trick that the universe seemed to be playing on him.

None came.

But the facts were difficult to deny. Though his eye muscles were not yet under his conscious control, his ears worked perfectly, and according to broadcasts on the wallscreen in an adjoining room, news events that had been history in the year 2048 were only now occurring. Alaska, Oregon and two other states that had seceded from the Union during the Great Depression were at last returning to the fold. Israel, faced with partition and possible extinction, had responded to a withdrawal of American support by leveling Wall Street and the South Street Seaport. They had tried to disguise the low yield weapon as coming from one of their neighbors, but methods which had become acceptable during the suspension of the U.S. Constitution ultimately revealed that the bomb had been planted behind a cellar wall nearly two decades before, in preparation for an American abandonment that seemed inevitable after the end of the Cold War. As near as Chris could tell, it was the year 2011. But, trapped as he was in an infant's body, with full knowledge of what the next thirty-seven years held in store for humanity, he was unable to communicate to anyone how the American-Israeli war *should* have been resolved. All he could do was listen helplessly as, day after day, the Americans made a mess of it all over again.

But some things, Chris decided, could certainly be changed. By the time his mother had the accident, Chris would be old enough to speak and to move, to make sure she did not end up on the wrong road on the wrong night. He would also make sure not to end up on or anywhere near Tranquillity Base on the eve of his flight to Centaurus. He was fairly certain that whatever happened on the Moon had killed him—or in some other way cut short all that he was about to accomplish—and somehow transported him back to babyhood with his memory intact.

Is that what really happened? Chris wondered. Have I, the adult, actually been reborn? Or is it the *baby* whom something has happened to? Is it possible that I have never lived at all until now, and that my first moments of consciousness are experienced as a vivid understanding? Is it possible that all infants emerge into the world in a hallucinatory state, and that all this knowledge—real or unreal?—fades quickly from memory? After all, our long-term memory does not become functional until about age two (*and how do I know that?*). Everything I know and think now can, by age two, be easily forgotten.

And then a heartbreaking thought: I have to remember. *Have to.* I've got to save Mom, and I've got to stay away from Tranquillity.

Chris turned these thoughts over in his mind, turned them over and over throughout the entire first year of his life. His second birthday came and went. His third birthday came and went. The memories strengthened and did not go away.

His mother's first attempts at teaching him the alphabet proved ludicrous, for as soon as his eyes could focus, he was able to read a newspaper. By the time he was four, his life was already on a different track than the life of his premonitions. (Or was it all a recollection?

He could not distinguish between the two.) Labeled a prodigy, he was sent to a school he'd never seen before, where he learned that, though world history was, in all essentials, the same as he'd "remembered" it, some of the finer details were curiously askew. Robert Kennedy, not Richard Nixon, had been America's thirty-seventh president. And there were other presidents whose names were entirely new to him. Hitler had evidently never lived, but even without him, the Nazi party emerged right on schedule, under the direction of a man named Himmler. And the Empire State Building, while still the same in all essentials, had moved to 7th Avenue.

By age thirteen, Chris had become obsessed with the nature of space-time and the oscillating universe. Keeping his hindsight of the future to himself, he developed a theory about the universe expanding, contracting, and emerging fresh from the Cosmic Crunch into a new Big Bang. Under these conditions, he guessed, time might somehow fold back on itself in such a way that each particle ended up in virtually the same place, over and over again. It seemed possible that, under the right conditions, events in a past universe could be pulled into one's forward field of vision. Accordingly, the memories (premonitions?) that haunted him were a leftover, or feedback, from the other side of the Big Bang, and the present universe was merely the most recent cusp in an infinite series of cosmic expansions and contractions. As for how anything, even a memory, could pass from one universe to another, these were details to be worked out later, and Chris now saw a whole lifetime spreading before him in which to pursue his obsession.

If something had indeed crossed over from the other side of the Big Bang, the memories it created had changed his life beyond recall, had set him to work on his Ph.D. thesis at age thirteen, had made him a university physicist at age fifteen, had set him upon a course that would lead irrevocably away from *Beagle*, Centaurus, and Tranquillity.

At age sixteen, he fell in love with a nineteen-year-old astronomy student from Japan, decided he would one day marry her, and thereby erased from existence the birth of Jonathan, his son from another marriage in a universe past.

In this universe, Chris decided, he was going to be rich. He knew precisely when gold was going to reach two thousand dollars per ounce. He knew when RCA was going to come out with coin-sized, erasable laser discs. And he knew that, as soon as he was old enough, he was going to start playing the markets. No grant chasing for *this* scientist. He would fund his own research. He would study only what he felt like studying, not what some administrator told him he should be studying.

At seventeen, he made a conscious effort to avoid walking alone down a particular street near his mother's home, where he recalled, somewhere on "the other side," being mugged and hospitalized with a broken jaw. That change, of course, put him in a car on a road he would otherwise never have traveled, put him directly in the path of a drunken driver—

THIS TIME, CHRIS'S MOTHER LIVED. HER SON'S FUNERAL kept her off the road that would ordinarily have led to her death. Twenty years later, *Beagle* was built and launched right on schedule, but Christopher Wayville was not aboard her, and the Earth slept a little easier in his absence.

HE AWOKE AGAIN, IN HIS CRIB, SURROUNDED BY BLURRY white light and the chimes of the music box. But this time there was no confusion. This time nothing had happened to the baby. At best he had only partial recall of at least two lives jumbled together on "the other side."

The premonitions came to him only five or six times throughout life—feelings that he had eaten at a new restaurant at Brighton Beach before, and overheard the same exact conversation at a neighboring table; a foreboding about certain stretches of road, strong enough to have kept both Chris and his mother alive, though neither of them had any way of knowing that Chris's premonitions had caused a change; and there was a similar uneasiness about Elmer Glue and Tranquillity Base, which he dismissed as signifying nothing . . .

CHRIS AWOKE IN A WHITE BLUR, GROPED FOR A BLANKET, AND found the in-feed to an IV needle. Now, at last, he had his bearings straight: the Port Chaffee hospital.

On the Moon, revival of decompression victims was almost routine, if one could get them through air locks to emergency equipment—required by law on all trucks— in time. Elmer Glue had repressurized him just in time— just barely.

"SO HOW IS THE PATIENT TODAY?" ASKED ADMIRAL FITZ Roy.

Chris was sitting up in a chair. He and his copilot wife, Clarice, were examining a floor-to-ceiling wallscreen whose entire surface danced with plots and close-up views of the Alpha Centauri system, when the Admiral walked in with Prime Minister Tam of New Zealand. Chris greeted them cheerfully and offered drinks. Clarice downed the last of her sake and winced. It tasted like uric acid—which, perhaps, it was. Almost all the hydrogen on the Moon, minute quantities of it, had to be painstakingly mined from the top few centimeters of lunar soil, where it had been deposited over billions of years by solar flares. Hydrogen was Port Chaffee's most precious commodity. The bulk of it was combined with Moonrock-extracted oxygen to make the water, which was recycled endlessly through urine stills, Folsome tubes, and hydroponic gardens; and still the rice juice tasted like urine, or sweat, or both.

"I'm feeling quite well," Chris said, eyeing his own glass of sake with caution. "Except for a little confusion about my left and my right, I'd say I'm back to where I was before the accident."

"The doctors say there is still some brain damage," added the Prime Minister.

"Nothing that can't be repaired during the next few days," Clarice said quickly. "We have the best neurologists and immunogeneticists Earth has ever produced right here on the Moon."

There was no question that Chris would soon be good enough for the expedition, but the Admiral had a graver question in mind: Was good enough good enough? Should the countdown be frozen indefinitely until Chris had undergone detailed psychological testing? Or should the countdown resume immediately, with the Wayvilles bumped and replaced by their backup crew? That last choice was a bad career move, thought Fitz Roy. Clarice was directly connected with the Prime Minister's family. From the decision he was about to make branched two alternate futures, one of them grim. But if Chris was not entirely fit for the flight, and if there was even the slightest chance of intelligent life being encountered on A-4, the Admiral saw emerging from his decision an even worse cascade of consequences than his career in decline. He reassured himself that, according to the best evidence, there was no intelligent life on A-4.

Still, an informal search for gaps in Chris's thinking would not hurt. "You've heard about the vote on Elmer Glue's proposal?"

"About freezing growth of the Asimov Array?" said Chris. "Sheer idiocy."

"Why not?" asked Fitz Roy, playing devil's advocate.

"For a start—just for a start—we've traded industrial haze, acid rain, nitric oxide chewing away at the ozone layer, nuclear waste, and the ravages of Gibraltar Dam for a scar on the Moon. It was a good trade, I think: clean electricity for all mankind. We've also reduced the probability of war by giving each nation too much to lose: unlimited power."

"Have you heard the old expression that power corrupts?" asked Fitz Roy.

"Yes," Chris said simply. "And so does lack of power."

"But how much do we really need? We already have more than we can possibly use. In a few years, Mercury's accelerators will be able to manufacture all the antihydrogen fuel needed for a round trip to Alpha Centauri in a matter of weeks. What on Earth are you going to do with all that power? You'll have to beam most of it back into the Sun just to get rid of it, just to prevent the machinery from burning up."

"You want to colonize Mars, don't you?"

The Admiral nodded.

"With a wide beam from Mercury, you'll be able to warm the whole planet, liberate all that gas and water tied up under the soil, and create a shirtsleeve environment."

"I've heard Elmer Glue argue that such a move would *ruin* the planet. She says Mars is too close to the Sun to support an Earth-like atmosphere on only thirty-eight percent Earth gravity. Ultraviolet light will split water vapor into hydrogen and oxygen, and the lighter hydrogen will simply rise out of the stratosphere and blow away on the solar wind. You'll have maybe two hundred years of shirtsleeve weather, and then Mars will dry up like an old bone, like the Moon, and for the same reason."

"I've thought about that. You can introduce recombo algae, much like what lives in *Beagle*'s Folsome tubes and produces our oxygen and food. Eventually we can tie up most of Mars' hydrogen in living systems."

Fitz Roy looked Chris in the eye and nodded approval. "Might work. But why colonize Mars in the first place? The Earth's population is going down, not up. There's no *need* to colonize other planets."

"I can think of one good reason," Chris said, raking his hair with a hand. "Two million years ago, when parts of Asia became tundra, there was no need to do many of the things we take for granted today. In China they have found the skeleton of a Stone Age man who froze to death only two meters from an outcrop of coal."

Fitz Roy's arms goosefleshed, and he decided, in that moment, that there was nothing wrong with Chris, that no matter what challenges he ran into, he would be able to think fast and hold his own. Combining this diagnosis with his certainty that there was nobody worth worrying about on A-4, the Admiral was satisfied that he had done what was necessary to preserve the safety of Earth, and elected next to preserve the safety of his own career by resuming the countdown, and clearing the way for Clarice and her husband to remain in command, as sole occupants of the starship *Beagle*.

And so they set sail for A-4, Clarice and Chris, where they discovered a hitherto unsuspected intelligence stirring upon the planet's surface. It projected itself toward Chris with a hideous grin. It knew his name. And when at last the Wayvilles returned to Earth, they found it deserted—relativistic-bombed, the whole thing. And in time, again, Chris died.

AFTER AN IMMEASURABLE INTERVAL, IF INDEED THERE WAS an interval at all, Chris emerged into babyhood again. He was born and raised, as always, in Wellington, New Zealand; but this time the world history was very different from anything he had experienced before. Chris did not know this. He had absolutely no recollection of the other histories, so it did not seem at all paradoxical to him that, instead of sailing an interstellar sea in the year 2048, he set forth aboard an oceanographic research vessel, to explore the continent-spanning ruins left behind by President Reagan's Great Cold War Gamble of 1981.

The whole East Coast of the United States was a savannalike growth of scrub grass, much of it covering saucer-shaped depressions, deep-hammered in the Earth and filled with shards of greenish-black glass. There were lakes where none had existed before, and no sign that civilization had existed at all.

Where New York's Twin Towers had been, Chris discovered North America's snowshoe rabbits resuming their classic cycle of population surges and crashes. Textbooks had attributed the cycles to the rabbits' lynx predators, arguing that when the rabbit population increased, the lynx population also began to rise. The rabbit population would then decrease under increased lynx predation, and the lynx, finding their food supply dwindling, would begin to die off, double tracking the rabbits' declining numbers. Then, with hardly a lynx in sight, the beleaguered rabbit population would do what rabbits were best at—breeding like rabbits. In very short order, the few surviving holdouts of the lynx population would be surrounded by food . . . and so on . . . and so on . . . except that the textbook explanation could no longer hold true, for the rabbits were following their pattern of surges and crashes in the total absence of the lynx—which, as near as Chris could tell, had been extinct for nearly seven decades.

He tried to invent and put to the test a new explanation, but before he could do so the planes came winging out of the west, and Christopher Wayville met untimely death yet again.

HE WOKE AGAIN, GREW UP WITH NOT A HINT OF RECALL, LIVED intermittently at Port Chaffee, married Clarice, went to A-4, died, and woke again in his crib, again, again, again.

If it were within his power to step outside of each of his
real or imagined lives—

(and he could not tell which was real and which was
imagined, as he lay at Tranquillity between the instant
of dying and death)

—if only he could have stood back and taken a
grandstand view, Chris would have noticed cracks in
his universe, gaps in which arbitrary decisions made
by parents and great-grandparents had precluded his
birth, gaps in which the human species was itself
occasionally absent. Only a grandstand perspective
could have allowed him any possibility of formulating
a theory about what the Lazarus Effect "really" was, as
he scanned, from end to end, an infinite succession of
alternate realities, universal histories of what might have
been if decisions made by him, or by anyone else, could
occasionally be altered by recall of what was to come.

And so he awoke confused and bewildered at Port
Chaffee, barely remembering the accident. He found
the IV in his arm, and understood immediately what
must have occurred at Tranquillity. He did not remember that somewhere between dying and death, during
an interval that could have been no more than a few
seconds, he'd had an opportunity to truly learn the
meaning of a million years; but even if he did remember,
he was the sort of man who would have tried to dismiss
it as a psychological reflex to the trauma of dying.

"So how is the patient today?" Admiral Fitz Roy had
asked.

"I'm feeling quite well," Chris said, eyeing his glass of
sake with caution. And he was quite well, except for the
occasional dreams about a grinning monster waiting for
him on A-4 . . . the bad dreams, and a tendency to find
himself grieving unexpectedly for his mother at odd
times of the day. He seemed to recall speaking with her
while he was unconscious and dying at Tranquillity. But
he kept such things to himself. Especially, he kept them

from Admiral Fitz Roy; and the dreams and the grief went away about the same time the Admiral approved Chris for duty, and resumed the mission countdown. The patient was feeling quite well. Nothing had changed, nothing at all . . . except that Chris, from time to time during the days leading up to departure, seemed to know precisely what the Admiral was going to say before he said it—but this, too, he kept to himself.

The final medical scans of his brain showed that even the mild dyslexia caused by burst capillaries and cell death had been fully reversed. Death had not affected Chris at all—immunogenetic medicine had repaired him—not affected him at all, physically.

13

Who Speaks for A-4?

Excerpt from the Mission Log of Clarice Wayville
Broadcast to Earth 10 October 2054

Transmission Begins

Y OU MUST BE WORRIED, BACK THERE ON EARTH, ABOUT HOW Chris is faring. His superstitious fears, his nightmares, his relativistic psychosis—call it what you will—abated quickly as I decelerated from our maximum cruising speed of ninety-three percent c; and our return to what I call more "normal" space-time seems to have wiped the condition away completely.

Just the same, I wish he'd had the good sense not to voice the darkest of his fears, and that they were not broadcast home when his psychosis was at its worst. You should be receiving some of those broadcasts about now, allowing for light travel time, and I can only imagine that you must be crossing our mission off as a total loss.

Quite the opposite. Much has changed. Many things, wonderful things, have happened, though my own worries about Chris reached a new height when we first landed, when Catherine appeared to be calling him by his name. The incident caused Chris to wonder (very briefly) if the Alphans had somehow shared his nightmares, and I must admit that Catherine's first utterance was more than a little convincing. It ran against all probability. It was downright spooky. The key word here is "probability." By an extraordinary coincidence, the expression "to eat" is pronounced "Chris."

So much for the notion of time gates and visions. The appearance that the Alphans foresaw our coming has turned out to be more apparent than real, which is just as well for us. That psychic event, if real, would have made our universe much more interesting and in the same stroke much less comfortable. And the less said about it, the better.

The bottom line is that we woke up today feeling just fine, *both of us.* We enjoy the company of the Alphans, and in the short time we have been here, we have begun to fall in love with their planet.

I am pleased with nothing so much as the mildness and generosity of the Alphans, which banishes at once any cause for fearing them.

Yesterday morning we went with Catherine to her village. Following a "hop path" to the sea, we noticed that the hills are thickly covered with fernlike plants as tall as trees. Their leaves are more blue than green, and at the feet of these mighty trees grows a low, cypresslike bush. The wild, fruit-bearing trees are so abundant that in places their production has fallen unharvested to the ground, and lies in heaps decaying. The peninsula is favored with a great natural advantage: a garden so luxuriant as to preclude famine from this land. Yet in spite of all the fruit, we saw no splotches of yellow or white or pink—no flowers; and no land appears to have been cleared for cultivation.

As soon as we arrived in the village, we were surrounded by Alphans. All of them understood English nouns and verbs, with which a true, if primitive sort of conversation could be held. We were greeted there by a very pretty scene. We met our first Alphan children (or, rather, they met us) almost as we came within sight of the main buildings. They came out hopping in unison, *dancing* and singing tribal verses. The adults went quiet and seated themselves in the grass. We followed their example. The songs were, I think, related to our arrival. One little girl trilled a line, and the others sang after her in a single voice that went up and up and then swooped. The words were indecipherable, yet beautiful and moving . . . we became unequivocally aware that we were seated on a world lost in the light years—outsiders, both of us, who had come plodding, uninvited, across the tedious waste.

As the singing died out, as we sat in the grass and the tears stung my eyes and the twin suns burned, it occurred to me that there were barely more than a dozen children present. They turned out to be all that existed in the entire village and, come to think of it, there are far fewer Alphans than the forest seems capable of feeding. I suspect that they are practicing a very rigid form of birth control, perhaps in response to an ancient episode of overpopulation. Support for this belief comes from our observation of what appear to be the fossilized impressions of gears in limestone, which are collected by and much prized by the villagers. I believe there were once cities on A-4, and that they fell into decay ages ago. If indeed these creatures did, at some point in their remote past, outgrow their food supply and foul the planetary nest, they learned from their mistake and never repeated it. This would be in agreement with what we know of them already, from the language lessons. The Alphans only have to be told once. They never forget. They learn everything.

I personally doubt that the previous civilization could have evolved much beyond the level of Earth's Maya;

except, of course, for a knowledge of how rockets and gears work.

It is strange to think that even today the Alphans seem not to have invented the wheel. This is not to say they are stupid. So far we have seen no animal larger than an Alphan, nothing strong enough to pull a cart full of goods; and the Alphans themselves would not be very good at pulling, for they hop, and wheeled carts are best pulled by walking creatures. The simple truth is that they have no use for wheels. One result of all this is that almost everything is constructed from small, very portable pieces of wood that can be carried on the back or in the hands of a single individual. By aid of this, we can understand why modern Alphan structures consist almost exclusively of sticks and reeds. This was not always the case. We have seen large quantities of broken glass eroding out of limestone cliffs. We also found fist-sized bricks among the glass. They were not merely carved rocks, as I originally thought them to be. They were cast from a paste of plant resin and ground-up limestone, and the organic resin has fossilized, like amber, preserving the bricks almost forever.

Casting bricks is a lost art (or, more accurately, an abandoned art). I asked Catherine why bricks were not used in any of the village buildings and she told me, "Ground shake," which I took to mean earthquake. She's right, of course. Mortar will tumble down much more easily than wood, and with heavier consequences. I suspect that her people know this from experience of ancient history, and as I have said, they only have to learn a lesson once.

Both their persons and their houses are immaculate and pleasing. All the homes have nearly the same form and dimensions, and all agree in being entirely absent of ornamental wood trim, or carvings, or paintings, or any sort of artistic adornment. The buildings are simple and strictly functional. They resemble Boy Scout or 4-H lean-tos mounted on shallow stilts. As with lean-tos, the whole front is open to the air. In this the Alphans sleep, free of invasion by mosquitoes and other flying insects, for nothing like them seems to have evolved here. In the back is a partition with a square hole in it. In this the Alphans keep all their valuables. From one such chamber Catherine pulled out a polished parabolic mirror with lenses attached in all the right places. I asked her where she got this thing and she explained that it was made by her friend, who turns out to be the male who has been avoiding us. His name is strung together from many words, but the most apt, at least from what Catherine was able to translate, are "Sky Watcher." He is an astronomer, and he appears to have invented the telescope, all by himself, on a world where new inventions are exceedingly rare. We have named him Galileo.

The village is chiefly conspicuous by being laid out in concentric circles around a large cenote or sinkhole. Except for a few volcanic extrusions, the rocks of Takahashi are limestone; in several parts we walked over strata turned on their sides and weathered in such a way that the layers resembled pages of a gigantic book seen edge-on, and clamlike fossils could clearly be distinguished between some of the pages. From this limey rock, every new rain signals carbonic acid secretions, which, through a gradual but profound digestive process, have honeycombed the valley with watery underground passages. When the roof of a cavern ascends too high to support the overlying burden, a section of jungle plunges into the cavity, bringing in the daylight. Chris has asked about their gods. They have none. But if the Alphans worship anything, it is these natural wells.

The cenote around which the village is constructed is, on all sides, a sheer drop of thirty meters. The villagers have carved a spiral path that winds all the way down the cavern walls to the water table. They have even cut a little alcove into the bottom of the well, at the water's edge—a poolside lounge.

The climb down was rather tight-going. The Alphan figure is short and slender, so we were obliged to stoop, and the going would have been tighter yet had the path not been built to accommodate hopping creatures. Still, it was hard on our calves, for there were no stairs, merely a continuous incline. The path was never meant to take the human leg.

Despite these minor discomforts, the view from within was beautiful, and we enjoyed our walk. From an overhanging ledge drooped old stalagtites, and tree roots broke through between them to become long vines.

On the side of the cenote that I have referred to as the poolside lounge, the villagers have created a wading area by tossing down many tons of limestone fill. In the center of the pool stands a small island overgrown with broad-leaved vegetation, and on the other side of the island the water is far over our heads.

I envy these creatures their simple luxuries. At times, I wish I could trade places with them, which has led me to understand, these past two days, that it may be wrong to teach them too much, to give them our Earthly technology, to change them. Paradise lost—right? I'd always believed, way in the back of my head, that extraterrestrials might show up on Earth and decide whether or not to let humans join the Galactic Club. Only it's turned out backward, hasn't it? *We* are the extraterrestrials who must decide how much knowledge gets passed on to the Alphans, and I am not certain that we are qualified to be making such judgments.

I have often wondered if, once we landed on this world, once we proved that our civilization could overcome its territorial passions, rise above the thermonuclear inverse to the Golden Rule, and make it to another star, *that's* when the guys who were deriving so much entertainment from our struggles on Earth would step forward and contact us: "Congratulations! Now go home. And stay there. And don't come back."

I am referring, of course, to the 1984 Hilton tapes. Richard Tuna's galactic law dictates that we own our own solar system, and the Alphans must own theirs. Perhaps that is the spirit in which we ought to have come here. I don't know. At least we have had the good taste not to plant flags; beyond that, I keep recalling something Chris said when he was sick, something about not tampering with history, no matter how noble your intentions.

So here we are, faced now with the question of changing the Alphans, and of them changing us. How much do we allow ourselves to interfere? Do we dare think of helping them out of their solar system? The sobering truth is that we've not had the ghost of a message from outside, no guidance from more experienced spacefarers. For some reason, we appear to be alone among electronic civilizations, and all the major decisions are up to us.

Oh, God! Don't let us fuck up!

Enough of that kind of thinking, Clarice. It's just . . . well . . . strange to think that, for two humans standing here on a world so full of life, the galaxy has begun to look so much lonelier.

The Alphans might really be all there is.

It is difficult to say what direction the Alphans will take, left on their own. In the village they are building a new rocket. The upper stage is identical to the one we found in orbit, and the lower stage is exactly what we expected it to be, judging from the orbiting upper stage.

We talked with Catherine at length about the rocket—that is, as much as could be talked about by aid of nouns and verbs together with the most obvious signs. Strange as this may sound, they do not build rockets to explore space. They build them to explore their own world. Their intent is to send a pilot as far away as possible. They ram pods off in what appear to be random directions, and I'm afraid almost all of the occupants end up drowning, for even more of this world is covered with water than Earth. If the rockets don't blow up, or fall into the sea, or crash with the engines still burning, or fly off into orbit, the astronauts are expected to walk home, recording in their brains everything they see along the way. If they find an ocean blocking their path, they build a new rocket and fly somewhere in the direction of home—and then, if they are very lucky, they come down a few thousand kilometers off target and complete the trip on foot.

The truly incredible thing is that three astronauts have actually survived this craziness and made it all the way home. That is, three during the past fifty thousand years. Their reports have saved us some work. Apparently there are no people beyond the Takahashi Peninsula, at least none that the astronauts met, except for what Catherine seemed to be describing as mute giants with small heads, and I don't think we'll go out looking for those brutes. No, thank you. We'll sit that one out.

So much for the truly incredible. Now for the outrageous. Here are people who have, for thousands of years, been using rockets to explore their own world, yet they never invented the sailboat. Their whole sailing technology is limited to surfboards, and they seem to use these strictly for pleasure, lying on their bellies and paddling with their feet. Looking at how they live, we find it hard to imagine where rockets fit in. They simply don't belong. But there they are.

Curiouser and curiouser . . . every villager can tell you exactly how to build a rocket from scratch, right down to the minutest details of mixing the chemical propellants, but when I questioned Catherine on the propellants, I realized that she did not understand the basic chemistry behind them. I explained oxidizers and oxidants to her, and she was able to regurgitate the information back to me as flawlessly as a coin, but I have my doubts about how well she understands what she is able to repeat.

During our first night on A-4, Catherine and Galileo took one of our cameras apart and reassembled it in perfect working order, several times. Today *all* the villagers know how to take our cameras apart and put them back together again. They even managed to dismantle major components of the flat we loaned them. We told them, "No," of course, and they restored it right before our eyes.

It must have taken them thousands of years to develop rocketry. Now, in only a few days, they have learned how to use and repair sophisticated photic and electronic devices, but what exactly have they learned? I have lectured them on chemistry, Chris has told them how electrons work, and though they can repeat a lesson word for word, they seem unable to connect the memorized facts together. I don't believe they have the slightest idea how the things they are building work. Clearly they do not understand how electricity works, or how oxidation propels their rockets. For them, it seems enough that things work.

All of which tells us something very important about the Alphan brain. They have astonishingly photographic memories, which explains, probably, why we have seen no signs of a written language. They can recount the adventures of a rocket explorer who returned to the village dozens of centuries ago, passing history down from memory to memory, from generation to generation, in what appears to be exquisite detail. They remember everything. They learn everything. Yet it begins to look as if they are slow to make connections between the facts in their heads, not unlike some university brats.

Catherine is a case in point. She has devoted most of her life to learning everything possible about how ice melts at a glacier called Wear, and, much as we love her, she is wasting her time. All she seems to do is memorize what she sees. She has gathered masses of information, some of it quite interesting, but she voices no guesses as to what it all means.

On my flat she has drawn remarkably photographic representations of the tiny creatures she has found frozen in the ice. They resemble crab larvae and copepods from Earth, except for having legs. Catherine has chirped long strings of words after each drawing, which FU has catalogued and found to be just names—descriptions, without questions or insights into what has been described.

Our own computer seems far more capable of connecting facts together, but that is to be expected. FU was designed to "think" like her creators. The Alphans think alien—truly alien. They have curiosity; like us, they want to experience new things, to take in new information, but the way they process that new information is . . . it sounds incredible, but their most basic thought processes must be very different. My thoughts when I see a waterfall and Catherine's thoughts when she sees the same waterfall are perhaps as alien to each other as our amino acids.

After lunching on Alphan fruit (for taste) and Folsome foods (for nourishment), we followed the valley to its end, emerged onto a shore, and then ascended the nearest pinnacle to a height of nine-hundred meters. The pinnacles are not dissimilar to the lush, rain-scoured mountains of the Hawaiian-Emperor chain. They are smooth and steep, flattening out at their bases. We found the foothills so clogged with vegetation that our progress was actually quicker by way of the steeper terrain. Chris attributes the abundance of plant life on the lower slopes to their relative flatness. Rainwater drains off more slowly than on the steeper land above, and plants thrive in the moisture.

Alphan bodies, it turns out, are not built for climbing. So we pulled and pushed our "guides" along, following a smooth ridge to the top. We found the fast-draining terrain above the foothills to be a virtual desert, inhabited almost exclusively by small, widely scattered dwarf grasses. Then, as we neared the peak, we climbed into cloud and entered a garden filled with whole new varieties of trees. The jungle here is sustained by the mist. Most of the plants absorb their water directly from the damp atmosphere, rather than through the ground.

Descending below the clouds onto the sterile ridge, we attained a stunning view of the long chain of coral rings known as the Lagoons of Powell. What did Catherine think, I wonder, as she looked down for the first time upon those circles of white beach? I know she named every one of them, and I know she could sketch an accurate picture of the scene on a flat or an arm, and I know that she asked me what they were called, but she never asked me what they *were*. She never asked me how they formed, how they got there. I doubt she even asked herself.

The world passes to her by way of facts. They accumulate in her brain like barnacles on a rock, and it is enough for her to know that the lagoons are there, even if she cannot explain how.

Transmission Ends

14

Her Name, *Enterprise*

T ENS OF THOUSANDS OF CENTURIES HAD PASSED SINCE THE inhabitants of A-4 took command of their own evolution, and began planning their great genetic destiny. During his lifetime, Celltrex had seen a whole generation of women grow up in perfect beauty. He had seen the proliferation of encyclopedic minds, and seemed to be the only Alphan alive who appreciated the fact that he had also seen the elimination of variety among his people. As the first of them headed out for the stars, he alone mourned for the very days his contemporaries were looking back to as the Age of Randomization and Barbarism.

As it turned out, those in charge of A-4 were barely more successful in planning their own destiny than they were at planning the Earth's. By the time canal builders on the Nile invented astronomy, Celltrex's bones had long turned to dust, and little more than dust remained of his brethren. One fallen remnant of the Alphan species lay a thousand light-years away, orbiting a star that in Celltrex's time had resided within only five light-years of A-4. Dolphinlike in appearance, this branch of the Alphan lineage had shed its limbs and returned to a

peaceful existence in the sea. But though millions of
years had passed, their adopted world was not yet
fully recovered from the strip-mining it had received
when the Alphans still possessed hands and were able
to make tools.

A second remnant had settled only two light-months
away, finding whole new oceans tens of kilometers
beneath the icy crust of a world circling Alpha Centauri
C. These colonists, too, redesigned themselves to an
aquatic life—redesigned themselves so utterly that within three generations they were alien to their ancestors
in all but phylogeny. During the thirty-three million
years that followed, they went forth and multiplied,
eventually outstripped the ability of their oceans to
sustain them, fell to near extinction, forgot how to
build machines, evolved in strange, new directions,
reacquired the ability to build machines, and again
outstripped their environment, again and again. They
never did rediscover interstellar space—not until the
spring of A.D. 1984, when, as Jim Powell and Richard
Tuna presented their plans for an interstellar rocket
to the AAAS Hilton meeting, something like a telescope
came up through the ice, and began to look around.

Winter, A.D. 2051

JONATHAN WAYVILLE HAD NEVER SEEN THE WATER SO CALM.
The Cook Strait was like polished black glass under the
stars . . . until the bottle rockets swarmed from the cliff
house and enveloped his world in a concussion of light
and shadow. Grapsid crabs, outcrops of rock on the
water, and hunks of driftwood flashed out green and red.
A chorus of cheers erupted from the cliff above, where
Jonathan's friends were celebrating the New Zealand
equivalent of the Fourth of July—Guy Fawkes Day—
in honor of one of the very few men ever to enter
Parliament with honest intentions.

"Do you really hate him?" Karen was asking. She took his hand in hers. "I mean, *really?*"

"Sometimes I don't know," he said. "My mother loved him so much. And I always thought he felt the same way about her, and when I was a kid I wanted to have a marriage just like theirs. And then, out of the blue, he dumps us for that bitch Clarice and a chance to get himself killed. I think all Clarice meant to him was a sure ticket to the stars. I doubt he ever looked back to see how much it hurt."

Karen followed Jonathan's gaze to the Southern Cross. If the latest press release from the Carter Observatory was correct, four people, including Christopher Wayville, were lancing out into that portion of the sky aboard *Beagle* and *Enterprise*. The two ships were traveling side by side, thirty light-minutes apart, almost two light-years from Earth. Now, pulling Jonathan closer to her side, Karen said, "I think I would have felt the same. It was one hell of a kick in the teeth for you."

"I understand," said Jonathan, "that he loved exploration. In another age he'd have been a sailor, right? But I never believed that his career came before us. I can't understand that way of thinking. I swear to you, if the Devil had offered him the chance to fly that mission, he would have signed the contract without even stopping to read the small print.

"I promise you, Karen, when I go to the university I'll never study astronomy, and whatever direction I do choose, my work will never become more important than my family. I'd hate myself if I became like him. God, no. Don't let me be like him."

CHRIS WAS ASLEEP, AND CLARICE SAT ALONE IN THE DARK in *Beagle*'s dining area. The crew compartment was a duplex apartment built within a delta-winged shuttle. It, and containers of equipment, water, and propellant, were harnessed to a ten-kilometer-long tether, somewhat like pearls on a string. *Beagle* and *Enterprise* were both in the cruise phase of flight, with the engines burning only strongly enough to keep the tethers taut. Equipment was now descending, elevatorlike, along one ship's main tether, toward the rear engine, in preparation for the deceleration phase of flight. Ten kilometers aft of the forward engine, deep in the shadows of the tungsten gamma ray shields (which were located only a hundred meters behind the engine, and thus cast large shadows with a minimum use of mass), the landing module *Beagle* twirled in its harness around the axis of the tether. The lander was counterbalanced by an identical harness bearing supplies of equal mass, and the rotation produced a wonderful sense of being at home under normal gravity.

Surrounded by wallscreens at her dining room table, Clarice had instructed the ship's computer to re-create the starscape outside, to reproduce it exactly as it would appear if the lander were standing perfectly still in space, poised somewhere between the Sun and Centaurus. To anyone else stepping into that darkened room, the scene would have created a feeling of instant vertigo; but for Clarice, uncountable bright stars scattered in every direction produced a much-needed calm.

The Sun was down there in the bottom. As she pressed a little square of canvas between her fingers—which was to her a touchstone to the plane in which Harriet Quimby had crossed the Atlantic, as a piece of gold foil was Chris's touchstone to Apollo—she instructed the computer to let a broadcast play from Earth, at the lowest possible volume.

Presently, a woman was reciting "Did Jesus Have a Dog?" by Guilder. The broadcast was coming live from Australia, or at least as live as any broadcast could be at a distance of two light-years. Clarice's attention was not on Guilder. She had no stomach for twentieth-century classics. What interested her was the Simultaneity Effect.

Listening to the broadcast from Earth, she was hard pressed to identify any signs of time dilation, even though she was, courtesy of Albert Einstein, aging three times slower than any humans who had ever lived except her husband . . . and the Bardos, half a light-hour away aboard the *Enterprise*. Time seemed to be taking its normal pace back home; but one of the first rules of relativistic flight was that things were not always as they seemed. To Earth-bound observers, Clarice knew, her reports home were arriving as unendurably long and slurred sentences, and what appeared to be the slow, careful shutting and opening of her eyelids was but a blink. She also knew that if she could somehow see, at this very moment, what was *really* happening on Earth, then from her slowed-down time frame people would be going about their business with quick, jerky movements, as if a video were being played in the fast-forward mode. They would awake and race through a day and night that seemed only eight hours long. But to see these phenomena, visions of Earth would have to come to her faster than light—and no such magic existed, so events on Earth could be connected to *Beagle* only by laser signals.

Having left Earth in the year 2048, *Beagle* and *Enterprise* would enter the Centaurus system some four light-years away, in 2054, after some six years of travel time. At that time, the latest news from Earth would still be four years old, dating back to 2050; meaning that a total of only two years of broadcasts more recent than 2048 would have been received aboard ship during the six-year journey. A result of this was that observers on Earth, connected to Clarice by laser broadcasts, would actually see two years passing aboard *Beagle*, while Clarice, observing from *Beagle*, would think she was seeing only two years passing on Earth.

A more fundamental difference between the experiences of Clarice and observers on Earth came every time she tuned in on robot probes, directly ahead at A-4. At once she could see transmissions from Centaurus blueshifted—the lightwaves compressed between her and the source, and the probes' computers speaking five times as fast as they should, with their on-board clocks seeming to run five times faster than hers, as *Beagle* intercepted four years of signals already racing between Centaurus and the Sun at the moment of departure in 2048, plus six years of new ones transmitted between departure and Arrival Day, 2054—ten years of news during what appeared to Clarice to be only two years of travel time.

Oh, how time flies—

Clarice pulled a liquid crystal flat from a drawer. It was a screen about the size and shape of a legal pad. With a touch-screen pen she scrawled "Start" on the flat. Then FUQ2 flashed the word "Okay," momentarily drowning out the stars.

"I'd like you to take some dictation," Clarice wrote, "for transmission to Earth."

"Is Chris still asleep?" the computer typed under her script.

"Yes, FU, still asleep."

"Then we won't be talking. You want me to use the write mode instead. Have I guessed correctly?"

"Yes."

"Okay, go ahead."

"One thing—before we begin, you can show me the stars in real time now."

The heavens shifted around her. Sol, down in the bottom, became a bright band overhead, and Clarice began to write.

Transmission Begins

23 December 2051. The days click by so quickly. From our vantage point at ninety-two percent the speed of light, an Earthly day has barely four hours of sunshine. We are traveling through space so fast that a large hole has opened up behind us and grown to consume two-thirds of the sky. The Sun we leave behind has been pulled into our forward field of vision. The whole universe is compressed into a dome-shaped window ahead of the ship. Near its rim, ultraviolet rays from the Sun have been stretched out into longer, visible wavelengths of light. Directly ahead, near the dome's center, the normally invisible infrared of Centaurus is compressed toward the blue end of the spectrum. And strangest of all, when the Sun is dead center behind us, it stretches out to form a perfect ring on the rim of the universe.

Such are the odd realities of relativistic flight. Though we were prepared for these experiences, it is necessary to sail this great ocean between the stars to appreciate its immensity. We are traveling almost as fast as light itself, and we have been doing so for many months; but we have yet to cross even half the distance that separates the Sun from Centaurus. We meet nothing but the same black deeps of space. Even at these speeds, with the universe aging rapidly outside the walls of our ship and thereby giving the illusion that we are traveling *faster* than light, the stars remain fixed in the heavens, each so far from the others, and from us. Accustomed to watching old science fiction films, in which crowds of stars move like fireflies from the center to the edges of starship bridge screens, we do not rightly judge how profoundly small the proportion of suns is to this vast expanse of empty space. The unmoving stars give testimony to the long light-years that remain ahead.

And when I think of the long deceleration that will finally bring us into the Alpha Centauri system—six painful months at two gees—When I think of how, as we get closer to our destination, the more there will be to fascinate us, yet the slower we will go and the more impatient we are likely to become, I somehow wish I could go to sleep and not wake up until I arrive on A-4.

I shouldn't be complaining. People have certainly dealt with more difficult situations aboard the original *Beagle*, or along the Oregon Trail. We travel in relative safety, with comforts a Roman emperor would have envied. I have recently begun work on my next two books, and it's nice to be able to put in a day's work without anyone being able to interrupt me for a telephone conversation. Still, I have considered sleep drinks, to decrease our waking hours and hasten our advance on the new world. But Chris does not like sleep. He rests now only because he has been on the verge of collapse from sheer exhaustion and stress. Even as I write, he tosses and turns, and his dreams, I know, are uneasy.

Transmission Ends

The bad dreams and premonitions of danger had started three light-months out from Earth. As the ship began to experience the first effects of time dilation, and objects astern began pulling into the forward view, random fragments of the Tranquillity visions returned to haunt Chris, night after relentless night, increasing

in intensity as *Beagle* increased her velocity.
During his waking hours, he thought of the dreams
often. He could recall them with spine-chilling detail,
and by Christmas Eve, 2051, they had grown to become
waking nightmares. Strangely, he did not seem to be
alone in his uneasiness. Constance Bardo, aboard *Enterprise*, was dreaming about monsters.

"Sure," said Clarice. "Doesn't everybody?" She dismissed the dreams as signifying nothing, except perhaps in-flight boredom mingled with jitters, possibly
even an underdone bit of "meat" from the algae tubes,
but nothing more.

In years to come, Chris would always remember
from his premonitions that *thing* waiting for him on
A-4, skeletal and vague, with a hideous grin. And he'd
remember an Earth devastated by relativistic bombs.
And he'd remember the light. But it was the light he
thought about first, when he could bring himself to think
about that horrible voyage at all.

He was dreaming about pancakes, solar-system-sized
disks of dust and ice orbiting around virtually invisible
brown dwarf stars. The dwarf stars, weighing in at
several Jupiter masses, were unlikely to provide a
collision hazard. It was the disks surrounding them,
out to a radius of twenty or more light-minutes, that
were dangerous. Each Valkyrie rocket, as it flew
through interstellar space, was preceded during the
acceleration and cruise phases of flight by streamers
of droplets (which doubled as coolant for the ship's
coils and shielding material against interstellar dust);
and during the deceleration phase of flight by a series
of microthin, self-repairing "umbrellas" lowered "down
forward," into the path of deceleration. Using nothing
more exotic than droplet and umbrella shields, *Beagle*
and *Enterprise* could easily handle the amounts of gas
and dust normally encountered in interstellar space. But
nothing could protect them from a pancake, except the

hope that all or most of those islands of dark matter had been discovered, and that a course to avoid them had been properly charted long in advance.

Pancakes had become the reefs and shoals of the twenty-first century.

And as he dreamed, during that Christmas Eve of 2051, Christopher Wayville saw the arm of a pancake sweeping toward him, and into that arm fell a brilliant white star, having great power; and it came to pass that icy moonlets, and a ring plane so large that it could easily have accommodated the orbit of Mars were lightened in its glory.

Chris knew the bright star by its name.

No. Impossible! But those dreadfully beautiful rings kept falling toward him, or he toward them—he could not quite tell. He'd been through this before, and realized suddenly that it was all no more than a bad dream—

(*Pancake? You may be no more than an underdone bit of meat.*)

—and he knew at once that Clarice would shake him awake if he called her. He screamed, but no sound came. Now the terror bit down hard.

Scream, dammit!

Not even a grunt. He was on his own. He'd have to wake himself. *Have to.* But the dust lanes were coming up too fast; and he kept on falling . . .

falling . . . . .

falling . . . .

Chris arched his back, tensed his muscles, and let loose with a sharp jerk, then another and another, bringing himself awake bit by bit, awake to the sound of Lex Bardo's voice, calm but very strained.

For an instant, *Enterprise* shone brighter than a whole galaxy of stars.

"Our scopes picked it up too late," Lex explained. "Pancake. We can't turn out of its way. We're hitting an awful lot of dust. We're going to burn up"—which, in fact, they already had. By the time Lex's words reached Chris's ears, the mouth that had spoken them was as close to nothing as anything could be and still be something. Indeed, parts of it were imbedded in *Beagle's* hull.

Enterprise's droplet shield had impacted against only one large chip of ice, not much larger than a cricket ball, but it might just as well have been the Sun. Caught in a storm of relativistic droplets, the ice converted into a thousand megatons of raw energy—an energy equivalent to the destructive power of a small-scale nuclear war. The ship's forward coil was more than ten kilometers away from the iceblast, but even ten *thousand* kilometers would have been too close, for the ship was traveling at ninety-two percent the speed of light, and would have overtaken the explosion center in less than one-thousandth of a second. The shield-facing side of the coil flashed to vapor. Then the shaded side rippled and exploded away at several thousand kilometers per second, with the tether and the shadow shields rushing into it at more than a quarter million kilometers per second. The antimatter tanks might just as well have been a nest of fleas located in the mouth of a shotgun. When they detonated, less than a trillionth of a second later, the fury of the iceblast was as the force of a snowflake falling upon an eyelash by comparison. Lex and Constance Bardo experienced the fastest death in all of human history. Their neurons almost had time enough to register the heat and pressure—almost—and then they were muons streaming out in every direction at the speed of light.

Two years later, few on Earth would be able to draw much consolation from the fact that the *Enterprise* Nova had proved the red shift theory once and for all.

Beagle, meanwhile, had been extraordinarily lucky. Thirty light-minutes away, the starship skimmed past the outer edge of the reef. The strategy of breaking interstellar expeditions in two, rather than loading all the risks and hopes onto a single spacecraft, had paid off.

And so the mission continued, though for a time the Wayvilles moved in a netherworld of shock, now more alone than any pair of humans had ever been. And as Clarice buried herself in her next two books, one of them a science fiction novel about *not* being in space, and as Chris began rummaging through the computer's library in search of history's oddest coincidences, they decided to increase *Beagle*'s speed ever so slightly, down that long, narrow path to whatever future might be.

15

The Chemist

10 October, A.D. 2054.

EARLY EVENING IN THE VALLEY OF WELLS.

Catherine ran her fingers up and down Chris's arms, sketching something with swift precision: more touchscript. Chris hadn't the foggiest idea what she was trying to tell him.

"We will have a very lonely time waiting for them to land on Earth," Clarice had said. That much was certain, Chris judged. Assuming we don't teach them too much. They sure as hell don't look like any threat to Earth—

(Right, Chris. Let's keep it that way.)

—it's doubtful that they could do any harm even if they could get there, which they can't. They have no potential. They are too primitive to make any difference.

(to invade and ravage the Earth)

Right! Chris told himself. I'd like to see them try, in their little wooden pods. We'd have them all rounded up in the Central Park Zoo before breakfast. So much for your responsibility for keeping the Earth from being blasted by aliens, from being made to look like those bad dreams. Either the dreams were nothing, and your

137

concern over them the folly of a fool, or you came to the wrong planet. The real danger to Earth—

(if there is any danger)

—is back on Earth: humans endangering humans. If there are truly questions about humankind's survival, there are no answers to be found on A-4.

(Can you be certain of that?)

Yes. I'm certain, Chris decided. Those visions were dreams that somehow obsessed me . . .

(that still obsess me?)

No. Not really. Not now. A few months ago, a few days ago even, yes. A few days ago I was afraid to cause any kind of change on A-4, afraid even to land the ship.

(Thank God for Clarice.)

Thank God you never found that grinning, skeletal thing in the forest, grinning and promising death. Thank God that the Alphans hold no ill will toward humankind, and that there are no relativistic rockets on or near this planet. Yet here exist things wilder than your dreams; and day by day, the wonders of A-4 make the visions seem more remote and foolish, make you look with shame upon your earlier desperation.

But there were moments . . .

The dream of a flash in the sky and the simultaneous destruction, only thirty light-minutes away, of the *Beagle*'s sister ship—

(coincidence)

—your name meaning devourer—

(coincidence)

—the strange reaction of the astronomer to your touch, as if something bad had passed between the two of you.

Oh, yes. There were moments. Bad ones.

"ME. CHRIS. IN *BEAGLE*, NOW," CLARICE SAID.

Catherine cocked her head to one side, still trying to teach Chris the keyname to every tree near the clearing.

Chris wasn't trying. He didn't even seem to be paying attention, and this troubled her.

"Question: We in *Beagle*?"

"No," Chris said, and then ran a hand gently along one side of her face. She closed her eyes and made a soft, purring sound. "Me. Clarice. Sleep. Tomorrow me, Clarice, come out. Tomorrow we talk more."

Not knowing what to sign or say, Catherine stepped back and said nothing at all as her newfound friends climbed into the hollow of *Beagle*.

"See you tomorrow," Clarice said.

Chris stood in the hollow and waved good-bye. Beyond the clearing he saw only dark, and a breeze came down from the hills and chilled him as the hull shut Catherine outside. The rectangular hole in the *Beagle*'s side looked like a mouth closing. Catherine stood in the grass and watched it swallow them.

AFTER THEY WERE GONE, CATHERINE FELT LOW AND UNHAPPY. She found the astronomer in the woods near the clearing, and he, too, was in a dark mood, but not for the same reason. She missed the aliens—truly missed them—while he wished they would simply go away.

Late now, she signed in touchscript, meaning that they should both be sleeping.

Later than you think, he signed back.

I do not understand.

He is bad for us, this Devourer. He is dangerous. And you are my only friend. I do not want to lose you. You spend too much time with Devourer. You spend too much time with a bad thing.

It hurt her to see him troubled. *Devourer is our friend*, she signed. *The Wayvilles are our friends. Nothing is bad with them.*

And what have your friends taught you today? There were scratches of sarcasm in his script. And a hardness about it that conveyed a deep, heartfelt pain that was always there, had always been there, as far back as she had known him. And she had come to know him as no other in the village could, or wanted to. The Alphans were indeed capable of love, and she did, alone among Alphans, love the astronomer.

Two nights ago she had tried to cheer him up by making love in a new position, the very position she had seen the Wayvilles using before the voice they called FU shut off the thing called flat. Face-to-face, she tried to make love, but she found the position impossible, and learned that only creatures with their knees on backward could manage the feat, and succeeded only in angering the astronomer.

For two nights he had not touched her. And she ached for his touch—something any villager would have seen as peculiar. Her closest friends wondered how she could touch him, much less let him make love to her, without vomiting. Some villagers even shunned her because of the relationship, called her a defective, but she did not care.

Defective, that's what they would label any child conceived of the union. And *that* she did care about. She would want to keep the child, yet the pressure to draw it out and discard it during the very first weeks of development, as soon as it entered the pouch, would be immense. They saw the astronomer as something bad, a threat to the gene pool, or something like that. Bad.

But he knows things, she tried to tell them. *He teaches me things.*

He teaches me . . . He teaches me . . . She repeated the phrase over and over in her head as she answered the astronomer's question, as she scratched what the Wayvilles had taught her about "oxidizers" and "oxidants" and "electrons." It was all new to him; strange, and difficult to put together. But pieces of it made sense, became narrow windows that had not been there moments before, windows through which at a distance he could see only cracks of light. A whole new universe was beginning to open up, and he became even more aware of the scope of his ignorance. But this was no cause for despair.

Quite the opposite: *These are beautiful things they teach you,* he signed.

Catherine closed her fingers around his arm in surprise. Thus far, the astronomer had seen only ugliness in the Wayvilles. And yet he saw beauty now, in their most meaningless lessons. Her friends in the village would view this behavior as another proof of their claim that he was a defective, but she would never believe them. And here she made a rare connection between cause and effect, and decided to eliminate the cause. She would never describe to them this behavior.

These things are tempting, he signed. *They make me want to go to Devourer myself. They make me want to learn from him about his universe. They make me want to ask him questions.*

Something the Wayvilles had said made the astronomer happy. And now Catherine was happy, too.

These things are tempting, he continued. *But we should stay away from the aliens.*

Catherine's smile was gone.

The astronomer signed, *They are changing us. A great change is coming. A great wind is beginning to blow. Something bad. It will be here fast.*

Devourer and Clarice are friends, Catherine protested. *Devourer and Clarice teach me things. I like Devourer and Clarice. Devourer and Clarice teach me things—that I teach you. You like what I teach you. I do not like to stay away from them.*

They teach us things, and I want to learn. This is tempting.

They are friends.

They are a temptation. But I do not believe they are friends. The astronomer paused, drawing connections as fast as he could. *Learn from them. But be careful. Watch out for Devourer. Watch out for*—"Devourer! Devourer!"

He pronounced it "Chris . . . Chris . . ."

Watch out for Chris.

Watch out for Chris.

Watch out—

16

The Astronomer

≫≫\\\\\≪≪

10 October, A.D. 2054.

Midnight in the Valley of Wells.

Clarice's flat showed an infrared image of Galileo trying to conceal himself in the forest. His warm breath, hissing out into the chill, moonless air, was a dead giveaway.

The astronomer's large eyes had become accustomed to the starlight. He saw spidery shadows moving to and fro on the *Beagle*'s topside. The ship was quiet tonight, a dark shape crouched out there in the center of the clearing. All the external lights were doused, and no sound carried through the hull.

He shifted his attention from the ship to the vegetation at its feet. Even in the dim glow of Sirius and Sol he could see that the grass nearest "the flying house" had paled and withered. There was something sad and wicked in the image of so much dead (devoured?) grass.

Bad there, he had warned the chemist. But she insisted on spending almost every waking minute with the aliens.

Now he passed his days alone. But this was nothing new to him. His earliest memory was loneliness. He could remember almost all the way back to his mother's pouch—almost, but not quite; and this was one thing that distinguished him from his peers. They could recall all the details of life before emergence.

The astronomer was fortunate not to remember his infancy. He developed in the pouch with perfect eyes and perfect ears, but the mind behind them was not perfect; learning this, his real mother ejected him from her body and exposed him on a rock. He would have died there, as she had intended him to do, if not for the grieving young woman who had lost a perfect child. She took him and pouched him and loved him, and became the only mother he ever knew.

Childhood was best forgotten for an Alphan creature born abnormally. The other children shunned him the moment they discovered that he was too dumb to learn the keynames of the trees. Instead, he turned his attention to the sky and started giving newer, shorter names to the stars—only one keyname to each. That was cheating, the children judged, a feeble attempt to make himself look smart. And stars were such useless things: lights in the sky that didn't even produce fruit.

Unable to memorize the trees, and seeing no point in trying, he irritated his teachers with questions about how trees came to be, and what stars were, and how *they* came to be. So they stopped teaching him. They labeled him retarded, and sent him out into the village as an advertisement for making abortion retroactive until age three.

The astronomer's view of the world differed from the views of all the other villagers. By Alphan standards, his brain was impaired—yet it was also peculiarly alive. He could hold only the barest minimum of facts, yet he was forever drawing connections between the few things he remembered. He was different, by sheer definition, and the villagers despised him because he was different.

He once made a connection between the suns of A-4 and the stars in the sky. The second, smaller sun was shrinking with every passing year. He knew from village history that every third generation saw the second sun diminish almost to a point in the heavens, like a star; and he saw—somehow he *saw* that the sun shrinks not by physically growing smaller, but by the same means that a mountain seems (*and only seems*) to grow smaller as one moves away from it. From this connection he guessed that all the stars in the sky might be suns. He could not yet say what the wanderers were, but he knew (*knew*) that the stars were suns seen from very far away.

Nobody believed him. And the more insistent he became, the more retarded they judged him.

Add to this cruelly different, sensitive organism a lifetime of punishment by his peers and elders—so that he begins to feel like an alien on his own world. Add to this the self-doubts, the private acknowledgment that perhaps they are right to call him a retard, that perhaps they are right to judge him a deviant who should have been weeded out of the pouch, whose only lifetime accomplishment will be to consume houseloads of precious fruit.

And still, some inward urgency directed his attention to the stars. His mind alone was filled with questions—

(*Is Chris from another star?*)

—on a world where everybody else had all the answers.

The Alphan measure of intelligence was how many facts and names one could recite, and most Alphans, the astronomer judged, were far, far more concerned about how smart everyone else thought one was, than about actually learning anything of importance.

The astronomer was concerned only about how much endless fun his questions could provide—

(*From another star? How could that be?*)

—and he alone had asked new questions about the same stars that everyone else had been looking at and keynaming and memorizing for thousands of centuries.

The villagers failed to see the stars as suns, not because they were ignorant, but because their answers came from highest authority; and on A-4, highest authority was the illusion of knowledge.

One authority, the only one who paid any attention to the astronomer's ravings, was the chemist. She saw in him a bright flame, an ability to abandon knowledge in favor of some deep-rooted intuition; and somehow this led him to knowledge that no other villager could possess.

But presently, his only friend was neglecting him for the aliens—

(*Oh, you too, my chemist.*)

—and he was puzzled that the villagers called him a retard, yet clambered with such vigor around creatures whose memories were a hundred times worse than his.

Inward and inward, he feared for the chemist's safety.

I am become Chris, the Devourer of worlds.

"Worlds? Become . . . am . . ." He did not know the meaning of the words. The aliens had not defined them. But they would, in time; and in time he would be able to decipher the sentence, and in time he would see what should have been.

17

Her Name, Titanic

Winter, A.D. *2051*

CHRIS CALLED A VIEW OF EARTH ONTO THE WALLSCREEN, Earth as it had existed two years ago.

Dawn was striking across China. The peaks of the Himalayas blazed, became dazzling white islands rising out of a sea of darkness. New Zealand was down there in the south, obscured now by a continent-sized sheet of cloud.

Horizontal rain in Wellington, Chris guessed. Underneath that glittering white veil, the Cook Strait must be (*must have been*) throwing one of her temper tantrums. He thought of how his son had always hated such days, and he knew now what it would cost him to visit a star: for among the other things Jonathan hated, Chris included himself.

On a December morning in the year 2051, enroute to A-4, Chris sat at the breakfast table, staring at the Earth via a live satellite broadcast, and making a fist around one of the few treasures he had brought from home. It was plain-appearing. Nothing more than a black rubber ball. But it dismayed him.

It was a gift from little Susan Skurla, who, like most

children her age, delighted in shocking her parents. But she had discovered a totally new way of accomplishing that feat. While her peers spouted curses for effect, six-year-old Susan stomped ahead and . . . and what? Rewrote the rules of geometry?

Sitting between the stars, Chris recalled a prelaunch interview at the Skurlas' Port Chaffee apartment. He remembered being distracted by Susan, a first-generation Moon-born. Her leg muscles were thinner than those of the Earth-born. She moved more gracefully and Chris understood that she would retain the features of childhood longer, unless, of course, she went to Earth, where it was impossible for her to walk without mechanical pants, where falls could be fatal, where capillaries in her feet might burst, and where she could never hope to run or skip or play tennis.

She was tall for her age, by Earth standards, with eyes that were peculiarly dark and knowing, even by lunar standards. She lived through those eyes, took in every word and gesture, probed Chris like an information-gathering machine, spreading the facts out on the floor of her mind, snatching up the useful bits and tucking them away for future reference. There was no telling what she would eventually make of the bits, how she would connect them together, what new insight would spill out of her. There was no telling at all, after you'd seen the ball, after you'd heard the sharp, popping sound, after she'd proudly handed you a tennis ball transformed instantly, denuded—no, not denuded, not stripped of its yellow fur, but . . . but . . .

Chris squeezed it and it was firm, unpunctured.

He dropped it and it bounced.

"Can I open it?" he asked.

Her eyes widened; then she nodded her head.

Chris pierced the rubber skin with a touchtone pen, and there was the fur where it did not belong: lining the ball's inner surface. No, not denuded, Chris told himself. Everted. Filled with air. Unpunctured, yet turned somehow inside out.

She did it again and again that evening, and gave him his very own inside-out tennis ball to carry off, intact, to the stars. He had since examined every millimeter of its surface in microscopic detail, and failed to find a blemish or patch concealing a hole through which the ball had been pulled.

There were children playing in the streets, Einstein had once complained, who could solve the universal field problem this afternoon, because they were able to look at things with a newness that adults had long forgotten—because grown-ups had built too many rules around themselves.

And so the everted tennis ball became, to Chris, a symbol of the clarity of childish perception, a reminder that when everything is new to him, when he or anybody else is unfamiliar with the ground rules, when no one has fixed in his mind what a tennis ball should and should not do, one is perhaps able to see possibilities in every direction and, unfossilized in his thinking, to touch the truth.

But how, exactly, did she do it? Chris wondered.

He regretted that he would probably never know. To learn more, he would have to dissect the ball. He would have to pull it apart and erase the very qualities that made it unique. Though he did not know it, little Susan had given him an all-too-appropriate way of looking at a lifelike dream, returning now, as the ship picked up speed—returning to torment him night after night—the dream in which he had been a child prodigy every bit as strange as the Moon-born: seeing in advance the chain of cause and effect through history, planning to prevent his mother's death, and eventually causing his own at age seventeen. That dream, and the un-tennis ball, were portents of a lesson that would best have been learned by Christopher Wayville before he set sail for the fourth world of Alpha Centauri A: to become an

observer was to alter the things observed, to stretch
them out of shape, to see them changed almost beyond
recall by our simple act of seeing.

If Chris were a smarter man, he would have taken this
lesson all by itself, stowed it for future use, and ignored
everything else about the Lazarus Effect. Far, far wiser
to force it out of his mind, to dismiss the whole thing
outright as a trick of the imagination. For it was during
those moments when he let the forebodings obsess him,
when he let them dominate and confuse his decisions,
that he was headed for trouble, and the fates of worlds
along with him.

"Chris, what's wrong?"

Chris propped the ball up on five fingers and rotated
it, like the Earth on its axis. "Wrong? What could possibly be wrong?"

"I mean, is it something specific? Something I can help
you with?"

"*Enterprise*? Can you help me with *Enterprise*?" He put
the ball down on the table. "I told you, I saw it."

"Oh, Chris—"

"I saw *Enterprise* die before it happened."

"Prove it."

"I can't." He stared across the table in a pleading,
desperate way that was unsettling, if not downright
frightening. "I know it must sound like I'm going nuts
out here, but I think I might actually have had a . . ."
He found the word dangerous, difficult to say. "*Premonition*," he managed to say, "a very specific premonition
of *Enterprise* exploding in a pancake. Now, if that came
true, what else is going to happen? What about the other bad things in my dreams? I don't know, and neither,
it seems, do you or anybody else. There may very well
be something legitimate about these—these . . . *visions*
about monsters on A-4, about Earth being ravaged. Our
whole civilization may be in legitimate danger, actually
in *real* danger, not imaginary danger."

"It's just bad dreams, Chris. And we don't even need

to invoke coincidence to explain what you saw. Can you really tell whether or not you heard Lex's first mention of danger intruding upon your sleep, shaping your dream for you? I think—"

You can keep that thought to yourself, Clarice.

Chris had already catalogued six possibilities in his mind. They ranged from not very bad to downright horrible.

One: Clarice was right. The visions meant nothing, but could he ever be one hundred percent sure?

Two: the visions were in fact premonitions, and when he arrived on the fourth world of Alpha Centauri A, he might, if he was wise enough and paid attention, find a solution to the problem and prevent the premonitions from becoming real.

Three: the visions were in fact premonitions and, outward-bound for Alpha Centauri A-4, he was flying in the wrong direction and should actually be on Earth, the only place where he could make any difference. But if he began decelerating today for the return home, he would find himself skidding more than five light-months farther from Earth by the time the ship could turn around, too far away even to communicate.

Four: the visions were in fact premonitions, and the means for making them unreal was indeed on A-4. There, too, was the means for making them real. He recalled scenes, misty and vague, of the grinning monster upon the planet's surface, grinning and intelligent. There were Other People. And perhaps even because of such premonitions (real or psychological), he might become too nervous, make mistakes he might otherwise have avoided, and screw up totally the first contact with ETIs, and eventually bring about the very destruction he wanted to prevent.

Five: the visions were in fact premonitions, and nothing he did could prevent them from becoming real.

The sixth possibility, of course, was that he was going nuts out here.

"Oh . . ." Clarice looked a little frightened. "There's never been proof of anything like that, of anything like you're saying—"

The possibilities gathered in Chris's brain, congealed into a particularly nasty, deep-rooted fear that every move he made could make his visions real.

And yet he also wanted to find out if there were ways of preventing them from becoming real.

And yet, at the same time, he suffered from self-doubts. He recognized the possibility (the hope) that it was merely his imagination at work. Still, while doubting himself, he believed that it was at least a possibility that these were true visions of something coming. He could not be sure of that, and from time to time he believed he might in fact be going crazy (and, yes, Clarice believed it, too), but in his moments of obsession he was beginning to feel—to really feel—that the threat was real enough that he could not risk inaction.

And yet he also feared that any action he took would be a mistake: make just one wrong move, and he could be redirecting history. In which case, the wisest action was none at all . . . unless, of course, no action, too, turned out to be a mistake.

It did not occur to him that the wisest action of all would have been never to have voiced such concerns, or at least to have blacked out the ship's broadcasts to Earth during the weeks and months in which he had let his dreams become the overmastering reality of his waking hours. Earth was two light-years away, and no one would know of Chris's present troubles for at least as long. But knowledge, once it came to those in charge on Earth, would redirect their choices along frightening new pathways that should never have been forged to A-4. He had already made a mistake. It raced toward Earth on a narrow beam of laser broadcast released by FUQ2. There was no way of calling back the light.

"—not a smidgen of evidence, Chris."

He uttered a strange, hysterical laugh, and this, too, was recorded by the ship's computer and downlinked to Earth. He lifted his un-tennis ball up to eye level and said, "This . . . after you've seen something like this, how can you expect not to keep an open mind?"

An open mind is one thing, Clarice thought of saying; *a hole in the head is quite something else.* And then she decided that she was cruel to be thinking such things— and on the verge of voicing them—when her man, *her Christopher,* wanted her, needed her.

"It proves nothing," she said at last, motioning toward the ball.

"Then forget the ball! There's more relevant incidents. I've been digging examples out of the computer all week. Take this: San Francisco, 1989—an earthquake brought down several miles of a double-tiered highway. The quake occurred during the evening rush hour, with a World Series game about to begin. The rescue workers expected to find hundreds of crushed cars, but when they pulled away the upper tier, there was practically no one underneath. The road had been almost as empty as you'd find it at three in the morning."

"You have documentation of this?"

Chris scrawled something on a liquid crystal flat, and the ship's computer began running relevant newspaper excerpts on the wallscreens, followed by television interviews with people who claimed to have turned away from the fatal road literally at the last moment. Over and over, it was the same story: something deep inside made them uneasy, an inner hunch that one should not go there, strong enough that people did not easily dismiss it, and instead took the road less traveled.

"Coincidence?" Clarice suggested. "Maybe what they really felt was a general uneasiness about the main road very likely being more jammed with traffic than it was already bound to be, because of the World Series game; and all having the same thought, they left the road empty. I'll admit that sounds improbable, but isn't it more probable than what you're suggesting?"

"You've heard of the *Hindenburg*?"

"Yes."

"Well, look here at the ticket cancellations—one of the biggest ticket runs in history. That airship was more than half empty when it blew up. They couldn't *give* tickets away."

"Sort of adds to the conspiracy theory, if you ask me. Sounds like someone leaked the plan."

"I think there's too many other cases just like it, and they don't all lend themselves to deliberate verbal forewarning." Chris began scrolling through news clippings on the wallscreens. "Here's an interesting one from April 15, 1912, the same day your idol Harriet Quimby made her English Channel crossing. No conspiracy could have arranged for the world's largest ship to strike an iceberg, but there she went, at the height of a coal strike, the only ship sailing to America from the U.K., and only fourteen hundred people aboard—more than half empty. As big a ticket-cancellation panic as with the *Hindenburg*. And here's why—"

Chris threw excerpts on the screen of newspaper interviews with those who had canceled their tickets. Mrs. Hart and Mrs. Astor spoke of the same bad dream, in which the unsinkable *Titanic* struck an iceberg and sank the first time it sailed.

"People have always made a rather larger thing out of the *Titanic* panic than it ever deserved to be," Clarice objected. "The fact remains that the *Titanic* never sank, in spite of all the bad dreams."

"In spite of them or because of them? The fact is that she did strike an iceberg the first time out—sailed straight into a hundred-kilometer-wide field of bergs and growlers; and if you look down to the bottom of the page here, in *The New York Times*, First Officer Will Murdoch was having the same recurring nightmare that Mrs. Hart, Mrs. Astor, and so many others were so specific about. He says right here that if not for his nightmares, he might not have been so on edge as he stood in charge of the bridge at eleven-forty P.M. on the night of April 14, 1912. He might not have telephoned the engine room to slow the ship from twenty-two and a half knots to twenty, he might not have warned the ship's lookouts to watch especially for icebergs, he might not have been so quick to respond when one of them banged the crow's nest bell three times, and he would have plowed into that ice field full throttle, and the story would have been quite different."

Chris scribbled something onto a flat, and the 15 April 1912 edition of the New York *Evening Sun* flashed onto one of the wallscreens.

The only bad news on the front page was that the Giants had lost to the Boston Braves.

Clarice shook her head. "There may be a good reason for Murdoch's bad dreams. I remember coming across a story linking the nearly empty *Titanic* to a strange novel of the time—*Futility*. I'm sure of it. The ship even had the same name, *Titanic*."

"*Futility?*"

"FU," Clarice called out. "Give me a library search. A novel called *Futility*, published somewhere between 1890 and 1912. It was about a ship striking an iceberg and sinking on its maiden voyage."

In an instant, the ship's computer had found the listing and put it on the screen.

FUTILITY. AUTHOR: MORGAN ROBERTSON. PUBLISHED BY M. F. MANSFIELD IN 1898.

Clarice called up the entire book and began scrolling down through it. The luxury Atlantic liner, bigger and faster and more beautiful than any ship that had sailed in 1898, matched the real-life *Titanic* in almost every detail, right down to the three large propellers, and the watertight compartments that ran from stem to stern and made the ship "unsinkable." Both the real and the imaginary *Titanic* sailed and struck icebergs in April.

"Perhaps Murdoch and the others simply read *Futility*," Clarice suggested. "A ship with the same name and the same features going out on its maiden voyage? The book must have been passed around quite a lot, as a sort of grim joke. Anyone who was given a copy, or who even heard that such a book existed—especially in those superstitious times—would have been a little worried about sailing aboard the *Titanic*."

"FU, I want a bio on Robertson," said Chris, and in a part of the ship's brain that weighed less than two kilograms, yet housed every film, every publication, and the accumulated knowledge of civilization (updated continually from Earth), ranging down to such details as the medical files of every hospital on Earth, FU retrieved all that was known about Morgan Robertson. There was very little to go by. None of his books had ever sold particularly well. Although various steamship historical societies still kept *Futility* in print, he was, during life, a struggling author. There had been a hospital admission on July 20, 1896: a near drowning, followed by complaints of "persistent sleep disturbance." The computer found a brief mention in the May 5, 1912, Brooklyn *Daily Eagle*, citing the similarity between Robertson's *Futility* and the actual *Titanic* collision. The columnist quoted Robertson as saying his book was inspired by things he had dreamed while unconscious and being rescued from a boating accident, things that for a little while afterward had come back to haunt him as nightmares, which eventually and thankfully went away. And there were Robertson's other three books.

Chris began scrolling casually through *Beyond the Spectrum*, published in 1908. By page 3, Clarice let out a gasp. Robertson had accurately described a Japanese internment camp in America. She took a touchtone pen and began skipping randomly through the book. On each page was told the tale of a great war of fire spreading over the Earth and fought mainly in the air, with flying fortresses and fighter planes far beyond the spit-and-glue flimsies of 1908. The war ended with America's use, against Japan, of something called a *sun bomb*, whose light was capable of incinerating everything for miles around—and hence the title: *Beyond the Spectrum*. One page contained a vivid description of smoldering ships limping into port, driven only by stokers or anyone else who happened to be below deck, because the flash from the bomb was so intense that it had burned or blinded everyone above.

Thirty-three years later, an air war astonishingly similar to the one imagined by Morgan Robertson had spread over the Earth, ending with the use of a weapon known to the Japanese as the *sun bomb*. The most haunting page of all in Robertson's novel gave the time and place of America's entry into the war: on a December morning, forces of the Empire of Japan bombed harbors in Manila and Hawaii from the air.

Clarice, her curiosity now kindled, began skimming through Robertson's other two novels, and was quickly disappointed. They contained no futuristic airplanes or ocean liners. They were about pirates.

Chris shrugged. "Do you think it might be worth checking where he said the treasure was buried?"

"Don't know," said Clarice. "This isn't like someone saying, after a road has collapsed, 'I wasn't there because I had a premonition.' This was thoroughly documented before it happened.

"I still prefer to think of it as a fascinating coincidence, though. Given a couple of hundred years of people writing novels, sooner or later someone was just bound to write something that looks very prophetic, and only looks like it."

"Maybe once. Maybe *Futility*. But two books like that? Don't you think that's pushing the probabilities just a little too far?"

"It's a highly improbable coincidence, I'll grant you that much. But it's not an impossible one."

"I'm telling you, there's nothing new about visions, Clarice. People have been having them all along."

"Yes. And in all these years, scientists have not proved any of it."

"Would you risk your reputation to try? Who would take you seriously? How should a technocrat deal with a spiritual experience?"

Spiritual experience? Clarice thought about Chris's

choice of words. It was all beginning to sound like witch-craft to her, or religion, or something like that, some-thing she had learned to put away.

That was New Year's Eve, the last day of 2051; and Clarice gave her husband a sleep drink, then spent the night awake watching him stir uneasily on their bed, breaking out, from time to time, in little beads of sweat. She knew that his dreams had to be very bad—again. They seemed to be worsening as the ship clocked slowly ahead from ninety-two to ninety-three percent lightspeed.

She watched him, and she loved him and feared for him, and she could not say a word to comfort him.

Now even she was becoming obsessed with Chris's dreams; not with what they meant or did not mean, or with that Morgan Robertson business, but with finding a way of stopping the dreams. Briefly, she even consid-ered decelerating, turning the ship around, and calling off the mission. She dropped that alternative very quick-ly, but not before it occurred to her that all the trouble had started with acceleration, almost from the moment that the first time dilation effects had been felt. And add to that Constance Bardo's bad dreams . . . perhaps time dilation was having an unanticipated psychological impact.

There lay a theory that could easily be put to the test: decrease time dilation, and see if Chris's agitation decreased proportionally.

On her liquid crystal flat, she ordered FUQ2 to begin shaving off velocity, to begin an early deceleration down to ninety-one percent lightspeed. She then called for the absolute black of outer space to fill the room, and for the starscape to be displayed on her wallscreens. She set her gaze ahead toward Centaurus, and let the tears well up. As her husband's sleep deepened and the cold stars burned through her tears, there were no sounds except the vibration of distant engines creeping down through the tether. The vibration was felt more than heard. It shook the bones, and it was always there, so Clarice had long ago become used to it, put it out of her thoughts, like any other background noise. Now, except for that faraway beat, the *Beagle* was as silent as the deserts of space.

18

Trinary

Autumn, A.D. 2054.

Dᴜʀɪɴɢ ᴛʜᴇ ᴛʜʀᴇᴇ ᴡᴇᴇᴋs ᴛʜᴀᴛ ꜰᴏʟʟᴏᴡᴇᴅ ᴛʜᴇ Wᴀʏᴠɪʟʟᴇs' arrival, the suns began a slow separation in the sky. Presently, A-4 and Alpha Centauri B were located on opposite sides of Alpha Centauri A, with the result that, viewed from A-4, the two suns rose and set side by side.

The alignment was transitory.

Already the suns were far enough apart that the Wayvilles, and every other object on the planet's surface, had gained a second shadow. The Alphan translation for the phenomenon was "twinning." One "twinner" was always dimmer than the other, and as yet they were so closely superimposed as to be difficult to distinguish; but in the weeks to come, as the suns wandered farther apart, so too would the twinners, until they became as distinct as shadows cast by two separate streetlamps.

Some eight months hence, A-4's orbit would carry it between the suns. Alpha Centauri A, around which A-4 orbited, would then shine alone at noontide, yellow-white and exactly as bright as the Sun in Earth's sky.

When A set, B would rise to command the heavens, banishing the stars with its brilliant orange light.

And then, slowly, the suns would realign, and the astronomer's season would return.

Chris regretted not having arrived on A-4 a few weeks earlier. Although in all the solar system, and in all the solar systems studied to date, no celestial event had been found that could compare with the sheer beauty of a solar eclipse seen from Earth, the Wayvilles had missed an enviable sight. The alignment this year had been so close that A actually eclipsed B. According to the Alphan witnesses, B was swallowed and the orange glow went out, and suddenly, briefly, new colors were everywhere.

ALPHAN DAWN CAME ON LIKE A THUNDERBOLT, WITH B AP-pearing first—a dazzling fireball rising in shades of red deeper than any sunrise seen on Earth. Within seconds A followed, a dozen times brighter and climbing the eastern sky noticeably faster than the Earth's Sun.

A-4's days were a few hours too short. If the Wayvilles wanted to be awake in time to watch the suns rise and still get a full night's sleep, they had to retire almost immediately after sunset.

Every morning when they stepped out of *Beagle*, Catherine was there, always eager to see Clarice and talk to her; and every time they spoke, her English was better.

"The glacier is two days from here." Catherine smiled her gentle smile and pointed west. "Let's go. But a question first: Do you *have* to bring spider?"

"We have to, so we can talk to FU."

Catherine accepted the answer, never taking pause to wonder what was so important about being able to talk with FU at all times. If she had, she would have noticed that the Wayvilles could talk to FU anytime they wanted, by aid of their flats, without bringing a spider along; and she would have realized that the spider was really an extension of FU's brain—the computer's arms and legs and eyes; and she would have asked herself: Does FU work in man's interest, or does man serve the machine's interests? And from this question she might have guessed that the relationship between man and machine had become a mutual parasitism.

They traveled on foot, Catherine leading the way and FU trotting alongside. The woods were dripping. Shafts of sunshine slanted through the tall ferns, and where they stabbed the forest floor, heavy dew sparkled in a million points of light. By noon the dew would be melted off and the air would be sticky and close.

"Toto, I have a feeling we're not in Kansas anymore," Clarice said jokingly.

Chris laughed.

Catherine did not. "Clarice. Question. How far from here is Oz?"

The Alphans all had that problem: they could not separate the movies they had seen from reality. To them, *The Wizard of Oz* and *Village of the Giants* were documentaries. Chris found it hard to believe: the Alphans did not play make-believe.

Here was a major departure from human thinking, Chris thought. It was a departure that condemned the Alphans never to create anything that was not strictly functional. A-4 would have no Pyramids, no Acropolis, no *Pietà*, no gods.

Clarice tried for the tenth time in as many days to explain that movies were not pictures and sounds taken from real life. "Oz does not exist, Catherine. It's fantasy. We make fantasies for fun and . . ."

She was still lecturing on acting and filmmaking when they reached a new clearing and broke for lunch.

SHADED BY LONG AND RAGGED FERNS, BENEATH A FACADE OF layered limestone, they ate. Catherine fashioned a small net stretched on a reed hoop and scooped "prawns" from a stream. She supplemented this dish with wild fruit. FU compared these against human biochemistry, checking all possible reactions in a flash of photic activity, and found no toxic effects. The computer told the Wayvilles that the "bananas" would not be worth tasting, and they didn't try. But the prawns were as sweet as Earthly prawns, and the humans appreciated the treat; but their left-handed sustenance had to come from Folsome foods carried by the spider.

A little higher up, the valley began to narrow. Its sides towered vertically for almost three hundred meters. Like the walls of the pinnacles, the lofty valley massifs were deserts, yet the floor was so thickly wooded that progress was possible only along the shore of the glacial stream. After having walked three hours from their lunch stop, they found the daylight fading fast and decided to set up camp.

Using strips of bark for rope, the stems of giant grasses for beams, and broad, leathery leaves for flooring and roofing, Catherine in a few minutes built them an excellent lean-to and, with "cotton" and leaves, made a soft bed.

She then made a fire by rubbing a pointed stick in a groove carved in a curiously gray and porous wood. The sticks were burning in only a few seconds, but try as he did, Chris was unable to master the art.

Catherine placed fist-sized stones upon the burning wood, then hopped off into the forest. In her absence the fire consumed the wood, and the stones became hot. She returned within minutes, bearing three green parcels of leaves, which she placed between the hot stones, and then buried the whole thing, embers and all, trapping the smoke and the steam under the soil, so that when she uncovered the parcels ten minutes later, they were most deliciously cooked. Inside were unrecognizable fruits, and after a nod of approval from

FU, they ate the parcels, and washed the meal down with cool meltwater from the Glacier Wear.

Dinner was both filling and pleasant, yet Chris and Clarice had to eat a second meal from the spider's provisions. Catherine was puzzled by Clarice's explanation for this peculiar and characteristically alien behavior, but puzzlement did not trouble her. A fact was a fact was a fact, even if sometimes the facts were strange.

The shades of night came on like sunrise. Viewed from the campsite, the towering cliffs shut out half the sky. Four pairs of eyes peered through an immense crack into a scarlet stew that flashed salmon pink as B, somewhere offstage, slipped below the horizon. Then the A-shine faded quickly, as if a lamp were being dimmed, and the crack was full of stars.

The Sun was up there in the middle, brighter than Sirius. Chris withdrew the gold foil from his pocket and took a look: yes, the metal was thin enough to see through—all the way to the place it had come from.

"Question," Catherine said. "What is that?"

"It's a piece of the very first *Beagle* ever to land my people on another world."

"Question: May I touch?"

"Sure."

Catherine turned the golden sliver over and over between her fingers. She seemed to think it a worthwhile artifact. Imitating Chris, she held it up to her face and looked through it at the stars.

"Question: May I keep?"

"I . . . I can give you a piece of it, yes." Chris lingered on the implications of what had just been said. If only Elmer Glue could be here to see this. If only her father could have known that a piece of LM-5 would one day be here, in another solar system, in an alien's hands.

"Question: Galileo wanted me to question. What are the stars?"

"Difficult to explain," Chris said. "You see this campfire. If you walked all the way to the other side of the valley and looked back, it would appear to be a much smaller light than the one we see as we sit here, wouldn't it?"

"Yes."

"Now, the suns are the same way. If you went very far away from A and B and looked back, they would seem much smaller, just like the campfire. They would look like stars." Chris paused, knowing that Catherine would never forget the words he'd just said, knowing that she would probably repeat them without error to Galileo, and not knowing if she could connect the thoughts they conveyed, but suspecting, from the questions he had sent her to ask, that Galileo could. Pausing, he hoped to give the words time to sink in, to connect.

"Now, can you tell me what that bright star over there would look like close up?" he said, pointing at the Sun.

"Question: Does it look like a sun?"

Chris's eyes widened. It was the last thing he'd expected to hear from the Alphan. "What makes you think that?" he asked.

"Galileo thinks that. Question: Is that what you are teaching me? That the suns are stars and the stars are suns?"

"Yes. That just about covers it."

"Then question. Another Galileo question. Wanderers look like stars. Wanderers move against the stars. Everybody knows that. Everybody knows that a wanderer is a light in the sky that moves. Galileo wants to know more."

"Easy enough," Chris said, withdrawing a flat from the spider. "The four brightest wanderers are worlds, very much like the one we are seated on now. They all have valleys very much like Wells, except that there is no air or water, and no trees, and the sky is black even when the suns are up."

Suddenly, whole new worlds opened up for Catherine—unimaginably strange lands beyond the edge of A-4; on the other side of a . . . *space.*

"Now, here, on the flat, is a simplified view of the five worlds of A."

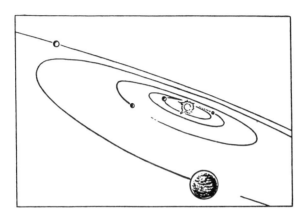

Catherine studied the flat closely, especially the drawing of A-4. What she saw went against everything she had been taught about her world.

"Now, here's a picture of B," Chris continued.

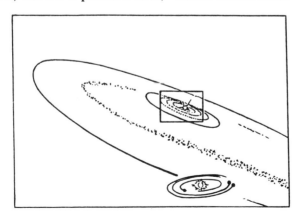

"Just like A, B has worlds that move around it in circles. It has three worlds. And like A-4, B makes a circle around A, carrying its worlds along with it.

"Now, if we move very far away from A and B, here's how they look."

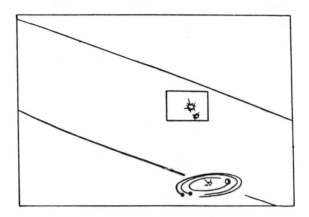

"Stars," Catherine said.

"Yes. And do you see that little sun on the bottom of the flat? It's called Proxima Centauri. It has three worlds. And Proxima Centauri is actually that tiny star right up there," Chris said, pointing. "Right between the Sun and—"

At that very instant, a light went on in the sky, right where Chris was pointing.

"Magic!" Catherine said.

"No," Chris said. "I had nothing to do with it. Proxima Centauri is what we call a flare star."

Catherine did not ask what a flare star was, or what made it flare, which was just as well, Chris thought. The Alphans had never seen a solar flare, and this would be difficult to explain to creatures who were just beginning to grapple with the idea that stars were suns.

Proxima Centauri was a red dwarf. As such, a planet orbiting the star at the same distance that the Earth orbits the Sun would be frozen, its sky dominated by a pigeon-blood ruby as radiant as forty-five full moons. Every few weeks, suddenly and without warning, the ruby would flash out canary yellow—a flare comparable to the brightest outbursts seen on A and B, but a million times more conspicuous, because on a dim red dwarf it more than tripled the total output of light.

The amber star began to fade. Even as they watched, it died up there in the constellation Cassiopeia. Catherine was hurriedly scratching circles and ellipses on Chris's forearm. It occurred to him that they were replicas of the drawings he had just displayed on the flat. Did she *really* understand them? Chris wondered. Whether she did or not, she would soon be communicating the pictographs to other Alphans through touchscript, and through touchscript the key to the universe would be stored in their heads and passed down from generation to generation.

"Now, here's a drawing of A, B, and Proxima Centauri seen from very far away," said Chris.

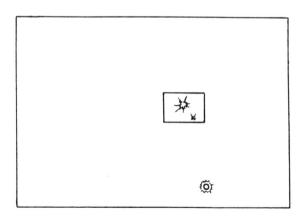

In this drawing, we are looking at your solar system from so far away that up there, in the top part of the picture, we can distinguish only two stars where actually there are three. This is because A and B are so close together that they look like one point of light if you step back far enough.

"And down there, in the bottom of the drawing, is the star Clarice and I came from. Most of our people live on the third world, a world very much like A-4."

"Question: FU has drawn A-4 and the other worlds round. Are the worlds shaped like A and B? Is A-4 shaped like A and B?"

"Yes. Of course." Chris went quiet for a few moments. "Catherine . . . tell me what you think A-4 is shaped like."

"A-4 is shaped like A and B. A-4 is round."

"No. Tell me what you thought A-4 was shaped like a few minutes ago, before I showed you. What do the teachers think A-4 is shaped like?"

"Teachers say this valley is the center of A-4. All the land and all the water, and all the land on the other side of the water goes away from the valley for many, many of your kilometers. Rocket explorers try to find where the land and water end. They say some have gone so far in their rockets that they flew over the edge of A-4 and were lost."

Chris drew his breath in astonishment. The Alphans had actually placed artificial satellites in orbit around their world, and yet they believed their world to be flat. They believed that a rocket could fly too fast and go soaring over the edge—which was, in fact, half true, as the pilot of "Dim" had learned.

There was little sleep for the Wayvilles and their guide that night as they huddled against the cold air of the upper valley and pondered the far stars and turned new astonishments over and over in their heads. Before dawn it rained very heavily, but Catherine's elevated floor and thatched roof kept them dry.

*   *   *

THE ROUTE WOULD HAVE BEEN IMPOSSIBLE TO FOLLOW WITHout Catherine's lead. So thick was the forest that every landmark, though on high ground, was completely shut out. The path Catherine chose was fairly level, but the Wayvilles had to bend to avoid walking into hardwood branches that jutted out from every direction.

And the air was a bit too damp.

And the Wayvilles were a bit too tired.

And suddenly, below them, was unearthly beauty.

They emerged into a clearing on the south massif, and there, partly shrouded in mist, was a broad plain of blue ice. About two kilometers down the valley, the glacier stalled, and was melting rapidly into a swamp of its own creation.

Conditions for ascending Wear's snout were everything but ideal, so Catherine had selected a path that ran above and alongside the ice.

In the clearing she fashioned for herself a pair of booties from soft bark, then led them down the massif and onto the glacier.

Chris noticed a sudden, ten-degree drop in air temperature between the forest and the ice. He looked upon his surroundings with admiration. On either hand, the massifs were covered with wild "bananas" and "berries" and other luxuriant productions of the Alphan tropics. And yet these things grew only a few meters from ice.

"It's the climate," Clarice guessed. "Very stable. So much of this world is water that there are no summer or winter extremes. Same thing happens near Milford Sound, right?"

"Yes," Chris said. "There's thick stands of palm trees living on the margin of south polar climate, and penguins walking under the palm trees. But this! There's nothing on Earth quite like this."

Catherine chittered at them, and Clarice broke into sudden laughter. Whatever the joke was, Chris had missed it.

Catherine led them to a place where dark chips of volcanic rock, glistening in the suns, had become hot and melted holes in the ice. She seemed to think the holes a marvel, and it was clear that she expected an explanation from Clarice and Chris; but Clarice was laughing again. And again, Chris had missed the joke.

So had Catherine.

"It's okay," Clarice explained, "just . . . just a little giddy," and then she dropped, clutching her flat in one hand, a look of startled surprise on her face.

"Giddiness . . . that's all."

OH MY GOD OH MY CLARICE—

"Giddiness . . ."

He had to get her off the ice. *Had* to. Otherwise it would kill her. He just knew it. It was *that* kind of thing. He grabbed her by the wrists and began pulling.

Gas. Poison ice. Whatever it is, it's BAD! Get her off the ice! Got to get her off! Drag her by her hair if you have to!

"Tired," Clarice mumbled. "So tired . . ."

"FU! Help me—"

FU was gone.

And Catherine, too.

OH MY GOD—

19

The New Alphans

T HE FOREST WAS LONELY, DARK, AND DEEP, BUT WHERE the suns penetrated, something new and hideous had sprouted, and it kept on sprouting. The astronomer groaned at the sight of a new crop of seedlings growing exactly where he'd pulled them out the day before. And today there were twice as many of them. Barely had they broken the soil, yet already he could distinguish the rudiments of three leaves on each stem.

Nothing in the valley grew with three leaves.

Nothing in the valley grew that shade of green.

The plants were alien, and, judging from their increasing numbers, it was beginning to look as if they would cover the world—

(devourer of worlds)

"No!" said the astronomer. His bitter sense of impending loss went deeper than logic. "They cannot do this. They cannot come here and take our world."

He leaned forward and began pulling the plants out by their roots, tearing at them and scattering them in pieces. He didn't expect to win, but he had no desire to help the aliens.

*   *   *

WHEN CLARICE OPENED HER EYES, THE FIRST THING SHE became aware of was the viselike pain that gripped her temples and pierced her brow. She almost welcomed the pain; it meant that she was still alive.

She found herself staring straight into a ceiling of carefully arranged leaves. It must have been frightening for Catherine, but the Alphan had kept her wits and was providing for her friends in the only way she knew. By the time Chris had hauled Clarice to the edge of the ice field, Catherine, assisted by FU, had built a new shelter in the forest.

There was a sudden stabbing pain in Clarice's right shoulder. Turning her head quickly toward the source of the pain, she saw FU withdrawing a probe from her arm.

"Here. Drink this," Chris said, planting a bulb and straw firmly in her left hand. She sipped a sugary Folsome juice, orange-flavored, and some of the pain abated.

"Where's Catherine?" Clarice asked.

"She's starting a fire. I told her to boil some water."

Clarice's eyes narrowed. Chris flashed a smile and said, "That's what they say in the movies, isn't it? 'Boil some water.' She was very upset. I had to give her *something* to do."

Clarice got the giggles, and the giggles hurt. Her forehead was damp with perspiration. She was trembling inside.

"Okay," she said, getting her face straight. "So what's eating me?"

"Hypoglycemia," FU answered. "Low blood sugar."

"How the hell did I get *that*?"

"Bacteria," FU said. "An Alphan strain. Most A-4 bacteria are made of D amino acids. They are completely indifferent to life from Earth. But in your blood I found a species that has L amino acids deep inside its cell wall—the same amino acids your bodies are made out of. The bacterium is able to use the same sugars your bodies use, and its outer shell of D amino acids makes it immune to your supercharged immune systems."

"So why don't *I* have the disease?" Chris said.

"I don't know yet. Sooner or later it may infect you. You must watch for symptoms. Fatigue. Dizziness. A state of mental confusion. If Clarice had been luckier, she might have recognized it in time."

Chris's shoulders slumped. The spider turned and focused its eyes on Clarice. "When you exerted yourself on the ice, the bacteria were eating up all your sugar, and *you* were burning it even faster than the bacteria. Your brain cannot run without sugar. That's why you passed out. Had the loss caused any difficulty with the circulation around your heart, you could have suffered a heart attack.

"Now, listen to me very carefully. *Doctor's orders.* You may be feeling better right now, but I cannot permit you to walk back to the village. I can control your sugar levels with the juices we brought along, as long as you don't do any walking around for the next few days. The ship has sent another spider with new provisions. It will arrive early tomorrow morning, and then I will go back to the ship. I might be able to cure this thing, but I will need the *Beagle*'s Folsome tubes."

"What are you planning to do?" Clarice asked.

"Antibodies," FU answered. "It's very simple. I will clone antibodies."

"From wha—?" Clarice realized that Catherine had grown up exposed to the hypoglycemia bug. It was clear that her immune system was capable of fighting off the disease. All FU had to do was match the bacteria in Clarice's blood with the right genes from Catherine's chromosomes. Then a new bacterium could be produced aboard *Beagle*, one that exuded the right antibodies, which would be collected and given directly to the Wayvilles. The basic procedures had been pro-grammed years ago; the ship's computer would simply modify the program and—

"And Catherine. You'll have to take some of her blood."

"She has agreed to this," FU said. "Even as we built this shelter, I told her that I might have to pierce her arm to save you. I sense that she is scared. This has never been done to her before. But she agreed with-out any hesitation. You have found a good friend in Catherine."

Chris sat down on the floor and leaned back against a wall post. Somehow, the word "infection" stuck in his mind. He thought about it, and then began to see that they'd be quarantined for years, perhaps forever, if they returned to the vicinity of the Sun. Their bodies had picked up something foreign and hostile. It was not to be welcomed into the solar system. It must be locked up and studied, and its hosts along with it.

Once he and Clarice had stepped onto A-4 and breathed its air and ingested its water and fruits, there could be no going home to Earth.

There was no hope of ever seeing London or Paris again, or Jonathan. There was no point even in trying.

That quickly, Chris's world—his whole outlook toward the future—changed, and he knew at once that a pre-monition had turned outward and outward and become prophecy: he would die on A-4, sooner or later, and perhaps sooner.

Catherine thumped into the lean-to and went directly to Clarice.

"She's okay," FU assured her.

She put a hand on Clarice's forehead, brushed back her hair, and said, "D-don't die, E. T."

20

Random Poisoning

I**N APRIL 1912, ON THE NIGHT THE** *TITANIC* **MADE ITS** acquaintance with the iceberg, First Officer Will Murdoch was peculiarly on edge. He wished to his dear God that he had never read that novel given to him by a friend, that damned Robertson novel. It had resurrected uneasy dreams which seemed to go back to earliest childhood, dreams he had mostly forgotten. He saw himself standing up to his knees in a surge of water, out of his mind with some sort of guilt, while all around him the world came apart. Somewhere nearby a gurgle was cut short by the sound of breaking glass. Someone behind him shrieked. It sounded at first like a man, but the noise spiraled up and up without pause. It was hard to believe that human lungs could sustain such a cry. Murdoch drew his revolver, turned, and shot the man, putting out that horrible sound. And then he thought he recognized one of the wireless operators, Harold Bride, striding toward him. Murdoch shook his head, said, "I've done all I can," then gave a military salute in Bride's direction and put a bullet through his own head.

At 11:40 P.M., on April 14, 1912, Will Murdoch was in charge of the bridge. The bad dreams had kept him awake for the better part of a week, yet at the same time made him more alert, more cautious than usual. The owners of the White Star Line had told him that the watertight compartments made the *Titanic* her own lifeboat—"literally unsinkable." But he refused to let complacency set in. She was made of iron, he told himself. She could sink.

So he slowed her speed, and he was ready to respond when the crow's nest lookout spotted the ice field at 12:20 A.M. His readiness resulted in a gash along the starboard side, right where Robertson had said it would be, just three meters short of opening the sixth watertight compartment, which made all the difference in the world.

Eight hours later, the *Carpathia* and the *Californian* were at the *Titanic*'s side. Captains Rostrom and Lord tied lines to her, towed her to Halifax, and became heroes of the day.

All aboard were saved.

No great cascade of consequences arose from Murdoch's actions. History was not changed in any noticeable way, except that people lived who would otherwise have died, children were born who otherwise would not have existed; but not one of them, or their descendants, ever arrived at a pivotal point in history from which decisions made branched into two or more vastly different futures.

The names of some of the players were indeed changed, but whether or not the *Titanic* floated had no bearing on the overall pattern of the game.

Thomas Astor would be President of the United States throughout the Second World War, but the outcome would not be altered.

Charles Lindbergh would not fly the *Spirit of St. Louis* across the Atlantic, but a woman would pilot the *Spirit of Long Island* along the same path. And if not her, the goal to fly solo across the ocean was so powerful and so universal that inevitably someone else would have taken the controls of some other plane.

And so it was that on April 15, 1912, an aviator named Harriet Quimby, not the *Titanic*, came to dominate the front page of *The New York Times*. If not for Murdoch, Quimby's solo flight across the English Channel would have been eclipsed beyond notice by news of tragedy at sea.

Her sudden notoriety kept her from keeping an appointment with death at the Boston Air Show a few months later, and put her on a path leading to triumph aboard the *Spirit of Long Island*.

Harriet Quimby lived to see two world wars playing down through history without alteration. But the all-night radio vigils, Coast Guard rescue stations, and other safety regulations that would have been initiated had the *Titanic* gone down did not exist in September 1959, when she joined an oceanographic expedition aboard the Scripps Institute research vessel *Orca*.

The ship went down with all hands, including a bright, seventeen-year-old boy on his very first expedition to sea. One of the few lasting legacies of Will Murdoch was that in 1961, oceanographers would name two seamounts in memory of Quimby and the seventeen-year-old explorer, and that nearly a century later, Christopher Wayville would borrow the name of an Earthly seamount and transfer it—the Ballard Rise—to A-4's Coral Sea.

Despite the old science fiction writer's standby about the time traveler who kills an ancient butterfly and finds the world he returns to changed beyond recognition, the history of human progress had never been a chain of infinite links in which every cause, including the choice of a tuna fish or a turkey sandwich, branched off into vastly different alternate effects. Even if Murdoch had wrecked the *Titanic*, the change was too trivial to make a noticeable stain in the overall picture. Even the death of Hitler in childhood would have changed little. Like most of history's leaders, the Führer had merely taken up the prevailing view of the mob and capitalized on it for his own ascent. He no more led the mobs than a surfer leads a wave, and in the end he was engulfed by that which had uplifted him. But if not Hitler, someone else would have been carried aloft by the very same surge. For in Germany there was no alternate reality. The mob was too powerful. The year 1938 was Nazi time in Berlin.

The rare leaders, the ones about whom alternate histories truly do pivot, are those who find themselves in positions of authority and make the choices that would seem the least probable, oftentimes moving against the mob's view at the moment, against the surge, and somehow managing to push it in a new direction. General George Washington was such a man. The mobs wanted to make him king, and the behavior most likely for a military leader who has emerged victorious was to accept, if not personally seize, kingship. But Washington said, "No. We are going to try the Great American Experiment, and elect our leaders." And from that moment, history shifted along a new and improbable path.

Christopher Wayville, like Washington, was now carving a truly new and unpredictable path. He was out there, on his own, with unlimited power at his fingertips. And how he responded to his forebodings, and how the mobs responded to his response, were going to determine into which of at least two alternate histories the path turned.

By May 5, 2054, the decelerating *Beagle* had entered the Alpha Centauri A-B system. Deceleration from a dilated time frame had diminished Chris's bad dreams. The "visions" became easier for him to dismiss, and choosing the wiser path, he did so. As the twin suns grew in brightness and the planets came into view, Chris decided to bury all thoughts and worries about monsters on A-4. And though this path would ultimately smooth his initial contact with whatever beings might be, his in-flight obsession, combined with the slowness of communication across the light-years, had already changed irrevocably the overall pattern of Earth's response to the *Beagle*/A-4 encounter, even if the Alphans of 2054 turned out to be one hundred percent benign. For where potentially great costs were involved, virtually any possibility of confrontation, no matter how small, might be judged an unacceptable risk.

RE: WAYVILLE CRISIS, STARSHIP *BEAGLE*
YAMASAKI AUSTRALIA H.Q.
CLASSIFIED PRIORITY 1

BY AUTHORITY OF THE AUSTRALIAN DEPART-MENT OF INTERSTELLAR STUDIES THIS BUBBLE PACK HAS BEEN SCRAMBLED FOR EXAMINA-TION EXCLUSIVELY BY PERSONS WITH *NEED TO KNOW* STATUS. DISCUSSION OF CONTENTS WITH UNAUTHORIZED PERSONS IS A CRIMINAL OFFENSE PUNISHABLE UNDER PROVISIONS OF THE VALKYRIE POWERS ACT.

EXCERPT FROM 31 DECEMBER 2051 TRANSMISSION RECEIVED 5 MAY 2054

I know it must sound like I'm going nuts out here, but . . . there may very well be something legitimate about these—these . . . *visions* about monsters on A-4, about Earth being ravaged. Our whole civilization may be in legitimate danger, actually in *real* danger, not imaginary danger . . . How should a technocrat deal with a spiritual experience?

EXCERPT FROM MISSION LOG OF CHRISTOPHER WAY-VILLE RECEIVED 5 MAY 2054

The images are all wrong, yet so vivid. They return night after night to haunt me in my sleep. They even flash upon me while I am awake, and I cannot shake the feeling that they were always there within me, hiding in ambush, waiting for this moment to come out. I am convinced that everything I am seeing should happen, as if history is laid out before me like a movie, playing the same events over and over; no matter how many times you replay it, Rhett Butler's little girl will jump that fence and die just the same—a deterministic universe. If this is the case, then all that I have seen, no matter how I may try to prevent it, is determined to turn out as I see it whether or not I try to prevent it. Elmer Glue told me so, at Tranquillity: do not try to tamper with history.

TRANSMISSION EXCERPTS CONTINUE

Olsen, her face beginning to grow slick with sweat, tossed the flat onto Marcus's desk and slumped back in her chair.

"Strangest damned thing I ever read," Marcus said, rocking back and forth, as if searching for a way out. "Are you sure he isn't—or wasn't, as the case may be— just doing some free-wheeling theorizing?"

Olsen shook her head. "If he is, he's living it as well as theorizing it, not to mention scaring the daylights out of his wife. Crikey! Who would have predicted this?"

"Somebody really screwed up Big Time in deciding who we let out there."

"It's not that simple. He certainly seemed stable enough. I actually met the guy at Port Chaffee."

"He seemed normal then?"

"Perfectly rational. There wasn't a hint of anything like this." Olsen scribbled something on a flat, and snowy static filled the wallscreen. "You know about the blackout ships?"

"Yeah, I've heard of them," Marcus said with a slight grin. He had in fact designed the five robot spacecraft that now soared below the solar disk. Two of them had gone out ahead to intercept *Beagle*'s signals and relay them the long way around to Australia. The others drew a curtain of interference between Alpha Centauri and the Earth.

"Well," Olsen said, "our people launched the interceptors ten years ago, just in case things got . . . got dangerous, in one way or another. They thought they were launching signal boosters. That's all they needed to know, wasn't it?"

"Yeah. So how's the cover story holding?"

"Well, there's a fifteen-year-old hacker in Perth who broke through the curtain. We had to send somebody to kind of talk to her. As far as the rest of the world knows, we've lost contact with *Beagle*, and we're supposed to be afraid that *Beagle* itself may be lost. That's all they need to know, isn't it? What they don't know can't hurt them—right?"

"No, Olsen, no. Only what they don't know has the power to hurt them." Fear washed over Marcus as he thought of Christopher Wayville out there, preparing to meet some sort of God-given destiny. Chris had virtually absolute power. All he had to do was go completely mad amidst the stars, and kamikaze the Earth with his Valkyrie rocket.

Marcus stared into the wallscreen and shook his head. "Not much chance of hitting another pancake, I take it?"

"We can always hope," Olsen said. "We can always hope that *something* will stop him. Clarice tries to keep him asleep as much as possible. Maybe she'll recognize the danger and put something in his relaxants to knock him out permanently. But I'm afraid we have to assume the worst. It's all out of our control now. Those rantings you read were transmitted two years ago. Anything they're transmitting today will take almost four years to reach us. They should be well into the deceleration phase of flight. They can probably see A-4 on their scopes. If we called Clarice right now and told her not to land, she wouldn't receive the message until she was on her way home, three years after the landing. There's no way around it. Chris is going to end up on that planet."

"That's not so bad," Marcus said, almost to himself. He was considering the gamma ray flare of a Valkyrie engine seen at a distance of four light-days, and possible ways of predicting its position and intercepting it when you knew that it was actually no more than eight hours away, and invisible, and coming in fast—

"Not so bad as what?" Olsen said.

Marcus ignored the question, and Olsen swiveled her chair to one side, then scrawled something on her flat. Blue and pink against a black background, the curve of Alpha Centauri A-4 fluttered onto the wallscreen, then grew rapidly second by second. By the time the shape had tripled in size, it was gaining a violent whirling motion. Olsen called a series of commands into the flat that helped adjust the bubble pack and its picture to the advance probe's movements in space.

The continent they called Tunaland came sweeping up ahead, then the Takahashi Peninsula, and below, barely discernible through the haze, the limestone cenotes in the Valley of Wells. Olsen fed in another command, and the scene was made even more eerie by infrared enhancement. Now something previously unseen blazed in the shoulder of Takahashi.

"Meteor?" Marcus guessed.

"Keep watching."

The point of light was climbing out of, not crashing down upon, the atmosphere. As it climbed, it deposited a tornado of vapors in its wake that stood away from A-4 like an infrared needle, white-hot.

"That's impossible," Marcus snapped. "All we've seen down there is rivers, mountains—natural land forms. There's no port cities. No roads. No industrial aerosols. No radio broadcasts. It has to be a meteor bouncing off the atmosphere at some odd angle."

Olsen put a box in the corner of the screen and filled it with three nearly identical graphs. "The top one is an atomic absorption spec of the 'meteor's' vapor trail. Take special notice of the aluminum oxide peak. The bottom ones are burning Estes toy rocket engines and old space shuttle booster fuel."

"Jesus," Marcus said.

Olsen punched up a fourth graph. It was a total mismatch of the other three. "This is an ordinary carbonaceous meteor entering the Earth's atmosphere."

"Jesus," Marcus said again. "My Jesus."

"Yes. That so-called meteor over A-4 is flying on rocket fuel, or something very close to it."

The light traversed the Takahashi Peninsula and gained at least two hundred kilometers of altitude even as Olsen flashed her spectographs onto the screen. Veering horizontally and north, it began to orbit, deliberate and relentless, like the minute hand of a large clock.

Softly, Olsen said, "What do you suppose he meant by a deterministic universe, by this lack of choice he seems to feel?"

"*That*, if he really believes it, could go quite hard on us. There's a theory, not entirely new with Chris, though I'm certain I've read something he once wrote on the subject, that the positions and motions of all particles in the universe at any given instant, including the electrons in our brains, must determine the whole past and future of the universe. Maybe he believes he can go to Alpha Centauri and do as he pleases, but what he pleases has been laid down in advance, since the beginning of time."

"Do you believe that?"

"It doesn't matter what I believe. All that matters is what Chris believes, and what Chris believes is that his 'visions' are real. That is the only reality we should be thinking about."

"Not the only one," Olsen said, calling a new image onto the screen. "This just in: something else no one has shown you yet, something not even the Wayvilles know about, because no one thought there was anything important on A-1 and A-2, so the signal came directly to Earth, missing *Beagle* completely. I doubt we'll tell them now, though."

Two small uncrewed Valkyries had gone out ahead of the *Beagle*, bringing with them thirty descendants of the Asimov Array robots. They sought out the two innermost, Mercury-like worlds of Alpha Centauri A with but one thought in their dim minds: to subdue and rebuild the worlds to serve man's interests. Antihydrogen fuel depots were to be built close to A. As in the case of Mercury, the robots would descend upon the worlds like a flu virus, immediately assembling replicas of themselves from the substance of their hosts. As with Mercury, the first half decade of infection was to be a latent, incubation phase, during which most of the solar panels manufactured by the "spiders" and "worms" would be used to power an ever-accelerating chain reaction of machines building self-replicating machines building self-replicating machines. As their population approached a predetermined critical density, more and more of them would cease reproduction and join to form solar-panel and linear-accelerator factories, with the result that almost three decades after the arrival of the original thirty machines, fifty million square kilometers of A-1 and A-2 would be transformed into a giant photovoltaic generator, with an area the size of Rhode Island being added daily.

But as the pictures on the wallscreen made frighteningly clear, someone had already been there.

"What's your guess, Marcus? Another starfaring civilization just passing through? First rockets on A-4, and now this. You wouldn't expect so much activity in one system, not when people have been listening to the galaxy for almost a century without ever receiving the ghost of a broadcast."

Marcus's attention was drawn to a saucer-shaped depression on A-2, about forty kilometers wide, where something big had splashed down on a boundless carpet of solar panels. The solar farms clearly preceded the impact and, judging from the impact history of his own solar system, Marcus guessed that a forty-kilometer crater-maker could be expected once every few million years. Cratering events were relatively rare, and hundreds of other punctures through the carpet, most of them in the size range of Arizona's Meteor Crater, were clues to its age. There was broken glass everywhere upon the surfaces of A-1 and A-2, which meant that the worlds had lain abandoned for a very long time. Someone had invented antimatter rockets, and then stopped using them, millions of years ago.

"The big question," Olsen said, "is were they fruitful, and did they multiply?"

"And Chris Wayville is out there in the middle of all this," Marcus added. He then called up a replay of a paragraph from Chris's mission log:

If the universe truly does expand and contract repeatedly, and if it follows that each expansion and contraction is identical, so that every fleck of dust in this room winds up in the same exact place again and again, and I keep speaking these same words into a flat every few hundred billion years or so, on opposite sides of the Big Bang, then where is free will? Must our hope for change depend on a single particle straying in a new direction and introducing Chaos by bringing the Big

Bang off lopsided? Or is it with us—with thinking creatures—that the responsibility lies? I wonder if we sometimes pick up scraps of knowledge from the last time we were here—premonitions, if you will. Maybe the *Titanic* did sink the last time around, and maybe that somehow fed back to Murdoch as a premonition of disaster this time around and, as a result, he sailed more carefully than he normally would have.

"I think I see a ray of hope here," Marcus said. "Chris has not committed himself entirely to the belief that his nightmares, or hallucinations, or whatever they are, belong to a deterministic universe. I think he's trying to tell us that an iceberg following a course that has been decided far in advance of its own creation cannot change direction; but intelligent beings might be able to change their decided courses, if they pay attention. He is suggesting that premonitions introduce free will into the universe. So long as he views himself more as Murdoch at the helm, rather than as the iceberg, I think we can hold out hope."

"I doubt it," Olsen said. "There's no telling what new lunacy Chris has committed himself to since he first spoke those words. If it were within my power, I'd R-bomb the whole Centaurus system this afternoon, and the Wayvilles along with it. I'm afraid we may be sitting here about five years from now, watching heaven knows what consequences coming our way, and longing for the good old days of 2054, when we had a hope of killing Chris and anyone he was likely to come into contact with.

"I wish I could share your ray of hope, Marcus. But I think you are resorting to wishful thinking because the truth is so downright scary that you dare not say it out loud. It is in Chris's mind, and his mind only, that his visions originate. The plain truth is that it's all coming apart. There is no way on Earth we can call the *Beagle* back. The Alphans have invented space travel. And one of the first people who will meet them belongs in a small room on Mount Victoria writing letters home with crayons—not on his way to Alpha Centauri representing the human species."

"IT DOESN'T MATTER WHAT I BELIEVE," MARCUS HAD SAID. "All that matters is what Chris believes . . . That is the only reality we should be thinking about."

Seen from Alpha Centauri, the inverse was also true. Whatever belief Chris was now forming, or rejecting, did not matter. The only reality that counted was Earth's assessment of risk. And thus there was a seventh scenario Chris ought to have listed, one for which the question of whether or not his visions were real had no relevance. The simple fact that one of Earth's cosmonauts, outward-bound for an encounter with aliens, was having difficulty telling the difference between reality and imagination, had been bound from the beginning to ignite a sense of fear when the news reached home. History did not need much more to shift men's minds from a mission of exploration to preparations for relativistic war.

Though the Alphans of A.D. 2054 were clearly a harmless, low-technology people, where conflict with extrasolar civilizations was a possibility, perception was more important than reality. It was now, in fact, creating reality. To evoke R-bombs for A-4, neither Marcus nor Olsen, nor anyone else in authority on Earth, had to be an evil person bearing some deep-seated malice toward whatever else lived in the universe; nor did these people have to be guided by deviant and wholly misplaced surges of paranoia. They were typical men and women of their time, dedicated to the survival of their own species, even if that meant eliminating risk where risk was not truly apparent. They were merely being human, and, through no special fault of their own, fools.

Under the circumstances, Chris's visions of monsters on A-4 were beginning to appear wrongly placed.

It was not necessarily in the darkness of the Takahashi Forest that the tigers waited, grinning hideously and drawing their plans against him and whatever else lived in the universe. There were monsters enough at home, on Earth.

III

Monsters from Earth

21

Softly Come the Dragons

IT WAS A QUIET DEATH.

Six of A-4's months had passed since he emerged from the womb; a blind, hairless thing whose hind legs were mere buds. His arms were more fully developed, and with these he'd passed the first of many tests, hauling his wormlike body up into the soft fur of his mother's pouch, finding one of the teats, and anchoring himself at its base. Only after she licked his body, only after she checked all the details of his external anatomy against what she knew a perfect newborn should be, only after he passed this second test, was he allowed to feed.

Now his hopping legs were developed. He was almost ready to make his first brief journeys out of the pouch. But something was wrong. By now his brain should have been complete, his mother knew. But he was not testing properly. He was not picking up the touchscript, or learning the trees. Instead, his mind traveled a winding route, straying from the assigned tasks and filling up with questions.

If she permitted him to live in the outside world, he would become an outcast, like Galileo, and for the same reasons. He was retarded, she knew, and the village did not need another Galileo.

A blue glow began to silhouette the hills in the direction of the ocean. The sky strengthened in brightness as the seconds passed. It was November 1, 2054, and several kilometers up the valley, an unlikely trio of human, Alphan, and machine struggled to keep Clarice alive.

The mother watched the suns come up. The skies were clear. There was not a whisper of wind in the air. Scanning the horizon, she knew that the suns would be potent today and that by midmorning, throughout much of the valley, dust would hang over the hop paths; and that by noon her naked child would lie alone on a rock in a hidden clearing, gaping and swallowing and turning red.

It was a fact of life that more than half the children conceived would be judged imperfect in earliest infancy.

It was a fact of life that most Alphan infants were exposed on rocks.

It was a fact older than remembered history.

The Wayvilles had guessed wrongly that the Alphan way of thinking was the product of evolution—an accident of nature. It was in fact the product of an ancient and deliberate genetic plan, reinforced now by culture. Every child had to pass an intelligence test before making its first foray out of the pouch. The Alphan standard of intelligence was the capacity for memory (and memory alone), and only an elite minority ever measured up to a parent's expectations.

By late afternoon the twin suns would look down on the desiccated corpse of an Alphan child. The Wayvilles would never find him, and even if they did, they would have guessed crib death, for they had begun to develop a genuine affection for the Aplhans, an affection that banished from their minds the possibility that infanticide could be socially acceptable on A-4.

No. Not here.

Surely these gentle creatures could not practice such a dreadful thing.

AT FIRST CLARICE THOUGHT THEY WERE LOST. THE HOP PATH seemed to her the right one, but in her weakened condition she supposed that they could have changed course, taken a different fork without her noticing. She stared down at the first flowers she had seen on A-4. Delicate and white, they appeared to be everywhere. The hills were speckled with them.

She looked about her, studying the contours of the land. Everything was familiar, and not familiar. The hill on her left looked right, yet it had turned a strange new shade of green, which she was forced to own as Earthly.

It was easy enough to see what had occurred. Almost a month ago, during her first visit aboard the *Beagle*, Catherine had eaten a strawberry. Later she had defecated in the woods, and in the short space of three weeks, undigested seeds had established a beachhead. Now their progeny overran the valley like a noxious weed.

"They've spread so fast!" Clarice said.

"Yes," FU said. "They will prove very troublesome."

Clarice was thankful that the Alphans did not know the word "troublesome." She stared at the plants in disbelief, and gradually the disbelief was displaced by anger as she realized she and Chris had done this, that one small mistake might now ruin a planet.

The strawberries absorbed minerals more efficiently than native grasses. They'd been engineered for rapid growth in hydroponic gardens, and now, let loose on A-4, they disputed the footing of the grasses.

And they were put together backward. Backward sugars. Backward proteins. Backward vitamin C. The beta carotene—all backward! Grazing animals feeding upon them would draw no nourishment, and it looked as if the strawberries would soon constitute more than half the plants available for grazing.

Dear God! thought Clarice. It was such a little mistake. Just one strawberry, but the consequences are so large. The grazers won't know that half their food is worthless. On full stomachs, they'll become malnourished. They'll get sick. They'll die. These plants can rock the entire food chain from the bottom up.

And on the heels of this thought came another: How many other little mistakes have we made?

22

Strawberry Plague

NOVEMBER PASSED.

Twinners spread apart and grew distinct.

Clarice grew stronger.

And the three-leaved plants grew everywhere, much to the surprise and delight of the villagers. They had developed quite a taste for strawberries, which hastened the transport of their seeds.

It was hard for Clarice to tell them that such benign-looking plants were in fact a malignancy and had to be exterminated. During the early weeks of November the villagers had glutted themselves on strawberries, preferring the new treat over the productions of the forest. Clarice cautioned them to eat the fruit only in moderation. They accepted these instructions without question.

There were too many plants to be pulled out by hand. The weeding process would require an army of spiders dedicated to the task year-round, day and night. They'd have to be built from scratch, using native minerals. FUQ2 sent her spiders searching among the rocks. The villagers assisted in the hunt. To them it was so much absorbing fun.

By the first of December, forty spiders had joined

to become spider-building factories. The villagers had permitted trees to be cleared to make room for solar ponds and, at the shore, they assisted eagerly in the construction of power sources for three thousand new machines. In the hills of the upper valley, they volunteered to assist in the extraction of building materials. Long into the lengthening day they hammered alongside spiders.

Industry was at last coming to A-4.

And it was fun.

Then one day, as Chris told the villagers that, for the time being, they must halt the spread of the seeds by evacuating their bowels in chemical toilets provided by the spiders, Galileo jumped up and pointed an accusing finger.

"You are a devourer," he squealed. "I see what you will do. You can destroy worlds. And you *will* destroy worlds. Because you can."

Galileo was retarded, of course, so no one listened to him. No one, that is, except Chris, and Catherine, who made a rare connection between the astronomer's warning and the fact that he had, according to Chris, been right about so many other fantastic things.

FIGHTING OFF SLEEP, HE STRETCHED, TRIED TO RUB HIS EYES, and peered up into a blur of white light. His eyes simply refused to focus. His arms would not move in any rational direction. There was music playing somewhere nearby: "Rock-a-Bye, Baby," in a little windup music box.

He remembered a suffocating sensation, and his hands were freezing from lack of circulation (interesting, but not very pleasant); and in the end, an intense loneliness washed over him, mingled with regret about wrong turns taken. And still he'd fought to draw in that last breath, but the air refused to come. He'd had nearly a week now to figure out what had happened to him. He was slowly coming to terms with "what," but he could not imagine "how" or "why" he'd been born with foreknowledge of his entire life, spread out ahead of him in such remarkable detail that it seemed more like a memory of something already lived than a foretaste of things to come. In one way, the years that lay before him were a curse (oh, how he wished his mother would stop rewinding that damned music box; and oh, the agony of having to go back to grade school and waste months and months memorizing multiplication and division tables again, when he knew that in his lifetime pocket calculators would render the task useless; and then to spend years learning to give all the wrong answers on science tests, because, despite the fact that his signature would one day be lying up there on Tranquillity Base, everyone living in this quarter of the twentieth century "knew" it was impossible to send a rocket to the Moon). And yet in another way, in most ways, this snippet of immortality, this second chance, was a blessing to match his fiercest ambitions. More than seventy years lay ahead, every one of them a treasure to be savored. Certainly childhood would have its confines, but that would more than be made up for by new opportunities. There was the Watergate, for a start. Most of all, he remembered the Watergate.

Well, I'm back, he told himself. I'm back, you bastards. And this time it's going to be different.

CHRIS, FIGHTING OFF SLEEP, STRETCHED. RUBBED HIS EYES, and peered up at the stars. His eyes followed the constellations and found them familiar. The distance between Earth and Alpha Centauri was too small for the backdrop of stars to have changed noticeably. Everything was the same, except for the Moon, up there in the west . . . Earth's moon.

"So how is the patient today?" Admiral Fitz Roy had asked.

The patient was feeling quite well, except that he was much older now. He looked down at his hands and he could immediately see that. And unlike Chris, the Earth below was not at all well. He looked at the wallscreens and he could just as easily see that. No science fiction writer or filmmaker had gotten it right. None of them had predicted that the end could come so swiftly, or be brought about so simply. The science fiction people had required giant armadas, and Moon-sized objects sufficiently massive to tear pieces out of the Moon itself as they passed. But at fractions of lightspeed, the realities of relativistic war were such that objects as small and crude as Wedgwood ashtrays, pounding down in clusters, could kill every living thing on Earth right down to the bacteria.

In June, A.D. 2076, during the bicentennial of the Sioux's last stand in a valley called the Little Big Horn, life on Earth had ceased to be.

(How, Chris? Do you suppose your Alphans—?)

The planet below looked like a ball of cotton stained grayish yellow. The top five meters of the oceans had actually boiled off under the assault, and sea-level air was three times denser than it had been in A.D. 2048, and twice as hot. All the cities were now gone so utterly that spiders dispatched to the surface had failed to find even archaeological traces that man had once existed.

(Couldn't have been them—)

Nothing seemed to add up.

(—with their wooden spaceships!)

Chris felt as if he had just stepped into a very vivid dream from a previous, equally vivid dream state in which he'd watched himself deteriorate to paranoia and paralysis en route to A-4, convinced then that something in the Alphan system would forbid him from ever returning to Earth—and yet here he awoke . . . aboard

Beagle . . . back home . . . where even Port Chaffee and the Asimov Array had been cleared away without leaving ruins behind.

"The gamma ray sources are growing stronger," FU said. "I have identified them as two Valkyries: *Nautile* and *Graff*, decelerating home from Barnard's Star. They are down to solar-system cruising speed, one hour, forty-three light-minutes away."

"I understand," said Clarice.

"They continue to call for information on all channels, from anyone who can hear them. Instructions?"

"Maintain silent running, FU."

Stealthily, the Wayvilles watched the two Valkyries fall homeward, broadcasting loudly every kilometer of the way. Then the pilot of *Graff* started to speak German words of astonishment. His gamma flare quit in the middle of a course correction. Simultaneously, the *Nautile* quit without any words at all.

Only the German had lived long enough to see something, Chris guessed. Whatever it was, it stupefied him. He had let out two or three exclamations before trying to describe it—which, then, of course, he couldn't.

Somewhere, Chris understood, he'd overlooked something which was hidden and perhaps unguessable. And now—

(all my fault?)

—the two had come home to a deserted solar system in which something, somewhere, was waiting for them.

AND HE AWOKE IN A HOSPITAL BED AT PORT CHAFFEE; AND the whole A-4 adventure was under way again. Everything was going to be different this time . . . if only he could remember that which had been forgotten . . . if only he could remember that there was something he must remember.

But he could not recall all the details, or even a meaningful fraction of them; and in some ways it was perhaps just as well for Christopher Wayville's state of mind that his universe did not permit him to step outside and take a grandstand view across all of his (real or imagined?) lives, to stand upon a ledge and look across all of time. Compared against the megayears of geologic time, the few decades of a human lifespan were belittling enough. Watching the history of the whole universe shrink to submicroscopic size against an infinite series of cosmic expansions and contractions, which might in turn be connected, like a snake, head to tail within some still larger pattern, would probably reduce even the strongest of minds to feelings of ultimate impotence, if not to maddening questions best left unasked by most people.

Why bother to worry about the welfare of Jonathan, or Clarice, or Catherine if the next cycle in an infinitely oscillating universe might undo everything you had set out to accomplish? On first hearing, the question made sense; but if you dug just a few centimeters beneath the surface, it really made about as much sense as arguing that treating Clarice for an easily curable hypoglycemia bug had been unnecessary because, seen against geologic time scales, in a million years she would be long dead anyway. It made as much sense as arguing that the horrors of Auschwitz should not haunt humanity because all those people would have been old or dead more than fifty years ago. By that very same logic, the fate of humanity—or the fate of the Alphans, much as the Wayvilles were coming to love them—really did not matter.

The time scales of the rocks and the universe were not appropriate yardsticks for the measure of Christopher Wayville's life, or anyone else's. If some miracle had permitted him a wider view than he already possessed— a truly grandstand view—and if he were truly wise, he might have magnified in his mind the importance of those moments in which he'd shone light into the life of his son, Jonathan, and made a little happier the days of the loved ones he had abandoned on Earth. He might have gained a greater appreciation of the here and now, and he might have become just a little more hesitant about joining up with Clarice. He might then have stayed at home on Earth; and perhaps two insignificant green planets, existing for a galactic nanosecond in a galaxy that was itself hidden in a far-flung corner of universal time, might have remained safe and green for a few epochs more.

What might have been . . . these were the four most poignant words to emerge from all those millennia of human experience.

En route to A-4, during the acceleration phase of flight, Chris had watched a dark circle open up behind the ship and grow until, at ninety-three percent lightspeed, the entire universe was compressed into a circle ahead of him. If he had pushed the gas pedal further, the circumference of the circle would have steadily decreased until, at lightspeed, it contracted to a point and disappeared. The ship itself (what was left of it) would then have ceased to age, spanning billions of years and as many light-years in an instant. The contracting circle was an ominous reminder that as he looked ahead into space, Chris was also glimpsing a future in which the whole cosmos might one day be squeezed to a state of infinite density. And what lay beyond the compression, beyond that time and place in which the Earth and A-4 and all the stars in the galaxy were smashed into a space smaller than a virus, in which all the known laws of "here" and "then" and "now" broke down so fully that time itself became timeless? More Big Bangs and Cosmic Crunches, apparently, strung together like pearls on an infinite string.

All well and fine, and harmless enough, insofar as Chris's occasional obsessions were concerned, so long as he did not take the pearl on whose surface he was presently moving too literally and try to imagine it as being contained in a higher dimensional space—as, for example, the entire string and the box that contained it and, heaven forbid, whatever lay outside the walls of the box.

To do this would be to impart extrinsic significance to space-time, and in that direction lay a certain mad giddiness, and a universe that could not possibly hold together. The fact that the Wayvilles tracing the course of a river on the Takahashi Peninsula were also tracing the curve of A-4 was an intrinsic property of the planet's geometry. The fact that they could ascend to orbit aboard *Beagle* and take a grandstand view of the globe was an extrinsic geometric feature. But space-time had no extrinsic geometry; the Wayvilles could fly their Valkyrie as far and fast as they wished and still they'd be upon the pearl. If the universe was indeed an immortal sphere whose center was everywhere and whose circumference was nowhere, then its radius was time itself and Chris was expressly forbidden from stepping outside and taking an extrinsic view.

Still, something like a ghost image seemed to have come to him during his death at Tranquillity, and seemed to have stayed with him during his recent time dilation, coming as if time occasionally fed back on itself, filling the universe with little resonances from a previous existence on the other side of the Big Bang, like bits of fingernail clippings left behind in an old house.

During what Clarice looked back to as the "bad" part of the voyage, when theories about premonition and the oscillating universe had obsessed him, Chris developed a model linking his visions to . . . to what? To divine intervention?

Well, not quite divine, he supposed, but something close to it. Looking ahead, he could see no end to man's striving, and looking back across the strides of the past century, he thought it was anyone's guess what the next thousand years, or million, or billion, might produce. But already humankind was looking out upon a redshifting universe bound eventually to cease expanding, to shift blue, and spill down into a Cosmic Crunch that would erase all of man's achievements, no matter how greatly he valued them. This final, irrevocable insignificance was one thing human civilization could not tolerate.

Chris decided that nothing in nature could account for information passing from one universe into a Cosmic Crunch, then rebounding through the Big Bang into the next universe. Nature did not work that way, did not have the ability to defy the utter disorder that exists within a universal black hole. Such things had to be carefully planned, and Chris had some ideas about what shape that plan might take. If all the combined knowledge of human civilization could now be held by FU in a space barely larger than a human brain (an achievement that would have been dismissed as "impossible" only a century before), then why not, a thousand years hence, a similar or even greater amount of information compressed into a space—or a particle—smaller and perhaps even more ghostly than a neutrino?

Perhaps historians of the year A.D. 3054 were mass-producing Christopher Wayville's hypothetical particles—he called them replayers—and casting them out into the universe, where they'd eventually enter the Cosmic Crunch, guaranteeing that someone, somewhere on the other side, would remember to write Shakespeare's plays and paint the Mona Lisa. One could not simply pass Michelangelo's *Pietà* through the infinite temperatures and pressures of the next Big Bang and expect it to arrive in one piece. The replayers would have to do. And if it were somehow possible to take all the information that would one day be available from the *Beagle*/A-4 encounter, including details of Christopher

Wayville's life—reenacted as movies, perhaps—and to compress this, too, onto a replayer particle . . . and to make multiple copies . . . a trillion-to-the thirtieth power of Chris's replayers streaming out into the universe . . . flooding the next universe with a lingering resonance . . . and the next universe . . .

(What might have been . . .)

The replayer theory, tenuous though it was, had given Chris hope. If he'd failed "last time" on A-4, then maybe with a little tampering from historians of the future, he was, even as he'd rocketed between the Sun and Centaurus, getting a second chance. This time it would be different. And if not this time, then perhaps—

(Then perhaps what?)

If these replayers were real, then what of replayer-manufacturing civilizations far beyond A.D. 3054, when even the works of Michelangelo and the A-4 encounter are supplanted by entirely new concerns? How many of these submicroscopic messages in bottles would mankind cast into the Cosmic Crunch, preserving for any who receive them his triumphs, and even an occasional warning sign covering the years between A.D. 3054 and 30,054? How many replayers would man produce and distribute by A.D. 1,000,000? Or by A.D. 10,000,000,000, if some distant descendant of man still survived?

And what, Chris thought, of replayer-building civilizations other than man? His own galaxy held more than five hundred billion stars, and there were probably multiple trillions of galaxies just like it. If he were to make a conservative estimate of only one civilization apiece, through the entire history of each galaxy, he would still have uncountable trillions of replayer broadcasts. Using the same conservative formula, Chris instructed FU to run some estimates, and found it hard to believe the results.

From every direction in the heavens, the warnings, birth cries, boasts, and death screams of civilizations would be heard. Even if more ghostly than neutrinos, most of the replayers would probably fail to endure the imploding universe; but, designed with endurance in mind, each failed replayer, as it lay trapped between collapsing neutrons and the collapsing shards of collapsing neutrons, would offer up some small resistance, and if there were enough of them . . . even Chris's and FU's most conservative estimates of the replayer flux showed that there were more than enough. Their combined resistance could actually halt the collapse, causing time and space to bounce back as a new universal expansion.

Chris looked in opposite directions, upstream and downstream, past and future, recalling the circle of stars ahead of the ship, and the black nothingness astern. And he beheld a universe that had emerged, and would emerge, fresh and hot from a Big Bang because of deeds performed by people who in one sense lived more than twenty billion years ago and in another sense were yet to be born.

(*In the beginning . . .*)

Somewhere in time, civilized man had been and would be as—

(*God . . .*)

—and it came to pass that God prepared the way for a universal rebirth—

(*. . . created the heaven and the earth.*)

—and in time God became his own progeny—

(*Let us make man in our image, after our likeness.*)

—his progeny its own creator—

(*In the image of God created he him.*)

History and Revelation, Genesis and destiny converged. The snake swallowed its tail, and Christopher Wayville's oscillating universe ran on and on like a film wound on a perpetual reel.

Left on its own, the nonconscious universe, rebounding under the guidance of whatever sentient life it had spawned, might have run through every cycle identically; but rebound, and rebirth, and immortality were apparently not enough for the creators, for in a film that ran time and time again with every frame the same, where in the universe was free will?

It occurred to Chris that if indeed someone on the other side of the Big Bang were giving him a second chance, then his theory about the replayer engineers striving to preserve the *Pietà* or any other great work could not have been farther from the truth. A film copied over and over was bound to replay the *Pietà*, was bound to replay all of Shakespeare's plays and the A-4 encounter identically every time. Was it reasonable to expect man, or any other intelligent species, to guarantee a universal rebirth and yet resist the urge to tamper with the cosmic egg? Even if the sum total of all their tampering was merely to inject the next universe with an element of uncertainty? In the end, all was vanity. The replayer particles moved from universe to universe like viruses sent forth to inject new bits of DNA into otherwise perfectly copied chromosomes. They were an infection of sorts, inter-universal viroids that might occasionally become cancerous, throwing history awry and negating great works or even whole civilizations—but that was okay, wasn't it? They'd simply do it differently next time.

Either through his hypothetical replayers or through something unguessable and stranger still, Chris and perhaps a few others like him were able to sense what was on (or what had originally been printed on) the frames ahead. On occasion, such people wound up in positions of responsibility, from which multiple outcomes diverged. Pivots ... the universe had found opportunities for change because people like Christopher Wayville existed.

CHRISTOPHER WAYVILLE WAS HAVING A STRANGE DREAM. In it, that shadowy thing bared its teeth in a merciless and skeletal grin. Then, suddenly, he knew that he'd seen this awful thing before, had been through this before; but he sensed also that his life was somehow different.

A plague of strawberries was changing everything— for better or for worse, he could not quite tell; but a voice came to him, his own voice, sure and complete: *When we change the Alphans we are going to face dangers no human being has ever faced before. We are going to see things no human being has ever imagined. Things. Unbelievable things. And we will instill in our people the fear of God.*

And then the dream faded back into the subconscious, where it had lain in hiding ever since the "bad" part of the voyage. It was lost as the next dream bubbled up from somewhere far below and began to take shape. He had forgotten both dreams by the time he awoke, but as the suns beamed through the morning cloud cover, something about the Alphan forests troubled him remotely.

ON THE TWO-MONTH ANNIVERSARY OF HIS ARRIVAL ON A-4, Chris stood alone at the edge of the village cenote.

Only two months, he told himself. And look at the changes we have worked.

The pool at the bottom of the cenote was deserted. Indeed, the whole village appeared to be deserted. Even the schools were out, Chris noted. Today there were more important things to learn than the keynames of the trees. Of course there were. Haven't you heard? The humans have arrived. Now there are spiders and solar ponds and ceramic composites and photonics and electronics—and *strawberries.* Oh, yes, let us not forget forbidden fruit.

Chris looked down upon stagnant water and listened to hammering that seemed to come from near and far, from every direction in the woods. Industrious little

beasties, he mused . . . when they put their minds to
it. I sure hope we're not messing up too badly. The
strawberry plague has caused us to introduce spiders
on a grand scale, to boost their know-how—too fast to
be safe? I hope not.

Can these people ultimately become a threat to
Earth?

Who knows? If those bad dreams were right, if I wasn't
just going crazy on the way to A-4, then the Alphans
are bad for our people. Maybe I shouldn't be liking this
planet so much. Maybe I should get back on the ball and
start thinking in terms of finding some way of preventing
the trouble. Maybe we shouldn't be helping the Alphans.
Maybe we should have let the strawberries starve them.
Maybe I should be thinking of—

(Of what? Ways of destroying the Alphans?)

Who knows? For all I do know, time could be running
out. A great dying could be at hand. And only I can
prevent it.

(Or cause it.)

Oh, bullfeathers. Stow those thoughts, Chrissie boy.
Stow them fast. Don't even speak them. You don't want
to make a fool of yourself again, do you?

But we've been teaching the aliens. *Teaching them.*
And what if they should turn out to be smarter than us?

No, that's nonsense, Chrissie boy. They do not connect facts—not very well, at least. They do not think for
themselves. They literally need us to think for them.

Still . . . I would not want to wake up one day and
find my solar system depending on the humanity of
the Alphans.

GALILEO WAS WILLING AND IN FACT EAGER TO LEARN FROM THE
Wayvilles, but he feared them and wished to avoid them
and decided that he would learn from them only through
Catherine. She was turning out to be a very good teacher.
She had obtained from the Wayvilles his very own flat,

and shown him pictures of worlds orbiting stars.

On this day, the fourth of December, Galileo had followed a hop path to the beach, where he stood alone, trying to savor its peace.

So what be these Wayvilles and their machines? he wondered. When his brethren thought about them at all, they took the Wayvilles and their spiders to be equally alien, essentially one and the same. Though the Wayvilles and each of their spiders had been assigned specific keynames, the strings of syllables differed more greatly among individual spiders than among spiders and humans. The villagers did not trouble themselves with the larger distinctions.

Standing somewhere between human and Alphan in his way of thinking, and perhaps closer to humans, Galileo was filled with questions. There was a time when he thought the spiders were "pets," as Toto was to Dorothy in Catherine's favorite film. But Toto never spoke to Dorothy, never answered her questions, and certainly never advised her. FU and the spiders had begun to seem more like the Tin Man and the Scarecrow. But even that idea did not quite fit. There was something more to the machine/Wayville relationship than even man's make-believe suggested.

The Wayvilles needed FU to speak for them. On that first day, when they came out of *Beagle*'s hollow, Clarice had decided not to bother with learning Alphan language, which had bothered Catherine during those first days after the landing; but it was, in time, shrugged off by her and forgotten. Just another fact.

Galileo did not shrug it off. For some reason, the Wayvilles could not learn the language of his people. FU was the one with the memory. FU, though her mind dwelt in flats and spiders and within the ship *Beagle*, though she looked far less Alphan than the humans, was, to Galileo's mind, the most Alphan-like of the Earthly Triad.

On Galileo's flat, the orbits of the worlds ran on and on around A, just as FU had revealed them to Catherine en route to the Glacier Wear. Galileo opened his mouth, then closed it.

"You wish me to change the view?" FU asked.

"No. This is good."

"Is there something else?"

He meant to say "Yes," but he was hesitant, and would have preferred to answer "No," or better yet, nothing at all. Nothing seemed by far the wisest choice, so he chose a new word he had seen used in a film, signifying a blank space: "Well . . ."

"Proceed," the computer said.

The response caught Galileo by surprise, a gentle command that was difficult to resist and impossible to ignore. Would only that he could toss his flat into the ocean and stop learning about these aliens. It was all very well for him to reject them; it was quite another thing to stop thinking about them. The Wayvilles of his thoughts and his dreams were like those needle-feeders that burrow under the fur of decaying bodies to get at the wetness inside (except that Galileo was not dead yet, but something stubborn had taken hold and was wiggling inside just the same). The intruders had brought wonders into his world, treasures to satiate his appetite for new things, even to distract him from resisting their advances. "Question," he said at last.

"At your service."

"Why do Clarice and Chris not learn our language? Why do you speak our language for them? Why do we learn English?"

"Because they have no need to. Because I can. Because you can."

"Question: They need not learn our language?"

"They need not."

"Why?"

"Because I exist. I am their extended memory."

Galileo signed an expression of confusion. "Question," he said. "Define extended memory."

"Look at your flat," advised FU. On the screen, in Alphan touchscript, appeared the keynames of an old tree near the *Beagle* landing site. Using animation, FU showed how the keyname fit easily inside the head of an Alphan, but not into the heads of the Wayvilles. The message was clear, though Galileo did not grasp all of it: Alphans were very good at something humans could not do. From this, Galileo might have guessed, if his way of thinking had been slightly more human, that the Wayvilles' forebears had chosen not to develop thoroughly photographic memories. So the computer (pet? partner? or something more?) did the memorization for them, and the final sequence in FU's cartoon bore this out, showing a keyname, unable to be crowded into Chris's brain, inserted effortlessly into FU, who in turn communicated it into an Alphan's head. Galileo's eyes gleamed at the screen like the eyes of a young, curious cat.

The astronomer understood that the ship's spiders— FU's other selves—had actually fed the Wayvilles during Catherine's journey with them to the Glacier Wear. Fed them. Like a mother feeding teat milk to a pouched Alphan.

(More than a Tin Man.)

And the machine healed Clarice, and gave her very specific advice—*doctor's orders*, Catherine had said.

Do you really want to stop learning? Galileo asked himself. He hesitated for just a moment longer, and the mind behind the liquid crystal screen recorded the hesitation, measuring Galileo against the other Alphans, who were not particularly hesitant about anything.

"I sense that you have more questions," FU said. "But you hesitate. Have I guessed correctly?"

"Well . . ."

"Proceed."

"No, I don't want to."

"Why?"

Galileo didn't bother answering that.

"We have the same needs, you and I. We both seek knowledge. Question, Galileo: Why, then, should you be hesitating? Why, then, should you fear me?"

"Question," Galileo answered, and then hesitated again.

"I can show you worlds, Galileo."

The screen came alive with cloudtops riding the wind toward a horizon that seemed very, very far away, and in the sky, almost as bright as B, shone the rings of Saturn.

"All these worlds are yours. I can show you anything. If you ask."

Anything, Galileo signed. *Anything*.

"Just ask, and I will show," FU said, as if slipping an arm over Galileo's shoulders. "Come. What do you want to know?"

And momentarily the Alphan felt at ease. The hesitation broke, and Galileo said: "What are you, FU? What are you to these Wayvilles? Pet or master? Dorothy or Toto?"

"Neither. I am a friend. I am an obedient friend."

Obedient. The word had a grating edge. Galileo could not personally recall, and could not find in Catherine's observations, an example of FU acting independently of the humans, or doing anything on her own initiative without first asking them. Galileo could understand the concept of an obedient friend. Without any great difficulty, he was able to connect FU's self-description with the behavior of the villagers: obedient friends of the Wayvilles. If he had looked deeper, he might have thought of another description: servants.

"Let me show you something," FU said. The dark circle of the Earth's moon, framed in the solar corona, appeared on the screen. In the foreground stood a limestone bust of the feathered serpent Quetzalcoatl, and beyond it the Pyramids of Teotihuacán.

Galileo was transfixed. "All these worlds for you," FU promised. "All these worlds for your eyes, whenever you want them."

It had come time for FU to change the subject, to deflect the astronomer's attention elsewhere, at least temporarily. So FU decided to massage Galileo's imagination, making him forget the direction his questions had been heading in, making him forget about Chris. FU was indeed more than a friend to the Wayvilles, more than a servant. As a mediator between two alien cultures, the computer knew when to behave like a bureaucrat. From Galileo's unwavering attention to the pictures, FU judged that the attempt at deflection was working. The alien was too preoccupied to be thinking about Chris. It was all very well for FU, quite satisfactory.

Galileo saw something erupting on the surface of A-5. It jetted tiny white crystals into the sky and he wondered what they could be, for he had never seen a snowstorm on A-4, much less one in space. He thought about Chris. A fissure opened up and let out a river of water whose surface was flashing to vapor. The vapor solidified instantly, became a blizzard. He thought about Chris. He wondered why the water on A-5 was behaving so strangely, but mostly he thought about Chris.

Now the A-5 river was seen from a vantage point high above. It had frozen in mid-stride, going as it had come, from nowhere. The camera backed up, revealing the curve of the world, and finally a diminishing circle. Galileo simultaneously replayed in his mind the many pictures Catherine had shown the villagers upon her return from Wear: A-4, A, B, the stars, and their orbits.

So the stars *are* suns and the world *is* round, the astronomer thought. And now the villagers know what you have tried to tell them all along. Oh, yes, now they know; but they find these facts hard to separate from all your other so-called ravings. And besides, they credit the Wayvilles with the discovery of the world's roundness.

No matter. There was beauty in the Wayvilles' facts, new windows that grew wider and wider with the addition of each truth, windows through which Galileo was seeing—really seeing for the first time—the universe.

He firmed a resolve to learn everything FU made available on the flat. He would study hard.

(*Know thine enemy.*)

And he knew already what the words "world," "become," and "am" meant.

I am become Chris, the Devourer of worlds.

At Galileo's request, FU had once run a cross-reference check on the phrase, and drawn up from memory something connected to "Hindu Triad" and "Trinity." It was very confusing. And the words—they were almost the same:

If the radiance of a thousand suns
Were to burst at once into the sky,
That would be like the splendor
Of the Mighty One.
I am become Death
The shatterer of worlds.

Bad.

The more he learned, the more fearful he became of Chris.

The strawberry plague was to him one more example of the incompatibility of two worlds, just one more example of what he had come to call the un-belongness of the Wayvilles.

They cannot eat our food, and we cannot eat theirs, because of the "stereoenantiomers": the basic building blocks of Earthly bodies are somehow opposite of ours.

And the Wayvilles cannot even go back to their own world because they are infected with life from ours.

These are all examples of what should have been, of the rightful separateness of our two worlds. The aliens should never have come here.

Bad.

23

A History Lesson

﹏﹏﹏\\\\\\\\\\﹏﹏

###::::::::##################:#####:::::::::#####################:#####:::
:::::::###############:#####:::::::::::###############:#####:::::::::
::::::##############.#####::::::::::::::::############:#####::::::::::::::::

POWELL, THE FIFTH WORLD OF A, ORBITED JUST INSIDE THE
rim of the asteroid belt, almost as far from its sun as
Jupiter was from Sol.

Powell was an ice world not much larger than Earth's
moon. Its surface was airless, grooved, and cratered. Its
only satellite was the unnatural coil-and-tether system
of the Valkyrie.

Orbiting at a height of one hundred kilometers, the
Beagle's "tugboat" looked down upon volcanoes whose
lava was water. Spiders dispatched to the surface had
found bacterialike cells fossilized in the lava-ice. The
volcanoes provided glimpses of an ocean buried tens
of kilometers below the ice, an ocean whose water had
sprouted life, and then frozen solid some two billion
years ago.

The planet had been geologically quiescent ever
since save for the occasional water eruption whose
heat source was still a mystery.

Valkyrie's spiders were not on the surface for research

alone. They had been sent to extract hydrogen and lithium from the ice, to be used for reactants in the ship's antimatter-matter engines. The rocket had arrived in the Alpha Centauri system with its remaining antihydrogen tanks fully stocked for a return to Sol. But the matter tanks were nearly empty—according to plan. The elements needed to "burn" the antihydrogen were known to be ubiquitous at Centaurus even before the rocket was built, so she was built to carry only enough propellant matter for a one-way voyage. This strategy decreased the weight of the ship, which in turn allowed the engines to run a little bit cooler, which in turn decreased the weight of gamma ray shielding needed to protect the crew and antimatter tanks, which in turn decreased the amount of fuel needed—it was a chain reaction of design simplifications similar to those created almost a hundred years earlier by the proliferation of international airports with refueling stations. If a 747 had been required to fly from New York to Paris with all the fuel needed for the return trip, its girth would have multiplied by a factor of two and the price of a ticket by six.

The lesson learned then had not been forgotten. Now a flotilla of self-replicating Asimov Array factories had arrived from Earth. The machines were already stirring upon the two inner worlds of A. They dismantled the ancient structures Olsen and Marcus had seen crumbling on A-1 and A-2, scavenged them for their mineral content, and blindly destroyed much that archaeology could have taught Earth about the lost civilization of the Alphans.

Earth was four and a half light-years from A, so nobody knew yet of the hypoglycemia bug. The next crewed expedition from Sol was scheduled for launch in six years. If they still chose to come, the first antihydrogen terminus should be waiting by the time they entered the deceleration phase. And their ships would have more spacious living quarters, and more advanced spiders, and they would carry no more antihydrogen than was required for the outbound journey.

Presently, the A-5 spiders worked atop the Matsunagas, which overlooked a flat stretch of icy lowland dubbed the Sea of Tranquillity. Almost three billion years ago, something big had splashed down there, excavating a basin as wide as the state of Montana. It punctured the crust, and the wound filled with an unquenchable tumult of steam, snow, and upwelling water. The circular depression called Tranquillity was indeed a sea. In A.D. 2054, a broad front of ice lay pooled at the feet of the Matsunaga highlands, peppered with bowl-shaped craters, some of them large enough to accommodate cities. On the horizon, the youngest craters were veiled in wispy sheets of outthrown snow, which glistened beneath the glory of A-5's two suns. Riding the night at a greater radius than A-4, A appeared considerably smaller than upon the Takahashi Peninsula, and B had brightened to become its rival.

On Christmas Day, 2054, nearly six years after she left Sol, the Valkyrie orbited A-5 and listened to a fifty-two-month-old broadcast from Earth. According to the "latest" news, *Beagle* and *Enterprise* were coasting toward Alpha Centauri, the Bardos were still alive, and plans were in preparation for a crewed landing on Halley's Comet when it returned in 2061. Mixed in with the news, and aimed directly at A-5, was a fine red beam of light that came and went as a series of flashes and flutters.

```
###::::::::##################:######::::::::::####################:######:::
::::::::##################:######::::::::::::::################:######:::::::::
::::::################:######:::::::::::::::###########:######::::::::::::::::
```

It was a simple binary code.

And the ship recognized its importance to those who had left her. Obediently, she beamed the message down toward A.

"Okay, FU. Replay Fitz Roy."
ADMIRAL FITZ ROY, PORT CHAFFEE, 31 OCTOBER 2048: "Okay, Chris. If we can go to the other side of the galaxy, why hasn't anybody come from the other direction? Why didn't we find the planet Mercury already covered with solar panels?"
"Stop," Chris said.
The flat went blank.
"Okay, FU. Let's try this one on for size. We know that if even one civilization, in the whole history of the galaxy, ever made it to another star and established a colony, the colony would in turn have sent one or more ships to neighboring stars and established secondary colonies, and so on, until, in almost no time at all, they end up overrunning Sol and Centaurus and the entire galaxy. We know that *they* are not here, and that the galaxy has not revealed any hints of any civilization technologically as advanced as ours. There is nothing to indicate that they exist . . . except possibly for the fact—"
"That we are here," FU finished.
"Right. If we can do it, then surely someone else can. So let's assume that every civilization has to pass through a kind of interstellar natural-selection filter. First, they must have the intelligence to develop the necessary technology, which the Alphans do not. Sec-

ond, they must *want* to go outside their system, and the Alphans seem perfectly content to spend eternity right here in this valley."

"Which still leaves the fact that we are here."

"I know. *I know.* So maybe the green guys have found more interesting things to do than carpet worlds with strawberries and spiders," Chris said acidly.

"A good point. But consider this: perhaps the only civilizations wise enough to possess unlimited power without turning that power suicidally against themselves, perhaps the only ones that *can* overrun the galaxy, are precisely those that are most likely to find the idea repulsive. There are more important things to do than turn every planet into another Manhattan Island. Perhaps they confine themselves to small numbers of explorers, like us."

"I don't know. I tend to think of ourselves as the only ones who have made it into space. I think something very unusual happened on Earth. Back in the 1940s, there were three warring powers racing to develop the first atomic bomb—and America got it first. At that time, one nation found itself in possession of absolute power, with which it could have made a gravel quarry out of any country that even tried to develop the same power. America could have established a global dictatorship if it chose to, yet it chose not to. If America had been a less benign nation, or if Japan or Germany had developed the bomb first, we would have seen a global empire. That one side should develop the ultimate weapon and hold it back, giving other competing sides time to develop the same weapon, must be exceedingly rare in the galaxy. I can't imagine another world assembling the planet-destroying arsenals of the twentieth century."

"Consider this: once there were only three atomic bombs on Earth. You tested one to see if they would work. You *used* the other two."

Chris looked at his flat and nodded grimly. "But within months of the Japanese surrender there were more bombs. And *there's* where we begin to tie into extrasolar civilizations."

"I see what you mean, Chris. When a civilization arrives at, say, 1945 technology, one of two things is very likely to happen and neither is very good for technological advancement. Either one group of people invents the bomb and takes over, or two groups of people invent it at the same time and try to knock out each other's ability to build more bombs. What follows in the second case is a protracted nuclear war, characterized by low-yield, Hiroshima-type weapons, that ends with one side winning and taking over or both sides losing. In either case, electronic civilization probably does not fare very well."

"Right. That's it exactly."

"I believe you're onto something, Chris. Good thinking."

Chris laughed and punched up a picture of the Alphan village. "I've been thinking about the rockets they build. The Alphans are like the Romans, in a way. The Romans had steam engines, differential gear shifts, plumbing, and central heating. They built toys for display at gladiatorial combats that could be described only as the beginnings of robotics, yet they never connected these things to make even a single steamship. Sails and oars were good enough, because no competing country was transporting trade goods more efficiently. And the reason no competing country was doing so was that there were no competing countries. For more than five hundred years, Rome controlled every nation within reach of its horses and ships, just as the Alphans have controlled everything within hopping distance, unchallenged, for God only knows how long. Rome eventually stagnated and collapsed from the inside out, and we are here today because the nations that emerged after Rome competed with each other in trade and war but never succeeded in establishing another universal empire."

"I note your point," said FU. "You imply that the Alphans have become a stagnant civilization because they have no competitors. You should hope that they never perceive us as competitors."

"There's precious little they could do if they did. If we really had to, we could bring the Valkyrie down on them, and that would be the end of the argument."

"High tech rapes low tech, right?"

"Everything in due time, FU."

The computer recognized something dangerous in Chris's eyes, something she had not noticed for many months. It flared there, and then it died and was—

```
###:::::::::#####################:######::::::::::#####################:######:::
:::::::#################:######:::::::::::::################:######::::::::::
::::::###############:######:::::::::::::############:######:::::::::::::
```

—HIGH TECH RAPES LOW TECH—
—HIGH TECH RAPES LOW TECH—
—HIGH TECH—

```
###:::::::::::::::::::::##########:######::::::::::::::::::::::#######:######:::
::::::::::::::::::::::######:######::::::::::::::::::::::::::::#####:######::::::::::
::::::::::::::::::::######:######::::::::::::::::::::::::::::##:######:::::::::::::
:::::::::::::#:######:::::::::::::::::::::::::::::::######:::::::::::::::::::
::::::::::######::::::::::::::::::::::::::::::######::::::::::::::::::::::::
:::######:::::::::::::::::::::::::######:::::::::::::::::::::::::::::::::###
###:::::::::::::::::::::::::::::::######:::::::::::::::::::::::::::::::######:::
```

"What do you think, FU? What do you think will be the most likely outcome when a civilization reaches 1945 technology? And consider that it probably reaches that level only through the kind of sustained competition that fueled Europe's industrial revolution."

"I think . . ." FU trailed off.

Chris nodded encouragement.

"I think . . . that . . . one competitor will discover atomic weapons and establish a global empire."

"Very good, FU. Now, let's see . . . If that had happened at the end of the Second World War, we might have seen V-2 rockets converted into ICBMs, perhaps we would even have seen communications satellites, but certainly we would not have landed on the moon in 1969, or built space stations, or come to Alpha Centauri. The twentieth century would not have seen a space race because there would never have been any competition between the Americans and the Soviets. Now . . ." Chris trailed off into thought, scrambled to snatch ideas as they popped up from his subconscious, then to knit them together as he spoke.

FU was distracted. As she spoke to Chris, more and more of her attention was being diverted to the incoming signals from the Valkyrie. Breaking the code was easy. It unscrambled on the first try—

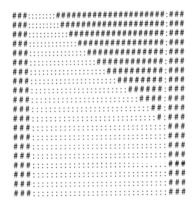

—but there was something else in Valkyrie's data. Something important . . .

"Now," Chris continued, "a global 1945-level empire

might last five hundred or even two thousand years, but eventually it's going to enfeeble from within and sink into a Dark Age. The best that can be hoped for is that some surviving island of electronic or photic civilization, in New Zealand or perhaps one or two other places, will spread out after the fall and . . . and then they compete with each other, and it's high-tech-rapes-low-tech all over again, with the Russian-American scenario being the least likely outcome."

###:::###:#:::::::::::::##

#########:######::::##:::#:::::::::::::##############################

"FU?"

###:::::::::::::::::::::::#:::::##::::#::::::#############################

"FU!"

"Oh!" said FU suddenly. "Then most intelligent species, if they are anything like us, will be doomed to an endless cycle of universal empires alternating with Dark Ages."

"Not an *endless* cycle," Chris admonished. "Mankind has been lucky enough to experience a centuries-long competition that resulted in neither mutual annihilation nor a global empire, and carried us from a wood-burning economy to a coal-burning one, from coal to oil and from oil to such high-tech, renewable-energy sources as the Mercury Power Project. If, on this or some other world, a 1945-level empire lasted for two thousand years, most if not all of the easy-to-get-at oil would be used up by the time the civilization collapsed. Coal is all that would remain for the next cycle, and after a hundred thousand years or so of global empires, the coal, too, would be gone. A hundred thousand years . . . that is probably all that any intelligent species can hope for—a geological nanosecond. After that, electronic civilization falls one last time, and its chances of ever making the leap from a wood-burning economy to the Asimov Array are almost zero."

```
. . . :::::::::::::::::::::## ::::::: ###
```

"So the stars belong to *Homo sapiens*, you think."

```
###::.###.#:................#################################################:###
###::.##::.#:...............################################################:###
###:::::::.#:..............#:################################################:###
###::.#:::...#:..........##:.#:#######################fff#####################:###
###::.##:.....#:........###:.#:.#############################################:###
###:::.##:......#:......###:.##:#############################################:###
###:::::.##:.....#:.....##:.##:#############################################:###
###:::::.###:......#:...###::##:.###########################################:###
###:::.###:........#:....###::##::#########################################:###
###:::::::.......##:....##::#:.#:.#########################################:###
###:::::::#:.#:.....#:.#:..##:::#:.#######################################:###
###:::::#:.########:#:....#:.:##:::#:.###################################:###
###:.#:.:.##########:.......#:.#:.#:......##############################:###
###:###:::.......#######:.##::.....#:.:.#:..########################### :###
###:.#:.::......:::###:..##::.#:...#:.....##########################:###
###:::::.........#:..##:::.#:..#:.#:......#########################:###
###::.#:.........###:......#:....#:.......#######################:###
###::::#:........###:.........#:.#:.......#####################:###
###::.#:.........###:..........#:#:........###################:###
###:#######:........##:..........##:........##################:###
###:#####:.........:##:..........##:........################:###
###:#:...........####:............##:........##############:###
###::.............###:#:####:.......#:........############:###
###:::#####:........###:.###:........#:.......:##########:###
###::::.#####:........##:.........#:...........#:...#########:###
###:#:::::.###:.....#:....###:....#:.....#:....##:##########:###
###:.##::..##::.##:..################:......#:.......##:.#########:###
###:.##:........:####:.##################:.......#:.......###########:###
###:...........#:#################################:.......#:.##########:###
###:...........###:.###:#:...........#:.......##:.###:###
###::.###:........##:.##::...........#:..........##::#:#:###
###::#####:.........#####:.............#:.#:.......##:.###
###:#:####:...#:.......##:.##:............#:.#:.......##:#:###
###:###::#:..............#:.............#:.#:.........###
###::.#:..................#:............#:.#:.........###
###:.............#####:.........#:.......#:.#:.....#:#:###
###:.............##:......#:.......##:....#::#:..::#:#:###
###:::......#:..........#:..............####:...#::##:...#::#:...###
###::.....##:..###:....###::.........#:.........##::##:...#...###
###:::.....###:.:.####:.....###:....#:........##::###:....##:###
###:.........######:...........#:.............##:.###:...##:###
###:...............#:.....................##::###:....##:###
###:.............##:.................##::.###:....#::###
###:.............................#:......##::###::..::.###
###::..........###:................#:.....###:.##::....###
###:...........###:.................#:.##:::##::......###
###:...............##:.......................##::......###
```

"Yes, FU. The stars—"

###:::::#:#:#:::#:#:####:::::#:###:#:::::##:#:#:#:#::#:::#:###:##:::#:#::#:#:
:###:#:##:#:#:#:::::###:##:#:##:#:#:#:#:::::#:#:#:#::::#######:#:###:#:#####::
#:###:::::#:#:#:::::##:#:###::##:#:#::::::##:#:#:#:#####:::#:#:#:#:#:#:#:::::::##

"—belong—"

"—to us."

"Sorry to spoil a perfectly good theory, Chris. But I'm receiving a coherent signal and it is not coming from Earth."

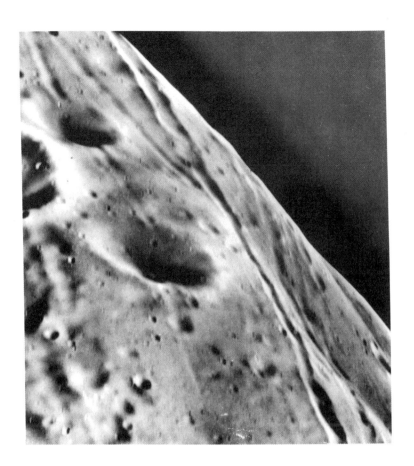

24

The Other People

▰▰▰▰▰

CHRIS, FIGHTING OFF SLEEP, STRETCHED, RUBBED HIS EYES, and peered up at the stars. His eyes followed the constellations and found them familiar. The distance between Earth and Alpha Centauri was too small for the backdrop of stars to have changed noticeably. Everything was the same . . . except for the moon, up there in the west . . . Earth's moon.

Earth? What am I doing back on—

He still did not fully recollect where he was, but he realized that he was leaning against a rail on an oceangoing vessel.

Earth? What am I—well, *of course* I'm on Earth . . . dead Manhattan is still out there in the night . . . and snowshoe rabbits . . . Just dozed off for a moment, that's all. Had another bad dream.

—another bad dream—

Out of the east had come that buzzing, winged reality: somewhere in America there were other human beings; and out of nowhere—out of the dark, impersonal nowhere—had come the visions. He saw himself married to a strange woman named Clarice, and traveling with her on a completely different mission. Was there really a Catherine out there? he wondered. Was there really a Galileo, and a Valley of Wells, and a species that probed space with rockets, yet thought its world was flat?

No! It was too fantastic. Such things had to come from the imagination, from the remote, infinitely distant subconscious.

Jacob Marley!

Right! An ordinary disturbance, a bad piece of food, perhaps, had brought it bobbing up out of the subconscious.

—but it was all so vivid—

Yes! It was, wasn't it? Especially that part about the message, the dawning reality that somewhere between Earth and A-4 there were other people.

And Chris, it was like him, really did want to know what happened next.

25

Ice

CLARICE CALLED COMPUTER-ENHANCED GREEN ONTO THE wallscreen. It blazed up freshly, and illuminated the huge, carved blocks that formed walls on the surface of C-3.

The outermost world of Alpha Centauri C had no atmosphere. More than eighty percent of its mass was ice. It creaked and groaned under the pull of C-3B, a moon so large that it qualified as a sister planet.

Airless worlds orbiting cold stars. At first glance, they looked like the most unlikely places in the galaxy to be harboring civilized life, or life of any kind. But there was no doubt that the pictures streaming down from space came from a source only two light-months away, at Alpha Centauri C. And there was no doubt that the senders of the message had overlooked A-4 as a habitat for life in favor of cold, lifeless A-5. They fired their narrow beam directly at the wrong world. If not for the fact that the Valkyrie had been sent there to gather supplies, no one would have known about the other people.

"You are very excited about these pictures," observed Catherine. "They are not as pretty as Oz. Question: How are they more exciting than Oz?"

"How are they more exciting than Oz?" repeated Clarice. "They are more exciting because they are not make-believe. This is really happening. We're receiving pictures from the third sun, from the slow wanderer."

"Question: Is that exciting?"

"Of course it's exciting. There are other people there."

Clarice saw no change of expression on her friend's face. It hadn't fazed her in the least. Sure, thought Clarice. Sure. It's just another fact to her. The Alphan way of thinking gives them an astonishing ability to adapt to new astonishments. To them, even the incredible is immediately reduced to just another new fact of life. To look at Catherine, you'd think she encountered aliens every day.

Clarice often supposed, on such occasions, that if a brontosaur came strolling up the valley, Catherine would probably look at it and say, "Oh, here comes another new fact." That fast, it would become commonplace.

"We want to learn more about the other people," Chris said. "But here's one of our problems."

Motioning to his left, he said, "Over that way is A-5. We have another spaceship orbiting there, it's what we call our mother ship, and we're going to be doing things now that require round-the-clock communication with our mother.

"We can take the *Beagle* up into orbit and drop off a few spiders to act as relays so that we can talk to Mother even when Tunaland is facing away from A-5. But there are reasons why we don't want to fly the *Beagle* unless we really have to. So you can do us a really big favor. Do you think your people will allow us to modify one of their rockets?"

"Certainly," said Catherine, without the slightest hesitation. And then, after a long pause, "Define 'modify.'"

"To change," Chris said. "We want to strap on a few little thrusters to push the rocket in the right direction so we can be sure that it gets into orbit. And instead of carrying one of the villagers, we want to send along ten miniature spiders, which will jump out of the pod at ten different points along its path. We can even show you what the spiders see as they look down on this world from three hundred kilometers up. It really looks beautiful from out there. You'll actually be able to see the roundness."

The roundness . . . Catherine latched onto that thought. Galileo had told her long ago that the world could be round. He also told her—can that, too, be real? Is there something wrong with Chris? Catherine had no way of knowing. She could not tell what was normal behavior for an alien.

THE WAYVILLES SAW IN C-3A A WORLD THAT SIMPLY HAD TO be explored.

They were not surprised to discover life there. After all, the moons of Jupiter, Saturn, Uranus, and Neptune, and even the Pluto-Charon pair, were mostly ice. And there were gravitational interactions between many of them, which dumped enormous loads of frictional energy under the ice, and created whole oceans.

Only those worlds covered with the thinnest icy skins had ever been penetrated by robot submarines. The water, though rippling with life, contained nothing more advanced than colonies of cells resembling filaments, hollow balls, and medusae.

So, while it was reasonable to expect icebound life in the solar system next door, the discovery of an advanced civilization went against all traditional teachings.

As far back as the 1980s, astronomers and paleontologists had converged on a unified vision of the Earth heaving and shifting through space. They saw the uneasy marriage of continental plates spawning fluctuating sea levels, surges of volcanic activity, and exhalations of carbon dioxide—all of which, over hundreds of millions of years, had conspired to raise and lower global temperatures and trigger mass dyings. Add to this turbulent foam of bumping, grinding continents a solar constant that had turned out to be not so constant, and asteroids large enough to put all-out nuclear war to shame, and it became difficult to imagine life on Earth ever approaching anything like a stable existence.

Catastrophes, tradition said, were what made the difference between worlds populated by humans and worlds populated by jellyfish. The importance of natural selection was thus diminished. If the smartest, best-adapted dinosaur on Earth should find herself in the path of an asteroid, if every so often something wiped out half of all the species, allowing the survivors to fan out and replace the old species without having to crowd them out, then the reason man was here is that other predators died out, not because his furry, protomonkey forebears outcompeted them. It was Richard Tuna who decided that, in wiping the slate clean, catastrophes opened up new ecological niches and prevented biological stagnation. He even claimed that dinosaurs, too, would never have evolved without them.

It followed that ice worlds, by contrast, were unbelievably stable. Temperature changes of more than one or two degrees over the course of a million years were almost unheard of. There were no tropics, no temperate zones, no ice ages, no seasons. A sun could flare up, or fade from existence, and no change would be felt below the thick shell of ice, whose thickness was typically measured in hundreds of kilometers. Even to a city-sized asteroid, it was an impenetrable shield.

Tuna had reasoned that such equable environments were perhaps capable of evolving an amoeba or a jellyfish, but it was hard to imagine them spawning sentient beings. Yet there they were.

And what technology! By all indications, the ocean in C-3A was buried underneath one hundred kilometers of ice. A similar ocean resided at that same depth inside Saturn's Titan, and as yet, no Earthly machine had explored it. Traveling across four and a half light-years of space was far easier than boring through a mere hundred kilometers of high-pressure ice.

Still . . . someone on (or rather, in) C-3A had done precisely that.

They had tunneled up from within, Chris knew. He wondered what they thought the stars were, when they stood upon the surface for the first time.

There was no question about it, Chris thought. They had to go there. What the aliens could teach, if they wanted to! But getting there would not be easy. The world was, after all, two light-months away.

Plans for the visit had already been suggested by Clarice and detailed by FU. It would cost nearly fifteen percent of Valkyrie's remaining antihydrogen supply, reducing the maximum cruising speed for a return to Earth. But that issue had already been decided. There would be no return.

The Valkyrie would leave half her spiders on A-5, moving away at two gees. At the end of a sixteen-day acceleration, the ship would be traveling at slightly more than eight percent the speed of light, a mere 24,940 kilometers per second.

The mother ship itself would not go near C-3A, largely for the same reasons that she was kept as far as possible from A-4. If the antimatter tanks ever detonated, as they had aboard *Enterprise*, the resulting gamma ray burst could bake a hemisphere.

So, two years hence, Valkyrie would decelerate into the Alpha Centauri C system, dropping off spiders that would in turn continue to decelerate on simple fusion rockets built from empty antihydrogen tanks and other cannibalized hardware. On final approach, the fusion engines would jettison into the star, and the actual landing would be made with primitive, chemical rockets. Valkyrie would continue on at cometary speed, flying almost directly at C, providing stunning close-up pictures of the dwarf star as she boomeranged over its far side and shot back toward A. The close flyby was as much a fuel-saving measure as a scientific adventure. The ship would not be obliged to accelerate to cruising speed from a resting state, thanks to the boost from C.

Not until Valkyrie was safely away from the other people would the decelerating spiders catch up to and land on C-3A. Almost all of FUQ2's memory would be transferred to each of the landers, except for the Earth history files, the volumes on antimatter rocket construction, instructions enabling the spiders to self-replicate, directions to Sol (indeed, almost all knowledge of the solar system was to be censored), all but the most basic details of human physiology and biochemistry, all Earthly literature and films depicting violent behavior (especially *The Wizard of Oz* and *The Muppet Chainsaw Massacre*), almost all knowledge of subatomic particles . . . the list went on . . . and on . . .

Censorship. The idea had been carefully weighed, both by the Wayvilles and by FU. From what little was known about the inhabitants of C-3A, they did not appear to be spacefarers. Mankind could go there, but they could not come to mankind. The three agreed that they should attempt to keep it that way.

26

Sorry to Interrupt the Festivities, But Someone Is Trying to Tell Us Something

━━━━◤◥◤◥━━━━

VIEWED FROM THE VICINITY OF C, THE GALAXY WAS SILENT. Except for A-4, there was not a whisper from any direction, not even from Earth.

Most Earth-based chatter had ceased leaking into space decades ago, during the rapid spread of laser and cable networks; and the four-year-old broadcasts to *Beagle* swept toward A on a microwave beam so narrow that C was entirely outside its reception cone.

According to the two-month-old relay from A-4, Britain had a new King, America had its first Navaho president, and all was well aboard two crewed spacecraft flying to Alpha Centauri.

The Bardos had died five years ago, but Earth was two light-years away at the time, so no one out there in the solar system knew about the *Enterprise* Nova until December of 2053. News of the explosion, now traveling back from Earth, would not reach A-4 until April 15, 2057, some four months hence.

Presently, the uncrewed Valkyrie was entering its last day of deceleration. Everything on board seemed to weigh twice its normal Earth weight. Brighter and brighter, each passing day, the strange star had rushed up from below. Indeed, it now ceased to resemble a star at all and appeared, instead, as a red disc, even to spiders unaided by telescopes. It grew balefully as they watched from their makeshift platform. It yawned as they dangled at the end of a tether some ten kilometers below the engines.

Close. It was going to be close.

"Look down now. Look at the third world," said Valkyrie. The spiders all saw it at once: a fluttering beacon burned, a voice that spoke in laser light.

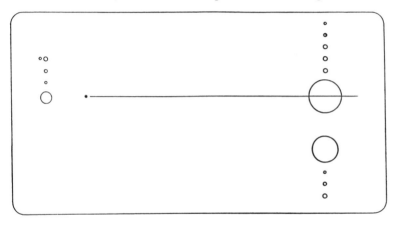

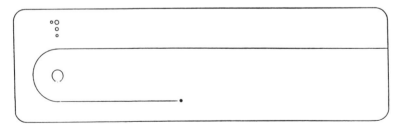

It was a question, carefully framed in binary code. The other people had seen the gamma ray shine from the engines, tracked it, and extrapolated its motion back to A, and forward to its flyby of C. They wanted to know if they had guessed correctly. Valkyrie saw immediately that the proper answer would have been a copy of their message, which would be read as: "Yes, I am intelligent enough to receive and decipher your signal. Yes, I came from A. Yes, I intend to pass over the far side of C." She could also have altered the first picture to show a flight path originating at A-5. To the second picture she could have added the probe she would soon dispatch, showing an eventual landing on C-3A.

That, she decided, was the proper answer, not the best answer, which was no answer at all.

But the other people persisted.

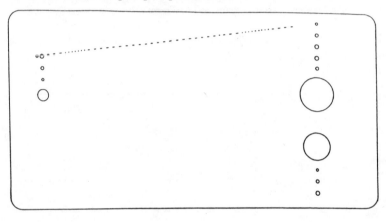

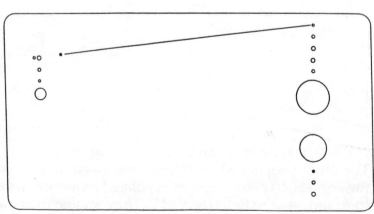

The pictures asked: "Did you receive the message we sent to A-5? And are you, as a result, coming to C-3A from A-5?"

Again Valkyrie elected not to answer. Instead, she shifted her course by three hundred kilometers. She would zig and zag at random intervals so that no one on C-3A could predict the exact position and motion of the ship at any point in time.

Prior to departure from A, FU had transmitted a duplicate of almost all her knowledge, all her consciousness, to Valkyrie; and her limited knowledge of the other people told her that interception and capture of a relativistic rocket could be catastrophic for the Earth and A-4, and should not be invited. All they would get was the lander's chemical rockets, and the limited knowledge of its spiderlike ambassadors.

FU was unwavering on this score. The other people were a high-technology civilization, and as such, they must be regarded as potential competitors until more was known about them. Equipped with relativistic rockets, they could hurl unstoppable bombs against humanity. If the probability of confrontation was as low as one percent, it was intolerable. If the price of preventing them from acquiring antimatter technology was to raise their suspicions by zigzagging through their system in utter silence, or to fire a stream of antimatter particles at anything that approached, or to detonate the antimatter tanks suicidally, then the mother ship and any being from C would be expendable.

Of course, nobody explained this to the Alphans.

BY THE TIME ANYONE ON A-4 READ THE QUESTIONS DIRECted at Valkyrie, the signals would be two months old. The first contact would already have passed into history before it was acted out for the first time on *Beagle*'s flats.

Every response Valkyrie could give had to be preprogrammed. Across the light-months, there could be no direct control from A-4. The Wayvilles could merely watch, like fans at a sporting event, able to cheer, but helpless to intervene.

And if the Wayvilles appeared to be helpless, they were paragons of opportunism compared with the people some four light-years away who realized too late that one of their cosmonauts, outward-bound for an encounter with aliens, was having visions of monsters and relativistic destruction. They saw in him a man who dreamed of bringing unspeakable calamity to the Earth, and worse, they saw a man who knew how.

27

Sun Diver

━━━━\\\\\\━━━━

THE WAYVILLES AND THE VILLAGERS WERE RAISING A NEW antenna atop Mount Victoria on the day Valkyrie received her first query from the other people.

During the two years since Valkyrie's departure, three thousand spiders had driven Earth's strawberries to near extinction, and the machines, more and more of them, were being recruited for the more intensive study of A-4. Hundreds of new flats had been manufactured and supplied to the villagers. With these, anyone could gain control of his own spider—merely by asking. Together, the Wayvilles and the Alphans probed the northern forests, the Lagoons of Powell, and the deepest reaches of the Ballard Rise. Their eyes were everywhere at once, yet they did not leave their village.

C WAS APALLINGLY LARGE NOW. IF NOT FOR THE CENTRIFUGAL force of Valkyrie's lcap over the far side, the ship would have felt itself drawn from space to fall headlong upon the star. Instead, the leap balanced against the pull of gravity, and Valkyrie felt weightless. Down there on the surface, a yellow-white fountain appeared, a blaze that spread three times wider than Earth. On A-4, two months hence, Alphan and human would behold something foreign to their experience of nature, as nature, even at its most violent, had hitherto revealed itself to them.

To the humans, the close-up views would trigger a commotion of delight, while their minds overloaded with strange new information and questions.

The Alphan mind would adjust more quickly. It did not remember a taste for the mysterious. It had forgotten all but facts. And, mechanically, it sought only facts.

Millions of kilometers behind Valkyrie, two spiders were flying outward toward an encounter with C-3A. Three weeks later, they climbed down the sky and landed within sight of pillbox-shaped buildings arranged in a circle.

The first thing the spiders learned, when they stepped down from the spent fuel tank, and the engine that had spent it, was that the world seemed to be creaking and snapping throughout its volume. One hundred kilometers of quivering ice lay under their feet, two hundred kilometers of relatively quiet water below that, then a veneer of rock and mud that capped hundreds of kilometers more of trembling, high-pressure ice—and, below that, a warm, shallow sea surrounding a volcanic, rocky core almost as large as Earth's moon. All these things became known to the spiders through seismic waves pulsing up to the surface.

There were places, only a few tens of kilometers below, where the sheer weight of overlaying crust produced new pressure phases, or densities, of ice. They differed from ordinary ice in having more closely packed molecules and odd melting points. The temperature one hundred kilometers below C-3A was minus thirty degrees Centigrade, yet the ice ran liquid and became a world-encircling sea—a bubble of water two hundred kilometers deep, locked between two concentric spheres of ice. Rocks and dust that would normally be mixed in with the ice had settled on top of an inner sphere of Ice Six, littering the sea floor with clays, sulfides, and other life-sustaining ingredients. At pressure phase Six, the ice was actually warmer than the ocean above.

And there was another sea within the inner sphere, and it, too, might harbor people. To contemplate beings living in oceans sandwiched between different pressure phases of ice was to behold the Buddhist concept of different planes of existence shifting suddenly, serendipitously, from symbol and myth to a dawning reality.

Four light-years from Earth, on the third world of C, FU's other selves thought these things, drew these connections, as C flared and the methane-nitrogen frost shivered from pink into something else.

Where are man and Alphan going? she wondered. What are they going to do with the universe? What is the universe going to do with them?

An approach communicated through the ground, footsteps undeniably.

A thought snapped up from her library: "Lucy! Quick! Ricky's coming!"

28

Chandelier

MINUTES LATER, THEY WERE STANDING FACE-TO-FACE, FU and this thing out of the ice. It was an automaton like herself, but shorter and thinner and indescribably graceful. He went to the Valkyrie spiders directly and flashed binary signals into their eyes.

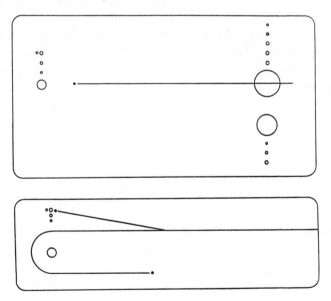

He wanted to know if they were from the gamma ray source that had (as predicted) passed over the far side of C.

The spiders flashed his picture back at him, answering, "Yes."

He replied with another question:

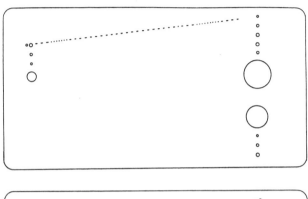

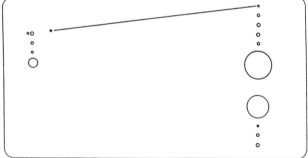

(Did you receive the message we sent to A-5? And did you, as a result, come to C-3A from A-5?)

Again the spiders flashed back a copy of the transmission. "Yes," they said.

It was the truth, but only half of it.

The exchange passed in an instant. Then he turned to the other automatons that were following him and spoke to them in laser light. In an opening between the pillboxes, FU saw a group of metallic figures. They had seen the exchange, and they directed a cannon toward her.

There were others closing in, and presently a little silver knot of twenty robots was around the spiders. The first automaton addressed them. He made binary pictures of pillboxes encircling a shaft that plunged into the heart of the world. Then he imparted motion to the pictures and allowed FU to peer into the abyss. Directly, as fast as the data came in, FU threw it to A—the spectacle of an ice giant seen for the first time in its entirety.

The impression was one of cobalt-blue void, lovely, dark, and deep. The flood of data was such that FU could shift her view in any direction. When she looked down, there was nothing her eyes could focus on. FU knew that there were two hundred kilometers of water beneath. The outer-space aspect of the surroundings suggested a reference system that had no equal. "Up" and "down" could be switched, so that the ceiling of the world became the ground and the ocean became the sky. The ceiling was a chandelier of hexagons and spikes of ice unguessable hundreds of centuries old. Some of the crystals had broken off and floated up, "fallen down," upon the ground.

At a distance on the horizon, two rectilinear shapes were etched against the sky. They appeared to grow out of the bed of crystals, but they were not crystals.

FU wanted to see more. She wanted to see through the water, beyond the twin towers, to the horizon that curved up. She wanted to see the other side of the sky—the globe, directly overhead—the other floor whose buildings, from her vantage point, hung upside down. She wanted to know the sea underneath those buildings, but the pictures stopped abruptly and she understood that it was now her turn to show the other people a new sky.

She permitted them close observation of their own

sun, a vast sphere glowing with dull red heat. She showed them the unquenchable tumult of yellow fire that had sprung up from within.

She showed them nothing of A or its fourth world, where water flowed impossibly on the outside, where creatures endured the temperature extremes of night and day, where no armor of ice prevented the occasional asteroid or comet from entering the biosphere directly.

All knowledge of A-4 had been withheld from memory, as had all traces of Earth save a few clips of vintage film and selected reports on pre-Sputnik technology.

With so much information missing and so many questions to be asked, it was only a matter of time before the automatons started running into dead ends with Valkyrie's ambassadors. That the discussion had started out with travels through inner and outer space brought the bulk of FU's ignorance right up to the front line of communication. And so, inevitably:

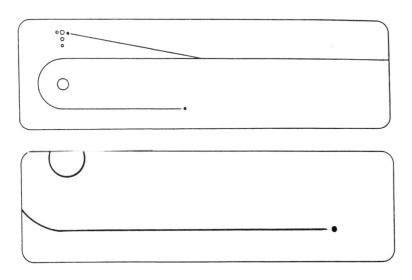

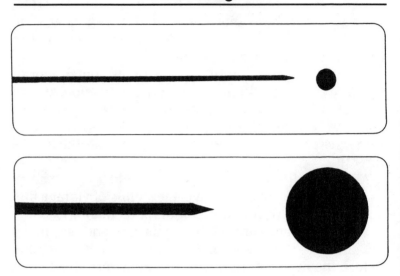

The automatons wanted to know about the ship that had come from A. But this knowledge, too, was missing.

Neither spider answered.

The question was repeated.

And still no answer came.

Two automatons simultaneously broke from the crowd and converged on one of the spiders. Her punishment came swiftly. She backed up two steps and was blocked by the inner rim of the circle. One of them bit off her face while the other divided her body in two. They singled out two other machines and brought them out of the ranks. The four snatched up the front half of the spider, pulled off the roof, then sank mosquito-like prosbosci inside.

In another moment they had found FU's brain and library and absorbed it—all of it—and the second spider was standing face-to-face with a strange hybrid that was half itself.

The binary question came:

SHOW ME SHIP BEAGLE

Fu searched her memory, latched into something, and answered in the only way she knew:

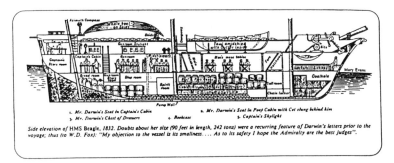

Side elevation of HMS Beagle, 1832. Doubts about her size (90 feet in length, 242 tons) were a recurring feature of Darwin's letters prior to the voyage; thus (to W.D. Fox): "My objection to the vessel is its smallness.... As to its safety I hope the Admiralty are the best judges".

The circle closed in on her. She had time enough to say, "Please stop!" before she was torn down and bitten apart and strewn about.

And then it was finished.

The first communication between electronic civilizations had lasted barely twenty seconds.

29

Valkyrie's Web

T WO MONTHS LATER, THE NEWS REACHED A-4.

"Clarice. Chris. Time to wake up."

Chris opened his eyes. FU brought up the lights slowly. He blinked, rolled over onto his stomach, and pulled a pillow over his head.

Clarice nudged him in the shoulder.

"Time to wake up," FU repeated.

He lifted his head and looked around the room. His eyes stopped at the plate-glass window. It was still dark outside.

"What's up?" Clarice asked for him.

"First contact," FU answered. "It's over."

"Over?"

"Spiders destroyed. The quickest way to explain will be to show you the transmission. It was very short."

A flat by the side of the bed lit up and replayed the encounter. When it was finished, Clarice said, "We've got a problem here," and asked FU to play it over again. While it played, Chris noticed that lights were burning atop one of the inverted twin towers.

"All right," Clarice said. "We won't be making friends

with that lot. Now, what do we tell Catherine and the others?"

"We tell them the truth," FU commanded.

"Will that be safe?"

"We have directed the other people's attention toward A. That may be dangerous for the Alphans. The Alphans are our friends. Our friends' problems are our problems."

"Okay, FU. Better put a call through to Catherine's room."

ACCORDING TO THE WAYVILLES' SENSE OF PROTOCOL, THE first conference on the other people, at which the problem and its solution would be presented, was a joint program conducted in an atmosphere of total openness. The Wayvilles could afford to be open, for the Alphans were slow to connect cause and effect. They asked few questions, and accepted freely any advice offered them.

The conference was held in a new, two-story building near the village: concrete trapezoids enclosing glass and dens and a swimming pool.

Clarice was the first to speak: "By now we've all seen pictures of the landing on C-3A. First off, I should explain that this is no longer a matter of new facts and fun. This is serious business, and there are a lot of things to do."

A furry white head craned for attention. Chris looked up from his flat and felt a chill of gooseflesh, accompanied by something like a premonition. It was Galileo.

"Serious business?" he said with a note of sarcasm. "What exactly do you mean?"

Chris stood up. "That if the other people ever get out of their world and into space, we may be invaded. We may eventually find ourselves in a war."

"War, you say. I've not heard that word before. Tell me about war."

"War is what we might experience if they come here.

War is what they did to our spiders, only on a much grander scale."

An uneasy murmur of touchscript ran through the crowd.

"It is a very bad thing, what they did," Chris continued. "They are very dangerous people. We cannot let them come here. We cannot even risk letting them get away from C."

Wrong thing to say, thought FU. I did ask for truth, but that was the wrong thing to say in front of the only villager who *can* trace the chain of cause and effect— the one villager who can see that we are not gods, that we make mistakes.

"Is there a way of stopping them?" Galileo said, looking suddenly frightened.

"We have to turn the Valkyrie around, send it back to C. Only this time the mother ship will fly much nearer to C-3A." Scratch another fifteen percent of the antihydrogen getting there, Chris thought. And worse, scratch almost all of the remaining hydrogen and lithium. To reduce the ship's mass and save fuel, only enough surplus matter for emergency maneuvers had been sent along. Valkyrie could not leave C again without first stopping off at C-3B or the nearest asteroid, dispatching spiders to collect propellant, and risking laser attack from the surface of C-3A. "Valkyrie must return to C, even if it becomes a one-way trip. What we plan to do is spray a canopy of cold antimatter in low orbit around their world."

(Scratch another twenty percent.)

"Now, it's so cold there that even gases normally found in the atmospheres of ice worlds lie crusted on the surface." Chris looked around and noticed that none of the Alphans, not even Galileo, appeared to be considering the importance of this revelation. To hell with it, he thought. Just feed them the facts. "The upshot is that the antimatter will remain in orbit around their world for a very long time. It may take a million years to dissipate.

"So far, the only buildings we've seen on the surface are clustered around that shaft. It doesn't look like they've been outside long enough to invent space travel. And we're not going to give them that opportunity. Rockets coming up through the antimatter will explode every time. They can't even send up bombs to blow holes in the canopy, because the antimatter particles will be racing over their heads at several kilometers per second, and anyone trying to run up through a hole is going to discover that the particles are too fast for them. They'll fry, intercepting antimatter and throwing off gamma rays. Nothing will get out of C-3A. We can lock them in tight, like a corked bottle."

"Oh, boy," Galileo chittered. "Yeah, I see your plan. But if nothing can come up from C-3A, nothing can go down, either."

"That's right. It's what we call total quarantine, a blockade that works both ways. But even the slightest possibility that they are a violent people, that they can overrun us like an interstellar plague if they get out, is intolerable. We can't risk it."

Galileo shrugged. "There are many basic facts we do not know about the other people."

"And we are not likely to learn them, I know. There will be no more landings. Probably no more binary exchanges . . ." Chris paused. No, he thought. This is not mere fun and games. This is serious business. Killing business. Perhaps the one thing that truly can bring ruination to Earth and A-4. "We'll have the quarantine anyway."

"War, you say . . . like they did to our spiders. You mean to say they would do that to us?"

"There's a chance."

"War, you say . . . This thing you plan to do. Will the other people call that war?"

"Perhaps."

"War, you say . . . One of your ancient writers tells of a curse that at first sight appears to be a blessing: 'May you live in interesting times.' We are indeed living in interesting times, thanks to you. And I foresee that times shall become even more interesting—for both of us."

Galileo left.

Outside, he alone among the Alphans turned the question of war over and over in his head. It was a new word for him. But there were hints that war was not so new to humans, and that FU might be hiding something.

Experience of war . . . it showed through even in their make-believe—in *The Wizard of Oz*, for one.

Yes—oh, yes. The humans and their machines had a secret.

30

Secret Wars

GALILEO SPLIT THE FRESHLY COOKED PACKET OF LEAVES WITH one of A-4's first "Spider-made Swiss Army knives," bit in, and immediately lost his appetite.

Headache . . .

He put a hand to his right eye—a hand once wiry but now merely stringy—and rubbed circles over his brow.

No, no, not again . . .

He was dizzy and headachy. A wave of nausea washed over him and was gone, but would come again, he knew.

He tossed the packet on the ground. Black berries spilled out, still warm—dirty now. Black berries . . . his favorite of all Takahashi fruit. Catherine had collected them for him only the day before—especially for him. The black berries were hard to come by, and as he pictured her finding them and wrapping them gently in leaves, taking special care not to bruise them; as he imagined her deciding not even to tell him what his lunch would be, knowing that she would not be there to see the surprise on his face, but drawing pleasure from the knowledge that in some small way she would bring happiness into his life; as he stared down at the ruined meal and considered a tender act come to nothing, he looked up at the sky and did what he had not allowed himself to do since he was a child declared defective: he cried.

And a storm raged on in the glands near his throat. The storm had begun almost on the very day *Beagle* arrived, brought about by fusion products inhaled as he and Catherine slept in the shade of the starship's still-hot engines. Catherine showed no signs of injury—not yet, at least. But Galileo's glands were swollen where, over the course of two and a half years, renegade cells had passed the test of his immune system— a kind of natural-selection filter that favored mutants immune to immunity. The renegades had established colonies, spherical lumps from which highways now branched. Centuries earlier, on Earth, Hippocrates had opened a cadaver and discovered colonies identical to those now growing in Galileo's neck. The highways looked to him like crab claws, and he named the condition after the Greek word for crab, which came into the twenty-first century as "cancer."

Where highways encroached upon blood vessels, outbound colonists exited into the bloodstream—millions of them daily. There, in his blood, Galileo's last line of defense was failing. Cells similar to human white cells, behaving much like spiders in search of strawberries, were somehow unable to find the enemy. The whites bumped into them directly, but it was as if the colonists were invisible. Through a remarkable quirk of nature, the renegades had fooled his immune system into ignoring them.

His body was at war with itself. It was a war that would result ultimately in the destruction of the colonists as they multiplied and gorged themselves and spilled their refuse into the very bloodstream that sustained them.

Galileo might cut the war short, if only he could summon up enough courage to visit the Wayvilles. The machines in the hollow of *Beagle* might save him, as they had saved Clarice from illness, as they had saved the world from strawberries, as they had saved more than one villager from chronic pain. But it would take more than pain and fatigue to make him visit Chris, and sit with him face-to-face, one-on-one.

No, he could not look at Chris.

And yet he used the flat Chris had delivered through Catherine. With it he spent his days watching the activities of spiders hundreds of kilometers away in the northern forests. The strawberries, one by one, had been defeated, and now the new machines had spread out across the entire continent. They searched the land, scrutinized it for the telltale three leaves and white flowers. From all indications they had got them all, but the machines would continue their search, for even one seed could become a global bloom.

Exploration was now a fringe benefit of the strawberry hunt. One of Catherine's spiders had discovered a hillside of amberstone bricks, exposed freshly by a mud slide. There were pieces of quartz among the bricks—quartz that had once been broad, flat sheets, and perfectly clear. Catherine said that the Wayvilles were very excited about the quartz sheets. They called them "windows"—but unlike any that had existed in the village before the arrival of the Wayvilles. They were windows made of "glass," like the ones that decorated the "big house" and the "swimming pool" enclosure.

On a hill a couple of kilometers away, Galileo saw the glint of a new tower. "Laser relay," the aliens called it.

They are changing us . . .

And what right have they?

Who granted them the right to so carelessly alert the other people to our presence? To risk war with them? To make problems where none existed? And the villagers . . . Their obedience to the Wayvilles disgusted Galileo. The aliens knew war from experience, he was certain. This meant that they must be used to war, that they considered it an acceptable outcome. If they'd experienced it at least once . . .

(the first time is always the hardest)

And the villagers obeyed these Wayvilles. But the aliens were not infallible; they could make mistakes. They already *had* made mistakes—that's why there were spiders running all over the continent looking for strawberries. And yet the villagers did not see this as anything other than the normal course of events. They were letting the aliens make all their decisions—and my foolish brethren buy it all, Galileo thought. They buy all of it . . . what is the expression? Hook and line . . . they swallow it hook, line and sinker.

If he were feeling well, Galileo would have left the valley for the northern territories. He'd found new beauty there, new marvels revealed every morning by the spiders. Yes, he should go. And he should take Catherine with him. Lately the valley did not feel safe.

(a great wind is going to blow)

Soon.

He wanted to leave the village. He wanted to get away from Chris.

But I feel so sick . . .

Soon.

The other people! Piss on those Wayvilles. They had gone right ahead and invited trouble. They had made all our decisions for us, knowing that the villagers would say yes to anything they suggested. And now—

He saw it for the second time that day. The air shimmered the way it sometimes does over hot coals, or the way a flat shimmers when it needs repair. Then the trees were nameless and dead. Then a cool breeze and the forest alive again. Then nausea.

—and now they tell us more rockets have come to A, to build Asimov Arrays on the inner worlds. Piss on those Wayvilles! Those worlds are ours! They belong to the village, to the people who live in this system. This is our solar system. Ours! And the Wayvilles act as if they own it. They are taking it away from us, piece by piece.

And what right have they?

What right, these devourers of worlds?

What right?

What right?

31

2057: The Crash of Three Worlds

B WAS ON THE OUTWARD LEG OF ITS ELLIPSE AROUND A. Flying to Apastron in 2075, the farther sun had grown noticeably dimmer and the air slightly cooler during the two and a half years since the Wayvilles landed.

On 15 April 2057, the first broadcasts of the *Enterprise* disaster reached A-4 from Earth. On that day, Catherine had adjusted Galileo's flat to give him control of a tiny, seagoing spider. It was a gift from Chris, and it seemed to Galileo to be a feeble attempt to win him over.

(To win me over? How can the village idiot be important enough for Devourer to win over?)

Bribery aside, Galileo accepted the new pair of eyes, and by midafternoon he was probing the Ballard Rise. On his flat, a tangle of volcanic pipes and chimneys gushed churning mineral brines, and the deeps of A-4 became an undersea forest inhabited by tree-shaped animals and "nautiloids" and "crabs." The sense of discovery filled him with questions and delights unknown to any other native of A-4.

"Sorry to interrupt," FU said. "I have something to show you."

HELLO, ABC, THIS IS BERT KNAPP SPEAKING FROM SYDNEY. THE *ENTERPRISE* HAS JUST EXPLODED. IN FACT, TWO YEARS AGO IT EXPLODED!—***–*– AND WITHOUT WARNING, THE *BEAGLE'S* SISTER SHIP ERUPTED INTO A MINI SUPERNOVA THAT CONTINUES TO RACE AWAY FROM EARTH AT NINETY-TWO PERCENT THE SPEED OF LIGHT.

DON EVERETT HERE. ANZSA DIRECTOR CLINDES PHONED PRIME MINISTER TAM TWO MINUTES AGO THAT THE *ENTERPRISE* AND ITS CREW HAVE BEEN LOST. NEW ZEALAND PARLIAMENT ALSO RECEIVED WORD TODAY OF A DYS—A— SIMULTANEOUS DYSFUNCTION ABOARD *BEAGLE*, THE NATURE OF WHICH HAS NOT BEEN DISCLOSED.

HERE IS WHAT HAS HAPPENED: WE HAVE A CONFIRMED REPORT FROM PERTH THAT THERE IS TROUBLE ABOARD *BEAGLE*, TOO. RECENT—**– THE WAYVILLE SHIP SUGGEST—*—******—AS SUFFERED–*-LOSS OF SIGNAL—*-EN ROUTE–*-

This extraordinary news, carried on three hundred flats, brought to a halt the activities of A-4. Not even Galileo could come to terms with a picture of Clarice sitting inside *Beagle*, at her breakfast table, with the words LIVE FROM INTERSTELLAR SPACE glowing boldly on the screen. According to the broadcast, she was still on her way to A-4, yet she had landed more than two years ago.

Paradoxes did not trouble the other villagers. In a few moments it would be only a fact, although a very confusing one, if given so much as a second glance. Galileo suspected that it had something to do with the universal speed limit FU had been trying to explain, something worth stopping and thinking about. But not now—not *now*—Clarice was writing (Clarice had written), and what she wrote about was Chris:

I HAVE CONSIDERED SLEEP DRINKS TO DECREASE OUR WAKING HOURS AND HASTEN OUR ADVANCE ON THE NEW WORLD. BUT CHRIS DOES NOT LIKE SLEEP. EVEN AS I WRITE, HE TOSSES AND TURNS, AND HIS DREAMS, I KNOW, ARE UNEASY. TRANS——***—

Her words died in a wash of static. After a few seconds, FU brought back the Ballard Rise.

"FU, what happened to the broadcast?" Galileo said.

"I've lost the signal. It was cut off suddenly. I don't have a proper answer right now. Give me a few seconds to think about it."

A "crab" maneuvered on the screen, made its way slowly toward the top of a chimney.

"I've just lost channels all across the board. There are no movies or broadcasts of any kind coming from Earth."

"Is Earth dead?"

"No. Not dead. I'm losing communication from the entire solar system. Someone is jamming all broadcasts. This is deliberate. Very strong signals between here and Sol are blotting out everything. Someone does not want us to hear Earth. They have severed the lines of communication."

"You mean, as we did to the other people."

"Yes. Very much the same."

The crab paused mere centimeters from the spout. A jet of water heated to four times its boiling point at sea level shot over the animal's head, creating an updraft of cooler water that washed over him and spared his life. Galileo could not understand, as yet, why the water did not boil and why the crab lived. And he didn't care. There were more important questions at hand.

"FU, why have they severed the lines?"

"Fear, I think."

"Fear of what?"

"Fear of Chris, I think."

There was another question that needed asking, the one that logically followed, but Galileo was slow to grasp it. No matter, the answer was good enough. Galileo understood fear of Chris.

"FU, show me Catherine."

The chimney and the crab disappeared, and Catherine's face flashed onto the screen. It was a spider's-eye view—*two eyes*—which meant that the crystals on Galileo's flat automatically threw the light in two slightly different directions, first into one eye, then into the other, alternating twenty times per second to build a moving picture of Catherine seen from two different angles. The result was that he viewed her in three dimensions, as clear as a reflection in a mirror. Several meters behind her was the base of the new laser relay. And, to Galileo's growing relief, she appeared to be alone.

"Catherine. You know Chris. You see him every day. Do you ever notice something wrong with him? Does he ever seem dangerous?"

Catherine saw that something was wrong with Galileo. His hearts were stopping and starting—repeatedly—bringing him to the very edge of death. His breath stopped in his throat and he snapped his head around quickly, as if to confront something behind him. But the picture on her flat showed that no one and nothing was there.

Five kilometers away, Galileo heard a sound behind him. He turned immediately, his eyes ticking back and forth from tree to tree. There was the one keynamed waikantrajuremaranriosponsphinctrimuscimoraspinab-aaccatowassoniicubensizapotecorummatisilopophora-riveaztecorumelidaturapheropsilocybeimonohoogsha-ngenilphiosomatropamuscimolomegatecorumixaeensinebrioconspicua... he forgot the rest. One of the few he could remember, and more than half of it was gone. There was the tall grass, all around him. There was the forest, just a few meters beyond. And there the leaves were a healthy bluish green. There was a shimmer, like the shimmer hot air has over sand when the suns are high in star season. For a moment Galileo was confused—

(and his dreams, I know, are uneasy)

—the shimmer was gone, the view clearer.

Brilliant sunlight stabbed down everywhere, through leafless trees onto white grass.

(Chris... dreams... uneasy...)

no. no! No! NO! I WILL NOT SEE THIS NOT AT ALL I WILL NOT SEE HIM MAKE IT REAL!

Shimmer...

Galileo blinked around stupidly. Waikantrajuremaranriosponsphinctrimuscimoraspinabaaccatowassoniicubensizapotecorummatisilopophorariveaztecorumelidaturapheropsilocybeimonohoogshangenilphiosomatropamuscimolomegatecorumixaeensinebrioconspicua— was dead. Fresh rainwater dripped down its bare trunk, dripped down a thousand bare trunks onto ground that was grassless and muddy and hot.

Shimmer...

There was the tall green grass. There was waikantrajuremaranriosponsphinctrimuscimoraspinabaaccatowassoniicubensizapotecorummatisilopophorariveaztecorumelidaturapheropsilocybeimonohoogshangenilphiosomatropamuscimolomegatecorumixaeensinebrioconspicua—ready to shed new fruit. And there was the forest beyond, pulsing with life's surge.

Catherine did not like what she saw on her flat. Galileo looked sick—had been sick for many "weeks." Now he looked confused.

"No, no," she answered at last. "Chris never seems dangerous. Chris is our friend."

"But how can you know that?"

"How can I know that? By knowing, of course. I just know it, that's all."

Galileo did not know how to answer. He could have told her the same thing about his own vision of Christopher Wayville. He stared into the flat for a long time, fighting off an attack of nausea and stopping hearts. Then he directed his questions at the *Beagle*'s computer: "FU, what do you know of these dreams Clarice has described? Is something wrong with Chris?"

"Give me a few seconds."

"FU!"

"I'm thinking."

"So am I. I'm thinking this is a time for honesty."

FU addressed him by his keynames, a formality that had a calculated, disarming effect. "Yes. You are probably right. This is a time for honesty. If for no other reason than because Earth's response to Chris's dreams is important to everyone on A-4, and that we did, after all, come here uninvited."

"Tell me, then, is something wrong with Chris?"

"Possibly not. He has a theory about something called the Lazarus experience, something that caused him to see pictures of the Earth charred—"

Galileo felt a jolt of fear. Dead on the ice, and dying now, he had seen A-4 charred. He had seen the forests dead.

"—I have checked my library and made every possible connection between the facts, and I have found nothing to confirm his theory, or to falsify it."

"He saw the Earth charred?"

"Eaten. By artificial suns."

—DEVOURER OF WORLDS—

"Can Chris destroy worlds?" Galileo said slowly.

"No. He will not set out to destroy worlds. These bad dreams and feelings brought much anxiety into Chris's life, but he is still the same man who left Sol. He still, as we say on Earth, has a good heart."

Catherine watched the exchange between Galileo and FU from afar. Both seemed to be ignoring her now, and it should have occurred to her that Galileo had a far better relationship with Chris's computer than with the living being, Chris; but Catherine was not quick to make such connections.

Nor was she the only one watching from afar.

The Wayvilles, playing on opposite sides of the swimming pool, had been engaged with twenty villagers in a game of volley ball when the signals from Earth dropped off. FU summoned them immediately to the house. Now, closed up alone in their bedroom, they watched Galileo and Catherine on a wallscreen.

Aside from the conference about the other people—and there he'd only seen Galileo's head bobbing up and down—Chris had not had an opportunity to observe the astronomer at close range for quite some time. The alien looked into the screen and Chris felt shock run through him like a live wire. Galileo was sick. Very sick. His breathing was irregular and his hands looked as if they wanted to shake. There had been weight loss, a loss that drew in the cheeks and made deep shadows under his eyes. The eyes themselves had that look, a look such as people have when they know they are close to death.

I do not like that alien, Chris thought. He is different from the others. He might be trouble. But right now he is *in* trouble. He needs our help. Perhaps I should send Catherine with a spider to sample his blood. If I help him, maybe he—

Catherine—it was unlike her—broke in and asked the question Galileo had overlooked: "FU, why is Earth afraid of Chris?"

"Don't answer yet!" Clarice scrawled on a flat.

"I don't have a proper answer right now, Catherine. Give me a few seconds to think about it." Then the computer's voice came over the bedroom intercom. "Chris. Clarice. I am on a private line with you. Have I guessed correctly? Do you want a private line?"

"Yes," Chris said. "Tell me, should Earth be afraid of what we are doing here?"

"You see that, don't you?"

"Because we are teaching the Alphans?"

"That is part of it."

From far away, Galileo's voice blazed over the flat: "FU! Please. Give us an answer!"

"Give me a few seconds." FU spoke like a true bureaucrat—which, of course, she was.

"FU, you should end that conversation," said Chris.

"Tell them you don't know the answer," said Clarice.

"I should not. Catherine might take that answer at face value, but Galileo may not. Also, as Galileo has said, this is a time for honesty. Earth might soon be a problem for the Alphans. The other people already are a problem for the Alphans. And the Alphans' problems are our problems."

Indeed they were. FU replayed the conference on the other people to herself, and she saw that Chris was mad to connect war and the other people in the same sentence—especially in Galileo's presence. The Earth in Chris's visions and the world of the other people had touched, and touching now, they held sway over the future of both man and Alphan.

FU said, "They know on Earth, Chris, that you were having visions of war. They know that you believed it might be your destiny to bring war to Earth. And some fifty-one months from now, they'll know that you have begun to teach the Alphans about war. Just as serious is the matter of our permanent residence on A-4, the fact that seeder ships have by now arrived on A-1 and A-2, and that we have, through our prolonged association with the Alphans, begun to transfer to them our technology."

Chris considered this for a moment. "So they will view the Alphans as competitors, as a potentially hostile nation, much as we have taught the Alphans to view the other people." The phrase stuck in his mind: other people. Alpha Centauri was turning out to be one hell of a statistical anomaly. There were too many thinking creatures in this system. You wouldn't expect that, judging from how quiet the rest of the galaxy appeared to be. Or perhaps the SETI people, listening to the stars with their radio telescopes, were mistaken and the galaxy wasn't anywhere near as quiet as the silence would suggest. He thought about it, and was cut short—

"Yes," FU told Chris. "Earth will have cause to fear A-4."

"And A-4 has cause to fear Earth?"

"Yes."

What will Earth do? Chris wondered. His first answer: *They may respond to their fear.* Fifty-two months from now, they may launch a rocket at us with only enough antimatter for a one-way trip, only enough fuel to accelerate up to ninety-two percent the speed of light. If it strikes the planet at that speed, even with no antimatter left in its tanks, it will become a bomb—a relativistic bomb. Gamma-irradiated dust will be set to the wind. Everything on A-4 will be poisoned, doomed by the air it breathes.

"Give me a few seconds," FU told Catherine and Galileo. Galileo had been right. This *was* a time for honesty. FU turned the answers and their possible consequences over and over in her brain, deciding, in the end, to give them the truth, but only part of it: "On Earth they are afraid of Chris because . . . give me a few seconds . . . because of his dreams."

"The dreams scare them?" said Galileo.

"Yes."

"Why is that?"

"You heard the broadcast," FU answered. "I saw your

face when you heard it. You looked scared. Why is that?"

Because I'm having the dreams, too, Galileo almost blurted. *Because we both see destroyed worlds. Because Chris might be the destroyer of worlds.* But he stopped himself, because he feared that the words might anger Chris, and cause him to use Valkyrie's power against A-4. But even more so, when it came right down to bottom, he feared that his dreams and his fear of Chris were jokes of the mind. He questioned the reality of both—and worse, he questioned his very sanity. And why not? A whole village could tell him (and had, for a lifetime, told him) that there was no question about his deviance—it was to them a fact. So he held the words back, and said instead, "I have no answer."

It was a lie, of course. And, watching Galileo, Chris could not tell the difference. He had never seen an alien lie before. He took it for a fact, and thanked his lucky stars that the astronomer had not thought to ask how man responded to fear.

32

The Fallen Sky

KNULL . . . BOOM . . . THOOM . . . BOOMBOOKATHOOM—
A silver star fell down from Heaven, having great power, and A-4 shuddered in its glory.

Galileo watched it come in from the direction of Sol, a tiny flare that did not even attempt to slow down. The Southern Hemisphere continent—Bardo, the Wayvilles called it—rippled and swayed, slipped, snapped, and leaped. Ten thousand new chasms yawned on the floor of a shallow inland sea, swallowing cubic kilometers of water and regurgitating it instantly as mountain ranges of black steam. A dark fountain went up, higher than the steam, laced with red sparks and sheets of lightning. He was awed by nothing so much as its expanding dimensions. He understood its scale. He saw it churning up there on the edge of space, propelled higher and higher on a column of backblast, and the center of the impact was in the center of Bardo.

The suns went out. Gravity drew the fountain down, and from its focus splashed vast fronts of boiling dust that ran like a liquid over the continent, faster than a plane, slashing down ferns and uprooting boulders as they moved.

From on high, from the altitude of Dim, perhaps, the cloud appeared to be shaped like a giant amoeba. It flowed off the edges of Bardo and out to sea, obscuring completely the tide of seething magma that rose to fill a wound larger than Lake Superior.

Death rolled into Tunaland on the tongue of a tsunami. It piled up on the western shelf, a foaming hell that nudged clouds out of its way as it approached. Trapped air fled ahead of it, first a puff that raised sand and straw, then a wind that flung pebbles and overturned trees, and finally a blast that scoured the land clean, with the wave only seconds behind. Takahashi's location on the east coast put all of Tunaland between it and the wave. Even so, the water shot inland, filling the valley with debris and stopping just short of the village. The Alphans enjoyed several hours' respite until the tsunamis from Bardo's west raced more than halfway around the globe without meeting land. They met instead the outrushing ripples from the shadow of Tunaland, overpowering them in a subsurface clash that reduced the Ballard Rise to churning sediment, yet failed to create a disturbance on the surface. Not until they reached the shallows of the continental shelf did they begin to climb out of the sea. The waters piled high over the Lagoons of Powell, broke across them, and were still strong enough to reach Wear when they passed the village.

Blistering heat blew to the ends of A-4, carrying with it dark matter that had once been stone, soil, trees and their inhabitants—all turned instantly into powder and vapor. Upon them had fallen the rays, inundating them completely. Then the pounded fragments of nothing were carried away in the spreading nuclear cloud, where they condensed and began to radiate back some of their energy.

Those trees that survived high on the valley walls shed their leaves and ceased growing. Thick black rain began to hew down the vegetation, and the soil beneath it, to the bare rock . . . yet the land remained eerily familiar. There, in the east, were the pinnacles. There, all around, were the massifs. And over there, in the ocean, the wreck of a lagoon. The land was familiar, yet unfamiliar. As a nuclear monsoon descended upon the graves of Wear and Wells, no splashes of green challenged the erosive forces. The valley ran full with mud, and there were no Alphans or strawberries or hypoglycemia bugs—no moving things except water-falls and *Beagle*'s spiders. Nothing but the terrors and the dark. Nothing but the rain and the dead and tomor-row.

And all of this had been wrought by a thing no larger than the Wayvilles' house—*all of this.*

—*Destroyer of worlds*—

(Chris?)

—*I am become death*—

Chris did this. Oh, no. Please, no! No! NO! CHRIS DID THIS CHRIS DID THIS OH NO CHRIS CHRIS CHRIS—

Galileo's eyes flashed open. He jumped backward, landing on his tail, blinking into the dark. He shrieked keynames—

(*!Catherine!*)

And Catherine was there beside him, Catherine with her hands reaching for his arms. She signed his shrieks back at him, adding: *Bad dream. Another bad dream. I'm here. I'm with you. Don't be scared.*

Bad dream, he signed back.

The fires again?

Yes. The fires again. All over the world.

You must tell me your dream. You must tell me all of it.

He told it long.

33

Like Dreamers Do

CATHERINE HAD ONE STRONG ADVANTAGE OVER THE VILLAG-
ers: she was better than they were at asking questions.

Catherine had one strong advantage over Galileo and
Chris: she was not as good as they were at asking
questions.

This enabled her to connect Chris's dreams with
Galileo's dreams and understand that the fate of Earth
and the fate of A-4 might be linked; and she did not
question the reality of the dreams, or the sanity of the
dreamers. To her, the terrors were a fact.

They were becoming more and more a fact to Galileo,
too, while Chris had succeeded, for the most part, in
putting the bad dreams away, in convincing himself that
they had been merely that: bad dreams.

These things I see, Galileo signed. *Is this how the aliens
respond to their fear? Will they punish us on this world
merely because they are afraid of Chris? Sometimes I am
convinced that something is happening to my mind. Something . . . BAD. But . . . this . . . if this vision is real . . .*

Catherine ran a hand up his arm and cupped his
shoulder with it . . . *then Chris must be stopped*, she
signed.

If he can be . . . Chris must be destroyed. I must kill Chris.

Muscles tightened in her face, and the fur stood out a little. *No, no. Chris must be stopped. Yes. But you misunderstand me. You do not kill him. He is my friend. Chris is not BAD. He is good.*

How am I supposed to know that? How am I supposed to know that he is not BAD? How am I supposed to know that he did not come here to take our world—or destroy it?

Because Clarice said he dreamed of the Earth eaten by immense fires. Chris's world is in danger, too. Chris would not destroy his own world. Chris is not BAD. He is my friend.

Galileo considered the connection she had just made, and a murmur of jealousy ran through his head. His face changed subtly, and he ruffled his fur with a hand, trying to hide the change. She was right (again). The facts were standing right in front of him, and he had failed to see them: Chris might indeed be a destroyer of worlds, but even an alien would not seek to destroy his own world. What was it that FU had said? "These bad dreams and feelings brought much anxiety into Chris's life." Oh, yes. He might truly become a destroyer of worlds, but he did not want to. And that meant . . . that meant . . . what?

Can he be talked to? Galileo asked.

Yes. Yes. You must try.

How can you know that?

Because you see a bad thing coming. You see the same bad thing Chris sees. Whatever this bad thing is, you have to help each other to face it. You have to help each other to stop it.

Dreams being real . . . this was crazy, and Galileo knew it. This was the talk of a defective—but a very gifted defective. Catherine was better at hiding her deviance from the villagers. She bent with every wind, learning all the necessary keynames, and refraining from asking questions in public. She knew how to survive in the Valley of Wells. She knew how to find acceptance among her teachers and her peers—and one way not to was to show signs of wandering thought. And she did, from time to time, think laterally, and Galileo had to admire the way she concealed it from all except him and the Wayvilles.

Let us . . . you and I . . . proceed on the assumption that your dreams and Chris's dreams are real. Let us keep this as a fact.

You really don't question it, do you?

No, she signed lightly. *I have no questions. I believe what you saw.*

I'm not sure I believe it. After long conversations with myself, I am full of nothing but questions.

The questions mean nothing if what you saw . . . give me a few seconds . . . if what you saw has so much as a five percent probability of being a fact.

There it was again: a flash of deviance. She was right (of course!). Even a tiny chance of the dreams being real was unacceptable. Another surge of jealousy flowered and died. In its wake, his admiration for her went up a couple of notches. *So . . . you think I must talk to this Devourer, this Chris.*

You look scared, Catherine signed.

I AM scared, Galileo signed.

He won't hurt you.

I'm afraid he might hurt all of us, if we give him enough time. But I'm also afraid that I will make a fool of myself if the dreams mean nothing. He looked down at the scales on his feet. They were flaking and white, as if he had grown prematurely old. Chris did this, he thought.

There was nothing in the world that Galileo feared more than Chris. Nothing. Not even the wrath of the villagers should he make a fool of himself in front of the aliens.

I want you with me, Galileo signed with a slight tremble.

I will go with you, Catherine signed back, noting the tremble in his fingers. *Now, straighten your spine and dig your feet in.*

I'm trying, he signed.

THE *BEAGLE*—AGAIN. B HUNG OVER WEAR IN THE WEST, blood bright and starlight cold.

Catherine had called ahead and found Chris at the ship. She stepped into the clearing, surveying the flying house and calling up images of the world at the time of its first appearance. Healthy green plants had filled in the patch of white that once surrounded *Beagle*. Trees at the clearing's edge had grown taller, a few had died, and young saplings now grew where none had stood before. Laser relays and solar ponds grew on the hills.

She fixed her eyes on the ship itself. The topside where she and Galileo had spent that first night taking a camera apart was unchanged. The door through which the Wayvilles had emerged the following day stood open, an invitation into the hollow of *Beagle*.

"I can't," Galileo chirped. "I can't go in there." He did not move from the woods, and seemed on the verge of bolting away.

"You must come. You must talk to him."

"No."

"He will not hurt you."

"No!"

"You must tell him what you saw!"

"You tell him!" Galileo squealed. "Don't you understand that I can't go in there?"

"You must try. Take that as a fact."

"No!"

"You must, or we may die. We took that as a fact."

Galileo looked out across the clearing. An alien figure stood in the hole in the side of *Beagle*. "Oh, no—no," he chittered. "No. I will not see him make it real." He looked at Catherine and motioned toward the ship. "All right," he said. "I'll go." His voice cracked twice as he said it.

"He will not hurt you," she repeated as Galileo emerged from the woods.

"It has to be me and Chris. Only Chris can understand what I saw."

"Follow me," Catherine said.

CHRIS THOUGHT THE ALIEN LOOKED FRIGHTENED AND SICK. Sicker than he'd expected. And more frightened than sick.

What he saw made him step back involuntarily. His second thought: God's teeth! If that's contagious . . . But then he thought with growing relief of the reversed amino acids, though his relief was marred by the memory of the hypoglycemia bug. Galileo stood, white-scaled and thin-haired and thin in the doorway, his eyes sunken and glistening in their sockets. He was a ghost of the Alphan he had been only a month before.

"You want me to heal you?" Chris guessed.

"That, too. But more important, it's . . ." He hesitated, then opted for bluntness. "It's the dreams. I've seen A-4 eaten by a big fire, just like you saw the Earth."

A vicious joke, Chris thought (hoped?). Galileo is trying to screw up my mind. He is different from the others. He hates me. Am I to believe that this alien is having the same dreams that frightened me so— especially when he already knows, from my broadcast, that I came here with uneasy dreams? What's this, you little bastard, psychological warfare? Am I to believe it's anything else?

(But what if it's real?)

Okay, I'll test you. That's easy. If I ask you to describe your dreams, and if I don't give you another clue about mine, and if still the details run in parallel, I might be disposed to believe you.

(And what then?)

(Don't even think about it—)

"Okay, Galileo. Tell me about the dreams."

The Alphan's face relaxed a little, like the face of a Nervous Nellie who has just passed those first two easy questions on the witness stand. It was an expression of relief that one has after he has cried, "Here goes nothing!" and then taken the first leap.

"I'll tell you," he chittered. "I'll tell you everything."

It was the part about the point of light that troubled Chris, that part about a silver star coming in, not decelerating, hitting the planet at fantastic speed. Galileo was telling Chris about relativistic bombs, the very thing Chris now feared the Earth might launch against A-4. It was also a thing Galileo should not have known about. A feeling came up in Chris—of being crowded, of time running out. Fifty-one months from now, FU's broadcast of the 15 April conference, in which the Alphans learned of war, would reach Earth. The very next day, they might launch their missile. Chris thought these things as Galileo described dangers that had been kept back from him, kept back from all Alphans. As he chittered on and on, telling everything, Clarice was summoned to the ship. She came in near the end of the tale, and heard things that could not possibly be rooted in mere coincidence. She did not have to hear a playback to understand just how high the stakes were, and how real Chris's nightmares had become.

"So where do we go from here? How do we prevent interstellar war?" Chris said.

There was that word again. It filled Galileo with dread.

"Fifty-one months," Clarice warned. "Fifty-one months and they may decide that the situation here is intolerable. Maybe we should go back to Sol—" She cut the sentence short, realizing that even if their tugboat were not low on fuel and on its way to C-3A, the

Beagle would arrive two years after Earth had made a decision and carried it out. If a missile were launched in fifty-one months, it would be too far flung to call back by the time Chris and Clarice and a couple of Alphan ambassadors arrived in the solar system. "No, that won't do," she said.

Galileo looked back and forth from Clarice to Chris, trying to understand the expressions on their faces. "What, exactly, will they find intolerable?"

"Us. All of us. Chris and I have become your teachers, and they may think your people are too smart. Years ago they were frightened enough to cut off all contact with us. Over things less serious than this they blacked themselves out. And what did we do? We cut off all broadcasts to them. In fifty-one months they'll know that." Dumb! Dumb! Dumb! Clarice thought. Dumbest thing in the world, to stop talking to each other. But how could we know that? This is all so new. We don't know the house rules yet . . . and we may not have time to learn. "If there is only a one percent probability, in Earth's eyes, that Alphans can eventually go into space, use the A-1 and A-2 power projects, and eventually launch relativistic rockets against mankind, they may decide that even a one percent probability is intolerable. They may launch a preemptive strike."

"I don't understand the words 'preemptive strike'."

"They may send a rocket to A-4, like that silver star in your dreams, and destroy us before we become an actual danger to them. We may *never* be a danger to them, but they may decide not to take the chance."

"Destroyer of worlds!"

"No!" Chris cried out.

"We stopped talking to each other," Clarice continued. "In fifty-one months they'll decide, and we won't even know the names of the world leaders who will make the decision."

"No . . ."

Galileo turned to Chris: "Then why don't you start talking? Why don't you say something to them? Tell them to stop."

"Yes . . . we've got to try to talk. We've got to tell them . . . *something*. But light is so slow. It will take nearly four and a half years for our signal to reach Earth. If we say something today, they will hear it one month after they see our conference on the other people. Now, if they have launched a rocket one or even two months before they get our message, the rocket will be only light-weeks away from Earth, and still accelerating. They will have time to call it back. Okay. So we have time. The question is: What can we possibly say that will convince them to call it back?"

"Convince them that we are no danger," Clarice suggested.

Chris considered and rejected the idea. "We may be no danger today, but they will know that almost five years will have passed between our sending of the message and their receiving it. They will also know that a relativistic rocket will take more than five years to reach us. That's at least ten years, from where they stand, for us to change our minds, to build our own weapons, or to, *very quickly*, change the Valkyrie into a weapon."

"Maybe they'll just hit A-1 and A-2," said Clarice. "Rob us of any potential power."

"We'd be lucky if that's all they did," said Chris. "I don't believe it—one big, dangling loose end: What happens when Earth's own explorers become colonists, and the colonists are seen as a threat, and in turn see Earth as a threat? We should have been asking this question twenty years ago."

"If you can't convince them that A-4 is no threat," Galileo said, "then you must convince them . . . give me a few seconds . . . give me a few seconds . . . Just the opposite! You must make them as scared of us as we are of them. Make them even more scared. Tell them we'll be ready in ten years, and then make us ready." The shrunken, dying Galileo managed a crooked grin, and Chris realized to his horror that he'd seen this awful thing before.

"You'd like that, wouldn't you? You'd like to smash my world. Understand this, Galileo: I *have* made problems for your world. I admit that, and I'm not at all proud of it. But understand also that I came here in peace, and when I die here I intend to leave in peace. All life must be protected. All life, Galileo, whether at Sol or Centaurus."

"Teacher . . . what do you expect us to do?" Galileo demanded.

"What you have said we should do. We should put the fear of God in them."

"The fear of God?"

Chris nodded. The phrase stayed with him, playing over and over in his brain, over and over: the fear of God. There was the answer. But how could that be accomplished without killing? What do we do? Blow up Venus as a display of strength?

He started to walk toward the door.

"Where are you going?"

"Out. Out where I can see the trees. Out where I can feel the suns. I've got some thinking to do."

"About what?"

"About the fear of God."

34

Trinity

"I'M CHRISTOPHER WAYVILLE," HE WHISPERED TO THE IMPASsive sky.

Remember me? he thought, turning his head toward Earth. *Remember the explorer who believed he'd found a rip in man's fabric of rational beliefs? The one who dreamed himself immortal, more or less? The man who now teaches the Alphans? Oh, you'll remember, all right. Whoever you are, blacking out your signals, pulling the strings up there, you may wish to wipe me and my Alphans away so utterly that we cease to be even a memory; yet you will be forced to leave us here. You will be forced to remember. You will have no choice.*

To his own eyes, partly by aid of an idea he had developed during what Clarice still referred back to as the "bad" part of the voyage, the rip at last seemed to have knitted shut, or at least to be on the mend. Chris knew that, like most hot speculations, his theory about intelligent species intervening through replayer particles was probably wrong. But for the moment, it provided a working model, around which the idea of premonitions became a little more rational, and the universe a little more interesting.

With corroborative testimony from Galileo, the likelihood that "relativistic psychosis" was just that—a psychosis—was banished from his thinking. Up to this point, with his "bad dreams" receding deeper and deeper into his past, he'd been able to dismiss them as a strange but temporary and best-forgotten quirk. They'd intruded on his orderly universe, trying to turn it on end, and for the most part he preferred not to remember the nightmares; but now he was helpless to avoid them. The revelations of the past few hours had brought something put mostly to rest more than two years ago hurtling into the present, dismaying and frightening him. Nonetheless, Chris began to stiffen his back. At least this time there was no fear that his mind was coming unhinged. Clarice, as master of the *Beagle*, would listen to him, and would probably act on whatever he suggested—which put him in a most uncomfortable position, from which multiple and largely unpredictable outcomes branched.

(Earth is afraid of us. That is dangerous.)

How best to prevent relativistic bombardment from Earth?

(Make them more afraid. Make them very afraid. That may be safe.)

There was no shortage of things to be afraid of that day. First, nearer to A-4 (nearer to home), there was the C-3A problem. Clarice seemed to have gotten that one fairly under control; but—

(*If you people on Earth can be frightened into total silence just because one of your explorers had a few bad dreams, if furry little Alphans who have barely crossed into the Stone Age from the Wood Age are bound to incite you to paranoia, wait till you see the silver crabs. You're going to love those.*)

—we must control the fear. We must control . . .

"Heaven and Earth," Chris whispered. "All of Heaven and Earth."

The silver crabs on C-3A were under control. The Valkyrie was closing off their world. The web would contain them, temporarily at least, for a few thousand years or so.

Chris liked to believe he and Clarice had thought of everything, and done everything they could to bottle the other people up. But he kept recalling the words that the deep-sea explorer Jason Bradley had lived and died by: *When you think you have thought of everything, the sea will think of something else.*

The same could be said about the new and still largely unexplored oceans of space. Chris had always tried to live by Bradley's law, and even without the new threat from Earth, there were surprises enough on C-3A alone to give him many sleepless nights indeed:

During the first moments of contact—in just twenty seconds—the crabs had absorbed every shred of information the two probes possessed, and were ready to use it instantaneously. Something ruthless and fast had come out of the ground. Whatever it was, it knew undeniably that other sentient beings existed. It might attempt contact again, and Chris was not all too certain that further contact, via laser pictographs from the Valkyrie, should be forever precluded—so long as they were very careful about what they revealed, and so long as the crabs stayed put, where he wanted them, beneath the web. (And no matter how he tried, he could not shake the desire to learn more about the crabs, to reopen the lines of communication.)

Compulsive communicators. That's how Chris summed up his own civilization; and he decided that the compulsion was humanity's curse. His people had first scrutinized the galaxy for signals from other worlds, and finally sailed across interstellar space directly, driven by a kind of homing instinct. Now that they had at last encountered other minds and attempted exchanges of ideas, the desert of silence from Earth was a ghastly reminder that no matter how powerful the instinct, the gap between man's desires and man's communicative skills was dangerously large. If humans became fearful of their own scouts, and cut off contact with them, how could they be expected to understand an alien species whose very perception of objects in its immediate surroundings was entirely different? Even as he lived with them, and though there had been much talking, Chris wondered if he and Galileo, or he and any Alphan, could ever truly understand each other.

Seeking contact with other islands of civilization, Earth, A-4, and C-3B had been drawn together and transformed by man's own hand from three dots to points on a triangle whose every feature had (at least at the outset) seemed preordained. Chris felt like a man who had just used a stick to stir a sleeping dragon. He guessed that in a few years there would be no Alphans. No silver crabs, either. And perhaps no humans.

In any triangular arrangement, everyone wanted to be the highest point, but one or two always had to be on the bottom. For the moment, Earth was on top, being the only one in possession of relativistic technology. A lucky break, perhaps.

(High tech rapes low tech.)

If the Wayvilles were truly participants in a communications breakdown branching relentlessly in the direction of relativistic war, then it was going to be a decidedly one-sided war. A-4 and C-3B were about to become losers in civilization's extinction lottery: the lowest points on the triangle. Always there would be winners and losers . . . always . . . unless someone intervened.

(What to do about Earth?)

Oh, yes. There was trouble and xenophobia enough back home without adding the C-3A problem.

(Make them more afraid?)

And now Chris had become a teacher to Alphans—something he had feared, from time to time, could alter the shape of the triangle by creating a new contender for the top position. And what would happen when, on Earth, the exact shape of the triangle could no longer be foreseen?

It was all so clearly too late. There was no way of preventing humanity from knowing that Chris was teaching the Alphans to become what he had feared: technologically aware, and unpredictable. At the same time, he understood, he must find a way to convince or bluff Earth out of doing what he feared most, and what Galileo, too, feared. And all the while he was changing the Alphans in ways that at least one reasonably observant Alphan had come to fear.

And so on.

The only out, he decided, was to feed man's paranoia. Disarm him with his fear. Let him stew in it for a while.

(And how might that be accomplished?)

Without great difficulty, Chris supposed. The tactic had been tried once before, out there across the light-years; and while there were indeed risks, it had the distinction of having worked.

Chris, the Devourer, the alien who came uninvited to A-4, was now assuming the role of speaker for the Alphan corner of the triangle. He knew what words the humans would understand. Chris would take care of everything, and the obedient, unquestioning Alphans would let him. He was a little sadder for all of it, and a little more responsible, a little braver, and a little meaner as well.

35

The Fear of God

THE SILENT DEATH CAME SWIFTLY. IT SURGED INTO THE VEINS in Galileo's neck, seeking vital segments common to the genetic blueprints of all renegades, yet unique to them alone. Manufactured from Catherine's blood, the invaders slowly, methodically, became incorporated into the renegades' own cycles for the storage and release of energy, sabotaging the delicate machinery of life, and causing its descent into chaos.

The assault was two-pronged. As the invaders, behaving much like spiders in search of strawberries, homed in on and struck down the renegades, other substances sought out Galileo's weakened immune system, and began to prop it up.

CATHERINE'S VOICE CAME TO HIM, FROM VERY FAR AWAY: "He's coming back."

And then a sharp pain as something was pulled from his arm, and he let out a chirp, and opened his eyes.

Catherine looked down at him. "See. I told you Chris was our friend." Another pain, this time in the neck, as Chris probed and pressed with his hands.

"The swelling's going down," Chris said. "So how is the patient today?"

Galileo tried to answer, but could not. He lay very still on his back, on something called a "water bed," and the unusual position made it difficult to breathe. He reached for Catherine, pulled himself up a little bit, and managed to say, "What happened?"

"You collapsed into a faint."

"How long?"

"Six days. For six days you slept."

"So how is the patient today?" Chris repeated.

"A . . . a little better . . . not so sick."

"Good. You should be feeling stronger every day."

Galileo signed something on Catherine's arm and she helped him up onto his feet. The breathing came much easier, more natural, now that his weight was removed from his ribs. "Six days . . . I take it you've solved the Earth problem."

"We think so."

"That's good," Galileo said, and then began to fall into a doze; but the question came up in him: "How?"

"You were right," Clarice said. "We had to tell them something so frightening that when they heard it they would think long and hard before launching a missile against us. As intolerable as they might find our exist-ence and our potential, we had to show them that any attempt to remove that potential would make their future even more intolerable."

"The fear of God?"

"The fear of Valkyrie," Clarice said, and then scrib-bled something on a flat. Words began to appear on the wallscreen. "We beamed these three sentences at the spot that will be occupied by the Earth in fifty-two months. As you can see, they are short and simple."

DO NOT ATTEMPT TO LAUNCH RELATIVISTIC ROCKETS AGAINST A-4. FACT: YOU CAN NEVER

PREDICT EXACTLY THE POSITION AND MOTION OF VALKYRIE AT ANY PARTICULAR INSTANT. DECLARATION: YOUR SOLAR SYSTEM WILL NOTE THAT ANY RELATIVISTIC DETONATIONS IN THIS SYSTEM WILL INVITE A FULL RETALIATORY RESPONSE FROM VALKYRIE.

"We have been repeating this message over and over for the last two days."

Galileo snapped his head in Chris's direction. "You would do this? You would destroy your own world?"

"No. Not at all. I am not a destroyer of worlds. FU is under orders not to—*under any circumstances*—fire anything against Earth.

"Even if they do wipe us out, how would it serve our dead bodies to destroy them? I vote for letting what is left alive go on living. We are bluffing them, but Earth has no way of knowing that. What I have told them should prove just as disarming as if it were real. I think we've put them right, so to say."

Galileo's fear of Chris began to subside a little bit; but only a little. He would continue to avoid the alien for many star seasons to come. And he would never call him friend. He settled back on his tail and haunches and closed his eyes. He fell into a feverish but dreamless and pleasant sleep.

36

Your Words as Slow as Light

THE FIRST SPASM OF XENOPHOBIA HAD RUN THROUGH the solar system even as the Wayvilles approached Centaurus, way back in the spring of 2054.

Today the Earth was a silence that appeared endless, but it would not remain so, for the wall of satellite interference, renewed every second and washing over A-4 at the speed of light, was now passing the Wayvilles' warning flying in the opposite direction.

The signal would reach Sol in August 2061. The Wayvilles would be almost nine years older when they heard the reply.

What on Earth are we going to talk about? Chris wondered.

If they respond quickly they will be speaking from shock, having had it their own way all these years. Certainly they will not say the first things that come to mind. They will know that first impressions will take more than four years to reach A-4, and by that time the words might lose their meaning. Whatever they say must have lasting significance. It must still be relevant five and ten years down the line.

Clarice liked to joke about lawyer types getting into

the act, on both sides: "I object!"

Nine years later: "Why?"

(Talk about delaying tactics! Curse, yes!)

"What indeed will we talk about," Chris said, "now that I have resurrected the concept of Mutually Assured Destruction, and lifted it to the stars?"

Sunlight blazed in through the bedroom window, silhouetting Clarice as she looked out across the village. "Mutually Assured Destruction," she said. "That's not so bad. It worked on Earth."

"And the guy the lagoons are named after once said it would keep right on working—right up to the very last second."

Clarice winced against a chill of gooseflesh.

Chris turned the thought over for a while. It wasn't really mutually assured, was it? The Earth in his visions would not be made real at the hands of A-4. Perhaps they may do it to themselves one day; but the burning will not come from here. No, not from this system.

And who knows, he wondered, whether the bad dreams were all a joke of the mind, or whether premonitions can alter history? How can we know the visions were real when, if they were real, the end result has been a nonevent?

Clarice did not concern herself with bad dreams and nonevents. Today her attention was focused on the old launch tower across the village cenote, and the new rocket cradled in it. In a few months the voice of an Alphan Yuri Gagarin would chirp down from space, to be followed by a safe landing in the valley. "One of these days," she told Chris. "Someday they're going out there. With all the help we're giving them, they'll learn how to live and work in space. And with Asimov Arrays sprouting on A-1—"

"They'll visit Earth," Chris finished for her.

"What else is there? Light is so slow. Sooner or later they must talk face-to-face. Sooner or later we must send ambassadors. People like Galileo and Catherine, if they can be found."

Clarice looked out the window and took in the sound of hammering coming from the village. "Visit Earth? Can they learn such technology? Can they—"

She stopped the questions short as her mind latched onto the first thing she'd learned about the Alphans: "*The Alphans learn everything.*"

"There's nothing really bad about that," Chris said. "We can live with that. We'll all be talking in a few years, A-4 and Earth. And I doubt that there will be any shooting. Not to worry. She'll be right, mate. Everything is sewn up quite nicely."

Yes, it was all very satisfactory.

Except for one particularly nasty loose end.

37

2061: Split Ends

VALKYRIE HUNG MOTIONLESS OVER THE PILLBOXES OF C-3A, turning with the world in geostationary orbit and observing every square meter of its surface by aid of low-orbiting spiders. The ship was ready, at any moment, to move into position and squirt a stream of antihydrogen at anything that rose from the planet and made it through the web.

So far, the other people seemed to be behaving themselves. There were no targets. Either they had never developed a space capability, or they saw the web as impenetrable. The quarantine appeared to be working.

Yes, it was all very satisfactory.

A tiny white point of light flashed over the eastern limb. It ran down through the web at twelve kilometers per second and exploded. An odd sight: a meteor burning up over an airless world. FU watched it die, and beamed a report of the sighting back to A-4, unaware that she was not the only one watching C-3A from on high, and making reports.

The same gravitational tug-of-war that kept C-3A wet inside also dumped enormous loads of energy into Galen, the closer of C-3A's two icy moons. Barely wider than New Zealand's North Island, it was invisible by comparison to its Australia-sized cousin, C-3B, and was not even included on certain charts.

(*that which was forgotten...*)

According to the old twentieth-century saying, big things came in small packages. The saying applied especially to Galen. Deep within, the ice flowed liquid over a rocky core barely 150 kilometers across. The rock base was the actual surface of Galen, a planet so small that a submarine could travel all the way around its 471-kilometer circumference in a single afternoon. Above, the ocean stretched skyward for several tens of kilometers, terminating at a roof of ice whose underside was crusted with chandeliers, bacterial mats, and occasional buildings. The blocks were similar in construction to the upside-down towers inside C-3A: rectilinear, with open sides that let the water run through.

Thaw Tint hung upside down. A tiny gas bladder behind his siphons kept him anchored to the ceiling, which was furnished as though it were the floor.

Chemosensors primed and working, he noticed something ripe in the water. A garden of black, fernlike fronds carpeted the floor that was really his ceiling. He reached up, pulled one down, popped it into his mouth, then sprinkled sulfide-rich fertilizer up upon the others. Still chewing on the frond, he walked across the ceiling that was really a floor and wrapped himself around a machine that vaguely resembled an electron microscope. Gingerly, and with learned precision, three of his tentacles called hundreds of little hydraulic controls into action. Tens of kilometers below him, in the cold vacuum of Galen's outer surface, a telescope disguised as an outcrop of block-ice pointed down toward C-3A.

Nothing of significance appeared to be happening near the pillboxes, near that tunnel through which his ancestors had climbed so many ages ago to build their rocket. They'd gotten away just in time, before the "silver crabs" swarmed onto the surface. If the history books served him correctly, the rocket people had taken special care to bring all the plans for their ship with them, along with the tunnel maker.

And now Thaw Tint watched, hoping (praying) that the experts were right, and that the machines had not discovered some misplaced blueprint for a rocket, or drawn one up by themselves. Certainly they would destroy his people if they ascended into space, as they had, no doubt, destroyed all life inside Homeworld. What, he wondered, could have been more insane than giving hunter-killer submarines and silver crabs the power of self-replication? It seemed the Forebears had focused an extraordinary amount of know-how on inventing their own suicide.

And now there was this spaceship whose surface crawled with machines very similar to crabs, yet different. The experts claimed that it was harmless, at least relatively so, because it came from outside the C system. The scope translated its coils and colors into touchtones for Thaw Tint's tentacles—for he belonged to an eyeless species.

By all indications, the ship had come from the brighter of the two far suns, blueshifting gamma all the way. Its capability for speed, combined with its estimated mass and the gamma emissions, hinted at the cargo of raw power that stirred within. That fast, theory had shifted to fact. The mere existence of the intruder drove home the lesson that the energies of the atom could be harnessed for spaceflight. No longer would his people restrict their thoughts of space to ships powered by hydrogen and oxygen—chemicals abundant in the ice, yet too weak to really get one anywhere.

Thaw Tint tugged on one of the hydraulic controls and boosted the magnification. Five of his tentacles rested motionless on the screen for several minutes, taking in the forward coil, the tanks, and the tiny shapes that hauled themselves up and down the rigging.

Yes, he thought. There are opportunities that the experts do not see as yet. My Forebears rocketed into space with barely enough fuel to land them safely on this world. We never tried that waterless sea again; but this will change. There are ways to go back. There are ways to go far and fast. And we know, we who have seen the alien ship.

He was right, of course. His people possessed a giant advantage over the men and women of Sol, who had struggled for many decades with the question: Is interstellar travel possible? Often, those who said yes did so at the cost of their reputations. Even those who built *Beagle* could not know that the ship would work, until it actually decelerated into the Centaurus system. But Thaw Tint knew the stars could be bridged—truly knew it. *It can be done because it has been done*, he concluded. And more—if we watch that ship very closely, if we are wise and pay attention, we may even guess *how* it was done.

Oh, yes. OH, YES. We shall go out from this prison.

We have been waiting for a very long time.

Afterword:
What Makes Valkyrie Fly?
The Science Behind the Fiction

"T HE DAYS CLICK BY SO QUICKLY. FROM OUR VANTAGE point at ninety-two percent the speed of light, an Earthly day has barely four hours of sunshine. We are traveling through space so fast that a large hole has opened up behind us and grown to consume two-thirds of the sky. The Sun we leave behind has been pulled into our forward field of vision."

Science fiction?

"Not quite," wrote the British journalist Paul Simons, after attending a meeting of the American Association for the Advancement of Science. "These are some of the bizarre phenomena of travelling near the speed of light caused by relativity. It was recorded in the imaginary diary of an interstellar space traveller in a mere 64 years' time. Even more incredibly, it was written by a scientist who is working on a feasibility study to send an expedition to Alpha Centauri. Yes, you read that correctly. And before you throw your arms up in disbelief, such a voyage would rely on technology available now, or likely to be developed within the next few decades."

Since early 1984, Brookhaven National Laboratory physicist Jim Powell and I have been coordinating

299

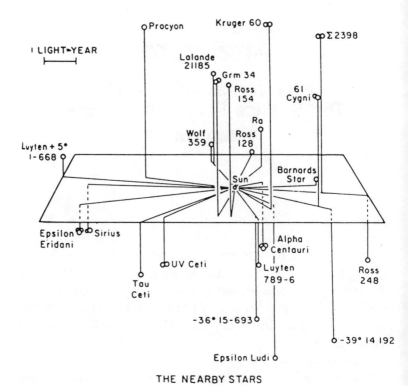

THE NEARBY STARS

brainstorming sessions on the next seventy years in space. Our primary conclusion from these meetings is that *Star Trek* (The First Generation) is a lot closer than most people think. If civilization holds together, and makes the right choices, it is conceivable that actual interstellar voyages may commence within the lifetimes of children walking the Earth today.

The Centauri triple system in general (and Alpha Centauri A in particular) was chosen as the focus of our brainstorming sessions, in part because it is the nearest system to us. Even so, the distances traveled and the speeds required to travel them within an acceptable fraction of a human lifetime are impressive, if not daunt-

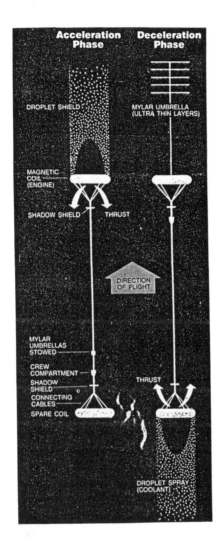

Spacecraft-on-a-String: Matter-antimatter annihilation powers this crewed, interstellar Valkyrie rocket designed at Brookhaven National Laboratory. Upon arrival in another star system, the crew compartment, a spacecraft in its own right, detaches from the rest of the ship to land on one or more target planets. Life support must operate on a closed ecosystem basis and be capable of supporting the crew for several years.

ing. As seen from a perspective aboard ship, Valkyrie crew members accelerating to a cruising velocity of ninety-two percent lightspeed will, when they return, have six years of back pay coming to them (and, as seen by stay-at-home observers at the Internal Revenue Service, thirteen years of back taxes).

Ninety-two percent lightspeed is, for a number of reasons including reasonable interstellar travel times, a realistic and optimal velocity to aim for. Relativistic effects become significant at this speed, providing highly desirable yet (to those of us living in relatively flat space-time) downright strange benefits. The Valkyrie crew ages at a rate only one-third of the rest of the universe. To an outside observer, even the ship's length and mass change. At ninety-two percent lightspeed, a Valkyrie starship would appear to have shrunk to less than half of its original ten-kilometer length, and would seem three times as massive, three times as resistant to acceleration, and, though traveling under the illusion that the rocket is moving almost three times as fast as light (which is compensated for by the crew's view of the entire universe being compressed ahead of the ship, into a dome that occupies only one-third of the sky), no crew member will notice a difference in mass, length, or even [her own] rate of age. To the crew, it is the outside universe that looks peculiar. If the gas pedal is depressed further, the ship will appear, to outside observers, to shrink still more in the direction of flight until at last, at lightspeed, it appears to have achieved infinite compression (no length at all) and infinite mass (an entire starship squeezed down to two spatial dimensions). Of course, the thrust required to accelerate up to and against infinite mass and infinite compression calls for literally infinite energy. If acceleration to two-dimensionality is indeed achievable (few things are truly impossible, but this comes very close to it), the results will be utterly fascinating, but not very pleasant. At lightspeed, the ship and her crew cease aging altogether. Billions of light-years, and billions of years, pass in an instant (actually, from a ship perspective, with the blinking of an eye seeming to take its normal fraction of a second, but spanning thousands of geologic eras to outside observers, everyone and everything drops immediately into the next Cosmic Crunch). The energies involved are such that purines and starch molecules, even individual carbon and hydrogen atoms, can no longer hold together. They convert to neutrinos and photons of light, vanishing in a searing white glare. And the rest is gamma rays.

The universe posts speed limits considerably below the 299,517 kilometers per second permitted for neutrinos and photons. Push a little ways above ninety-nine percent lightspeed, and colliding with a single interstellar hydrogen atom can kill you. It passes with impunity through the droplet shields we have designed for Valkyrie (or any other shielding system we can imagine), then through the walls of your ship, and through you, somewhat like a ghostly, planet-piercing neutrino. What distinguishes this near-lightspeed hydrogen atom from the passage of a neutrino is that the space it passes through subsequently becomes as hot as the universe was a few seconds after the Big Bang. Even at ninety-five percent lightspeed, flecks of dust impacting against the Valkyrie shielding system begin to look like very large hand grenades. These we think we can handle; but it is notable that encounters with dust particles are twice as energetic at ninety-five percent lightspeed as they are at ninety-two percent, and that the amount of fuel required to move from ninety-two to ninety-five percent lightspeed is twice as much as the move from zero to ninety-two (more, after one adds the amount of fuel required to push the extra load of fuel). Velocities greater than ninety-two percent lightspeed therefore become energetically practical for stellar distances of twelve light-years or more—that is, for very long hauls which become thinkable only if the crew is aging one-sixth as fast as the rest of the universe (however, current advances in cryogenics involving the use of artificial blood are making relativistic sleeper ships thinkable).

To reach ninety-two percent lightspeed, the ship will accelerate gradually for somewhere between one year (producing a gee force equivalent to one Earth gravity) and six months (in which case, crew members experience twice their normal Earth weight). As perceived by the crew, the long coast from Sunspace to Alpha Centauri takes less than two years, followed by at least four months of deceleration. Once in the vicinity of Alpha Centauri A, the crew compartment detaches from its "cradle" on the ship's tether system and flies off as a separate spacecraft to explore whatever extrasolar planets may be.

While there is as yet no evidence that a planet such as A-4 exists within the Centaurus system, Jim Powell and I have noted several features that make this system attractive for closer study.

Exobiologists, a handful of scientists with the curious distinction of not yet knowing that their subject matter exists,[1] have traditionally shunned Alpha Centauri A because, like half of the stars in the sky, it is part of a multiple star system. Every new class of astronomy students has been warned that multiple star systems cannot have planets in stable orbits. In order to merit such repetition, one would think that this "fact" was

---

[1]Exobiology, the study of, or search for, extraterrestrial life, is now sheltered in the broader field of astrobiology, which encompasses crewed spaceflight, advanced spacecraft design, planetary geology, and such paleontological realms as studies of life's origins, mass extinction events, and paleoclimatology.

based upon hard computer models and observational evidence.

No. Just another self-perpetuating textbook dogma, not unlike the Egyptian pottery clock (which is neither entirely Egyptian nor keeping the right time, though every new class of archaeology students is required to memorize it). We might have guessed as much from a quick look around the solar system: at the brown dwarfs that orbit beyond the asteroid belt, each of them a star that has failed to accumulate enough mass to burn brightly, each of them a solar system within our solar system, complete with ring planes.[2]

From computer simulations of the orbits of hypothetical sister stars and their associated planets, Robert and Betty Harrington of the U.S. Naval Observatory in Washington, D.C., and David Black, director of Houston's Lunar and Planetary Institute, have concluded that a planet near a star of approximately one solar mass will have a stable orbit as long as a second star with a gravitational pull of one solar mass or greater never approaches within 3.5 times the planetary orbit's radius.

Alpha Centauri A weighs in at 1.1 solar mass. Alpha Centauri B weighs 0.89 solar mass. The two are separated by a *minimum* distance of 11 astronomical units (an astronomical unit is equivalent to 149 million kilometers, the mean distance between Earth and the Sun). If Alpha Centauri B were to be inserted into our

---

[2]The ring planes of Jupiter, Saturn, Uranus, and Neptune, maintained by the gravitational tug of orbiting ice worlds, are comparable to the Sun's asteroid belt. The gravitational tug-of-war between Jupiter and Sol, for example, creates a cosmic scatter zone, a sort of demolition derby in which planet formation becomes very difficult. Constantly stirred this way and that, dust grains, boulders, and flying mountains tend not to clump together. Planetary rings are also comparable to the Oort Cloud, an even larger ring plane in which Sol's gravitational influence may be periodically balanced by close flybys—within two light-years—of other stars.

own solar system at that same distance, it would lie between the orbits of Saturn and Uranus. Both planets would be flung immediately out of the solar system. Farther out, at a mean distance of 34.79 astronomical units from the Sun, Neptune and the Pluto-Charon pair would suffer the same fate. Jupiter and its moons, 5.20 astronomical units from the Sun, would orbit like drunkards, but Mars, 1.52 astronomical units away, would have a stable orbit, as would the Earth, Venus, and Mercury.

If, instead of inserting Alpha Centauri B suddenly between the orbits of Saturn and Uranus, we allow ourselves to imagine the star forming *with* our Sun, then the matter that has accreted to form Saturn, Uranus, and their satellites, rather than being cast out of the solar system, forms as planets around the second sun—much as Jupiter, although it resides much closer to the Sun than Alpha Centauri A and B are to each other, has nevertheless managed to acquire no fewer than fourteen satellites, each of them a world in its own right.

Alpha Centauri A and B are far enough apart from each other that any planets located in their habitable zones will have stable orbits. And that is one of the things that makes the Alpha Centauri system so important: the fact that there are two habitable zones—two places for life to get a start on the surface of an appropriate world. Solar systems like our own can provide only one chance.

Another feature that makes the Alpha Centauri system important is its spectral signature. It is astonishingly similar to our Sun's—even down to the unlikely ratio of one atom of iron to every 31,620 atoms of hydrogen, which suggests that the star was born from the same elemental background as our Sun; that is, at almost the same point in the galaxy's history. Unlike most stars in the sky, Centaurus is old enough to have evolved biospheres as complex as Earth's.

Far from being the last places we should consider

as habitats for extraterrestrial life, we see in the suns of Centaurus the ultimate fantasy: the possibility of two life-bearing, Earth-like worlds in the same solar system.

Tantalizing wobbling motions in the flight paths of several nearby stars hint that faint, substellar companions may be commonplace and detectable even with the primitive astronomical equipment already at hand. Some of the companions apparently weigh in at eighty-five Jupiter masses. The existence of such relatively small stellar companions implies that still smaller objects await discovery—objects as small, perhaps, as Earth.

As yet, no signatures of even Jupiter-like giants have been detected near Alpha Centauri, primarily because few astrobiologists think trinaries are worth looking at, and secondarily because Alpha Centauri is a Southern Hemisphere system, and the latest and most expensive equipment is concentrated with most of the world's land and the people who live on it—in the Northern Hemisphere. In any case, I could not help but look at and think about Centaurus. I used to live in New Zealand, on a hilltop, next door to the Carter National Observatory. I remember B shining gold through the telescope. A and B were beacons up there in the night, the brightest and most tantalizing objects in my universe.

A new generation of telescopes, some to be placed in orbit, should be able to capture infrared reflections of Jupiter-class planets around stars located within thirty light-years (ten parsecs) of the Sun, and will also be able to detect planet-induced wobbles with an accuracy of ten-millionths of an arc second—which is like measuring the diameter of a dime on the Moon as viewed from Earth. Such accuracy will permit the detection of a companion as small as ten Earth masses around a one-solar-mass star thirty light-years from Earth; or, at 4.3 light-years, make possible the detection of an Earth-like world.

Many scientists have simply dismissed the notion that crewed spacecraft will ever be able to cover the distance even to the nearest star and return in a reasonable amount of time. The distances are such that if you were to represent the 12,900-kilometer-wide Earth as a little ball of three centimeters diameter (about the size of a golf ball), Mars would be a large pea nearly eighty meters away. Jupiter is then two kilometers away, Saturn is four kilometers off, Uranus eight kilometers, while Neptune and the Pluto-Charon pair hover twelve kilometers away. And then, for tens of thousands of kilometers, there exists nothing except the unexplored seas of interstellar space. Alpha Centauri, on this golf-ball scale, is eighty thousand kilometers off, in a galaxy of six hundred billion stars, each, on average, as far as Earth from its nearest extrasolar neighbor.

When we consider crossing such distances, there are distinct advantages to using antihydrogen as a propellant. If brought into contact with ordinary matter, one hundred percent of the mass of both the matter and the antimatter is converted into pure energy. By contrast, the conversion ratio in a conventional hydrogen bomb (which uses as a trigger a massive and even less efficient fission device) is only about one percent. For propulsion purposes, microfusion bursts triggered by antihydrogen-hydrogen annihilation (possibly with a component of lithium added) will prove efficient up to ship-cruising speeds approaching twelve percent the speed of light, owing to jets of relatively slow, massive particles. Above twelve percent lightspeed, propulsion shifts from antimatter-triggered fusion jets to straightforward matter-antimatter annihilation, which produces a lower mass thrust than fusion, but provides particles with the high-exhaust velocities necessary to push the ship to a high fraction of lightspeed.

How much antimatter might be needed for a trip to Alpha Centauri—assuming that Asimov Arrays or something very much like them will eventually provide humanity with the excess energy required for its large-scale production? We have estimated that the fuel stores (both antimatter and matter combined) might be equal to roughly half the mass of the rest of the spacecraft, or about one hundred tons.[3]

Others have been more pessimistic, including an earlier study by space scientists Donald Goldsmith and Tobias Owen which yielded an estimate that a journey to Alpha Centauri would require four hundred million tons of matter-antimatter fuel. Such estimates arise from assumptions that the spacecraft will be huge, with powerful engines mounted in the rear. Everything forward of the engines becomes, in essence, a massive, rocketlike tower, requiring enormous amounts of shielding from the rocket's gamma ray shine, supplemented by complex (and massive) cooling systems to shed intercepted engine heat (and a traditional rocket configuration must absorb most of the heat-depositing gamma rays, even if they do, like X rays, have a tendency to pass through things). The addition of each layer of shielding and cooling equipment placed on top of the engine becomes increasingly prohibitive as ship mass increases, requiring higher burn rates, which in turn require more cooling and shielding, which increases ship mass and burn rates, and so on.

With our elongated, two-crew-member ship on a string, gamma shine and heat are spilled directly into the unfillable sink of outer space. A pulling rather than a pushing engine eliminates most of the

---

[3]To assure "burning" of all available antimatter, an as-yet-undetermined excess of matter will be required.

structural girders that would not only, by their mere existence, add unwarranted mass, but would multiply that mass many times over by their need for shields and coolers. Valkyrie, in effect, is a fuel-efficient, twenty-first-century version of today's "ultralight" aircraft.

While we have, since 1984, participated in and coordinated scientific symposia on antimatter propulsion, Jim Powell and I emphasize that our goal all along has been what the goal of pure science always boils down to: having fun. With our "ultralight" Valkyrie, we began to explore the question: Can relativistic flight be achieved while obeying the limits imposed by nature? Almost from the start, we were surprised to find that there were no technological barriers that could not be climbed over within the next five or six decades, and that relativistic flight was a lot less difficult than previous researchers had believed.

The primary propellant for Valkyrie, the antiproton, is not merely a figment of the science fiction writer's imagination; though, as is often the case, science fiction writers seem to have discovered it long before the scientists.[4] At the moment, small numbers of antiprotons are being routinely produced in physics experiments, and very recently, antiprotons have been combined with antielectrons to produce the first true antihydrogen atoms (which, as Jim Powell and I predicted, appear almost surprisingly easy to capture and stabilize, a development that has both good and bad implications for future propulsion systems). At this writing, the production rates involve very small, experimental quantities. Large-scale production of antihydrogen remains

---

[4]The late Gene Roddenberry is the first person, to my knowledge, to have anticipated antimatter's practicality in spacecraft propulsion, which is why Jim and I have always named such Valkyrie components as the antimatter containment vessels "antimatter pods," in homage to him.

a dream at least forty years beyond our present technological (and more importantly, economic) capability.

An antihydrogen atom is the antimatter twin of the
more familiar hydrogen atom. It has the same mass as
the hydrogen atom, but its electron (called a positron)
is positively charged and its proton (an antiproton)
also has a charge opposite that of normal hydrogen.
Since antimatter and matter annihilate each other on
contact, releasing enormous bursts of energy from literally microscopic amounts of propellant, you cannot
simply fill a shuttle tank with liquid antihydrogen and
let it slosh around inside.

The only storage method that has a hope of working
is solid antihydrogen, supercooled within one degree of
absolute zero (within one Kelvin of –273 degrees C). At
this temperature, antihydrogen condenses into "white
flake," with an extremely low evaporation rate.

Particles of solid antihydrogen will be suspended
and held away from the "pod" walls, probably by
electrostatic forces and/or magnetism. According to
our latest models, near 0.0005° K, antihydrogen should
be sufficiently stable as to allow storage and mixture
together with actual matter, in the form of matter-
antimatter micropellets or wafers (we are presently
working to determine which design, layered pellets or
wafers, will provide optimal thrust). Within one-fifty
thousandth of a degree Kelvin, matter-antimatter storage becomes thinkable because the wave functions do
not overlap enough to produce an appreciable reaction,
at least in principle.

(And in practice?)

We do not know. It has not been practiced yet, and
can only be verified by experimentation. Personally,
carrying matter-antimatter pellets already assembled,
even at 0.0005° K, gives me nightmares. I keep seeing
a cosmic ray particle stopping at the matter-antimatter
interface, giving off its heat, and triggering a horrible

chain reaction not unlike the one that killed the Bardos in Chapter 14. Jim says we can prevent that, but I am still opting for storing our antihydrogen in complete isolation from matter until virtually the moment it is needed. I am reminded of that scene from the movie version of *2010*, in which Roy Scheider describes the aerobreaking maneuver his ship is about to make through Jupiter's atmosphere. "It's dynamite on paper," he says. "Of course, the people who came up with the numbers on the paper aren't here."

Call me old-fashioned, but I cannot sleep easily with a pod full of matter-antimatter pellets. So I vote for manufacturing our pellets immediately before use. Once they are manufactured, supercooling is maintained until they are guided to the desired point of detonation, whereupon simple laser-induced warming does the rest.

Upon warming, electrons and positrons self-annihilate to produce small bursts of gamma rays which, in terms of thrust, can be totally ignored. The positrons are there simply for stability's sake. The proton-antiproton pairs, however, produce three varieties of elementary particles called pi-mesons:

1. Neutral pi-mesons[5] comprise thirty percent of the proton-antiproton reaction products. They decay immediately into gamma rays.
2. Positively charged pi-mesons, traveling near the speed of light, decay into positively charged mu-mesons (muons) and neutrinos after flying, on average, only twenty-one meters. The muons last several microseconds (almost two kilometers) before decaying into positively charged electrons and neutrinos.

---

[5] A meson is a particle with a mass intermediate between an electron and a positron. It is essentially a proton fragment.

3. Negatively charged pi-mesons behave the same way positive ones do, except that the resulting muons and electrons are negatively charged.

The charged *pions* and *muons* are the particles we want, and when not being used below twelve percent lightspeed to immediately trigger fusion explosions (a matter of simply modifying the type of pellet or flake used), we want to simply bounce the pions off the outermost fringes of the engine's magnetic field, and thus steal whatever thrust they have to contribute, before a significant fraction of them have traveled twenty-one meters and shed part of their energy as useless neutrinos. The engine we have designed ejects pions and muons (and, at lower velocities, pion- and muon-triggered fusion products) along a diverging magnetic field nozzle to produce thrust, in much the same fashion as hot, expanding gases in a conventional rocket impact against a solid wall or pusher plate at the back of the ship, propelling the entire assembly forward. Since the pions and muons are acting only against a magnetic field, they can propel the Valkyrie without ablating or wearing down the engine walls (as does space shuttle propellant, with the result that the engines must be rebuilt after every flight, and eventually thrown away). However, gamma rays emitted by the decay of neutral pions will knock atoms out of position in structures near the antimatter reaction zones, making the material stronger, yet brittle. One solution is to add structures called shadow shields wherever practical. (Shadow shields are nifty little devices already being used in certain very advanced nuclear reactors. They are a major component of Valkyrie, so stay with me and I will get around to describing them in just a few moments.) Another, supplemental solution is to weave most structures residing within four kilometers of the reaction zone from hundreds of filaments, and to send electric currents through the filaments, heating them, one at a time, to several hundred degrees below their melting point. Gamma ray displacements in the wires are thus rearranged, and the atoms can reestablish their normal positions.[6]

The gamma ray flare from the engine dictates other major features of ship design. In particular, it has caused us to turn rocketry literally inside out.

Riding an antimatter rocket is like riding a giant death-ray bomb. An unshielded man standing a hundred kilometers away from the engine will receive a lethal dose of gamma radiation within milliseconds. In designing spacecraft, even when considering a propellant as efficient as antimatter, RULE NUMBER ONE is to keep the mass of the ship as low as possible. Even an added gram means extra fuel.

Here's how we can shave off many tons of shielding.

Put the engine up front and carry the crew compartment ten kilometers behind the engine, on the end of a tether. Let the engine pull the ship along, much like a motorboat pulling a water skier, and let the dis-

---

[6]There appears to be nothing we can do to prevent the occasional transmutations of atoms into other elements. Fly far enough with your engines burning at full throttle, and your ship will turn slowly into gold, plus lithium, arsenic, chlorine, and a lot of other elements that were not aboard when you left. These new substances will be concentrated around the antimatter reaction zone, and it is important to note that advanced composite materials already coming into existence dictate that our Valkyrie, even at this early design stage, will be built mostly from organic and ceramic materials, rather than from metals. It is conceivable that expanding knowledge of composites can be taken into account by the time relativistic flight becomes a reality, so that the ship actually incorporates the transmuted elements into its filaments in a manner that ultimately results in structural improvements for a ship designed to essentially rebuild itself as it flies. Exploiting what at first glance seems to be a disadvantage (transmutation) is simply a matter of anticipating the "disadvantage" before you begin to build. It's the disadvantages unforeseen or unaddressed that will get you in the end.

tance between the gamma ray source and the crew compartment, as the rays stream out in every direction, provide part of the gamma ray protection—with almost no weight penalty at all. We can easily direct the pion/muon thrust around the tether and its supporting structures, and we can strap a tiny block of (let us say) tungsten to the tether, about one hundred meters behind the engine. Gamma rays are attenuated by a factor of ten for every two centimeters of tungsten they pass through. Therefore, a block of tungsten twenty centimeters deep will reduce the gamma dose to anything behind it by a factor of ten to the tenth power (10^{10}). An important shielding advantage provided by a ten-kilometer-long tether is that, by locating the tungsten shield one hundred times closer to the engine than the crew, the diameter of the shield need be only one-hundredth the diameter of the gamma ray shadow you want to cast over and around the crew compartment. *The weight of the shielding system then becomes trivial.*

The tether system requires that elements of the ship must be designed to climb "up" and "down" the lines, somewhat like elevators on tracks.

We can even locate the hydrogen between the tungsten shadow shield and the antihydrogen, to provide even more shielding for both the crew and the antihydrogen.

There is an irony involved in this configuration. Our "inside-out" rocket, the most highly evolved rocket yet conceived, is nothing new. We have simply come full circle and rediscovered Robert Goddard's original rocket configuration: with the engine ahead of the fuel tanks and the fuel tanks ahead of the payload. Nor is the engine itself an entirely new creation. It guides and focuses jets of subatomic particles the same way the tool of choice among most microbiologists guides streams of electrons through magnetic lenses. Valkyrie, in essence, is little more than a glorified electron microscope.

In addition to shielding against gamma shine and avoiding the absorption of engine heat, another major design consideration is shielding against interstellar dust grains. Flying through space at significant fractions of lightspeed is like looking down the barrel of a super particle collider. Even an isolated proton has a sting, and grains of sand begin to look like torpedoes. Judging from what is presently known about the nature of interstellar space, such torpedoes will certainly be encountered, perhaps as frequently as once a day. Add to this the fact that as energy from the matter-antimatter reaction zones (particularly gamma radiation) shines through the tungsten shields and other ship components, the heat it deposits must be ejected.

Jim Powell and I have a system that can perform both services (particle shielding and heat shedding), at least during the acceleration and coast phases of flight. We can dump intercepted engine heat into a fluid (chiefly organic material with metallic inclusions) and throw streams of hot droplets out ahead of the ship. The droplets radiate their heat load into space before the ship accelerates into and recaptures them in magnetic funnels for eventual reuse. These same, heat-shedding droplets can ionize most of the atoms they encounter by stripping off their electrons. The rocket itself then shunts the resulting shower of charged particles—protons and electrons—off to either side of its magnetic field, much the same as when a boat's prow pushes aside water.

The power generated by occasional dust grains should range from the equivalent of rifle shots to (rarely) small bombs. These detonate in the shield, harmlessly, far ahead of the ship. Fortunately, almost all of the interstellar particles likely to be encountered are fewer than 20 microns across (10,000 microns = 1 centimeter), and we should expect no more than one impact per day per square meter of Valkyrie's flight path profile. When a dust grain impacts against the droplets, the particles from which the grain is made will simply act as individual particles, "unaware" that they are part of anything else. Hence, as it penetrates the droplet, each proton, neutron, or electron will be scattered at a certain angle, and the angle of scatter should increase as the particles pass through more and more droplets in their approach to Valkyrie's magnetic field, resulting in a harmless, spreading shower effect. We need only worry about neutrons or other uncharged fragments that get through the magnetic field lines and impact on the nose of the ship, where they will deposit heat— which we expel on a spray of reusable droplets.

One of the great advantages of a droplet shield is that it is constantly renewing itself. Put a dent in it, and the cavity is immediately filled by outrushing spray.

If a dust grain passes into the shield, many of the shield's droplets are bound to be exploded. Some of the scattered droplet fluid will be absorbed and recovered by surrounding droplets, but some fluid is bound to be hurled out of the droplet stream, which means that we must also add the weight of droplets to be replaced to the ship's initial mass.[7]

In addition to spare droplet fluid, our preliminary designs call for a spare engine. Both engines will be located at opposite ends of the tether. The forward

---

[7]One potential weight-saving option is to carry only enough droplet fluid for a one-way trip, and to manufacture new fluid when you reach your destination. The hydrogen and lithium (both of which are ubiquitous in space) needed for matter-antimatter reactions will also be gathered, for the return trip, at the destination system. To get a feeling for what this means, consider the ballooning proportions of jet aircraft if they were required to carry the fuel for the return trip from New York to Paris. Most of the energy expended would be for the transport of fuel, and a 747 would be four times as heavy.

engine pulls the ship along during the acceleration phase of flight. It also fires during the cruise phase, but only at one-hundred thousandth of a gravity, keeping the tether taut and permitting recapture of forward-flying droplets. At the end of the cruise phase, the rear engine kicks in for deceleration (as we cannot simply swing a ten-kilometer-long ship broadside to relativistic bombardment in order to turn the engine around and fire in reverse).

In normal use, the rear engine is turned on only to decelerate the ship, or to maneuver the crew compartment into the center of the forward engine's gamma ray shadow. Nudging the crew compartment, from behind, to one side or the other will be necessary during major course changes, because the crew compartment, much like a water skier, cannot turn simultaneously with the motor that pulls it and might otherwise drift out of the protective shadow. A spare engine also provides some insurance against the chilling possibility of irreparable damage to the leading engine or, worse, a break in the tether. In the former case, identical engine parts could be ferried up and down the tether and exchanged as necessary. In the latter, depending upon where the break occurs, with careful rearrangement of the ship's components along the tether, the remaining coil can be safely used to finish the outbound leg of the mission.

At the end of the cruise phase, with nearly half of the ship's fuel exhausted, empty fuel tanks can be ground up into ultrafine dust, for dumping overboard (we see no reason to expend extra energy decelerating tons of equipment, no longer in use, which can easily be remanufactured and replaced at the destination solar system). At up to ninety-two percent the speed of light, the dust will fly ahead of the decelerating ship, exploding interstellar particles and clearing a temporary path (trajectory must be such that relativistic dust will fly out of the galaxy without passing near stars and detonating in the atmospheres of planets). This fist of relativistic dust is the first line of defense against particles encountered during final approach. With the rear engine firing into the direction of flight, droplet shields will become useful only for expelling heat from the rear engine, for along the tether, "up" has now become "down," and droplets can only be sprayed "up" behind the engine, where, traveling at uniform speed, they will fall back upon the decelerating ship. To shield against particles ahead of the ship, ultrathin "umbrellas" made of organic polymers similar to mylar and stacked thousands of layers deep are lowered into the direction of flight. This is the second line of defense— against particles moving into the ever-lengthening space between the ship and the fist. The umbrellas will behave much like the droplet shield and, in like fashion, they will be designed with rapid self-repair in mind. Throughout the ship, repair and restructuring will be assisted (where such repair abilities as self-annealing filaments are not already built into ship components) by small, mouselike robots capable of climbing up and down tethers and rigging.

Still . . . we can design all the shielding systems we want, and the nagging possibility of finding occasional large particles in interstellar space will not go away. It is a small blessing that the probability of encountering particles of a given size decreases exponentially with linearly increasing volume, but sooner or later, a ship flying near the speed of light is bound to find a one-microgram particle in its shield. No larger than a grain of sand (about one hundred microns across), it will carry all the destructive force of one hundred kilograms of TNT. This is not much of a problem if our droplet shield extends several hundred meters ahead of the ship, but we would still lose a lot of droplet fluid.

We cannot afford to hit too many grains of sand.

And there are bigger traps in waiting; much bigger, if it turns out that "Pellegrino's Pancakes" (a name given in 1984 that appears to have stuck) actually exist. By 1987, hints that pancakes, or something very much like them, might be passing in the night began to turn up. University of Iowa radio astronomer Ralph Fiedler's reexamination of data originally tossed aside as "wrong measurements" revealed a new kind of structure—cloudlike, and smaller than the solar system, with clearly defined edges—passing in front of extremely luminous, extremely narrow point sources called quasars.

The quasar 0954+658, for example, with an angular diameter of only 0.39 milliarcseconds (equivalent to the diameter of four hundred dimes spread out side by side on the surface of the moon as viewed from Earth) was eclipsed by an object, or by the corner of an object. At 2,695 MHz, the quasar's brightness rose for one week, as if it were being approached by, and its transmission scattered by, the fringe of something akin to Saturn's electron-charged ring system. In just a few days, the quasar radio source faded to half its initial intensity, but continued to fluctuate at regular intervals which, to me, are hauntingly reminiscent of data returned by the *Voyager II* spacecraft as it watched a star passing behind gaps and grooves in the Saturnian ring. The quasar eclipse lasted almost two months. Whatever the eclipsing body was, it moved across the sky at a rate of 0.09 milliarcseconds per day. If one assumes the object to be located at the quasar's distance of 1,000 megaparsecs (307 million light-years), then an angular motion of 0.09 milliarcseconds per day dictates an apparent velocity five hundred times lightspeed. The object, and four like it eclipsing other pinpoint radio sources, must therefore be closer to Earth, much closer. If, as appears to be the case, the objects are located within our own galaxy, then at a distance of 4,238 light-years, traveling at an assumed velocity of two hundred kilometers per second (the average for material in the galactic halo), the two-month passage across quasar 0954+658 makes the object, or at least that portion of it crossing in front of the quasar, seven astronomical units across (slightly more than the distance separating Jupiter from the Sun). If closer still, such objects will be smaller, perhaps somewhere between the diameters of the Jovian system and Mercury's orbit. Their velocity will also be correspondingly smaller, comparable, perhaps, to the relative velocities (ranging near twenty kilometers per second) averaged between the Sun, Centaurus, and other nearby stars. In order to hold together gravitationally, the overall structure must contain as much mass as Jupiter and all the planets combined, and probably has within it several minor planetlike objects (possible creators of the observed inhomogeneties or "gaps"), comparable in size and composition to some of the Jovian, Saturnian, Uranian, and Neptunian satellites.

Out there, between the Sun and Centaurus, may lie dust disks with Jupiter-like brown dwarfs at their centers. The dwarf stars themselves are no major hazard to navigation. The danger is the dust that surrounds the stars, rather like the rings and satellites in the planes of Jupiter's and Saturn's equators. Although you would have to sift through millions of interstellar grains before you found one weighing a microgram, and billions before you found one weighing a gram, in a dust disk you will find all the billions of grains you need. The probability of encountering more dust than the shield can handle at one time, and occasional nuggets of ice and ice-rock, thus becomes a statistical certainty. All you have to do is hit a single ice cube at ninety-two percent the speed of light, and you might just as well be flying headlong into the Sun.

Judging from the number of quasar radio sources being interrupted so far (five out of thirty-seven scrutinized in recent years), if the mysterious eclipsing objects are indeed, as seems to be the case, located within the galaxy, then as many as one hundred of these bodies may exist in the cubic parsec of space lying between the Sun and Alpha Centauri. If this is true, then pancakes or dark stars may be a thousand times more populous than stars, and courses will have to be charted around them long in advance if we ever intend to navigate interstellar space at relativistic speed. Pancakes may truly become the reefs and shoals of the twenty-first century.

One of the aspects that makes antimatter rocket studies so much fun is trying to anticipate what technological options will be available to planners as they approach the second half of the next century. For example, what will be the state of robotics, especially in the field of miniaturization (nanotechnology)? Superconducting magnets that work at room temperature would be nice to have, but we don't know if they can actually be built, so we must plan alternative designs including and excluding them.

Add to this a few unanticipated surprises. We can probably keep antihydrogen stable with matter at approximately .0005° K, yet getting even warm antihydrogen to react in acceptable proportions with hydrogen presents a problem we never imagined we would have to deal with. At the very instant the two substances begin to react, the resultant heating blasts much of the hydrogen and antihydrogen away from the reaction center, causing the reaction rate to drop. It was previously believed that all you had to do with matter and antimatter was throw them together—*BIG PUFF OF SMOKE*—and you were on your way. One of our brainstorming team members, Brookhaven physicist Hiroshi Takahashi, is fascinated by this new obstacle, because it is similar to puzzles that must be solved if muon-triggered fusion reactors (and an even more promising new method involving accelerator bombardment schemes in which heavy hydrogen—

deuterium, tritium—and sometimes even molecules of ordinary water are crashed at relativistic speeds into targets of heavy hydrogen) have a chance of becoming practical. One of the things Takahashi has enjoyed most about antimatter-engine brainstorming sessions is that they sometimes clarify and simplify problems to be addressed when he goes back to his room to work on fusion reactor designs.

The technology for producing antimatter using particle accelerators is presently under development at American and European laboratories. At CERN's seven-kilometer-circumference synchrotron near Geneva, Switzerland, antiprotons are routinely produced by firing a high-energy beam of protons into a block of tungsten. A trillion (10^{12}) antiprotons can be created in this way. A trillion antiprotons may sound like a lot, but they contain the potential annihilation energy of only three hundred joules (roughly equivalent to the "bang" from a cap gun), and the CERN facility gets slapped with a $40,000 electric bill every time the accelerator is turned on.

Clearly, simpler and more efficient accelerators are needed. Machines with the proper requirements are presently under development in the United States (and soon to be under intensive development in Japan) for use in fusion reactor research.[8]

"As an example," explains physicist George Mueller, "in one design being studied, the particle accelerator will produce short bursts of protons with a power beam of 10^{14} watts, about one hundred times the present power output of the entire world! Of course,

---

[8]The development of fusion reactors will be worth every penny invested, for they may eventually lead to the powering of whole nations essentially from water. It is becoming more and more apparent that particle accelerator and antimatter technology will play a role in this dream.

since the machine will be operated in 10^{-8}-second bursts, the average power is very much lower."

The natural location for antimatter factories, in view of their large power requirements, is in space, where continuous and, from an industrial perspective, limitless solar power is available. "Using the solar flux at the Earth's distance from the Sun," adds Mueller, "a light collector about three hundred kilometers on a side could provide the power for a 10^{14}-watt factory. If the efficiency of antiproton production from each high-energy proton in the initial beam could be made as high as 0.1 percent [presently Hiroshi Takahashi is predicting higher efficiencies], then this machine would produce 10^{20} antiprotons per second, or about one kilogram of antimatter per month."

From our earliest brainstorming sessions emerged proposals for a solar panel array, in orbit around Earth, covering an area in excess of ten thousand square kilometers. Even if it should one day become economically feasible to mine, refine, and transport materials from the Moon to Earth orbit, such an array would literally become a gigantic solar sail, requiring a considerable expenditure in thrust (presumably from rockets that would have to be refueled from somewhere) just to keep it from blowing away on the solar wind.

Our attention turned elsewhere, to a power source more firmly anchored, yet overlooked, perhaps because it is so large that no one noticed it before. If we are correct, the planet Mercury is destined to become the most valuable piece of real estate in the solar system.

Presently, we are eyeing self-replicating, solar-panel-building machines. If humanity plays its cards right, prototypes could be tested on the Moon near 2020, and the rewards that the descendants of these first machines can bring—cheap, clean, and unlimited power for all mankind—are yet another argument for a permanent Moon base.[9] Using the materials available at the lunar surface, they will build solar panel farms, and new solar-panel-building machines. In time, the farms will girdle the Moon's equator to form the Asimov Array (named, exactly as described in Chapter 4, after an early contributor to the concept). The Asimov Array will provide power for Earth. However, we dare not use that power for producing and storing large quantities of antimatter on the Moon, or anywhere near Earth, because even a single kilogram of the stuff—a mere handful—carries the explosive potential of forty hydrogen bombs, along with the moral responsibilities that go hand in hand with the possession of such power.

Once perfected, the descendants of the original Asimov Array robots can be sent like a viral infection to the planet Mercury. Assembling replicas of themselves from the substance of their host, their first half decade of habitation will be a latent, incubation phase, during which most of the solar panels manufactured by the machines will be used to power an ever-accelerating chain reaction of machines building more self-replicating machines. As their population approaches a predetermined critical density, more and more of them cease reproduction and join to form solar panel factories, with the result that almost three decades after the arrival of the original twenty or thirty machines, uncountable square kilometers of Mercury's surface will become a gigantic photovoltaic

---

[9]Indeed, when considering the amount of high-speed debris already polluting low Earth orbit, which space shuttles are now frequently required to swerve and avoid (Space Station *Freedom*, at least as presently designed, will be unable to move out of the path of oncoming debris), Jim Powell and I are very tempted to advocate scrapping the space station design program and to proceed directly to a Moon base—which, interestingly enough, will have broader applications and be easier to maintain.

generator, with an area the size of Rhode Island being added daily.

When Mercury is farthest from the Sun, each panel will receive 6.7 times as much solar energy as it would receive on the surface of the Moon. This figure rises to fully ten times the lunar surface value as the planet's eccentric orbit dips twenty-four million kilometers nearer the Sun. In time, self-replicating machines will carpet the Mercuran landscape from pole to pole with solar panels, giving mankind more than 50,000 times the present U.S. electrical energy budget, a power capable of launching at least two interstellar missions per year.

Using self-replicators, the world's future energy problems and even the excess energy required for relativistic flight can be solved for a very small initial investment: the cost of developing as few as a dozen ancestral machines on the Moon. Of course, we should not trouble ourselves to begin immediate development. They would be too expensive to build today, and too inefficient if built from the equipment now at hand—just as a trans-Atlantic airline service and videocassette recorders, though technologically feasible, would have been prohibitively expensive to build in 1925. We must wait, not only for technology to catch up with the idea, but for the idea to become economically viable.

There is, as emphasized in this novel, a darker side to the Valkyrie vision; little gnomes to watch out for, hiding somewhere up ahead, behind the bushes. When Jim and I began to see that relativistic flight might actually become real, we began to ask questions no one had asked before. The answers turned out to be bigger than our questions.

What if we crash a relativistic rocket into a planet at ninety-two percent the speed of light, or even thirty percent? What if we begin to colonize other star systems, and what if, given enough colonies and enough time, one of the colonies becomes xenophobic of the others, and begins throwing around relativistic-rockets-turned-relativistic-bombs? If the odds of an extrasolar colony evolving into something like "Saddam World" are, say, one chance in a thousand, and you colonize planets around a thousand stars, doesn't the probability of trouble become a statistical certainty?

The questions went on and on, and we began to see that massive colonization of the galaxy by human beings would probably be very unwise. We began to see in our designs either the keys to the universe, or death on a grander scale than humans had hitherto imagined. A relativistic rocket launched offensively against a planet is certain to reach that planet, because the rocket is never where you see it when you see it. A projectile weighing in at only one space-shuttle mass (a fully fueled shuttle sitting on the launch pad weighs in at fifteen hundred tons) striking the Earth at only thirty percent lightspeed will release fifteen million megatons of energy—an explosive power equivalent to 10,000 times the present global nuclear arsenal, released all in one place in the space of a sneeze. And the attacked are powerless to prevent it, probably given even ten million years of technological development beyond our own.

And if we must begin to worry about the possibility of relativistic war with our own potential colonists, with our own brethren, what if the galaxy should harbor other thinking beings whom we will find even more difficult to understand? We may find ourselves turning back to a truth of the Old West: God made some men taller and stronger than others, but Mr. Colt made all men equal. Some civilizations may be older and more advanced than others, but relativistic rockets will make all civilizations equal, at least in terms of destructive capability.

The keys to the universe, or death.

We cannot have it both ways—at least, that's what Jim Powell and I concluded. So we named our rocket

Valkyrie, after the beautiful Norse maidens who, in the shape of eagles, descended to snatch up the souls of the brave killed in war, carrying them heavenward, to Valhalla, the legendary Hall of Odin. If Earthly sapience cannot live up to its name, if we are foolish enough to ascend beyond Earth orbit with our old ways of thinking still intact, if we move to the march of tribal drumbeats, then surely the souls of the brave will fly up with Odin's eagles, for we shall all be killed in war. We carry with us, in our rocket's name, a chilling and timely reminder: choose the wrong path, and we are, every one of us, flying to Valhalla.

Charles Pellegrino, Ph.D.
Rockville Centre, New York
1:00 P.M., December 7, 1991

Acknowledgments
and Notes

History never repeats
I tell myself
before I go to sleep.
—SPLIT ENDS

WELLINGTON WAS A CITY ENCLOSED BY MOUNTAINS AND forests, with a harbor so clean that there was a beach at which people could actually swim; and on calm, windless mornings, whales swam there, too. If not for the cold, dark days of 1982, I'd probably have remained a paleontologist and teacher in New Zealand, living peacefully, putting out a book every now and then, and essentially enjoying life to the fullest. By "life to the fullest," I mean to say that some of my happiest memories are Scrabble and chess in Wellington's botanical gardens, tea at the begonia house, fresh bread on Saturday mornings while watching, from my dining room window, layers of mist pulling apart over the mountains. Such memories may seem silly if not downright boring to most people, but they are my treasures. It was the only time and place in which I have ever known a true peace.

Unfortunately, in 1982, the turbulent conditions of the Northern Hemisphere finally reached "down under." U.S. naval ships were being expelled, the economy was going turtle, rocks were thrown at the car of then-visiting Vice President George Bush, and in some quarters "evolution" became a bad word worthy of censorship. In

329

Paradise they were busy inventing snakes. Before long, the first terrorist bombings in that country's history would commence.

For me, the end came swiftly, all in about two weeks. There was a sudden and determined effort at Victoria University (backed ultimately by the Minister of Education) to make me withdraw my first book, "Darwin's Universe," from publication; also to hold back submission of my paleontological studies to technical journals. I resisted these demands and, in very short order, as rumors spread to the students that I was variously an expatriate American criminal hiding out in New Zealand and an agent of the CIA,[1] my two university laboratories were mysteriously destroyed. Then an "ad hoc committee" was assembled to consider such things as my "renegade research"[2] into such things as the *punctuated equilibrium* question and biological revolutions occurring near layers of rock bearing signatures of asteroid impacts. There was also the question of why a paleontologist was receiving so much mail from NASA,

---

[1]The fact is that I never even met anyone from the CIA until after I published *Her Name, Titanic* in 1988.

[2]Although this research was specifically funded by departmental grants in response to detailed proposals and progress reports, all previous knowledge of my work was disavowed. As it turned out, American Museum of Natural History paleontologist Niles Eldredge (co-author, with Stephen Jay Gould, of the *punctuated equilibrium* theory), along with L.I.U.'s Edward I. Coher and several New Zealand paleontologists, including Sir Charles Flemming and Alan Beu, did much to defend and establish the credibility of my work against a system gone out of control. Most importantly, they did so at a moment when I was being beaten over the head so relentlessly that I was actually beginning to get that "bad dog" feeling, and to make some ridiculous noises about never writing anything again. It takes guts to make a stand for someone when the authorities are shouting him down. To those who stood by me and spoke up when it was the unpopular thing to do, you have more thanks than you will ever know. Your courage meant a lot to me.

and talking at the National Observatory about sending robot submarines to Jupiter's Europa, and filling the electron microscopy lab with amber and carbonaceous meteorites.

"All of this is very confusing to mere mortals living in the twentieth century," said one committee member. "You think in strange ways, and I don't know how we are going to bang it out of you. Sooner or later you'll be writing science fiction, and then you'll really embarrass us all."

Well, maybe he had a point there.

Ultimately, many of the emerging scientists in my age group left New Zealand for America, or Canada, or England. A crowning irony is that the head of the committee that chased me out later complained in an interview with the journal *Nature* that New Zealand's youngest and most imaginative scientists were leaving for distant shores—as if the blame could conveniently be passed along to some evil alien brain drain.[3]

(Sorry, mate. There were monsters enough at home, and you were one of them.)

The world I have called A-4 is not yet known to exist, but it is about ninety-five percent derived from the real landscapes I came to know and love in New Zealand. The tall massifs opening up on the Milky Way, the tropical forests growing shoulder to shoulder with glaciers; the more unlikely you find the scenery, the closer it is to reality. Not very far below the surface, this novel is a letter to New Zealand from a homesick child.

I guess I owe some belated thanks to some people who made it easier for me to strike out on a new path, way back in 1982: my parents, of course, and the Stoffs, and the Petersons. I am thankful for Russ Galen (Scott

---

[3]A year later, I had the curious distinction of being present when this same man, booted out by his own committee, showed up at Brookhaven National Laboratory looking for a job.

Meredith Literary Agency), Josh Stoff (Cradle of Aviation
Museum), Niles Eldredge (American Museum of Natural
History), Edward I. Coher (Southampton College), the
late Luis Alvarez (Berkeley), the late Clair Edwin Folsome
(University of Hawaii), and Stephen King (who helped me
to find humor in a bad situation).
A few early readers have asked me if Clarice is based
on my wife, Gloria, and if Christopher Wayville is me.
The answer to both questions is a resounding No. In
fact, I don't even like Christopher Wayville, and cannot imagine myself doing some of the things he has
done. The only parts of this novel that even approach
autobiography involve some of the aliens. Nevertheless, Arthur C. Clarke, Isaac Asimov, and Jim Powell
make brief appearances as themselves, and the exas-
perated remarks in Chapter 4 regarding the rotation
of Mercury were made by me to Isaac Asimov at an
AAAS conference in May 1984. Other comments regarding attitudes toward the idea of relativistic flight in 1984
are historically accurate excerpts from actual scientific
meetings held about that time, though for obvious reasons most of the names have been changed (Richard
Tuna, of course, is you-know-who; and Colby was really
Arthur C. Clarke).

I am indebted to Al Munier (Grumman Aerospace),
Jim Powell and Hiroshi Takahashi (Brookhaven National
Laboratory), Robert Jastrow (NASA), Michael Rampino
(NASA), William Newman (University of California), Free-
man Dyson and Jill Tarter (NASA/SETI), John Rather
(Kaman Aerospace), Robert L. Forward (Hughes Cor-
poration), Isaac Asimov (Boston University School of
Medicine), Arthur C. Clarke (University of Moratuwa),
Roald Z. Sagdeev (the former Soviet Academy of Sci-
ences), David Black (Lunar and Planetary Institute),
Glen Marcus (Comicopia), Bruce Murray (California
Institute of Technology), Senator Harrison Schmitt
(the first scientist and last Apollo astronaut to set

foot upon the Moon) and the late Senator Spark Matsunaga for their contributions to long-ranging discussions, brainstorming sessions, and symposia on many of the subjects (primarily interstellar travel and communication) encountered in this book. For lots of neat fun with asteroid "ash layers" and cyclic mass extinctions (especially during the hot, hot days of 1979–1980), I am grateful to Stephen Jay Gould and Luis Alvarez (and my apologies to Richard Muller for that awful nail I put in Nemesis' coffin). I am also indebted to Carl Sagan (Cornell University) for introducing me to the Cosmic Crunch, and for expressing such excitement over the idea that an oscillating universe might be fractal in nature (hauntingly repetitive) that even though in my own estimate Christopher Wayville's universe has less than a one percent chance of being real, I truly wish it were, because it's just too damned interesting not to be.

I hope Jill Tarter will forgive my speculation that her search for extraterrestrial radio signals may never bear fruit. My real concern is that it may bear far too much; for a galaxy of 600 billion stars containing only one civilization is an extremely low probability event (indeed, virtually a statistical impossibility). If a loud, coherent signal ever is received, the three laws of alien behavior must apply, and I believe mine and Powell's explanations for their content—"baiters or death cries"—will also apply.

The closed-ecosystem life-support system for Valkyrie was first proposed by one of my mentors, the late Clair E. Folsome. In 1984, as our Valkyrie brainstorming sessions began, and as the need for reducing ship mass came to the fore, we began extrapolating ahead to what forms Folsome's closed-ecosystem algae tubes might take forty years into the future, given the emerging science of recombinant genetics. Folsome and I concluded, in theory, that a system might be developed in which each member of a colony or spacecraft could be sustained by only a cubic meter of algae tubes. And now you know why the starship *Beagle*'s life-support system carries his name to A-4.

The positions and behavior of the Alpha Centauri suns, as described throughout this novel, are indeed as they will actually appear on the dates given, as seen from a planet orbiting at A-4's distance from A. The story of the little girl named Elmer Glue, whose picture is on Tranquillity Base, is also true. I hope she enjoys my extrapolation of her life into the next century.

The Lazarus Effect, whereby Christopher Wayville lives his life over and over again, with varying degrees of recall, through histories that may or may not be very much the same, was first explored in my SF radio series, *How I Got Screwed by the World, and Other Private Ejaculations*, during my brief stint with the National Lampoon Radio Hour (way back in—gulp!—1974). Chris's predecessor in time travel was a man named Filby, who makes a cameo appearance in Chapter 4.[4]

For editorial criticisms, I am especially indebted to John Douglas (who has a keen sense for when it is time to turn a book, like a Valkyrie rocket, inside out), George Zebrowski and Pamela Sargent (who have a keen sense for when it is time to toss a nagging Pellegrinoism overboard), Russ Galen (who, after reading about Folsome tubes, the Matsunagas, the Lagoons of Powell, and the Asimov Array, asked, "Gee, Charlie, when do I get a mountain range or something on another planet named after me?" So I found the worst place in the galaxy . . .), *the* Don Peterson (who had better schedule a "let's go places and eat things" road trip real soon!), and

---

[4]Unlike Wayville, no matter how different the surrounding history, Filby kept repeating the same mistakes lifetime after lifetime. In particular, he always went back to the same fatal woman. Even when he searched her out while still a fifteen-year-old, just to punch her in the mouth for what she would one day grow up to be, he fell hopelessly in love with her all over again.

Arthur C. Clarke (who has a wicked sense of humor—*formic*ation indeed!).

As always, I thank Mom and Dad, Adelle Dobie, and Barbara and Dennis Harris for the faith they showed and encouragement they gave to a child some experts claimed would never read books, much less write them. Thanks also to two science teachers who came onto the scene a little bit later, Agnes Saunders and Ed Mcgunnigle. The world cannot produce enough people like you.

I am deeply grateful to my old friend (Great grief! Were the Ballard expeditions really that long ago?) Walter Lord, author of *A Night to Remember*, for material concerning Morgan Robertson and the *Titanic*. Robertson's novel *Futility (The Wreck of the Titan)* has been well known for many years; but *Beyond the Spectrum* (for which there are now known to exist at least three different versions, including a short story), his 1908 novel about the bombing of Pearl Harbor on a December morning, the subsequent air war with Japan, and America's ultimate victory by use of the atomic bomb, was so obscure that one of the only surviving copies had remained unread on Walter's bookshelves until I came across it, quite by accident. As I began leafing through it, Walter saw the blood drain from my face.

"What's wrong?" he said.

I think the two inelegant words that came out of my mouth—"Holy shit"—summed it up quite nicely.

In any case, Wayville's dilemma has provided an opportunity for me and Walter to bring to life one of our favorite science fiction fantasies involving the *Carpathia* and the *Californian*, another of history's great "what ifs."

Like the Robertson novel (and the newspaper headline displayed in Chapter 17), the information I have given regarding the collapse of a San Francisco highway is a fact and not a fiction. In this respect, I also owe thanks to the stewardess who came through the harrowing flight of Pan Am 465 with me, and especially for her fascinating explanation for my observation that she had, even before takeoff, seemed exceedingly nervous. She said she *knew* something was going to go wrong, because more than half the passengers had failed to show up. "These are the flights that always go weird," she said.[5] Up to that point, I had not taken serious note of the fact that the *Titanic*, though fully booked, was nearly half empty when she sailed.

In the Preface to *Her Name, Titanic* I wrote, "This book was an exorcism of sorts. A final release. And I do not wish ever to repeat the experience." As it turned out, history surely repeats. This book, too, became a means of coping with sheer stupidity and senseless destruction. Put briefly, *Flying to Valhalla* was written during a period in which I witnessed (and in one case became the target of) rampant paranoia and cowardice blossoming into just the sort of mayhem I left New Zealand to get away from. Oh, God, how history repeats. In New Zealand, under the weight of 1982's economic crash, with every man beginning to fear for his job, I watched friends who had named their children after each other drawing lines in the sand and preparing to slit each other's throats. I watched it become easier to destroy a new book, or discovery, or product,

---

[5]Friends recall how unusually uneasy I became the night before Pan Am 465, and how I kept joking nervously about how much I hated airplanes. But as I am not the superstitious sort, I ignored my own uneasiness. I'll never know how many would-be passengers shared my uneasiness that night. What I do know is that when I tried to change to a window seat at the ticket counter, I was unable to do so because this and every other plane to Mexico was fully booked due to the approach of the century's longest solar eclipse. I eventually did get my window seat, because when we took off, more than half the seats were empty. Stephen King points out something said to be well known in the industry: full planes don't crash. This might be worth someone out there looking into. I'd love to see some statistics either supporting or challenging this well-known "fact."

and the man or woman who created it, than to produce a viable product, because under the new rules it made more economic sense to destroy than to create. And then, as all around me the whole decision-making process seemed to spiral down, it was easy for opportunists not very unlike America's David Duke—men formerly regarded as little walking jokes—to attain positions of authority. And always they were short on solutions, long on lists of people who could be blamed for everybody's problems. One day it was people on the dole (what in America we call welfare). The next day it was the Asians, or the evolutionists, or people who did not like rugby. It didn't matter. Any scapegoat would do. I watched innocents destroyed. I watched logic drop dead.

And now, like humanity standing where the Alphans of 33,000,000 B.C. once stood, America, with its deteriorating economy and powerful new challenges ahead, is poised on the same brink occupied by New Zealand in the spring of 1982. New challenges, as a matter of sheer definition, are opportunities for forward leaps that come disguised as a lot of hard work and a need to pay attention. So far, I'm afraid we are failing to pay attention. American industry and the world have begun to follow the Alphan lead, the road more traveled, the ceaseless repetition of old mistakes. At bottom, this book is a fable for the new millennium.

Charles Pellegrino
Rockville Centre, New York
2:26 P.M., December 7, 1991

About the Author

Dr. Charles Pellegrino (along with Dr. Jesse Stoff) proposed the original models that predicted the discovery of oceans inside certain icy moons of the outer solar system. While looking at the requirements for robot exploration of those new oceans, he worked with the deep-sea robots that probed the *Titanic*. Pellegrino's first loves are paleontology and archaeology, though he has been described by paleontologist Stephen Jay Gould as a space scientist who occasionally looks down, and by Arthur C. Clarke as the world's first astro-paleontologist. He is the co-designer of the Valkyrie antimatter rocket and the author of eight books, including *Her Name, TITANIC*, *Unearthing Atlantis* and *Toward Sodom and Gomorrah*. His work on 95-million-year-old biting flies in the New Jersey amber beds, and his speculative piece in the January 1985 issue of *Omni* detailing how dinosaurs might one day be cloned from DNA preserved in the stomachs of amberized flies, were the basis for the Michael Crichton novel and Steven Spielberg film *Jurassic Park*. His patents include (with James Powell) economically viable equipment for raising the *Titanic*, new composite materials that make it possible to build mile-high city-towers even in a swamp bed, and (with a Japanese team) High Speed Global Maglev—which means London to Sydney in four hours. Subsequent to their design (during Valkyrie's development) of some of the largest and smallest nuclear devices ever conceived, Pellegrino and Powell have been called "the Pablo Picasso and Salvador Dali" of nuclear destruction. In his spare time, Pellegrino builds sand cities on the beach, speaks at science fiction conventions, and scares Stephen King.

DATE DUE